TANGLED DARKNESS

MM Desch

Cover Art Design by: Kelly Moran/Rowan Prose Publishing
Photo Credit: Adobe Images/Deposit Photos
First Edition
ISBN: 978-1-961967-54-0
Rowan Prose Publishing, LLC
www.RowanProsePublishing.com
Published in the United States of America

ACKNOWLEDGEMENTS

Thank you to everyone at Rowan Prose Publishing, especially Kelly Moran and Shakera Blakney for your brilliant editing. Kelly, you've navigated me through the publishing process, kept me on track with patience and grace, and listened to my personal challenges complicating the home stretch. I'm especially grateful for your leadership—often exercised with humor—and your determination as you juggle plenty.

So many people helped me develop Tangled Darkness from its inception during the COVID lockdown. Angela M. Sanders, a fabulous author and book coach, thank you for your developmental edit, offering a critique group, and your steady encouragement as I sought "my PhD in writing" with Tangled Darkness.

To all those members of Angie's critique group, and the subsequent critique group through Willamette Writers (you know who you are), I thank you for your helpful feedback, your support, your ideas, and especially your time as you read through my early drafts.

To all my siblings who read an early draft and listened to me talk endlessly about my writing project on our weekly Zoom calls, I love you and thank you. Thank you to my brilliant nephews

Ted and Griffin who gave me ideas about the IT elements in the book and phone calls to seal my understanding. And to our friend Marty, the retired police commander who shared her time and experience to help me understand law enforcement's culture and procedures, thank you so much.

My Portland, Oregon, Twin City, and other author friends in the US and UK have been so generous and helpful. I thank you all and hesitate to name names lest I forget someone, but here goes. Dian Greenwood, my friend, thank you for sticking with me from the start. You are my superhero writer ideal. You taught me whatever happens, just keep writing and it's never too late. To Deborah Jiang-Stein, we go back a long way, and your writing passion was always an inspiration to me. Thank you for being my friend over decades and encouraging me to join the writing community. To Laura Stanfill, Nancy Townsley, Dana Haynes, Suzy Vitello, Michael Keefe, Tammy Euliano, Lisa Mathews, Kaye George, Marilyn Levinson, Elin Daniels, and all the members of the Author Avenues and Let's Talk About Writing groups, thank you for taking me into your circles.

No thanks would be complete without acknowledging the many resources and generous authors within the Sisters in Crime, Writer's Digest University, Curtis Brown Creative, and Willamette Writers communities. Workshops, conferences, email boards, individual authors who provided information and feedback, help with that query letter and synopsis, the whole shebang. Thank you all so much.

Finally, I've saved the most and best for last. This book is dedicated to Liz Hay, my beautiful and patient marital partner. Thanks, hon, for all your encouragement and patience. For your willingness to support my "beyond focused" passion for writing. Your understanding of the written word, creativity, spirit, and love for fun helped to infuse this story with a certain edge.

Oh—and you came up with killer title ideas. So, let's go have some fun!

"The past is never where you think you left it."
-Katherine Anne Porter

One

Wednesday, October 9th

Leslie Schoen glanced at her desk clock for the umpteenth time in an hour—five minutes had vanished since her last check. Izzy should have called by now. If time had to drag, at least she was waiting in a cozy, lived-in room. Stacks of medical books, journals, and files insulated her downtown Portland clinic office from the outside world. The early twentieth-century building held high ceilings and finished wood floors. Art and her credentials covered the walls. She easily connected with clients face-to-face from her little nook—settled behind the desk with an open side extension facing the room. The cherry furniture complemented the floor and its oriental rug. Floor lamps and spacious windows provided end-of-day light, and comfortable leather chairs added to the room's warmth.

With all appointments completed and phone calls returned, Leslie stared at her mobile, willing it to ring. She fed her day's schedule through the shredder under her desk, noticing her in-box sat empty for once in a long while. Her eyes took in a neatly organized desk. The day's appointments passed quickly. As a psychiatrist, she juggled mundane paperwork and intense personal connections. Whether managing prescriptions or leading an emotional therapy session, her job was never dull.

Through her open office door, she gazed at the now-empty hallway where, just minutes before, colleagues had chatted, phones had rung, and staff had made periodic trips to the sample closet at the hall's end. The clinic's activity had dwindled to silence. Damon Grady, her medical assistant, spoke softly into his phone at his desk across the hall.

The phone rang as she rose for a view from her streetside window.

At last. "Hey, hon, what's happened?" She sat again.

"I have the best news," Izzy spoke in a hush. "I'm still in the exam room. The doctor's coming back any minute."

"What news?" Her heart skipped a beat.

"I'm pregnant."

She sat forward in her chair, glued to the edge, as shock rippled through her limbs like a charge of electricity. A new reality formed in her mind: motherhood before forty—she'd just make it. "Oh. My. God."

Izzy's breathing punctuated the sudden quiet between them.

Leslie sprang to her feet. "Wait. I'm closing the door." Damon materialized just as she stepped toward the doorway. His sharp-angled cheekbones, dark circles under his eyes, and overgrown curly black hair made him look tired and thin, older than his thirty-two years. She pressed her phone to her chest to cover the microphone.

"You heading out soon?" He extended a handful of envelopes.

"On the phone. It'll be a while." She accepted her mail and closed the door. "Izzy?"

"I'm here. They're getting info about our next steps, reminding me of all the other times. I keep running through our false starts while I'm waiting."

Their last pregnancy flashed through Leslie's mind like an old-fashioned horror story. "What about the labs? The blood test?"

"This time, I hope it's different." Izzy paced her words. "But the number is sky-high. It's a definite positive, along with my exam."

"Oh, sweetheart, we did it!" She harnessed her energy by walking back and forth. "How are you? Tell me everything the OB said."

"Hold on." Izzy sounded out of breath. A door closed in the background. "Gotta go! I'll tell you all the details at home."

Leslie's face relaxed as Izzy's enthusiasm swept through her. She snatched her coat, reflecting on the challenges fertility treatment dwarfed: all she'd endured to get and keep her Oregon medical license, finish psychiatric training, and start her practice.

She grabbed her purse and noticed a Personal and Confidential envelope from her licensing board among her tossed mail. Tearing it open, she read the opening line with confusion before starting again.

You are hereby notified that the Oregon Medical Board has opened an investigation into your potential misuse of the patient sample medication: buprenorphine and/or Suboxone (the combination drug with buprenorphine).

She didn't prescribe Suboxone.

Her hands shook as she read the letter for the second time and grasped the allegation—that she had swiped controlled drugs. Potentially addictive drugs. The board's assertion baffled her. Where would she even access Suboxone—the potent opiate buprenorphine, a DEA Class III with serious abuse potential and street value? The allegation made no sense.

"Really? Who would do this?" Images of Bryce invaded her mind—her officemate whose addiction treatment program dispensed Suboxone samples. She considered Michelle, their nurse—eccentric perhaps, but her unwavering commitment to patients was clear. And Sloan worked longer hours than any psychologist she'd encountered, his office well-worn after decades of service. She reread the letter, her gut seeping dread.

The complainant is, at this time, unnamed in our investigation. Your written response, required within fourteen days, will precede a formal interview. Potential consequences of failure to respond include, but are not limited to, suspension of your medical license.

Leslie threw the notice—the lie—back onto her tidy desk. This inquiry would stress her family just as she and Izzy reached for their dream—the pregnancy. Was it a mistake? Samples placed in the main sample closet instead of Bryce's private safe?

After three years, she knew her handful of coworkers well. Despite sharing Bryce's lease and renting his employees' services, she intentionally kept her practice separate from his. If narcotics truly had vanished—if this wasn't merely an administrative mix-up—the allegation must've been instigated by someone in his practice.

Was this payback? No doubt, Bryce's attitude toward her had soured since she questioned his billing practices after their office manager left.

Leslie glanced at her closed door. Damon worked directly across the hall, but was like the younger brother she had never been given. No chance it was him.

She rose and moved to her far office window, the accusation's weight pressing against her chest. Taking measured breaths, she tried to focus her scattered mind while overlooking a blustery downtown Portland, Oregon, at dusk. Wind swept the leaves into small, helpless spirals, its faint whirring audible through the glass. While viewing the street from the third story, trees and people walking the sidewalk apace drifted further away like in a murky, surreal dream.

Bryce alone distributed Suboxone samples and other buprenorphine opiates in their office. Had she misjudged when agreeing to share both staff and a lease with an addiction psychiatrist and his rehab team? While her adult psychiatry practice shared similarities, her focus on legally connected mental health cases distinguished her from the group. Remaining outside Bryce's practice created enough distance. People with opioid addictions dotted her client list too. Still, she rejected his practice of treating opiate addicts with long-term opiates. When tampered with and misused, buprenorphine—bupe for short—was potentially lethal.

She caught a glimpse of herself in the window's reflection—her long bangs pulled to the side from a casual side part, the sunlit highlights in her chestnut hair dim. She scarcely recognized herself. The board notice drained the color from her face, making her cheekbones and narrowly defined nose stand out starkly. At thirty-nine, this transformation had descended without warning—her brown eyes appearing black above the tight line of her rounded lips.

She hurried back to her desk and texted Bryce, who was lounging somewhere on vacation.

Need a call, must talk.

Her gaze fell to the letter again. Its bureaucratic language heightened the sting of being called a thief. Back in the day, she'd weathered far worse slurs. Strange incidents plagued the office lately—like the last office manager's hurried exit, quitting without notice. Despite her growing list of office oddities, this accusation exceeded all the others.

With a quick sweep, she gathered her laptop case and other belongings for the trip home. As she opened the door, Damon stepped out of the main sample closet at the end of the hall.

"Time for home?" He offered a weary smile.

"Yeah." Though they'd been on the same team for years, Leslie's gut said, *wait*. Did she misread this kid? She hoisted her bags onto her shoulder.

"What's going on?" Damon's brows rose as she brushed past him into the hall. He'd always been good at reading her.

Keeping quiet around a once-friendly coworker tested her resolve. She used to find him approachable, but now her wife was the only confidant she craved. Tonight, of all nights, Izzy would be waiting at home, probably wondering what was keeping her.

"I can't go there right now. I'll see you tomorrow."

"Wait."

She stopped and turned.

"Hey." His pitch dropped. "You're worrying me. Did something bad happen?"

Maybe she should have asked him what he knew about opiate sample deliveries, but he looked exhausted, and she needed to collect herself before broaching such a sensitive topic.

"Sorry, I've got to go, Damon. Bye."

As Leslie drove through downtown Portland in the six o'clock rush hour, steam rose from manhole covers like apparitions haunting the cracked sidewalks. Homeless tents lined Burnside Street leading to the bridge, markers of lost hope. She recalled a stint with her licensing board a decade earlier. The dump she'd inhabited alone, a barren apartment, matched her emptiness while getting sober under the monitoring program required to keep her medical license. Surviving those first alcohol-free years tested her resolve daily, but meeting Izzy at two years sober multiplied their individual strengths—one plus one became three. Their synergy, connection, and eventually marriage buoyed her through varied, sometimes brutal changes.

Having to bring Izzy this bad news during their pregnancy celebration simply stunk.

As she veered onto Sandy Boulevard, the fading early evening light threw the surrounding trees into an altered dimension. With no reply from Bryce, she turned into a northeast neighborhood and tapped her dashboard for a Bluetooth call.

"Doctor Bryce Nelson. Message at the tone." *Beep.*

"Bryce, I need your input on an office situation. Reach me as soon as you can."

His failure to respond to her text typified Bryce's recent behavior. Since persuading her to attend rehab for alcoholism years ago, he'd changed so much. Her mind flashed on the moment he convinced her that a life of sobriety was essential if she wanted to keep practicing medicine.

Now, so much more stood on the line. Her expanding family depended on her. This allegation threatened more than just her career. The DEA might investigate her narcotics prescription authority, risking many of the anti-anxiety and insomnia medications she prescribed. At least they wouldn't impinge on her antidepressant prescriptions. Legal charges? Jail or probation? Loss of her license? Who knew? With her board history, scrutiny would intensify for every practice decision she made. What would the charge do to her relationships with her office clan and her arrangement to share handling after-hours calls with her friend and colleague, Susan Blake?

Her throat tightened as a tear rolled down her cheek, her skin burning underneath. She wiped the droplet away as though denying her tears would deny the fear behind them. Clamping her lips together, the certainty of panic pooled in her limbs, tingling in her fingers. Her vision blurred. She pulled over to a curb just as a flood of emotions—fear, anger, worry, love for her wife, their home, and the life they built together—spilled over into sobs. She leaned against the steering wheel as her shoulders rocked and the tears streamed down at a steady pace. The specter of old demons clamped down on her chest. As her tearfulness waned, she let loose the tension in her hands and shook them.

Remembering others who shared her struggle, Leslie took a deep breath. Izzy and their pregnancy needed her attention. The two of them had already endured so much together. She and Izzy had seen enough loss in the last year to overwhelm a funeral director. Her lawyer would compose and send a response to the board within two weeks. She planned to call him in the morning and sat taller. She reached into her bag for a tissue and told herself to snap out of it.

The mirror reflected a face drained by the emotional blast, but some healthy color had returned to her cheeks. She brushed her hair back to graze her shoulders. This crisis screamed, "Call your AA sponsor," but the woman left on her honeymoon two days before. In the meantime, Leslie texted another program friend to arrange a call.

"I'm home." Leslie stepped into their kitchen, speaking above an over-the-stove metal exhaust fan attached to the ceiling between maple cabinets and blowing like a turbo engine.

Izzy faced the range, her shoulder-length shock of wavy blonde hair visible above a sturdy camo apron splattered with droplets of simmering sauce. Its rust and sage colors blended into the warm palette of the room. The kitchen surrounded them in a cozy envelope of cream walls and burnt orange accents, with granite countertops featuring flecks of copper within caramel and cream swirls. Pendant lights hung from the ceiling, casting a honey-colored glow across the wood floor, stained to a rich amber that mimicked the cabinets' tone. Steam from a stovetop pot rose and whirled before her as she stirred the pan.

Leslie inhaled the warm dinner scent from their home's hub—their sanctuary. Breadcrumbs and a serrated knife rested on a bamboo cutting board. Warmed bread. The sizzling of sautéed mushrooms and onions filled the air, accompanied by an occasional pop and crackle.

Baby J, their intrepid border collie, met her and sat neatly with her head bowed. The dog's tail wagged in earnest, sweeping the wood floor.

Izzy quieted the overhead roar and turned. "Oh, hey there. What a day. Geez, this hood fan is the worst purchase we ever made." Pulled back from her face, her hair cascaded just below her shoulders, framing fair, creamy skin, vivid blue eyes, and a distinct, nearly Roman nose. Though just a couple of years younger than Leslie, Izzy passed for twenty-something even though she was in her mid-30s. She reached for a hug while Baby J nosed her way between them, her rear end swinging as they kissed.

Leslie leaned back to explore her wife's face, holding her shoulders. She stood on tiptoes to counter their two-inch difference in height. At five-four, she had the perfect position to nestle into Izzy's shoulder during a hug. Her face exuded a rested elegance.

"You're beautiful, pregnant lady."

Izzy smiled, blinking. "Let's sit in the living room. We can finish dinner later." She turned off the stove and led Leslie to the couch alongside the fireplace and facing the foremost part of their house. Their broad front windows opened wide to a blanket of auburn and crimson leaves rustling gradually in the wind's ebb and flow. This room captured Leslie's heart with its full-bodied, original mahogany woodwork, the wide fireplace with custom teal and taupe ornamental tile, and the stuffed, upholstered furniture.

The photo displayed on the mantel, the two of them with Leslie's mom at the ocean in Yachats just the year before, constricted Leslie's heart. Freedom and joy marked that day. She often caught herself disbelieving her mother's absence.

Baby J settled near Izzy's feet at the end of the couch. Even after a long day, Izzy showed care and attentiveness. Her temperament suited a nursery owner whose heart belonged most fully with her hands buried in the dirt. If it were possible to become grounded tonight, Leslie was closer now. Her wife's blue sapphire necklace, given for their fifth anniversary, sparkled with a color matching her eyes.

"Okay. Tell me everything the OB said." Leslie balanced on the edge of the couch, her hands on top of Izzy's.

In a momentary pause, the dog's soft snoring rose from the floor. They broke out in giddy laughter, clinging to each other and falling onto the cushion. The emotional roller coaster of recent months brought them to this summit, the highest point of their difficult climb. Their laughter shifted to a fusion of tears and giggles as they righted themselves again.

Leslie brought her hand to the side of Izzy's face and softly brushed some of her hair away. "We're pregnant," she whispered, smiling as her hand drifted down Izzy's arm to the couch.

"We did it." Izzy wiped her eyes and sat straighter. A flushed intensity filled her cheeks. "I'm fine. More than fine. This isn't like any of the other times. I feel different. It's hard to explain."

Their donor insemination efforts had spanned more than a year, creating a timeline of heartbreaking comparisons. The final and most devastating came with an early second-trimester miscarriage right after Leslie's mom had died.

"I'm telling you, this is the real deal. I don't want you to worry." Izzy placed her hands over her lower belly. "The doctor thinks I'm around six weeks. Wants me to have an ultrasound at eight weeks." She raised her index finger to her lips. "No sharing this until after. You know, because of before."

The wince on Izzy's face reflected Leslie's pain. They both quietly nodded. Leslie swallowed against the lump in her throat.

Was this the right time to mention troubling news? They stood at the threshold of their shared dream—expanding their family with a child they both fiercely desired.

Izzy gave her a gentle kiss. "Let's get some dinner."

They gathered at the table with a buttered baguette, a bowl of spaghetti with mushroom sauce, and a salad.

"So, what took you so long to get home?" Izzy twirled noodles with her fork.

"What?" Leslie tugged on her ear. "Oh—a software problem with my accounting, but I figured it out."

Dodging the truth left her uneasy. She glanced out the window at the patio wisteria vine, realizing she'd never lied to Izzy. But they surely didn't need another stressor affecting Izzy and the pregnancy. Best to postpone the news for a few days. "I'm still goosey about my billing records, I guess."

They exchanged a telling glance.

"Well, no surprise," Izzy said. "Thank God for your consults with lawyers."

Leslie's income dropped sharply when the office manager, who handled her billing and all office billing, vanished. Fortunately, she'd seen some relief through her mental health work with the legal system.

"Really." She nodded. "I want to understand what happened with that guy, but everyone is so closed-lipped about it. Kudos to our new biller, a gem, for getting the money to flow again. She had no idea what she walked into."

Izzy's forehead furrowed. "More problems?"

"It's already fixed." Leslie reached for her hand. "Forget about it. The baby! Let's celebrate."

During their relationship, she'd dragged Izzy through a myriad of nerve-wracking stressors: her medical license monitored for years, her early sobriety, and leaving the security of a large corporate medical group to start a private practice. With today's joyous pregnancy news, she wouldn't let her potential legal problems steal attention from her wife and the baby. She lacked the stomach to bring Izzy into another minefield, at least right now.

The board complaint would crumble once her lawyer took action. Resolving again to call him tomorrow, Leslie planned to update Izzy afterward. Just a day or so of delay.

She laid down her fork. "How about I draw us a luxurious hops bath?"

Izzy's face relaxed with a grin. "It's a date."

When unable to sleep, Leslie rarely followed the advice she gave her patients. Tonight, around midnight, instead of reading something boring, she sat in front of her garage workbench, finishing her latest jewelry creation—an interlocking teak necklace hung from a gold chain. With practiced fingers, she prepared the last chain piece for attachment.

A buzzing phone interrupted her work, her medical assistant Damon calling. She debated answering, since he had helped her with a computer problem after hours a few weeks before.

However, given the direct call to her mobile rather than going through the answering service, she let it go to voicemail.

After attaching the final chain piece, she listened to Damon's message:

"Hey, Dr. Schoen." A muffled cough preceded, "I know it's late, but..."

The message momentarily went silent.

"I've been having a rough night and wanted to talk. I debated whether to call."

More silence.

"My mom's in the hospital again. I'm worried, but she always seems to pull through." He sighed. "Between her and all this overtime work, I'm exhausted."

She pictured how tired he looked earlier.

"I'm probably just missing my ex and her daughter. It's frustrating, you know?"

An abrupt crashing sound interrupted him. Damon had mentioned his former girlfriend and her daughter several times before when sharing his eventual plan to move back to Wisconsin.

"Sorry, just knocked my hard drive off the table." Scuffling sounds and his breathing ensued. "To top it all off, I had a strange visitor tonight. Brought me a gift out of the blue. It just left me longing for an old friend. I'm... uh..."

He let out a deep sigh.

"Sorry. I'm talking too much, but I didn't know who else to call this late. I considered Michelle, but... she'd just yell at me for calling in sick. I'm not feeling too well. I don't think I can make it to work tomorrow. Bad tacos, I think. My stomach's wrecked. I know it's last minute, but I need to take a sick day. I'll call Michelle with an update tomorrow."

She set her phone down, puzzled by the strange call. Damon had never contacted her about taking time off before, and his mention of overtime concerned Leslie. He was working from home on extra tasks, not anything she assigned. Bryce must have given him an assignment to work on after hours. *What exactly was Bryce having him do?*

While putting away her jewelry supplies, Leslie made a mental note to check in with Michelle first thing in the morning. She resolved to subtly investigate what after-hours work Bryce had given him. Something about the arrangement troubled her. Exploitation of staff wasn't right.

What an odd ending to a strangely mixed day.

Two

A week later—Wednesday, October 16th

Bryce Nelson chose the monogrammed handkerchief and folded a pocket square. He reached for the intercom at his clinic desk with renewed vigor. Its light and dark brown cloth harmonized nicely with his sandy hair and brown eyes. Although a bit of gray sprinkled his full head of hair, it hadn't invaded his heavy brows. He'd checked that morning before leaving for work. The spiderweb of lines surrounding what was left of his lips had eased somewhat with time off and sun. What he wouldn't give to return to his fifties.

"Good morning, Lynn. Would you kindly bring me my schedule?"

He glanced at his desktop piles an hour early for work and settled back into his cushioned leather chair. The memos fanned out before him. At home in his clinic office, he glanced around the room, calculating gains and losses. Everything occupied its rightful place. The dusty credenza piles were just as he had left them weeks before. Unlike the cramped quarters he'd been forced to endure on vacation, his oversized leather furnishings catered well to his six-foot frame. Lynn Tidings, the front receptionist, arrived in her typical perfunctory style, blonde hair tied away from her drawn face in an orange patterned scarf wrap. She carried files and a notebook.

"Here it is, Doctor." Her face remained expressionless as she presented a page pulled from her pile. Behind thick glasses, her gray eyes held weariness but vigilance. Her thin, straight nose led to a small mouth often caught between just enough truth and necessary silence. She laid the sheet down. "There's a message from your lawyer on the rearranged federal agent meeting. I left it on top."

He leaned forward while thumbing through quickly and separated one. Marveling at the timing of things, he only wished he'd held his tongue with his key referral source before the would-be inspector arrived, but that proverbial horse was out of the barn. His task now was to reassure that same referral source. Fortunately, the wheels were in motion to eliminate their shared problem.

Lynn adjusted her thick glasses and sat on the bulky couch near his desk, her feet failing to rest flat on the floor. "I need to get back to your patient, Larry Bridge. He's lost his job and insurance. Says he can't afford the Marketplace and wants to know if you'll do a sliding fee until he finds another position. He doesn't want to risk going off his medication. Will we enroll him in the drug company's assistance program?"

Bryce rubbed the side of his face, an "uh" escaping his breath. The patient's story was too much like his son Dan's. Though Dan hadn't lost his position, their family's health insurance was history—a financial deathblow given Danny Jr.'s muscular dystrophy. Nearly three years later, the system left them falling through a crack the size of the Columbia River Gorge. Bryce lifted his chin and fingered the handkerchief. The topic brought to mind a real son-of-a-bitch—his own father, Daniel.

"Get Michelle going on the drug company program for his meds." Perfect job for the nurse.

He considered how his father would handle Larry Bridge's dilemma. Almost hearing his typical cut-and-dried quip, *You run into an obstacle, you remove it*, Bryce was certain Larry would be sent packing.

"And the sliding scale?"

In the distance, the waiting room door closed.

"No, I won't reduce my fees." Some deserved extra help and some didn't. "Get working on referring him to the public health system. We'll carry whatever balance he can't pay. He can work out a payment plan with Pearl." Their new office manager's responsibility—every provider's billing. Problem solved.

Another door closed, signaling they weren't alone. Sloan Mannon stood in the doorway, a light Burberry scarf draping his coat collar.

"Hey, welcome back. Again." His pale complexion framed hooded eyes summoning charm and fitting his perfectly pressed clothing.

Although this was Bryce's first day at work after three weeks off, he'd returned to town on Monday—just in time to attend their addiction treatment team meeting under cover of vacation garb.

Sloan toted a signature plaid briefcase. The shine of his shaved head under office lights matched his clean-shaven face. "Can we talk? I've got some updates after getting current with the rehab clinic counseling records."

Decades of labor in a psychologist's chair had left few facial lines on this man in his early sixties, the same age as Bryce. With their type of work, Bryce was surprised he didn't look older, but then, he'd probably cheated with facials and Botox.

"Thanks, man. I'll catch you in the kitchen after we're done here."

"Sure," Sloan waved off.

"Anything pressing with the medical board?" Bryce turned to Lynn.

"The usual. The director is asking for a call." She stood and smoothed her skirt. "And you'll be having lunch at twelve-fifteen with Dr. Schoen."

Bryce raised an eyebrow. "Surely, we can reschedule. Look at this desk."

"No, sir." She held his eyes without seeming to breathe. "I've given my word."

He sighed, knowing he had to speak to his key referral source soon and call his lawyer to discuss the arrangements made with the DEA agent, the details of which he was still unaware. But those weren't things he would deal with in a lunch hour. He'd brush Leslie off in a few minutes.

"All right." He rose from his desk and handed Lynn a message. "Will you get this lawyer on the phone for me?"

Overhead lights illuminated the clinic's waiting room at seven-thirty as Leslie arrived for work. Every light visible in the suite was ablaze, unusual for the hour, and the reception desk was unoccupied. She crossed the square area, empty chairs lining three of its walls, toward the door to the back office next to Lynn's window.

Setting her purse and laptop bag on the providers' inbox counter, she turned to notice Bryce's door was closed. With a few steps down the hall, pausing outside his door, she registered muffled voices and returned to the counter to organize her day's schedule.

After touching base with her lawyer yesterday, Leslie harbored a growing sense of irritation because they'd made no progress in learning who'd filed the complaint against her. She considered whether the last office manager was the culprit since he left under a cloud. His replacement, Pearl, was quite unlikely, and blaming either was a stretch. If the drugs were truly missing, Leslie doubted they'd been lifted from the hall sample closet. Michelle and Damon's thorough inventory yesterday, under her oversight, found everything in order. Of course, that didn't speak to the past.

In just a few hours, Leslie would finally question Bryce about the missing opiates since he'd ducked every effort she'd made to reach him on vacation. His closed office door clicked, and Lynn emerged, dressed in brown professional attire except for a floral paisley hair scarf.

"Morning." Leslie greeted the trustworthy receptionist, the glue holding everything in their busy office together. Lynn would never tamper with Bryce's safe.

"Hi, Dr. Schoen." She rested her files on the counter, offering a meager smile.

"Is Dr. Nelson in already?"

"Yeah, he's got a pile in there." Her porcelain face held scant cosmetics. "You know how it is after a long vacation."

In fact, Leslie had never taken a long break. She'd hardly call rehab a vacation. Maybe in about seven or eight months, it would be different.

"Anyone else here?" Leslie checked the time.

"Just Dr. Mannon." The shadows under Lynn's eyes were uncharacteristic.

"Didn't you stay overtime last night? And here you are again, early."

"I had a late meeting yesterday."

"On my way out, I saw you heading into Pearl's office. Same scheduling thing?"

Lynn nodded. She looked the worse for wear. Her lips pressed together as she glanced somewhere over Leslie's shoulder. The pattern was repeating itself. Lynn had been increasingly alone with the former manager and now with their current biller, Pearl.

Leslie pictured the former manager's last day at work. Bryce had stormed out of his office after the man confronted him, the door wide open.

"Have you heard about Suboxone or buprenorphine samples going missing around here?"

Lynn straightened. "What?"

"Is it possible our former biller was angry enough with Bryce to take opioid samples from his safe the day he quit?"

"Are you kidding me?" Lynn hitched a shoulder before turning toward Bryce, who exited his room. She grabbed her files as he passed on his way to the restroom, his head down, staring at his phone.

Leslie doubted the man's involvement, but maybe Lynn had seen something to implicate him. Leslie and Lynn had been present that Friday when the last manager, who'd had enough of Bryce, left the job—leaving no one to manage the books for weeks. He'd been alone in Bryce's office long enough to have accessed his safe. All the while, she and Lynn stood by, watching the whole drama unfold.

Gesturing toward her office, Leslie snatched her mail and mouthed, "Later" to Lynn. After pouring a cup from the coffee pot, bold comfort rising in fragrant steam, she settled in at her desk. Nothing like getting lost in morning patients' issues—a welcome reprieve from her own.

At twelve-fifteen, she set her lunch bag on the kitchen table. Bryce entered the room with a cell phone at his ear as she bit into a turkey sandwich. He scraped a wooden chair across the tile floor, exchanged the phone for a handkerchief from his jacket pocket, and launched himself into the seat. His graying flock of sandy hair framed brown eyes and an angular facial shape with a fresh tan.

"Welcome back, Bryce. You look rested." Leslie squinted at him.

"I have little time, Leslie." He sprang from his seat and headed to the refrigerator, where he grabbed a sandwich and tore the wrapping apart. "Okay, what happened while I was gone? Did my on-call team handle everything?"

"I need to talk to you about your bupe samples, Bryce. I have nothing to say about your on-call coverage. Are you missing Suboxone or other buprenorphine samples from your safe?"

He studied his sandwich for a bit too long and took another bite. His once-handsome features had hardened into a mask of preoccupation. He chomped at a moderately quick pace gazing at the wall behind her.

"What's this about?"

"The medical board sent me a notice. Someone alleged I stole opioid drugs—Suboxone or similar—from this office. That has to be from your practice. They aren't saying who made the complaint yet."

A tightness at the edges of his eyes hadn't been present when he sat down. His glance moved from her back to his lunch. As he continued to eat, the hair on the back of her neck stood on end.

"Bryce, I don't need to explain how disturbing this is." He was well aware of her story—her entire life history to age thirty. "You must know something about this. You're the only one giving out bupe samples around here."

He swallowed the rest of his sandwich and wiped his mouth with his handkerchief. There was no masking the glint in his eye. "There'd better not be bupe missing. God knows you've got plenty of experience with the medical board, Leslie. I have every faith in you and your attorney's ability to deal with them." He glanced at the wall clock.

Her hand closed into a tight fist as she resisted the bait in his patronizing tone. Not only had he evaluated her alcoholism for the state's physician health program a decade before, but he was still the Board's addiction expert. He tried to feign ignorance, but it wasn't working. And she'd learned from experience that pressing Bryce was like circling in a revolving door with no exit.

"You're not answering the question. Is your sample safe missing buprenorphine?"

He stood abruptly. "Let's find out. No one else is telling me bupe is missing from my safe. We'll do an inventory of all office samples right now." He turned to leave.

She opened her mouth to say the hall sample closet review was done yesterday, but he was gone.

THREE

Wednesday, October 16th—Early afternoon: Clinic

An after-lunch brief walk downtown helped to clear Leslie's mind. She returned to the office and peered at two men sitting together in the reception room. Dressed in dark suits with thin ties, one with a briefcase, they looked more prepared for a business meeting than a couples' or family mental health session.

The check-in window was closed, with at least eight other people waiting. She passed through to the back hallway.

Gesturing at the front counter, Leslie caught Lynn's attention. "Something's happening. Are you free to sit down together?"

After a quick nod, Leslie led Lynn to her office and closed the door. "So, what's with the two fellows out there?"

Lynn laid a business card on the desk and hiked her glasses, her forehead furrowed. "Drug Enforcement Agency."

Leslie's breath caught. This might connect to the board allegation. But in yesterday's call with her lawyer, she'd been reassured there wouldn't be any DEA interviews unless the claim was confirmed. She cautioned herself to chill. This wasn't about her.

"So, an inspection of the MAT clinic?" They often shortened Bryce's opioid addiction program to "Medication Assisted Treatment," or MAT.

"Yes. An agent and an inspector auditing Bryce's practice," Lynn said. "I told Drs. Nelson and Mannon. They're both busy with patients right now."

Missing opiates? DEA? Too close for comfort. A creeping dread burrowed through Leslie's chest.

"Are Damon and Michelle aware?"

"Yeah. I know those two are working a lot of overtime, but they've been acting weird toward each other lately. Really distant since their team meeting on Monday. They wouldn't even look at each other."

"I noticed, too."

Leslie was surprised Lynn had mentioned it. She'd expected Lynn and Michelle would be closer, both Portland natives in their mid-forties. She later learned both had a parent with addiction or alcoholism. No surprise for rehab practice employees.

Michelle had met Bryce fifteen years earlier in the hospital's addiction treatment department. She was a registered nurse for the program, and he was their treating doctor. Over time, he convinced her to work for him. She'd once said Bryce's charm and good looks captured her. He often brought her sweet things to eat. But she wasn't into him like that. Bryce must've been the opposite of Michelle's father, whom she had called a horribly abusive addict, dead long ago. Had he lived, her dad and Bryce would've been about the same age.

Leslie knew Michelle looked for Bryce's approval. He supported her decision to throw herself into her job after her divorce since she didn't have kids. He helped pile the work on with praise for her dedication.

"Dr. Schoen, can I mention one more thing?" Lynn spoke in a serious tone. "I've had this feeling something isn't right ever since Dr. Nelson's addiction treatment—you know, the MAT clinic—patient load increased so much this year. I can't put my finger on it, but a man came in last week for the MAT clinic." She aligned a pen and sticky pad on the desk. "I knew the guy but couldn't place him. It was like he'd been a patient here in the past, but the name and information he gave didn't appear in the database. He was self-pay, not unusual for a MAT client." She repositioned her glasses. "I mentioned him to Michelle, but she blew me off. And something is off with Damon, too. I've had my eye on him now for a while. He changed his system sign-in a couple of days ago after telling me he'd changed it last week. It's not like him. He makes killer passwords."

"I hear you. I've noticed the circles under his eyes." Leslie handed the DEA agent's business card back to Lynn.

Damon had appeared painfully exhausted that morning, his eyelids purple and swollen. He'd been so removed lately. Nothing like the energetic, funny guy she'd gotten to know. She flashed on the joy, the quiet pride he'd shown two years before after solving her laptop theft issue. How different he was now. He'd only begun talking to Michelle again.

"Have either he or Michelle talked about the bupe samples? Maybe concerns with how they're delivered or stored?"

Lynn frowned. "I need to think about it. Nothing comes to mind right away."

Lynn's can-do attitude and resourcefulness had made her indispensable around the office. She reliably gave consideration when asked.

The timing of all of this was too much for coincidence. Leslie wasn't sure she believed in coincidences.

"Okay, let me know. Let's go to the front." It struck her: Michelle hadn't directly addressed her questions about bupe sample deliveries during the hall closet inventory. "One thing, Lynn. I know sometimes the DEA simply does unannounced inspections of Suboxone clinics. Maybe part of this is that simple."

Lynn nodded and hurried down the hall.

Right now, Leslie needed to pin Michelle down about pharmaceutical sales reps and samples in Bryce's safe before she got busy with the DEA.

Outside the nurse's room, Leslie paused. Michelle spoke with a stern tone, the actual words muffled. The waiting room door closed with a bang, and Leslie spotted Bryce leading the DEA agents into his office. She quickly stepped into Michelle's work area.

"Hey, Michelle, can I—?"

"So, I'll come by with the material we talked about Monday." Michelle was facing Damon, fully engaged.

No doubt about it, Leslie had interrupted quite a focused exchange.

The nurse's work area spanned the front corner of a large work area opposite the inner hallway. Between her desk against the wall and her bookshelves lining the adjacent wall, she operated out of an L-shaped nook, fielding patient calls, responding to pharmacies, and a myriad of healthcare matters. Directly behind her and on the far wall, a door into Damon's office closed with a thump.

Michelle reached for a bagel resting on a napkin, inhaled a bite, and sat chewing. "What's new?" Her tall stature seated in a high-backed chair left her head even with Leslie's shoulder, nearly erasing the six-inch gap in their heights.

"I need to hear more about the sample closet inventory. Let's meet in the kitchen after my last patient."

"Sure, if I'm not busy with this DEA thing," Michelle spoke with a wrist in front of her mouth, her brunette hair loose around her shoulders, and bangs swept back behind her ear. Her pale skin stretched tautly over her rounded face and drooped around her eyes, but the tension in the lines around her mouth was evident. Dressed in hospital scrubs, she turned her five-foot, ten-inch frame back, reaching to tap her blinking phone. The intercom channeled Bryce.

"Michelle, I need you to take these agents and meet with them in Sloan's office."

"Right away." She steadied her bagel on a napkin and licked a finger. "Excuse me." She darted into the hall.

Leslie headed to her office, intent on getting Michelle to talk about the Suboxone sales representative and the log of dispensed bupe samples. She barely settled behind her desk when a bang sounded from Damon's office across the hall. Heart in her throat, Leslie hurried out to realize someone must have shut his office door so hard it had bounced ajar. She cracked the opening slightly, finding Bryce and Damon in conversation.

After checking to ensure no one was around, Leslie leaned into the crack, planning on seeking supplies in the closet to her left if someone entered the hall.

"Listen, Damon," Bryce spoke with a low pitch. "You must get those chart edits done. Today. I told you three weeks ago to get current." Something landed with a slap on a desk or counter. "Put off everything else and text me before you leave. I want it updated. Now." His voice shifted even lower. "Sloan has the goods on you, man. Let's not air dirty laundry."

Leslie held her breath and waited, the tick-tock rhythm of Damon's plastic travel clock counting in the background.

"Doctor, I know this is important. I'll get it done. I'm a team player. And what I shared with Dr. Mannon years ago stays with him. He assured me it would. But you're right. Stinkin' laundry is foul. Yours included."

"Do it." Bryce was seething, his tone and huffed breath revealing his anger. How had he become such a Class A jerk?

A doorknob's click from the psychologist's room next to hers sent Leslie back to her office at full tilt, her pulse in her ears. She shut herself in and plopped into her desk chair.

This was it—time to ask Damon about the missing opiates and the medical board. He was so pissed with Bryce. Whatever might've held him back was probably history. The hostility between them was boiling over. She jotted some notes while breathing deeply to slow her pulse.

Chart edits?

What does Bryce have on Damon that's compromising?

Is Damon's knowledge of Bryce's "stinking laundry" about the missing drugs?

Would her questions put Damon in a bind? His phone call in the middle of the night last week came to mind. *Bad tacos, my ass.* No, he'd been reaching out about something. She cursed herself for not understanding he needed help.

A buzz sounded at her desk.

"Dr. Schoen, your next patient is ready."

Leslie reached for her afternoon schedule. She'd speak with Damon before Michelle after her last patient. If he got tied up with the inspection, she'd do it first thing in the morning.

FOUR

Thursday, October 17th

Leslie settled into their home's kitchen breakfast nook while the coffee maker bubbled and hissed, brewing a strong early-Guatemalan blend. She inhaled its rich complexity. As a holding station for miscellaneous items in front of the door to the garage, their wooden table and chairs endured plenty of wear. The nook's bay window featured a full view of the backyard and patio garden. Across the table, Izzy sighed and rubbed her warm mug.

Why am I really holding the board complaint back from her?

"Earth to Leslie?" Izzy dinged her cup with her spoon.

"What?" Leslie startled. "Oh, sorry! I've got three priorities on my mind at once."

"What three priorities, exactly?"

"Well, I wanted to catch Damon early about a couple of things." She'd failed to speak privately with either him or Michelle yesterday.

Izzy's eyebrows lifted. "You're ignoring a few important personal details with everything going on at work." She shook her head. "All you talked about last night was the office. Yeah, it's crazy over there, but what about all your mom's stuff in the baby's room? Are you avoiding the boxes her friend packed for you? We need to prepare the nursery."

True. Leslie also wanted to get going on plans for the baby. After the miscarriage, they'd tossed so much—out of sight, out of mind—behind the room's closed door.

"Those were your mom's treasures. We—*you*—should look at them."

Leslie's mother had lived in a Phoenix, Arizona, townhouse several years before a heart attack caused her unexpected death. "You know what they say. Never look back." She shifted in her chair. "I'll do something with those boxes, I promise, but right now, I need to take a shower."

Izzy wadded her napkin and tossed it on the counter. "What an un-shrink-like thing to say." Her cheeks bloomed crimson. "We've got to get ready for the baby. And since when do you skate around sharing what's on your mind with me?"

"It's the same old tune, Iz. Will this office remain stable? Should I move my practice? Yada, yada."

"Bullshit. Leslie, what's happening with you?"

Tightening her grip on the cup, Leslie took a deep breath. "Okay, maybe it's insecurity about becoming a parent again." She avoided Izzy's stare. "I'm grappling with having one original family member left. My father might be dead. I haven't seen him since I was seven." She pushed herself back from the table. "I've got vague memories of him. Thankfully, Gramps and my mom's cousin Grace saved our asses after he bailed." She tussled the hair on Baby J's head as the dog crowded her. "At least I still have Grace."

Quiet descended on the room. If she hadn't succeeded in diverting Izzy away from her secretiveness, at least Leslie had lightened the twist in the pit of her gut. Oh, Grace! Like an older sister, funny and quick as a whip, if not with her own flights of fancy. She missed her.

"We need to get in touch. It's been so long," Izzy said finally. Leslie kept silent.

"Right. Ms. Never-Look-Back." Izzy stood behind her chair and shoved it into the table. "You are full of it today." She forced a hard smile.

Again, Leslie didn't answer. Her mom, Jean, had often been a bone of contention between them. Whenever Izzy had asked pointed questions, like why her parents had separated, all Leslie offered was her mother's defense—her father had bailed during trying times. Right after her father left, her mom had taken a nosedive, abusing weed and prescription medications. They'd lived in their car for a month.

"Look, we have some time." Leslie bit her lower lip, checking the clock above the foyer entry. "Let's open the top box. It'll take ten minutes."

Izzy ran her hands through her hair and squinted. "Okay."

They went upstairs, past the study, to the room at the end of the hall. In the quiet early morning, the only sound was Baby J's toenails clicking on the floor.

Leslie crossed through the mess to open the blinds, illuminating the crib trapped behind a stack of boxes. Next to a portable bassinet, five bankers' boxes were stacked high, reaching eye level. She pulled the top one down and ripped the packing tape away while Izzy stood in the doorway. Baby J had picked her spot and lay on the rug between them. Leslie's eyes fixed on a small wooden box underneath letter bundles and photos.

"This looks familiar." She dislodged it, sitting cross-legged on the floor beside the dog.

As she opened the lid, a folded page that had stuck to the bottom of the box fell into her lap. The faint odor of rosewood prompted an image of her mother. "It's my Badger necklace!" She sprang to her feet, grinning.

"What?" Izzy walked into the room and grabbed the paper from the floor. She read,

"The Badger's Medicine. Invokes warrior courage and fighting spirit. The white stripe shows its openness. Its powerful jaws tie to the word, recalling the magic of storytelling. A digger, the Badger sees beneath the surface of all things. This solitary animal teaches comfort with self and encourages inward seeking. The badger's bold and ferocious spirit demands, 'Never surrender.' We love you, Leslie. Mom, Gramps, and Grace."

"I got this when I was eight years old." Tears brimmed in Leslie's eyes as she placed the leather cord with its carved rustic amulet around her neck. "After Mom pulled herself together for a while." She held the wooden badger in her hands, running her fingertips along its smoothed edges. "We went on a driving trip to Colorado, crossed the Nebraska Sandhills. I found this in a little truck-stop trinket place in Broken Bow."

Izzy smiled. "Your power-animal object."

Baby J's tail wagged as she nosed her way in for some scratches.

"Very late '80s, huh?" Leslie beamed. "It meant so much to me. I wore it all the time. My mom told me over and over, 'Seek your inner self, your bold, ferocious spirit. Never surrender.'" She placed a hand over the necklace on her chest. "I think that's what she was trying to do. I'm not so sure about the 'never surrender' part for me these days."

"There's the old mojo." While one arm encircled Leslie, Izzy used her other hand to caress the dog. "But we really need to unload this room."

"Absolutely. I'll schlep these boxes out of here first thing when I get home."

"Thanks, Pearl. Come on through."

Leslie leaned toward her office desk intercom, doubting the timing of her scheduled video call with her accountant. Luckily, their new office manager, Pearl Blanco, was on her way in to help create some order. With all the stacks on her desk, Leslie had lost the instructions she'd printed. At half past eight, the workday and her office were disorganized with Damon not in yet.

The sound of a quick knock drew Leslie's attention to greet Pearl. The woman's flowing skirt and heavy, lived-in sweater hugged a robust figure. Beneath her professional demeanor, fine lines around her eyes revealed life's hardships and moments of joy. Her full mouth often curved into a knowing half-smile. After two months in the job, she'd already proven her steady hand during rough waters.

Pearl sat across the desk with a direct, unblinking gaze. "What do we have?" Her alto voice was calming and intense at the same time.

"Will you please show me how to access my last quarterly financials? I can't find the new system directions, and I've got a Zoom meeting with my CPA about my line of credit in an hour."

Pearl had upgraded their bookkeeping software.

"Of course." She came around to view the laptop. Her eyes narrowed as she took charge of the keyboard, narrating instructions in a paced fashion. The tight kinks of her dark hair stood high on her head with a few salty sprinkles in contrast at the temples. A faint, earthy aroma with subtle citrus undertones surrounded her as she demonstrated the software. The reports were generated within two minutes. Leslie jotted down the essential path.

This close, Pearl looked squarely middle-aged. Leslie marveled at her smooth, dark brown complexion, with rich mahogany tones that nearly defied wrinkling. Beyond the woman's talent for numbers, she'd already demonstrated her shrewdness by restoring Leslie's cash flow to normal.

"You make it look easy. I've got it now, thanks. Have a seat."

"You're welcome." Pearl took the same seat again and gazed at the wall piece next to the window, a woodcut with a winding path through forest greens. The stonewall-bound passage led into dark woods, with an unclear end. "I like this print." She turned her head to face Leslie. "Would you want me to join you on the Zoom? I'll school the accountant about what she needs in ten minutes. You introduce me and drop out."

"Deal. I'd love to bow out. Has Damon arrived?"

"No, I haven't seen him yet this morning." Pearl shifted forward in her chair. "But I know Lynn's tried to reach him twice. She talked to him last night after everyone was gone. He said he'd be in early."

A woman sobbed in the next room. The psychologist, Sloan Mannon, had started working with clients.

Leslie gestured toward the wall. "Things get a little sensitive around here sometimes." She pictured their previous hot-headed biller, who'd been nothing like this poised woman. "How are you doing with the job?"

Pearl let out a deep breath. "Doctor, now don't get me wrong. I am very grateful for the work. I've got a ten-year-old son at home." She flickered her gaze. "But I'm in kind of a bind."

"You're spending lots of time with Lynn on the scheduling. Frankly, your predecessor had some real difficulties tying it all together." She moved her laptop further to the side. "By now,

I'm sure you realize how separate my practice is from Dr. Nelson's clinic."

"Yes."

"Have you heard anyone around here talking about medication samples or the medical board? Apparently, there are missing opioids, and someone's trying to pin it on me." Leslie lightly cleared her throat.

Pearl's brows rose. "Oh, now that *is* some stormy weather coming in." She fixed her gaze on the bookshelves behind Leslie's desk. "No... but I did—"

The noise in the next room settled into soft whimpers.

"What?"

"Dr. Schoen, I came upon Dr. Nelson and Michelle in the kitchen the other day, right before his vacation. The door was opened a bit." She paused. "He told her she'd be moving into your office soon." Pearl tipped her chin down. "I got out of there right away."

Heat rose from Leslie's chest into her neck as her breath caught.

Ah, Bejeezus!

She was the scapegoat for missing drugs. It was Bryce's plan to get her out of there.

Around midmorning, while tapping on her laptop, Leslie finished a note at her desk with laser focus. Her office door opened after a brief knock. Lynn popped her head in.

"Doctor, your next patient wanted to be rescheduled. Dr. Nelson wants you to come to his office and talk about how we'll deal without Damon today. The DEA is busy with Dr. Mannon right now."

"Did Damon call?"

"No. No one's heard anything."

Leslie nodded. A plan for the short-staffed day was needed. But facing Bryce, knowing what Pearl had overheard, would be a challenge. She decided against addressing it with him, not wanting to put their biller in a tight spot. Maybe Leslie's lease expiration in eight months was perfectly timed after all.

She centered herself, gazing at the art piece hanging on her office side wall. A person walking away from the viewer carried a crimson backpack, the only color in an otherwise gray winter scene. The solitary figure trudged along a narrow, uneven brick path exposed to falling snow between tall buildings.

A question formed in Leslie's mind as she focused on the red knapsack. *Why does Bryce want me out, after he did so much to recruit me?*

She closed her laptop and followed the aroma of freshly brewed coffee to Bryce's door.

Leslie hated his office—its dark furnishings, expensive, and ginormous. He'd chosen every piece of furniture for someone six feet or taller. Heavy drapes covered the windows. A stuffed couch sat too high off the floor. Every shelf was overfilled with mementos, books, and tchotchkes. The sizes of the furniture pieces were simply too large for the space, making it an obstacle course to move through the room. Michelle sat opposite him, elbows on the mighty teak desk. Bryce leaned away in his custom swivel chair, grimacing, looking so different from the smiling man in his ridiculous framed credenza photo with the governor.

"Hey there." She sat, not waiting for a reply. "You wanted to talk about no Damon today?"

"Listen, Leslie." Bryce hovered over the desk with dissatisfaction, his dark eyes flashing with threatened authority. "We want to know where he is."

"Dr. Nelson always relies on me to get everything done." Michelle had settled upright in her chair. She'd pulled her hair back into a tight braid, highlighting deepened hollows beneath her high cheekbones. "And I can assure you I'm ready. I'll juggle whatever DEA-related tasks are needed as well."

Something more was going on here. Michelle sounded ready to pop, her voice climbing high and tight. It was as if her blood pressure was maxing out, her orblike face was so reddened. She was more tightly wound than Leslie had ever witnessed.

"I have three people who need nursing or medical assistant attention today. Would you like their names now?"

"Dr. Nelson wants you to check on Damon," Michelle blurted, the whites of her eyes growing larger as she leaned forward. "You can go to his apartment and text us when you find him."

"I'm calling for no such thing." Bryce kept his voice at an even pace. His breathing sounded through flared nostrils as he frowned at Michelle. "You often seem to think you know what I prefer. And here, you are incorrect. To the contrary, I'm opposed." The muscles in his jawline contracted and relaxed. "But I believe you know where Damon is, Leslie. You two have become so chummy."

Now, she was definitely worried about Damon. Checking on him would give her a perfect chance to find out what he knew about the missing bupe. He'd looked so drained lately. Maybe he'd gotten into the opiates—taken the drugs himself. But he'd never shown pinned pupils or appeared intoxicated around her. Or had withdrawal signs like sweating and shakiness.

"I wish I knew where he was." Leslie kept her expression fixed. "But I have no idea. How will we get everything covered today? I am willing to check on him after my work's done."

"I'm the one who's covering for Damon." Michelle tapped her hand on her heart. "Good—you'll look in on him. Let me know what's needed. I'll address questions and discuss charts with the inspectors." Her speaking pace had quickened. "Pearl can get messages at my desk. She'll process the mail. We'll get it all done."

Leslie stood, with Bryce now between her and the door.

"You're involved in some way with Damon's absence." Bryce pointed at Leslie, his tone menacing.

She softened her face into an amiable smile, reaching back to performance skills from a college theater class. In a couple of weeks, she might be talking to the medical board with him in the room. He was already coming after her. *Time to tread carefully.* "I don't know why you'd say that, Bryce. Your reactions baffle me sometimes." She rose, her throat tight, to make her exit. "Lynn left Damon a message. I'll swing by his place later. I'm concerned about him. He's never not shown without calling."

"Of all days," Bryce muttered something more under his breath. "Michelle, get Pearl to help. We're done."

He waved Leslie and Michelle away.

Having circled the block at nearly six-thirty after work that day, Leslie pulled her Subaru over to the curb outside Damon's place in Grant Park. She peered at the expansive, corner Portland-style home. Painted periwinkle blue with cream trim, its center steps led to a full-width porch. Two stories rose above, hinting at a possible finished attic, while the elevated foundation suggested the basement apartment below. Dark, blinds drawn, there were no signs of people anywhere, including at Damon's basement apartment.

Everyone in the office had been dealing with the DEA when she'd left. Again, she'd had no chance to talk with Michelle privately.

Leslie sat for a minute in her car and continued to watch Damon's place—a west-facing basement apartment with its own entry. A small courtyard with a patio table and two chairs decorated the lower-level side entrance. Briefly, she scrolled through her phone history. She hadn't spoken with Izzy since breakfast.

"Leslie?"

"Hey, Izzy. I'm finally done at the office. Things were too crazy for me to check in at lunch. Where are you now?"

"In the kitchen with the dog. What's going on?"

"Where do I start?"

She filled Izzy in about Damon's disappearance and the latest audit news. "I think they found problems with the inspection, but I don't have specifics. Lynn told me their log of active patients taking bupe wasn't current. Of course, it's Bryce's fault. But Damon never came to work today or called. It isn't like him."

"Does anyone have an idea where he is?"

Leslie glanced sideways to check the sidewalks behind her and across the street.

"No." She cleared her throat. "Bryce was a complete ass when Michelle and I met with him about covering for Damon. Michelle's in some sort of crazed robot mode. Sloan stayed out of view. I suppose the DEA isn't as interested in a psychologist." She sat taller for a better look at the home's side yard, where a weathered wooden fence stood in the fading light, partially intact. "Damon has this apartment in Grant Park close to us. I'm sitting outside his place now."

"What?"

The dark gray clouds overhead gave way to some western light, rendering a surreal three-dimensional cast to the old homes and mature trees in the neighborhood.

"Okay, it started with Bryce, Michelle, and me in his office. Michelle had this psycho moment, saying Bryce wanted me to go to Damon's apartment to check on him." Leslie turned her car off. "Then Bryce got steamed and told me to forget it."

"So, have you checked on Damon yet?"

"No." Leslie gave her earring an absent-minded tug.

"Weren't you telling me he didn't look good?"

"Yeah." She lingered on the image. "I'm about to head to his door now." Leslie pulled the car keys out and pocketed them. "I'll call you right back." She ended the call.

Damon's front door housed three vertical glass panes resting above a ledge in the entry's upper half, but nothing was visible when Leslie peeked in. The blinds on either side of the door were drawn. She knocked and rang the doorbell, called him, but got his voicemail again.

Deciding to leave a message through the main house letter slot, she headed back to her car for some paper and a pen. She noticed nothing unusual when walking around the house, except that his dining room window was partially open. A yell inside roused nothing, no one. Within minutes, Leslie was back in her car.

She planned to call for a police welfare check if he remained silent until morning.

FIVE

Friday, October 18th

At midmorning, multiple police cruisers swarmed the streets surrounding Damon Grady's basement apartment in Grant Park. Neighbors gathered, necks craned to catch a view. Barricades linked with bright yellow tape roped off a spectrum of shocked faces as a drab, cloud-packed sky created odd shadows on the residence's front patio.

"Hello, Jeannette?" Detective Aaron Davis emerged from the compact apartment, bending forward to clear the entry at six feet three inches while stuffing a notebook into his rear pocket.

He greeted the Multnomah County Deputy Medical Examiner, whose composed refinement belied her proximity to corpses. With her dark hair pulled into a neat ponytail, her face revealed nothing but prominent cheekbones and a defined jawline. As far as Davis had seen, she'd always maintained her composure around mortality's darkness. Conferring with her over a suspicious death case was becoming a regular habit.

"Hi, Aaron." The doctor pulled disposable gloves from her leather satchel as her mouth curved into a measured smile. She tugged on the mitts. "I spoke with your assistant on the phone earlier, but will you review this morning for me, from the top?"

"Sure." He listed the neighborhood beat officers who'd completed the early morning welfare check. No neighbors questioned had seen Damon Grady since Wednesday. The homeowner was at the coast, so they'd forced entry after finding the apartment doorknob and deadbolt locked. After discovering a dead man in the bathroom, they called for a detail team and preserved the scene. Mr. Grady's wallet, found in the apartment, contained his driver's license, giving a preliminary corpse ID. An Oregon criminal history records check landed a remote DUI arrest giving his fingerprints. A confirmation of the body was anticipated. The investigative supervisor reached the Medical Examiner, who elected to postpone responding until homicide detectives completed an initial assessment.

There was something about a closed space with a corpse, the air's stillness and weight, that troubled Detective Davis. Cold memories produced a crawl of goosebumps along the back of his neck.

Inside the apartment, less than nine hundred square feet, he stood next to his junior detective while they both spoke with the CSI team supervisor. Adrienne Levy, his right hand for three days and a rookie to Homicide, had already made a name for herself at the Bureau. That's what worried him.

An overview of the apartment began with a cluttered desk, including gaming equipment along the north wall. Bookshelves flanked the bedroom doorway on the south. An under-porch mudroom connected the bedroom's second door to another apartment exit, which also led to the front patio. The dining area's egress window provided natural light and opened to the property's backyard. Flanking the dining area, which was open to the kitchen, the bathroom contained a tub-shower, while the U-shaped kitchen featured abandoned dishes and take-out containers. Everything screamed bachelor living.

Davis and Levy's pairing was a first within the PPB: a seasoned Black detective with a rookie white woman, the only woman in the Portland Police Bureau's Homicide Unit. Levy's late-twentysomething frame spoke of strength and stamina. She was a gym rat. The bulk of her muscle showed in her shoulders, but overall, she was fairly light—maybe five feet seven and a hundred forty pounds. Davis zeroed in on her face, framed in short, dark curly hair, an olive skin complexion, and the signature mole above her right cheekbone that drew people's eyes. Her thick eyebrows held steady as she shot a glare at him.

He supposed their acceptance into PPB Homicide was what they had in common. He stood eight inches taller, and his experience exceeded hers by a decade. He liked to defer to his wife, Rochelle, about his appearance: years of police work had etched thoughtful lines around his mouth, and his deep brown—sometimes black—eyes radiated calm authority nestled within his mahogany complexion. She called him towering and solid, but he leaned toward his unyielding determination, tempered only by an essential compassion, as the driving force behind his achievement in this senior homicide position. They entered a small bathroom reeking of vomit and soiled briefs. He paused between the sink and the toilet to view the body while Levy began snapping photos.

"A pretty strange position," she remarked, waving at the bathtub corpse, her navy-blue nail polish visible under latex gloves.

What once was Damon Grady knelt in the tub, face leaning into the faucet, showerhead pointing down on him. In all of Davis's years at the Bureau, he'd seen plenty of dead bodies in bathtubs—on their backs in a pool of bloody water or puddles of blood, riddled with bullets. Lots of face-upward situations, but never like this. His jeans, socks, and a T-shirt were jammed into the space between the toilet and the bath. What looked like dried puke was stuck on the tiled wall.

"He looks pretty lightweight, maybe five feet eight inches. About a hundred sixty pounds." Davis activated his phone's flashlight. "How he got into this position—or better yet, why—that's the question."

He nosed around the bathroom, carefully avoiding possible evidence. Multiple investigative team members worked in the apartment, clicking photographs, dusting for fingerprints, and scrutinizing the deceased's belongings.

"Looks like shower water came down on him, based on his hair and the look of his briefs." Levy pointed to the back of the corpse's head where thick black curls flattened in the middle and pressed against the skull. Matted cloth over the buttocks stuck to the skin. Above the bathtub, a curtain ring hung on chains, dropped from the ceiling. The plastic liner rested on the outside of the bath, gathered against the far wall.

"If the water came down, who turned it off? Or on?" Davis scanned the ceiling above the tub.

"Good question. Plus, I don't see evidence of multiple or longstanding injection marks." Levy moved to view the body, although the shower-tub arrangement abutted the wall, preventing her from circling it. "The ME's call."

The corpse's right arm hung down to the bath base, palm partially open. Davis leaned in to discover a syringe, needle, and tourniquet next to the hand. Some discoloration of the tub surface looked like possible blood. Directly above the compression tie, at the inner aspect of the elbow, remnants of a puncture wound included some bleeding. The corpse gripped the hot water faucet on the other side.

Levy stopped taking photos and stepped back. Davis made some notes in his journal. He pulled on disposable gloves and approached the body.

"The skin is ashen with darker discoloration at the lowest parts, such as from the knees to the feet." *Livor mortis.* "Swollen face, especially under his open left eye. I have trouble seeing the right side. There's a dark triangular spot in the white part over here." He carefully touched the corpse's upper arm, pushing lightly. "Cold body. Stiffness." *Algor mortis. Rigor mortis.*

"Levy. Did you get a photo of this?" Davis illuminated an area surrounding the dead man's ear, partially covered with thick hair.

"Looks like some capillary breaks. Maybe there are signs of bruising on his scalp." She bent down to observe.

"I'll get zoomed in." She prepared her camera.

Davis pocketed his writing gear. "When you're done, Levy, step in here."

He circled around a small dining table in the kitchen opposite the bedroom, quietly scrutinizing the east end of the dining area. Above a window seat, an egress window provided an exit to the property's backyard. Cold air blew in on an investigative team member dusting the casement for fingerprints. The opening was ajar a few inches, with no screen visible from the inside.

He retreated to join Levy in the living room.

"Are you about done?" Davis's head barely cleared the venting in a dropped ceiling area. He found her standing with her hands on her hips, weight on her toes, almost bouncing.

"Betcha twenty on time of death. Twelve hours." She screwed on a sassy smile. "Wanna play?"

Davis frowned. "Watch yourself, Levy. Can the shit. You're here to learn the trade, and I'm your boss."

She looked down at her notes.

"Dr. Taylor will tell us the time of death." He rubbed the side of his nose. "At first glance, I thought possible suicide or overdose. But with the strange corpse position, the egress window, deadbolt locked, and a probable blow to the head, it's definitely suspicious. What else did you notice in the apartment?"

His partner moved easily around the space cramped with several investigators. How to keep the fresh homicide rookie busy but on a leash was his next worry.

"A stash of drugs and paraphernalia in the bedroom. To my eye, it looks like oxycodone tablets and some heroin, but the lab will confirm. Maybe he smoked the powder with tobacco or cannabis. There's loose-leaf marijuana, buds, and rolling papers. We've found no other rigging—simply the syringe, needle, and tourniquet in the bathtub."

Davis nodded. Levy pointed at the counter and a flat screen on the north wall of the living room.

"Probably a gamer, looking at his computer equipment. I think we'll have more to work with once the forensics lab gets into his gear."

A team member was already dismantling and packing the desk area. "Do we know who lives above in the main house?" Davis pointed to the ceiling. "And where are they?"

The three-level property rose high above the sidewalk. The generous front porch was surrounded by wooden railings. Under the portico, the second doorway connecting the basement residence to the outside had also been dead-bolted. The two west-facing access doors to the deceased's apartment sat behind a side cement patio inside retaining walls.

Detective Levy read from her notes, "A neighbor said the landlord is at his house on the Coast, in Manzanita. He's been gone a week. I have his number." She returned her notebook to her back pocket. "We've got officers canvassing more neighbors for information right now. I want to get with them about possible witnesses—anyone noticing visitors lately."

"Good."

"Oh, yeah, two more things." Levy gestured excitedly while speaking, her hands arcing and twisting. "We haven't found a cell phone or a landline. A couple of printed pay stubs are over on the desk. We know where he worked, as of last month on the fifteenth. A psychiatric group downtown." She reached into her pocket again. "Bryce Nelson, MD. The website shows a partnership, a psychiatrist and psychologist together, including an opioid addiction clinic, Psych Recovery. There's a link to another doctor's info at this address. It looks like a solo psychiatrist, Leslie Schoen, MD, is also working there. Not a partner."

"Wouldn't you know?" Davis didn't miss the irony. The dead guy, seemingly overdosed on heroin, worked at an opioid addiction treatment center. "For the love *of*—" He let out a breath. "All right. You do the neighborhood interviews while I head to the office site. Text me those links." He turned, adding over his shoulder, "I'll talk with the ME before I go, let her know the plan. Will you come back to her?"

Levy didn't answer but nodded curtly.

"A pain in the ass," Davis muttered under his breath as he walked toward Taylor. He would've much rather started off training Levy with a typical domestic homicide than on a case like this. But he supposed they'd find they had more things in common, like trying to fit into the culture at the Bureau. Although their strategies for surviving were probably as similar as instinct and logic.

He'd relied on his record, without deficiencies, while withstanding various tests as he rose through the ranks. In over fifteen years on the job, he'd reached Homicide through conscientious work, an uncanny ability to relate to almost anyone, and an unwavering drive to achieve better community conditions.

He refused to take his peers' bait with overtly racist remarks and veiled insults, and had honed the skill of suppressing emotions to an art. The key was maintaining his cool and keeping his mind in analytical mode, no matter what.

Word had it that Levy had grabbed every opportunity to advance, even if it meant stepping into hot water at times.

With sharp eyes that dissected instead of observed, she promoted herself as if she missed nothing. She'd sometimes confronted fellow street beat officers over minor matters and pushed her way to gain the next rank. Davis had been watching her rise for quite some time. She lifted serious weight at the gym, but rumors circulated that her actual power lay in stubborn manipulation.

With what he'd learned so far, Davis expected they'd need to work closely together, and he had no idea how that would go.

Six

Friday, October 18th—A few hours earlier: Clinic

In the lightless hallway, while most of Portland still slept, Leslie handled a key to their office suite, the sharp, astringent odor of chlorine filling the air. She yawned, rubbing her eyes while scanning for the cleaning personnel. The early work meeting had been arranged yesterday, after Pearl had finished the conference with Leslie's CPA, and the day had ended without Damon. Leslie's worry level had only escalated since then. She hadn't anticipated having to call for a police welfare check on Damon. Despite her brief, skimmed sleep, she remained determined to discover how the missing opiates allegation connected to Damon's disappearance.

As she flipped on the lights, a bundled figure rounded the corner in the outer hall. Pearl approached with a briefcase dangling off her shoulder, unwrapping a long, bright red scarf from her neck.

"Damn, it's cold out there." She joined Leslie in the waiting room. "I'm keeping track, lady. This is favor number one." She looked around, her expressive eyes containing a mark of wisdom beyond her years. "What if Damon appears while we're in here?"

"I wish he would. If he does, he'll be the one with the worries." Leslie torched the back hall lights. "Let me do all the talking if he shows. And this would be the second favor, after a bailout on the credit line. Thanks again." They made their way to Pearl's office.

"Listen." Pearl plopped her bag down. "I did my job yesterday. And this is me trying to save my ass today. If I don't get the billing together with the MAT clinic, I'll be at risk. I'm betting you can help."

Damon's inner office door was closed. "I understand. We may be in the same boat. Different deck chairs. Same Titanic."

Pearl let out a low hum. "You got it."

Their eyes met as Leslie opened Damon's office and turned on the light. "How about your son, Pearl? Isn't it a couple of hours before school starts?"

"He has an extremely involved uncle."

Leslie scrutinized Damon's things: a Lake George Rhinelander coffee cup, an old hoodie on the back of his chair, a little girl's photo—maybe six or seven years old—and several charcoal drawings on the walls. She crossed to the desk and tested the middle drawer. Locked. A faint odor of unwashed laundry led her to open the hallway door.

"What are we looking for, exactly?" Pearl faced the bookshelf on the opposite wall, scanning its shelves.

"Good question." Leslie leaned into the lateral file with a hand at her chin. "It's possible Damon might've taken the missing bupe. Did you hear how the audit went yesterday? Any problems with the opiate count?"

"No, but I wouldn't be surprised if the count was off. The way Michelle and Lynn were huddling yesterday, kind of whispering. But I'm not in their loop."

"Well, assuming opiates really are gone, maybe Damon filched them. I've seen Michelle send him in there before when she's busy." Leslie stood upright. "You know how he's looked lately."

"Oh, yeah."

"So, I guess we're looking for something about the bupe samples. Or anything that looks different. Maybe find his calendar, too." She tested the file cabinet, yanking on the top drawer.

While rifling through side cabinets, Pearl settled into the desk chair.

"Suppose Bryce found the medicines missing and planned to use them to send me packing—by making the board complaint." Leslie opened the hanging files and looked in the back of the bin. "How much time before you expect Lynn?"

Pearl checked the ticking plastic clock. "We've probably got a half hour."

"Hey, wait." Leslie reached to the back of the drawer. "What's this?" She unearthed a spiral notebook, missing many sheets but with a paper note folded into it. Minor doodles marked a few pages, and a phone number next to the name "Allison" filled another. Pearl looked over Leslie's shoulder.

"His sister. He called her a few weeks ago, I remember," Pearl said. "And he mentioned he spoke to her the other day when he talked with his ex-girlfriend, Sheri. The picture must be Sheri's daughter, Morgan. They all live in Wisconsin." She pointed to the corkboard holding the only personal photo in the office.

"Look, another drawing. It's got a funny backdrop." Leslie held out the flattened sketch. The likeness of a man's head in partial profile, drawn in pencil, included an extended disfigurement across his cheek. In the background, various numbers aligned in multiple rows and columns, each having five or six digits.

"These numbers aren't in any order I recognize." Leslie scratched her forehead. How to handle this? After all, it was Damon's private stuff. Maybe he called Bryce last night to check in. Should she put everything back where she'd found it?

"I'm not sure what to think. I don't recognize this man. Do you?"

"No. The sketch looks partially done." Leslie laid the notebook and drawing on Damon's desk. "I'll snap a couple of photos. Then we can put it all back. We'll leave the room as we found it, okay?"

"Sounds right."

Leslie turned the pages, capturing images. The hinges of the waiting room door creaked as metal scraped against metal, interrupting her concentration. She steadied her shaking hand for the final click and turned to Pearl. They both held a finger in front of pursed lips.

Leslie pointed to the exit toward her office. Nodding, they stepped out into the hallway.

A moment before, Michelle Wichim had balanced her bulky shoulder bag with a stack of files and her lunchbox in her arm as she slipped from the outer third-floor hallway into the clinic's waiting room. The night's short, disordered sleep left her jumbled. Their four-story building was a century old, at least, constructed in red brick and reinforced concrete with architectural terra cotta for decoration. Despite its age, the lighting timers to dim the interior usually worked. Noticing the lights on, she dismissed it. *The maintenance crew.* In the early morning quiet, she paused to scrutinize her reflection in a glass-covered wall piece.

Taking a deep breath, she straightened her shoulders. No workplace scrubs today. Her brown hair tumbled free with a few waves to her shoulders. In her mid-calf flared skirt, hip-length sweater, and high-necked blouse, she dressed much like she had as a kid for Sunday school, washed clean after her parents' Saturday night debauchery, as if getting holy would rub off on them.

That morning's nightmare hadn't visited her for quite a while, but when it recurred, it stuck like tar on a rutted pothole. The overhead light flickered, startling Michelle as she pulled her sweater closed over her chest. Tired and distracted, she attempted to force herself to focus on her morning routine. Through the interior waiting room door and into the inner hallway, she rounded the corner next to the check-in desk, finding her work area in the shared large room with file shelves and equipment. She stopped at the periphery of the room, the remnants of violent, chaotic scenes lingering at the edge of her awareness.

As if she were wiping away her history, Michelle rubbed her forehead with force. Dealing with the DEA agents and everything thereafter had left her with a hangover of crisscrossed emotions refusing to settle.

She tilted her head back sharply, flicking her hair over her shoulder in a quick, defiant motion, her eyes squeezed tight, and hurried to the safety of her desk. With her jacket hung on a creaky chair, she dropped her bags and files with a thud and booted her computer. *Every time I look up, here I am again.*

Her stomach growled. Although disturbed sleep had stolen her appetite earlier, she made sure to pack breakfast and lunch. As she reached for a small package in her purse, she sensed a faint breath approaching from behind, near the doorways to Pearl's and Damon's offices. Her heart smacked into her throat as she grabbed the parcel, tossed it into a desk drawer, and slammed it shut.

"Hey, Michelle."

She turned with a hand to her chest. "My God, you two scared me!"

"We didn't expect you so early." Leslie waved off with a retreat to the back hall. "I've got a phone call to make."

"Gosh, I'm sorry." Pearl clasped her hands in front of her chest. "We didn't mean to alarm you."

The waiting room door closed with a *thunk*. Michelle turned her head sharply. Lynn arrived at her window, hoisting her purse to the counter. "Good morning."

"Have you talked with Dr. Nelson about those billing issues?" Pearl searched Michelle's face.

"Would you get off my case?" Heat rose from Michelle's neck to her ears. "It's not as if we've had nothing happening lately. I'll address it."

The topic kept reappearing. When would these billing managers understand? Dr. Nelson didn't want a new scheduling program—and he had to have a good reason. She'd managed to deal with the last guy by sitting on her hands each time he complained he'd gotten no response from the boss. He pleaded for her help to get Bryce to act before the big blowup. Now, this new biller was stuck on the same problem. But she had to give credit to Pearl. Her delivery was much calmer, more polished. And she stuck at it like a penguin ready to breed.

"It's been weeks, going on months. We have to deal with this." Pearl shot Michelle a moody stare and gestured as if hitching a ride. "I've got to eat something. Let's talk in the kitchen."

Glaring at the woman's back, Michelle grappled with the challenge of how to act by omission again. She'd have to go through the motions. Probably warn Dr. Nelson. She turned to the bookshelf next to her desk, reaching for her lunchbox as the beep and whirl of Lynn's computer announced her return.

"Who's been messing with my stuff?" At eye level, Michelle's bookshelf held a small fairy garden scene with seven miniature statues placed in and around an open house. A tiny dog, his tail erect and carrying something in his mouth, lay next to another minuscule figure. She handled a compact "man" with care, stroking the smooth edges of his painted hair with a finger, and shoved it into her purse.

"I don't know anything about your stuff," Lynn said.

"Good. Since we've got the DEA out of here, we can get back to the real addicts who want help—what's really important." She snatched her lunchbox.

Lynn dismissed it. "You know better than I."

Indeed, she did know better. The memory of her early morning nightmare summoned her brother Andy's face. Now *he* had been a real addict. Since her mother had moved to the dementia home, this dreadful dream had been visiting her more often. With an eerie cry for help, the vision of a teenage Andy had advanced to an old man with sagging jowls and open wounds.

Shake it off.

Lynn stared at her computer. "We *do* have the MAT patient roster current, right?"

"It's fine." Michelle picked at a hangnail. The DEA had found them out of compliance because not all active MAT clients were on the roster. But she'd had good fortune—the chance to update it before the audit was finished.

She made her way toward the kitchen but stopped at Lynn's desk. "We're good now. If you'd only alerted me that we were behind, we wouldn't have fallen short."

Lynn avoided looking at her. "Not my job."

Michelle often steered Dr. Nelson to complete the required tasks before handing new MAT patients' names to Lynn for roster entry. The man was so exasperating. When she told him what he needed to do, he pushed her away. When she left it all to him, he blew things off, getting them all in trouble. She did everything within her power for him, but his organizational skills were horrid.

"Did Damon return any of our office messages?" Michelle tossed some loose hair over her shoulder.

Lynn swung around in her chair. "I've heard nothing from him. But I got a text from Dr. Nelson. He has a late patient start today, and he's behind schedule. Should be in around ten."

"Yeah, okay."

Michelle cursed Nelson's sloppiness affecting the clinic *and* the last-minute patients Pearl was about to bitch about. A little benign neglect went far, but not always. Pearl was waiting, so she'd have to find another way—like heaving a pile of work on her to keep her quiet.

Michelle grumbled to herself on the way to the kitchen—a short trip, across from the providers' in-box counter and next to Dr. Nelson's office. *What time-consuming credentials project will I busy Pearl with?* Maybe it was time to centralize all the doctors' certifications, licenses, and continuing education records electronically. That might derail her.

She found Pearl chomping almond butter on well-done toast. The blended aroma of charred bread, nut spread, and freshly brewing coffee made her famished. Now after eight, it was past time to eat.

The compact room caused them to bump into each other if occupied by more than three. Pearl's good manners led her to sit at the table in the corner chair. Four chairs, a table, a sink, a counter to hold a microwave, and a coffeemaker filled the room. Not much else fit except the refrigerator. Fortunately, people had been keeping their dishes clean of late. The "lived-in" smell of last week had dissipated. She settled into a chair and unpacked her lunchbox.

"Listen, Michelle." Pearl bobbed the tea bag in her cup. "You promised you'd get my letter in front of Dr. Nelson for an answer." Her voice lowered. "We have to fix this."

Dr. Schoen walked in with her nose in her cell phone. The conversation stood still.

"Don't mind me, you two. I'm here for the caffeine." Leslie crossed to the counter.

Pearl sighed. "By the way, Michelle, that skirt looks good on you." She set her toast down, apparently believing you catch more bees with honey.

"Thanks. But you were planning to take this scheduling problem back to Damon for changes." Michelle prepared her cereal. "What happened?"

"Let's hope Damon reappears while we're in here." Pearl exchanged glances with Leslie, then turned to Michelle. "Same result I got after going to Dr. Nelson weeks ago—nothing. Nelson sends me to Damon. Damon files it under forgotten." She sipped her tea. "I told them both. We can't be documenting two people seen by the same provider at the same time. It's a big red audit flag. You know those insurance companies—the ones we're asking to pay us? They can look into our records. All it takes is one mistake to be scrutinized for financial fraud." Her fingers worked the beads of her necklace. "I tried to help Damon understand several times. He obviously didn't absorb it because nothing's changed."

Leslie's head rose. She stirred her coffee, making a soft spoon-on-cup clink.

"That's why the two of you sounded pretty heated the other day." Michelle poured milk into her cereal.

"Yup, we got into it." Pearl raised her hands as if in surrender. "I went to you for help when Damon was a lost cause, and now you've failed me, too. Here's the problem: when an unscheduled add-in patient gives us money to be seen, we have to record an invoice—the billing for service. Otherwise, the deposits we make don't balance with the total services provided. The improvised system I inherited leaves a trail to the date and time of service when the provider may be billing for a different patient. So, if one provider bills for two separate people at the same time, and one of those bills is sent to an insurance company for payment, it's insurance fraud. With the current system, this *will* happen, sooner or later."

"That's not happening here." Michelle laid down her spoon. She had to slow this train down. "Let's talk about the software first. Find some addendum schedule field we can use to tie every appointment to billing, even same-day, last-minute people, and don't worry about what time it happened. And I'll put improving communication with you about add-ins on our MAT team agenda."

Pearl buried her face in her hands, and Leslie crossed to join them at the table.

"Not to rain on anyone's parade, but the prior biller went through the software with a fine-tooth comb. What you're proposing isn't possible, Michelle. It's why he insisted on a new scheduling program."

Michelle brushed cereal crumbs from the front of her blouse to the floor.

"Did the DEA find bupe missing from Bryce's safe?" Leslie's eyes were fixed on Michelle.

These two were on the same team. The hair on Michelle's neck bristled with their nervy intrusions. Leslie wasn't even a *member* of Psych Recovery.

Then she considered, with satisfaction, that Leslie would be defending herself soon enough over her own issues: missing narcotics.

Seven

Friday, October 18ᵗʰ—Early morning: Clinic

In more than thirty years as a psychologist, Sloan Mannon had never drifted so unmoored. He'd already steeped chamomile tea at his clinic office-based tea station. The confidence he'd gained from his Brioni suit evaporated at the office suite doorway when he arrived at eight-thirty. Nor were the recently updated office digs lifting his spirits as he sat at his trendy minimalist desk spreading glue on diploma frames for wall cushions. His sleek teak workspace featured three angular client chairs, streamlined side tables, and a floor lamp. The only somewhat bulky item was the lateral file in teak, but its top made a nifty spot for a kettle and tea selection, along with a slim cooling fan. The acrid glue odor reminded him of building model airplanes in his tweens, a lost time of innocence and an untroubled life.

He lifted the last frame and found the shop receipt underneath. Another detail to throw in his taxes folder. Flipping open his wallet, he tucked it in and lingered at the photo under his fingers. Though he loved to gaze at that hunk of a man, there was little time to pine over his ex, with his broad, easy smile and those haunting eyes.

A rap on the door made him flinch. He quickly shoved his wallet away. Turning to face Leslie, he drummed his fingers on the desktop. This wasn't a good time. His planned meeting with Bryce was the next priority. As she entered wearing slacks and a shell top, despite her diminutive frame, she projected an inner toughness. Her chestnut hair framed a carved face and resolute brown eyes—or were they hazel? They changed color at times. Those gym workouts she'd rattled on about last week were showing results in her toned, muscular arms and shoulders. She studied his new Persian rug and the modern art covering his walls.

"Hey, Sloan." Leslie stopped in front of his desk. "Have you heard anything from Damon?"

"Not yet."

"Hm, Lynn told me about your late night here. Do you know if the DEA found bupe missing from Bryce's safe?"

He crossed his arms as he sat back in his chair, clenching his jaw.

Leslie sniffed and glanced at the tube of glue. He gestured for her to sit.

"Yesterday was a long day. We finished the inspection." Sloan tracked her gaze moving from his desktop to the wall by the light switch.

"Are those your credentials?" She studied his psychology diploma, which was centered in a glossy frame, with furrowed brows. "You got your PhD at the University of Minnesota, the same year Bryce graduated from residency? Did you know each other back then?"

Whatever calming effect the chamomile tea promised dissipated as Sloan sipped again.

"Ancient history, but yes, we were there at the same time. I had to bring my license and training diploma in for the DEA inspectors right when they were being reframed." He cleared his throat. "I'd love to share some stories about those days, but not now. I've got a few things to do before seeing patients."

"Right, so I'll let you go." She rose and moved to the doorway. "But did you know about the missing bupe?"

"Not my territory. I don't have to tell you this—psychologists don't prescribe medication in Oregon." He brushed the smooth, shaved surface of his head as he made his way around his desk.

"Okay." She paused with her hand on the door frame.

He reached to swing the door partially closed. "Sorry. I'd better get to work."

Grateful he hadn't needed to literally push her out, Sloan closed the door behind her. Her meddling questions rattled him almost more than dealing with the DEA. Of course, he knew about the DEA's drug count, but he planned to talk it over with Bryce before anyone else.

Then there was the matter of no Damon. Broaching the problem with Bryce would surely result in an order for him to find a solution. That's how it always went. But if they didn't address Damon's continued absence, those needy MAT clients he routinely handled would demand someone else's attention. More for Sloan to handle with Michelle.

Another rock and a hard place. Sloan slipped his thumbs under his belt and cursed. Bryce would never have finished his psych residency if it hadn't been for Sloan's guidance. The man created messes wherever he went.

Time to deal with him.

Leslie walked along downtown Portland's Broadway Avenue before noon, anticipating a late morning meeting, her head down in deep reflection. Dodging pedestrians and crossing the avenue at the light, she struggled to keep her attention on the busy downtown activity. Cars honking, an ambulance or police siren in the distance, and a number of people clearly contending with no housing brought her attention to the present. She jammed in her earbuds, expecting the call from Izzy. Or maybe the police. Where was Damon? Was she simply going to keep editing out the board complaint with Izzy? Nearly ten days had gone by. The written response to the board would be due soon.

Her delay in talking with her wife about the drug theft allegation wasn't *only* due to the fear of causing another stress-induced miscarriage. A sinking gut accompanied Leslie's sense of déjà vu. At what point would she stumble and forget she was concealing the whole thing?

With Izzy in her mid-thirties, after the previous failures to conceive and abandoning the sperm bank for a known donor, who knew if they would succeed in getting her pregnant again? Was Leslie's dishonesty at all tied to doubts about becoming a parent? She'd talked this entire lie-by-omission over with another woman in her recovery program, who'd suggested journaling it out as part of one of the Steps, but that action wasn't getting her the self-awareness she craved. Plenty had happened in ten days. Now they were waiting for a welfare check on an MIA Damon.

Fast-moving clouds threw shifting shadows along the wet sidewalk. Her walk to the restaurant had fallen between showers, at least. The ring of her phone pierced her ears.

"Hey. It's eleven-thirty." Izzy sounded hungry.

"Yeah, I'm walking to Revolución now. Be there in five."

"Right. I'm nearly there."

They arrived at the coffee shop almost simultaneously. The spicy scents of traditional Mexican baked goods hit Leslie as she opened the door. Strong cinnamon intermingled with robust coffee and fresh bread made her mouth water. She and Izzy placed their orders and took a table by the window. For a midday Friday, the place was unusually empty.

"Did you hear anything from the PPB?" Izzy had all the language down about the Portland Police Bureau, with her dad being a retired homicide detective. Getting a welfare check on Damon was smoothed by some inside pull.

"Nothing yet. I was going over the list of weird office happenings lately in my head. Let me show you what Pearl and I found in Damon's office this morning."

She updated Izzy on her early meeting with Pearl to search Damon's room and what they'd found. When she showed Izzy the drawing, her wife grimaced.

"The scar-faced fellow is pretty strange—especially with all those numbers in the background. Based on what you overheard Bryce and Damon saying Wednesday afternoon, I wonder if this guy—assuming he's a real person—is part of the 'dirty laundry.' Didn't Bryce say Sloan had 'the goods' on Damon?" Izzy gestured with air quotes. "What do they know to hang over the other's head?"

Leslie sighed. "No idea." The shop worker brought them drinks and food.

"It's hard to imagine Damon having any sway over Bryce or Sloan. Plus, why would any of them seek an advantage? Unless Bryce was trying to get extra work out of Damon."

"You've inherited detective skills from your father." Leslie grinned.

"Or my mom. You know she solved plenty of mysteries in her nursing career." Izzy played with her food. "My mother's a keen observer."

Izzy had a talent for reading people as well.

"Do you think Damon developed a drug problem?" Leslie's attention turned to the dinging door as a new customer entered the shop. "With the missing bupe, and now him gone—"

"What missing bupe?" Izzy leaned in, frowning.

Leslie stiffened at the slip, a warm flush extending into her face. "Oh my god, I forgot to tell you." Leslie avoided her eyes. "I learned from Lynn this morning, after Michelle and Sloan stonewalled me. The DEA found Bryce's supply of buprenorphine samples short. I don't know how much is gone, but plenty must have gone missing."

"All right." Izzy set her sandwich down. "This is getting creepy." Her voice dropped. "Why are you turning all red?"

"I—uh—" *This is it. Here's your chance.*

"All right. There's something more to this you're not telling me." Izzy rested her hands on the table. "What is it?"

"I learned what the DEA found this morning." Her pulse bounded. *Kick in. Give me the words.* "Too much happening at once."

Izzy shoved her chair back. "This is like the other night. There. Is. Something. Missing."

"Listen." Leslie focused on not blinking. "I'm telling you what I learned this morning." There was another lie. "Here's the rest of it. Damon was a patient of Sloan's right before he took the job with them. According to Lynn, it was a single visit, and before I joined."

"Your office drama is over the top." A vein in Izzy's forehead had popped out. "Forget it. We should talk about the baby's room. I've got too much work at the garden center this weekend. Will you finally clear out the room so we can start getting ready?"

"Of course."

They sat in silence with Izzy staring at her phone. More customers entered the shop, the door chiming with a notice each time. It wasn't too late to cop to the board investigation. If only she could go back to the day the letter arrived and tell the entire story. She winced at the itty-bitty chorus of judgment inside her head. Dangerous territory.

The buzzing in her pocket drew their attention.

Leslie tapped. "Yeah?" The knot of tension in her stomach dropped a few inches. "I'll be right there."

She looked at Izzy.

"What?"

"That was the office—Lynn." Leslie tossed her bag over her shoulder. "There's a detective waiting. He asked for me and Bryce."

At a bit beyond noon, Sloan sighed with relief behind Bryce's closed door, walking further into the overstuffed, dusty office. He'd endured a four-hour wait for the meeting. While Bryce was out of town, he offered a cleaning service for the man's workspace, but the unyielding dolt refused. Soon Sloan would need antihistamines before entering the congested, old-fashioned room.

"Listen, Sloan. There's a detective in the kitchen waiting for me." Bryce turned from his computer screen at his desk, his face somber. They locked eyes.

"Shit." Sloan swallowed, unable to grasp—from the DEA yesterday to the police today. "Were you going to tell me about the missing bupe? What do they want?"

"Lynn alerted me on instant message. I had her put him off for a minute, saying I'm with a patient. I've delayed so we can talk." He stood, taking a step around his desk. "Did you hear from Damon at any point after Wednesday night?"

"No. What's the detective here about? What's happened?"

"Leslie apparently called for a police welfare check on him after he didn't respond to our calls, and he didn't answer the door last night when she went to check on him." Bryce shoved his hands in his pockets. "This detective has to be about Damon. What else? Leslie left here not an hour ago. Shit. I should have put my foot down about her going over to Damon's."

Sloan jammed a finger in his ear to stop the ringing. This wasn't looking good. After an uncomfortable silence, his ear quieted. "I told you Finn tracked me down the other night after Damon went missing. He was so pissed I expected he'd level me. Now what?"

"Damon really failed us. I don't think he listened to me about getting current on MAT patient files. He looked wasted on Wednesday." Bryce looked out the window.

"Wait a minute. You texted me to bring my MAT charting up to date when your vacation started. You knew the DEA was coming?" He raised his brows. "And what's with the missing bupe?"

"Yeah, well." Bryce sighed. "I didn't tell you about an unexpected expense with my grandson's medical care. Told myself you'd understand. I took the bupe samples. The DEA agent showed up right when I was leaving for my long vacation." He ran a hand through his hair. "Of course, with my lawyer's help, we got them to reschedule for my return. That's why I texted you about your MAT work. Texted the same to Damon and Michelle." He settled into his chair. "So, right as I was about to get a long break, it hit me in a flash. This was the perfect opportunity to solve our problem."

The number of problems on their list was long.

"Which problem?"

"After the old biller left, Leslie's cash flow took a big hit. She started asking questions about our billing practices—why the prick quit without notice. I mentioned her snooping to our *key* referral source a couple of months back. He insisted we get rid of her. So, I figured we'd move Michelle into Leslie's office. Told Michelle as much before my vacay." Bryce checked the clock. "You know how the pregnant opiate addicts get the pure bupe product. It's a much higher value opportunity. We need Leslie gone and Michelle in her office to grow that patient group. We can't have Michelle seeing patients in the kitchen. Right now, her desk is wide open to other staff, and there's no other room. Michelle must be in a private office."

Sloan bit his tongue. Leslie was still nosing around their practice. "Aren't we showing Leslie the door when the lease expires?"

"By the original plan. But I had to scramble for an explanation on short narcotics right quick." He grinned. "Bingo. We'll get her out faster this way, and the DEA has an answer on the drug count. At least for now. Leslie's not going to stick around here with this board problem going on. All handled with an expedited complaint to the licensing authority." He reeked of self-satisfaction.

Sloan's mouth dropped open in disbelief. *The balls on this guy.* With his position at the board, he must be planning on steering their investigation.

"So, voila. Two birds with one stone." Bryce pursed his lips, his nose wrinkled. "What better way to motivate Leslie's expedited departure. A doctor who's a recovering alcoholic stealing opiates? She'll be out of here in a few weeks. Problem solved."

The gears in the idiot's head were churning. Sloan willed himself to avoid showing disgust. The risky times he'd spent with Bryce over thirty years were too many to count. Charging insurance companies for more expensive treatments than were provided. Altering charts after the fact while under insurance payor reviews.

But Sloan kept his mouth shut. They'd each stockpiled plenty of secrets about the other, and Bryce routinely threatened him with the career-ending skeleton. Decades ago, being outed as gay in the Midwest might have had serious ramifications. Not true in recent years—but the sexual relationship with a male patient was a different story.

Of course, he knew Bryce's next strategy. "You'd better be sure Michelle is a convincing witness for the medical board." Sloan crossed his arms over his chest. Leslie would eventually sort out what was happening, given her friendship with Damon. She'd probably gotten information from him already.

"I'll take care of Michelle. I always have, haven't I?" Bryce rolled his chair back. "The DEA is done, and I think they bought the explanation. I gave them a copy of my board complaint against Leslie for the missing samples. That'll stump them. Maybe they'll drop it. Michelle will do whatever I tell her to do."

"If you say so." Sloan stepped further into the room. "So, what about Damon? Did *you* hear from him at any point after Wednesday night?"

Tread carefully here.

"I'll tell you what I'm worried about." A quick sniff punctuated his point. "The little shit got with Leslie about the missing drugs. What if she bent his ear about the board complaint and recruited him to come to her defense? What a tight little pair." He let out a sigh. "There's no way Damon knew who really took the drugs. Am I right?"

For a moment, Sloan's focus faltered, but not enough to notice Bryce had avoided his question. "This is getting over my head."

Bryce rose and paced a few steps in each direction. "Listen. Here's what we've got to do. Convince your man, the slimeball Finn, I'm the boss. I call the shots. We'll have none of their referrals coming through the MAT clinic a second time as a different person. Ever. The one who got through is the first and the last." He pointed at Sloan's chest. "And deal with the issue Pearl's stuck on: how we're billing add-in patients. Fix it. Maybe we see them and not bother with billing."

"Right." Sloan inhaled sharply before returning to his office. He had to disengage from this clinic—this maniac—at his earliest chance. Bryce was one cocky bastard. There was a detective in the waiting room, goddammit.

After starting the kettle for more calming tea, he drummed his fingers on the counter, waiting. The medical board was Bryce's turf, and he should have it. He had all the sway there, given his position. But how to convince Finn Connor of anything was beyond Sloan. The creep took the slightest clash as provocation. Maybe Sloan's bookie friend, Stan, would help. After all, Stan was the one who connected him with Finn and his big boss. Would he get them to back off?

Sloan's water boiled, and a fresh cup of Darjeeling was soon steeping as he moved on to the next matter.

Was the Pearl problem fixable? If they stopped billing those add-in patients, would she back off? Or could they stuff the toothpaste back into that tube?

EIGHT

Leslie rushed down the outer hall of her office building, trying to catch her breath. A detective waiting for her had to mean the welfare check was done. "Please be okay, please be okay," she muttered to herself as she crossed the waiting area. Lynn elevated her head as erect as a security guard, waving Leslie to come back to her desk.

"Dr. Schoen." Lynn adjusted her glasses. "He's in the kitchen. Here's his card."

Detective Aaron Davis, Portland Police Bureau.

"Is it about Damon? Is he okay?" Leslie scanned the office behind her, finding doors closed and Michelle engaged on her phone.

"He didn't say." Lynn's color resembled beige paint. "I put him in the kitchen. I think you can just go in."

Leslie nodded. As she approached the kitchen, a man's resonant voice made her pause. She strained to hear.

"Suspicious death... yeah. My initial view was suicide. Or OD. Or both."

Leslie curled her shoulders as if punched in the chest. *Damon. Oh, no.*

Her forehead broke out in chilly dampness. She grabbed a tissue from her purse and wiped her head and neck.

"I haven't spoken with Taylor since her first look," the man continued. "Levy is there with the Deputy ME now."

Pages ruffled. The sounds drifted at a funereal pace, like an old record player losing power. Leslie fell into an unending tunnel.

"I'm at the workplace." The man's voice traveled through a fog.

A chill ascended the back of Leslie's neck as she fought panic. *Run.*

But an eerie silence descended, as if she were six feet underwater, the world muffled and distant. Into her visual periphery, a dark field inched its way forward.

Squeezing her eyes shut, a pop and whistle exploded around her, like an old camera flashbulb. She pushed her fists into her temples.

The landscape of her childhood home unveiled itself into a different scene: her parents arguing in the kitchen. Her father's booming voice. Her mother's high-pitched protest. A young Leslie crouched beside the dining room door, rubbing the cords of the thinned braided rug, curling herself into near nothingness. Sunbeams through the front window broke the early morning darkness, catching the intricate woodwork of her grandparents' tea cart. The worn, expansive sideboard, its lower cabinets large enough to crawl into and hide. The smell of burned toast.

She clung to every image without moving, clutching as if to keep from falling into the end of something, a void. But there again—the wrinkling paper, like pages of a book turning.

No. No. She didn't want to hear it. But she had to. *Get a grip. Be here, now.*

Squeezing the tissue into a ball, she focused on the softness beneath her fingers, its moistness against her skin. *You're going in there to find out what happened.*

She dragged her concrete legs into the kitchen, taking a deep, slow breath. Straightening her spine, she returned the tissue to her bag.

A lanky, middle-aged Black man stood at the table with a poised, composed expression exuding confidence. He wore a dark suit and tie, with a white shirt, and held a pocket-sized notebook. His symmetric face presented a closed mouth suggesting a possible overbite, while a small scar near his right eyebrow hinted at untold stories. His short, neatly trimmed hair displayed a natural texture. Leslie chewed on her inner cheek as she met his dark eyes, his gaze conveying an analytic mind. She reached out to greet him.

"Detective, I'm Dr. Leslie Schoen." Her face hardened, mask-like, as stiff as the tone in her voice. He shook her hand and eyed the door, appearing to carefully weigh the situation with empathy. He waited for her to close it.

"Dr. Schoen. Detective Aaron Davis, Portland Police Bureau." He handed her his card.

She nodded.

"I'd like to speak with you about Damon Grady. Are you one of his employers?"

His watchful eyes were direct and steely. She failed to sort whether the pain behind his orbs was his or hers.

"Yes... well, technically. My office-share colleague, Dr. Bryce Nelson, manages the payroll, but I'm essentially Damon's boss."

The detective's strong jawline projected steadiness, and his expression was muted.

"Is he okay? I'm the one who called for a welfare check. He's been missing since Wednesday night."

Davis tipped his chin down. "I'm sorry to tell you this, but he was found dead in his home early this morning."

The message penetrated as Leslie took a step back, a palm over her open mouth while the room swayed slightly. She grabbed a chair backrest, picturing Damon's deep brown eyes sparkling as he broke into laughter.

"No." She braced against the horrifying news, bringing her other hand to grip the chair. Damon hadn't even seen his thirty-third birthday. "What happened?"

"Doctor, when did you see him last?" His notebook surfaced in his hands. He clicked his pen, his expression unmoved.

Leslie scraped the chair across the floor and caved into it. "I—I, uh, left here Wednesday night around six, I think. Damon was working in his office."

Davis remained standing, jotting a note. "And you said he hadn't returned to work since then?"

"No. Let me get some water." She used a coffee cup at the cooler, her mouth dry as autumn leaves, before settling again at the table. As she recounted what she knew about Damon's absence, a sinking realization emerged—she was now on her own about the missing bupe. Any knowledge Damon might have had was gone.

Leslie's chin trembled. Her eyes burned with tears as she willed them to stop.

Beyond the kitchen, voices exchanged unclear words before footsteps passed by. She reached for her cup again, emptying it. Should she take a break to make a fast call to Izzy?

No. Not yet. "Detective, I think we should continue in my office. People often use the kitchen around this time." Standing, she pushed a few things about in her bag to find her phone. "I'm going to message my family I'll be home later than planned." Her voice sounded flat even to her ears.

He nodded slightly.

Emptiness numbed her chest.

Davis leaned forward in the doctor's office, seated in a too-comfortable leather chair facing Dr. Schoen's desk. The small-framed psychiatrist looked sickened, thin as six o'clock. Her blanched complexion contrasted with her dark auburn hair as she sat silhouetted against the gloomy sky visible through the windowpanes to her right. What he believed were green eyes now looked nearly black in her oval face, her expressive eyebrows telegraphing suffering before she even spoke. The room's windows let in pasty gray light as if it were dusk, though the clock over the psychiatrist's shoulder read early afternoon.

He had never gotten used to bearing news about death. After he delivered the message, Dr. Schoen froze in genuine shock, her eyes wide with distress. She leaned forward intently, causing her necklace to swing forward—a carved wooden dove with a jewel eyepiece. He'd hardly been a messenger of peace.

"I'm aware you initiated the welfare check." He braced himself against the uneasy sensation in his neck. "Can I get some background on the deceased?"

"Yes." Leslie dabbed her eyes. "I'll share what I know."

"First, do you have Mr. Grady's phone number?" Davis glanced at his buzzing cell, sticking the note she provided to his pad. She didn't have to search long for his info—two mobile taps. Sitting more upright, he detected a shift in her demeanor, her body tensed, and her gaze sharpened, putting him on alert. Slipping back into familiar territory, he steeled himself, ready to query the information she held.

They reviewed several recent work events, happenings she labeled "unusual," ending with the DEA visit on the day of the deceased's disappearance: disputes over scheduling last-minute patients, the precipitous departure of their last billing manager, Damon Grady's exhausted appearance before he went missing. The day before, she had overheard a heated conversation between Damon and Dr. Nelson. She and the new biller had searched his office, looking to understand his disappearance. After expressing her concern about him, she showed the photographs on her phone of Damon's notebook and drawing—a figure with columns of numbers in the background. He zoomed in on the photos, especially examining the strange, numbered background in the sketch.

"Would you forward those photographs to me?" Davis shared his contact details. "Do you recognize the man in the drawing?"

"I don't know who it is. I'm sure I haven't covered every curious thing around here lately. This number is his sister's. Allison. In Rhinelander, Wisconsin, I think." She paused while he copied the information. "I went to look in on Damon at his home after work yesterday—no answer. No response in the main house, either. That's why I called the police."

She looked away and down. Davis continued taking notes. "Had you been to his place before?"

"No. After I got home last night, my wife and I discussed calling for a welfare check. Her father is a retired Portland detective, so we ran it by him."

"And what's his name?"

"Brad Turner."

He stopped writing, suppressing a new tension in his forehead.

"Do you know him?"

"Yes. We've worked together. Good man." A buzz sounded from his coat. "One moment." He listened and nodded, uttering "Yeah" before ending the call. "That was my partner, Detective Adrienne Levy. She'll be joining us shortly."

Damon Grady had apparently been this woman's friend. Or at least they'd been friendly coworkers. Her reaction to his death struck Davis as visceral. She'd obviously spent long hours in this lived-in office. Every available space held facets of her daily grind or decoration. Yet her arrangement with the other practice and her manner of speaking about them made her seem an outsider. Outsiders were easy to spot.

"What time did you go to Grady's apartment last night? When did you arrive home?"

"Let's see. I called Izzy." She scrolled through her phone, facing him directly. No crossed legs or arms. "I probably got there around six forty. I'm sure I was home by seven. We live close by."

She didn't avoid eye contact.

"Do you know of anyone who might've wanted to harm Mr. Grady?"

"No, I don't." Her arms remained at her sides. "We were friendly, but I wasn't aware of his personal life." Her voice broke. "I cared about him—I really did." Davis detected a tone of regret, noting the rosy blush on her ears. "I'm reminded of the conversation I told you about between Damon and Dr. Nelson on Wednesday afternoon."

He sat quietly.

"I know I can only guess what was meant by 'dirty laundry' and 'chart edits,'" she continued. "But those things I mentioned earlier, along with Damon looking so exhausted, led me to wonder about the MAT clinic team. Then the DEA showed up. Our receptionist told me there were problems identified in the audit, but I'm not in on the details since I'm not a member of their practice. I have my own general adult psychiatric practice with a side interest in medical-legal cases." She fiddled with an earring.

"Lynn might be able to clarify those audit results and whatever Damon said to her Wednesday night."

"MAT?"

After a quick knock at the door, Detective Levy entered, her lips pressed thin with seeming determination. Her short black curls and navy hoops drew attention to the dark mole over her right cheekbone and her intense eyes.

"Detective Levy." Davis motioned for her to sit next to him. "This is Dr. Leslie Schoen. We were getting background on the decedent and his work." As the women shook hands, Levy looked down.

"I should add that the MAT clinic is our shorthand way of saying 'Medication Assisted Treatment.' Suboxone treatment—which contains the opiate buprenorphine—is a prescription for opioid addiction. The MAT clinic treats a group of patients under Dr. Nelson's care."

She sat straighter in her chair, rolling it forward, and cleared her throat. "I've recently learned that some buprenorphine samples are missing from Dr. Nelson's safe." She checked her phone on the desk, briefly looking away. "Last week, I got a letter from the Oregon Medical Board about a complaint alleging I took them. They haven't identified the complainant to me yet, but I expect the details will come out when I meet with them." The reddish flush extended in front of her ears.

"I see." Davis ignored Levy's raised brow.

Leslie's jaw muscles clenched. "I didn't take them." She kept her eyes on Davis's.

"You said you'd never been to Damon Grady's apartment before Wednesday night?" He rubbed the side of his nose.

"Yes, that's right. Lynn gave me his address." Leslie shifted in her seat. "I was worried about him."

Levy craned her neck to check Davis's notes. "Dr. Schoen, where did you spend the rest of last evening after you visited Grady's apartment?"

"At home, like I told Detective Davis."

Levy crossed her arms and frowned. "Alone?"

"No, I was with my wife, Izzy."

Levy's eyebrows lifted again.

Does she have a problem with that?

"Did you leave the house? Like, go out for anything?" When the doctor didn't reply immediately, Levy tapped her navy-blue fingernails on her notebook.

Was there some insecurity emerging as aggression? Davis made a mental note to talk privately with her.

"No. We both stayed in until the next morning." The doctor paused. "You can confirm with Izzy if you'd like."

Davis's grip on his pen tightened with the palpable tension between the two women, but he stayed silent. Better to let things unfold.

Levy tilted her head and resumed. "So why do you think someone alleged you took the drugs from Dr. Nelson's safe?"

Dr. Schoen looked steadily ahead, her mouth clamped tight. "I've been debating that myself." She turned to Davis. "Is it known yet how Damon died?"

"It'll take some time to determine."

The slightly sickened look on her face returned.

"I'm thinking about his family." Leslie winced. "As far as I know, Damon didn't have relatives in the Portland area. I think they're all in Wisconsin. I'll want to speak with them at some point."

"The ME's office will notify." Levy's matter-of-fact tone lingered.

Davis shifted back to the edge of his chair. "I texted the sister's name and number to the ME, Dr. Jeannette Taylor."

"I see." Leslie's brows lifted as she reached to bring a bag to her lap. "Detective Davis, I've told you everything I can think of right now. I need to be with my family."

She rose along with Davis, while Levy remained seated. "We may get back to you later. Would you add your mobile number?" He handed her one of her cards. "Please reach out anytime if you think of something more." He stepped toward the door with a nod to his partner. "We'd like to speak with your colleague, Dr. Nelson, next."

"Have a seat in the kitchen again. I'll see what I can do."

NINE

Friday, October 18th—Early afternoon

A tense, usually short drive from her office had turned into a long journey for Leslie. She squeezed the wheel as she parked at the curb and looked at her in-laws' home in Portland's Irvington neighborhood. Their grand three-story Prairie School home, with its broad eaves and horizontal lines, nestled within enormous, mature trees. The area's urban forest canopy and period-revival homes failed to draw her attention as they typically did. She'd stopped once on the way to breathe through a flood of foreboding, and now she longed for a nap. Damon was dead. Detective Davis's voice *...initial view was suicide...* echoed in her mind, piercing its way into her heart.

Sounds of life carried on around her while damp coldness seeped into her bones. A smacking racket brought her attention to a neighbor's house, where workers pounded with nail guns. *Thud. Thud. Thud.*

Covering her ears to block a distant memory failed, as she scrunched her face sharply. Her chin trembling, she braced against the erupting impression. Her father had left. By seven years old, she'd already been taught how to call for help when in danger.

She was seven again, skipping along while unbuttoning her collar, the plains breeze, which failed to bring any relief, rustling and waving leafy trees. It was searing hot. The promise of shedding school clothes and running into the woods for serious play propelled her three-block journey home.

Finding the door unlocked, she tossed her schoolbag on a chair and yelled, "Mom!" Running straight into the kitchen for cold milk and sugar cookies, she stopped to listen. *Where is she?*

The only sound, a tinny radio with static-filled crackles, intertwined with her uneasiness. Her heart pounded. Something was wrong.

"I'm home! Where are you?"

Running through their half-duplex took forever.

Dining room. "Mother!"

Mudroom. "Hello?"

Her own cramped quarters. No one was there.

The bathroom—empty.

Her mother's bedroom, its entry mostly closed. She swallowed against a parched throat, peeking in.

An arm and hand were visible through the crack. She's on the bed.

"Mooooommm!" Running towards her.

The high-pitched scream reverberated from a source unseen, shaking Leslie to the core.

Thud. Thud. The nail gun blasted from the Irvington neighbor's home. She found herself again, inside her car in front of her in-laws' residence.

As if in an old elevator dropping a foot without warning, Leslie's gut fell. With her face in her hands, a mixture of tears and snot smeared her palms. She leaned into the steering wheel, sobbing, struggling to release the memory, to let it wash through.

Another thump, flatter this time, drew her attention. She turned to find Izzy pounding on the glass.

"Leslie!"

She wiped her mouth with her sleeve and found tissues in her purse before reaching for the door against a force like moving through quicksand. After swabbing her hands and face, Leslie exited the car to find her wife's arms open.

"Oh my God, are you okay?" Izzy scrambled to grab her. "What's going on?"

They gripped each other until Leslie's weeping wore itself out.

"Whew." Leslie clutched once more tightly. They swayed together, then moved slowly toward the house, arms interlocked.

"You're okay. We're good. Come inside and talk."

While entering the Turners' expansive home—once filled with their seven-member family—Leslie both longed for and dreaded the web of family connections. A few minutes later, Izzy, her father Brad, and Leslie sat around the kitchen table while Izzy's mom Kathy clicked on the kettle. Her wavy blonde-gray hair mirrored Izzy's as she stood at the tea station, a practical nurturer. Kathy's fair complexion bore laugh lines that framed her expressive mouth—evidence of a life filled with more joy than sorrow. Her demeanor reflected nothing but thoughtful regard.

As Brad reached over for Leslie's hand, his strong jawline softening with a concerned smile, she found familiar, wide blue eyes surrounded by weatherworn lines—the still-penetrating eyes of a detective, even if retired. His wiry, overgrown salt-and-pepper eyebrows moved upwards. Taken together with the sparse hair on his head, he looked perpetually windblown.

"Wow, I am so beside myself." Leslie's only impulse, to state the obvious, surfaced from a deadened pool of blankness. The background scent of freshly baked bread drew her attention to the counter, where a cooling rack held a perfect loaf.

"Sweet one, not to worry." Brad gently combed his fingers through his messy hair, massaging as much scalp as anything else. "What's going on, honey?"

Leslie looked down at the table. "Damon's dead."

"No! What? What happened?" Izzy's eyes widened.

Why hadn't Leslie looked into Damon's midnight call? Why hadn't she reached out as he looked increasingly exhausted? She winced at the slam of smothering regret in her chest. Had she only pushed things and questioned Damon—she'd had plenty of chances—maybe this whole situation would have fewer complications. Maybe Damon wouldn't be dead. But now, she had to keep so many things straight. One lapse with Izzy, and—

Oh God, is Damon's death tied to the missing opiates?

Her monotonic recap of the events since she'd left Revolución sounded like a court reporter.

"And I heard the detective on the phone before he saw me—" Her face grew hot, her eyes watery. She faltered and swallowed. "Saying it was a suspicious death... maybe suicide..." Her head dropped, with the catch in her voice.

Kathy was at her side in an instant. Her mother-in-law, a former nurse whose eyes were identical to Izzy's, only softened by wisdom, missed nothing while judging little. "Leslie, what else? Something more is getting to you."

"Oh. I—" Leslie turned, crossing her legs. "It brought me back to my mother's suicide attempt. Because the detective said at first, he thought Damon had killed himself. It—it must be the grief—the loss of Damon, my mom." She rubbed the side of her neck. "It was after my dad left. She was such a mess."

"My God, honey." Kathy rubbed Leslie's shoulder. "What suffering for a child to go through."

Leslie shifted again in her chair. Maybe she'd have to understand why Damon died to find out what happened to the missing opiates. "But let me finish about the police."

She resumed the story, falling back into colorless mode. Brad threw a knowing glance at Kathy with the mention of Aaron Davis.

"You worked with Detective Davis, right, Dad?" Izzy asked.

He nodded. "We were partners for several years. When I retired, he took my old job. Good man."

"Did you work with Detective Levy too?" Leslie turned to her father-in-law, her hand closed into a fist. "She judged me in a minute. Not in a good way, either. I don't know why."

Leslie braced against a chill and cupped her hot teacup.

"No, I never worked directly with her. But I heard she was an up-and-comer in the Bureau. What was the 'not good' part?"

"Her tone, I guess, when she asked what I did and where I went after checking on Damon last night. She acted like a crime had happened, and I was the criminal." She sighed. "Did Izzy tell you about Bryce's unannounced DEA audit?" Brad and Kathy nodded.

"Told them while we were waiting for you." Izzy cleared her throat. "And some of the other things you've mentioned about work lately. You know, like the billing manager change."

Fairly certain Izzy hadn't shared their pregnancy news yet, Leslie shot a cautionary glance at her. The slightest movement of Izzy's head confirmed.

Leslie absorbed the anticipation on all of their faces. There was no way she'd cop to the board complaint with Izzy's parents present. It'd be another matter if she'd been honest from the start. This wasn't the time.

She slipped her hand into her jacket pocket, recalling what she'd chosen to accompany her that morning. "I learned from some of the staff that the DEA discovered opiates were missing from Bryce's safe."

Brad puffed out a breath. "Whoa. That's serious."

With her thumb tracing its familiar carved edges, Leslie clutched the wooden badger. The old childhood talisman pulsed with warmth against her skin. A sudden clarity cut through her fog of grief, as the words formed in her mind: *The badger sees beneath the surface. Time to channel that spirit and dig deeper—before whoever killed Damon comes for someone else.*

Turning, she met Brad's knowing stare.

Ten

Friday, October 18th—Early afternoon: Clinic

Detective Davis grew restless waiting for Dr. Bryce Nelson to appear. Levy flipped through her case notes. Resolving to stay on task, though he would've rather partnered with his best bureau friend, Brad Turner, he settled on training the rookie.

"Hey, Levy, I want to hear more about the neighbors' and the ME's impressions. I'll update you on my interview with the doctor before you arrived. Let's brief each other in a minute." Lunch was definitely off, and he wanted to create some momentum. "I'll go check on the receptionist."

In a few minutes, he returned to the kitchen, finding Levy still reading her notes. The news had traveled fast: from Leslie Schoen to Bryce Nelson, to the front desk. Apparently, Nelson was already on the phone with his attorney. The billing worker had agreed to meet with them after the receptionist.

"Okay." Davis took a seat. "Lynn Tidings will be here in a few, then Pearl Blanco." He flipped through some pages in his notepad and shared some details of his contact with Dr. Schoen, including the photographs.

"What a piece of work." Levy huffed, her novice status on display. "What's she doing rifling through Grady's office so early in the morning with another worker and possible suspect? Taking photos? I mean, she went to his house last night. There are missing opiates from this office. She's formally the suspected thief in a board complaint." She puffed. "Come on."

"You better cool your jets, Levy. Don't jump to early conclusions." He returned his phone to his pocket. *She might be inflexible, might need more direction.* "The doctor's situation appears to have some complexity. She had a visceral reaction hearing Grady was dead. But then again, she looked a bit like death warmed over even before the news." He frowned. "Said she was concerned for at least a couple weeks about him, and for longer about the disrupted flow around here. I agree, Dr. Schoen has to be on our list. She's definitely holding something back... but so, it seems, is everyone at this clinic."

"I'm behind you, boss." Levy cracked her knuckles, arms extended. "I can tell you about the deputy ME and the neighbors in a bit. Let's see what other types hang with the mental pros."

Forty minutes later, with Lynn at the table, they'd gathered a wealth of information about the place, its history and staff, and usual practices. The receptionist, her forehead lined with worry, had become matter-of-fact soon after her initial tears. Faint freckles upon her pale complexion had surfaced over her nose during her most distressed period. When informing them she needed to meet with Dr. Nelson after his next patient, she shifted into mechanical recollection. Her body posture stayed erect, her glasses slipping occasionally, and she often tightened her ponytail.

"Where were you last night, Ms. Tidings?" Levy scooted her chair closer to the table.

"Home with my husband and kids. I grabbed some dinner on the way from work. We sat down to eat at seven." Directly looking at Levy, then Davis, she straightened even more. "I stayed in all evening and got back here around eight this morning."

Davis scratched a note. "I have a few more questions before we finish."

Levy put her pen down. "So, both Dr. Schoen and Dr. Nelson were concerned about Grady not showing for work yesterday."

Lynn nodded.

"You gave Dr. Schoen Grady's address to check on him," Davis repeated her report.

Another nod. "Dr. Nelson was especially upset that Damon wasn't here, I think because of the DEA inspection. He wanted Damon's help. The software program froze on Wednesday, so they needed a second day to finish. We all had to scramble to cover for Damon, but we did it."

"Did any office member mention problems uncovered in the audit?" Levy asked.

Lynn shifted in her seat. "The active patient log was two weeks behind. We brought it current before they finished. Michelle told me sample medications were missing from Dr. Nelson's safe. I have no more details."

"Who has access to his safe?" Davis asked.

"Only Dr. Nelson and Michelle, as far as I'm aware. Damon mentioned he was backlogged and trying to get current on Wednesday morning. He looked exhausted this week. Most of us were here late Wednesday, except Pearl and Dr. Schoen, who left around their usual times."

"When did you last talk with Mr. Grady?"

"I was concerned about how tired he looked. I called him at home that night, not long after he left. He rushed out in a hurry, saying he had to do something." Lynn pushed her glasses into place, opening a scratch pad. "I jotted some notes."

An outer door closed. Levy waited for footsteps and voices to pass in the hall.

"About when was the call?"

"I can tell you exactly. My phone's in my purse."

Levy scribbled a note. "We'll come back to it."

"I'd usually never phone at night, but Damon was so stressed. He mumbled something about 'doing the right thing' and 'just in case, someone should know where...' Then we got interrupted by something on his end. I asked him what he'd meant, but he didn't answer." Lynn looked down. "He cut the call quickly, saying he'd be in early, and we should talk more then." Her chin quivered. "I didn't talk to him again. Or see him."

Davis exchanged a glance with Levy before he produced a photo on his mobile, holding it out for Lynn.

"Ms. Tidings, do you recognize the man in this drawing? Do the numbers mean anything to you?"

He zoomed in on the photo.

Lynn examined the phone closely. "No, I don't." She looked away, whispering, "I can't believe he's gone."

Davis scanned her body posture. Open. Tense.

Levy checked her recorder. "And you said you saw him changing his computer sign-in more often than usual in the last two weeks, right?"

"Yes. Oh, and I remembered something else."

"Yeah?"

"The MAT team met last Monday. The bupe clinic. Dr. Nelson prescribes buprenorphine for opioid-addicted patients. Like, Suboxone. After the meeting, Michelle and Damon acted angry with each other." She chewed her bottom lip. "Or, at least, they didn't interact much for a while. But they had to work together. I mean, she's the nurse and he was her medical assistant. Then the DEA audit started, so they had to work together even more."

"Did either of them mention what happened between them?" She jotted a note.

"No, and I never asked."

Davis leaned back in his chair. "Were there any other differences lately in people's office relationships?"

Lynn tugged again at her hair tie.

"Only the face-off with Pearl and Damon a couple of weeks ago. I didn't hear the whole thing. She called him out on patients getting seen by a doctor without being officially scheduled. It messed with her balancing job. I mean, it was a big frustration for Pearl. Damon got a talking-to for not following the policy."

Davis looked at Levy, then back to the receptionist. "Thank you, Ms. Tidings."

"Here's my card. Call anytime with anything to add." Levy extended her information. "Oh, and one last question, Lynn. How did Damon come to work here?"

Lynn shrugged as she rose and headed toward the door. "He was someone our psychologist, Sloan Mannon, knew. Maybe Dr. Mannon can tell you more."

A chime sounded from Davis's phone, the one he'd assigned to his former homicide partner, Brad Turner. He checked the text:

On for racquetball tomorrow?

The question would usually bring on a smile, but this time he wavered. He needed a court blowout to clear his head, but should he cancel, given Brad's daughter-in-law was on the suspect list?

He glanced at Levy, who was inspecting her nails.

You're on. Prepare to lose.

Davis scanned the bookshelves in Damon Grady's office. How could anyone work in there with the clicking noise of a plastic clock's second hand? At least it showed the midafternoon time. His and Levy's interview of Pearl Blanco had started in the kitchen, another cramped space. This room was slightly larger, with a desk, a desktop computer, a bulletin board, a desk chair, a lateral file, some drawings hung on the wall, and a bookshelf—pretty basic. After getting an initial read on the biller, the fact she'd aided Leslie in scouring Grady's office led him to suggest they relocate.

Before they met with Pearl, Levy had updated Davis on what he'd missed after leaving the crime scene: Grady's neighbors added nothing except that the man next door had seen a woman at the property around six-thirty the prior night. His account was in line with the information Dr. Schoen had given. The ME confirmed the decedent's blunt force head trauma and the suspicion of foul play, pending autopsy and lab results, including tox. Plus, the CSI team had landed fingerprints—two full, one partial.

Davis expected the body would be at the morgue by now. They'd arranged a meeting with the nurse at their offices in another hour and scheduled the other doctors for the evening at Central Precinct.

Pearl, a relative newcomer to the office, had outlined her job duties. The practice had suffered for nearly three months without an on-site billing manager. Their outsourced billing effort was haphazard, in her opinion. It took her a month to sort things and get current, but she'd gotten on top of it. She found Lynn Tidings to be a great resource, not least for learning what went wrong with the previous biller. Main issues: last-minute appointments were never scheduled or properly billed, though patients were paying for the service. Lynn and the previous biller had created an accounting method based on deposit records to help with balancing incoming money with services billed. Apparently, the last biller had tried, like Pearl Blanco was trying now, to get a system in place for improved efficiency to reduce their exposure to tax audits. Another concern was the problem of appearing to double or triple-book time, which would be found in an insurance audit.

"Ms. Blanco." Davis looked at her squarely. "Did you have it out with Mr. Grady over these billing problems?"

The corners of her mouth lifted. "I told you, please call me Pearl." She turned to Levy. "And that goes for you too, Detective Levy."

Her hands clasped, she paused before smoothing the front of her skirt.

"Damon and I had a coming-together moment over this, about two weeks ago. After I went to Dr. Nelson about the issue, he referred me to Damon since he managed add-in appointments as the medical assistant." She paused. "I'd been harping on the topic practically since I got here, but I came away believing Mr. Grady either could not or would not act. I brought it to the practice nurse since she works so closely with Dr. Nelson."

Levy jotted a note. Pearl had said earlier she knew little of Grady personally. "Tell us what led you and Dr. Schoen to go through this office earlier today?"

"Yes, Detective." Pearl offered a cordial, even-tempered manner. "My understanding is Dr. Schoen wanted to look for an itinerary or a calendar to get an idea of where he might've gone. I assumed she was anxious about being short-staffed. I told her I'd be glad to let her know if anything was different in his office, since I'd been in here often recently."

"And was there anything out of order?"

"No, sir. Not to my eyes."

Davis prepped his phone to show Damon's drawing. "Was the man in this picture anyone you recognized?"

"No, sir. I'm good with numbers, but I don't understand what those are for, either."

Davis scanned the room again, noting the odd combination of an earthy, smoky scent he assumed was Pearl Blanco's, against the obvious smell of well-worn sneakers in the corner.

"Please tell us your whereabouts last night after you left work."

"Of course." Her matter-of-fact tone squared with the paced rhythm of her speech. "I headed directly home. My son and his uncle—his father's brother—arrived shortly after I did. I'd already planned dinner. We all ate and spent the evening together. I have a guest area for Merle's Uncle Willard when he spends time with us, which he does often since my husband died last year. Let's see. I went to bed about ten after Merle settled in his room, and Willard and I had talked a bit. Couldn't sleep. Headed for milk about midnight." She smiled, and with a light laugh added, "Found Willard in the kitchen with the same problem."

The detectives waited.

"Finally fell asleep and was back here at the office by seven thirty."

The sound of pages ruffling turned Davis's head toward his partner.

Levy looked back at her notes. "You said the prior biller was Patrick Walsh, correct?"

"Yes, Detective."

"Have you spoken with him during your time here?"

"Oh, no. He moved out of state. That's what Lynn told me."

Davis reached into his pocket, finding his card to extend. "We thank you for your time. Please call me if anything else comes to mind." Pearl left the room, closing the door.

"I get a funny feeling about her," Levy said. "She's too cozy with the Schoen woman."

"Your feelings aren't running this investigation." Davis buttoned his outer jacket. "We're going by the book."

Eleven

Friday, October 18th—Late afternoon

Michelle muttered to herself as she entered the PPB North Precinct. Its reception area greeted visitors with a dreary functionality—hard plastic chairs bolted to the floor, bulletproof glass separating staff from visitors, and fluorescent lights overhead. An unmistakable odorous mix of industrial cleaner, stale coffee, and paper files, with a faint trace of desperation, hung in the air. Rehashing her parting conversation with Bryce, she substituted what she wished she'd said. Once again, his needs trumped hers, causing a delay in looking after her mother.

Tapping the bell at the unmanned reception counter, she gripped the miniature troll attached to her pocketed keys and stroked the dwarf's hair. At half past four, she was already hungry for dinner.

Michelle unwrapped a chocolate square from her purse with a huff as she waited.

The front door opened, and two uniformed officers, one on each side of a disheveled woman, blew in with the cold air. A familiar sour odor, fresh alcohol upon years of soaked-in booze, wafted by as Michelle popped the candy in her mouth. An officer came to the counter as the trio of newcomers exited to the back.

"I'm here to meet with Detectives Davis and Levy. Michelle Wichim."

She took a seat. Getting out of the office had been a dance. The long and short of it was, at the detectives' insistence, she'd agreed to stop here on her way home. Bryce had demanded they rehearse the details of who had access to his safe.

"Please follow me, Ms. Wichim." The receptionist walked her back to a small conference room. "The detectives will be in shortly."

"Thank you." Michelle sat at a stark table with plastic chairs and took a look around. The space was bleak and stale, with empty walls and a hard painted floor.

This is a trial run for Leslie's complaint review hearing.

As she unwrapped the second chocolate, those details rehearsed with Bryce surfaced again—who, besides her, had access to his private office sample safe.

Remember—the safe combination.

The door gave way to the two detectives, Levy entering first. The woman started talking before they were seated. Michelle leaned away from them.

"Thank you for coming, Ms. Wichim. I'll be recording our conversation." Detective Levy clicked her device, setting it down after marking the time and those present.

"May I have a glass of water?" Michelle buried both hands in her coat pockets.

"Sure." Detective Davis turned to his associate. "Levy?"

"Of course. I'll be right back." Det. Levy left a closed folder on the table as she ducked out.

"Let's start with some basic information." Det. Davis asked about Michelle's job, when she was hired, and her duties. The other detective returned with the water and quietly began taking notes. Michelle's time working at a local hospital, meeting Dr. Nelson, and how she came to work at his office led to the topic of Dr. Nelson's opioid addiction clinic. After answering some work relationship questions, the sudden noise of a door slamming somewhere made Michelle jump, right after she'd denied any recent conflicts with Damon.

Det. Davis exchanged a deliberate glance with Levy—his forehead creased—and set his pen down. "Where were you last evening, and into early today, Ms. Wichim?"

Michelle adjusted her raincoat.

"I got home from the office around seven, starving. Had dinner and went to bed. I stayed in all night and woke for work about six."

"And who lives with you?" Levy asked.

"Until a few weeks ago, my ill mother. She moved to a dementia facility." Michelle folded her hands on the table. "So now I live with my cat. I'm divorced."

"Is there anyone who can confirm you were home alone?" Det. Davis stared at her. "A neighbor? Any phone calls?"

"No."

"Do you have any idea who would try to harm Damon Grady?" The detective's eyes narrowed.

"No. I knew little about him. I mean, he was my medical assistant. We worked together. But I keep strict boundaries with coworkers. It's not for me to be his friend, but to supervise him."

Chilled, Michelle's toes curled in her shoes. She draped her scarf over her neck.

"We're aware some medication went missing from Dr. Nelson's lockbox recently." Det. Davis leaned back a bit. "Tell us what you know about that?"

Michelle scooted her chair back from the table an inch or two.

"I expect to be interviewed about it by the medical board. Dr. Nelson is confident Dr. Schoen stole opiates from his safe. Buprenorphine, to be exact." She adjusted her scarf. "She has an addiction issue, and he's the board's expert in addictions. He examined her for them some years ago. You know, for her license and safety and all. When doctors have these substance abuse problems, the board calls on Dr. Nelson to evaluate them. I'm sure you're savvy about addictions. Some people want help, and others—"

"Is buprenorphine a drug a person gets high on?" Levy pushed the folder a few inches.

"It's confusing to some." Michelle placed her hands on the table. "Like methadone, buprenorphine is a treatment to reduce opioid craving and withdrawal. But it's also an opiate with abuse potential. So yes, it can intoxicate. It depends on the route and the dose."

"The route?" Detective Davis paused his notetaking.

"Swallowed, dissolved in the mouth, snorted, intravenous. The way it's ingested."

"Do you know why Dr. Nelson is so confident Dr. Schoen stole the drugs?" Levy leaned an elbow on the table, resting her chin in her hand.

"Because I saw her. She was at my desk a few weeks back, in my middle drawer where I keep the safe combination. The same morning, she went in and out of Dr. Nelson's office alone. It's common sense. There's no other explanation for it."

"Did you see her with the combination at your desk?" Det. Davis tapped the point of his pen.

"Well, no. But she looked guilty."

"Did you ask her what she was doing?" Levy's question came quickly.

"Of course. She said she was looking for a message pad. The ones with copies of phone call notes. I found one for her."

"And did you see her with any drugs coming out of the doctor's office?" Davis and Levy exchanged rapid-fire queries, like opponents in a tennis match.

"I don't know what was in her pockets. She wasn't stupid enough to walk out with them in her hands." Michelle drank some water. "I told you, she looked guilty."

"So, you did not witness her accessing the safe." Davis repeated what she'd said.

"No."

"And when was this again?"

"I'll have to check my office calendar. But several weeks ago." Michelle cleared her throat.

"In the last few months, has Dr. Schoen been impaired at work?" Det. Davis steadily wrote notes.

The air in the room hung without movement.

"I can't always tell. The typical drug addict is sneaky, often dangerous. Even if they *do* want help." A metal-on-metal clinking rose from her pocket as she squeezed her keys. "You have to be on your toes with those people." She shrugged. "And what did Damon know about the stolen drugs? I wonder if he figured out she took them." She made a point of looking at each of the detectives directly. "Dr. Schoen's got some problems with boundaries."

The detectives exchanged glances before Levy spoke. "What do you mean?"

"How friendly she and Damon were with each other. The afternoon the audit started—they met in his office with the doors closed. I believe Damon and Dr. Schoen shared things. You know, personal concerns."

"Did you hear them talking about the missing narcotics?" Det. Levy spoke at the same moment a fan kicked on, sending a blast of needed air into the room from a ceiling vent.

"No."

"Did they find a short supply of drugs in the recent DEA audit?" Det. Levy pressed.

"Of course." Michelle frowned. "Dr. Nelson was forthright about it. He showed them a copy of his complaint letter about Dr. Schoen to the medical board."

Det. Levy opened the folder and placed a drawing on the table. Some guy. Rows and columns of numbers were faded into the background.

"Ms. Wichim, do you recognize the man in this picture?" Det. Davis's eyes moved toward her keyring jingling in her pocket.

She let go of her keys and studied the drawing, wincing at the marked face.

"No. I've never seen him before." She folded her hands in her lap, picking at a rough edge around her nail.

Levy returned the page to her folder.

"We need to step out for a few minutes." Det. Davis stood and gathered his notes. "We'll be back to finish. Would you like some more water?"

"No."

After the door closed behind them, Michelle searched her bag for more chocolates. None left. Her gut quivering, she yanked the troll from her pocket again to stroke its hair. Dry but smooth, the material calmed while her mind drifted to the prior Monday's team meeting.

The four of them had sat in Sloan's office: Bryce, Sloan, Damon, and her. She'd rubbed her eyes as if to wipe out the exhaustion of the prior week. Her mother hadn't adjusted yet to her new location, and Michelle was also tapped out by an incident with a patient needing a domestic violence shelter. It was difficult to focus.

Bryce, with way too many patients, needed her and Damon to get his notes completed. Sloan had less time to screen potential referrals because of his own client growth. There was too much cash in Sloan's and Bryce's deposits. What a problem!

Damon was barely staying even with the chart edits he needed to do. A recent new MAT clinic intake had been a prior patient—a fact clearly unsettling for Bryce, as the recognition only came after the patient was in his office.

"Damn it. We are not doing doubles. One got through, but no more." His face reddened. "Sloan made it clear to his referral source—F—already."

"And like I told you, he said his boss—R—is calling the shots. You're going to have to meet with R." Sloan met Bryce's eyes directly. "Maybe we should halt the key referral growth until we find some resolution. We should slow down to settle into the pregnant women's program."

"I'll say." Michelle leaned forward. "One lady last Monday was crazy. It took me hours to get her situated. If we grow the MAT pregnant women segment, there'll be more domestic violence to deal with. We've got to have a shelter ready to take our clients in need. We're following so many people who require real help, and we need to have time for everyone."

"All right, already." Bryce's patience wore thin. "We're not halting growth. We want more clientele, not less. Sloan, you get with me after this. We'll plan my meeting with R and a strategy on the deposits."

Michelle pivoted to Damon, sitting next to the floor lamp. His skin tone was gray—ghoulish—and the purple circles around his eyes had worsened. That look, the one she'd seen so often on her father's face, set off a volley of rolling unease.

"On the cash issue, I've got an idea," Damon contributed after a long silence. "Let's have the new R and F referrals bring a larger down payment. Then we'll make follow-ups a draw-down against the credit balance. It'll be easier to time the big cash deposits."

Bryce brightened. "Sloan and I will discuss the idea." He turned to Michelle. "We're trying to get more provider attention for everyone who wants help, Michelle. I'll let you know the details after I meet with Sloan."

Michelle nodded, still fixated on Damon's ashen complexion. To her, he looked sixty, not thirty-two. There was something about his color, an unsettling signal. His dark, short, wavy haircut and the faraway look in his eyes struck a chord.

A burning fury rose in her chest as she now understood what her eyes had missed then.

Crushing her keys in one hand while gripping the troll's hair in the other, Michelle's focus came back to the police precinct. She slammed the key ring on the table.

Even though it should have hurt, it didn't.

Emptiness covers me completely.

Michelle floated from the chair, the room, the station, even the memory provoking her wrath. A numbness encased her, like ice covering the trees and sidewalks on a frozen Portland winter day.

The door opened. Detectives Davis and Levy entered.

"We have one more question, Ms. Wichim." Detective Levy spoke first. "You told us you have Dr. Nelson's combination in your desk. Have you used it to access his safe?"

Michelle's shoulders tensed upward toward her ears, pulling her back into the room. "Yes, of course. That's why he gave it to me—to get into it *for* him when he's busy."

"What does he keep in there?" Detective Davis sat at the table again.

"Highly controlled medications—the drugs with buprenor-phine."

"Anything else?" Detective Levy remained standing by the door.

"Just his gun."

Twelve

Friday, October 18th—Afternoon's end

Bryce checked the time as he walked the Greenway Path along the Portland South Bank. With an hour until dusk, he'd bitten off plenty to accomplish before having to speak with two police detectives. Tugging at the leash, he coaxed his Boston Terrier, Milo, out of a sniffing fest. The bench marking his destination rose on a hill twenty yards ahead. With an unfocused view, it floated in the choppy waters of the Willamette River.

On any other day, he would enjoy the view, this interwoven tableau of river, skyline, urban life, and surrounding landscape. The Willamette's surface churned below, its waters reflecting fragments of the downtown cityscape. That faint river stench—part decaying plant matter, part industrial runoff—filled his nostrils, a reminder of secrets easily swallowed and carried away.

He unclenched his jaw as he rubbed at his aching head, sensing the stubble of his beard, like fine sandpaper against his fingertips. The entire day had turned into an annoyance. Never relishing time with Rafael "Rafi" de Leon, his '*key*' referral source,' he looked forward to this evening's meeting about as much as a colonoscopy prep. With his IT point man's untimely departure and the sudden need to be interviewed at the Portland Police Bureau's Central Precinct, the day had not only become jammed but tricky.

The water's frothy scum bounced off boulders at the river's edge. A gold rush of fall colors across the way opposed the foul, stagnant water below. He rubbed the margins of his hairline. *How did I get connected to this guy?*

Sloan came to mind, and a similar autumn landscape around the Mississippi River at Minnesota's Twin Cities. Some thirty years before, they'd met in Minneapolis, also under difficult circumstances.

Bryce considered Sloan more a coach than a business partner. Had they not met when Bryce finally had a shot at achieving something for which his father would be proud, he wasn't sure where he'd be now. But Bryce's actions back then had jeopardized the successful completion of his psychiatric training. In Sloan's opinion at the time, his hubris would get him kicked out. A theatrical hospital ward rant in front of a supervisor, his peers, and the patient's family had bought him a ticket into the residency complaint review committee. Of course, no one grasped his brilliant point, but that didn't matter when the department chair called the shots. As Sloan had predicted, Bryce was close to the chopping block.

Now he sneered at the memory of having to accept personal supervision with Sloan's psychology department chief to stay employed. Once again, his father had intervened, making the deal to save his ass, along with a big hospital foundation donation. But the plan led to Bryce and Sloan's relationship deepening. Their friendship, greased by scratching each other's backs, led to Sloan's guidance, teaching Bryce how to "fake it" to meet expectations in the world of medicine. The vital formula—hiding his self-interested arrogance when in the field, developing the mindfulness to catch himself when using the "wrong" approach, and limiting his boasts to time with Sloan.

Each man had learned the other's weakness, connecting them even tighter over the decades. Oh, the schemes they had concocted. Those paper chart revisions back in the day to squeak through an insurance audit. The adjustments in billing codes to maximize payments while documenting false patient encounter times. Stacking patients in single slots to increase charges—effectively double-booking, then shorting treatment time to get more people seen. The list continued, but this latest project took the cake.

Bryce fidgeted with Milo's collar as he stroked the panting dog. Before his vacation and Damon's disappearance, he'd scheduled this rendezvous. At the time, he mentioned Leslie's prying to Rafi, especially her questions about the last billing manager's departure. What a mistake. The news so incensed Rafi that it was nearly impossible to get the man relaxed. No matter what happened today, Bryce wasn't about to try to cancel or reschedule this meeting with him.

He waited near the bench's edge as footsteps approached from behind. Bryce scratched Milo's ears and moved further to the end, lifting the dog and tucking him under his arm.

Rafi sat and stared straight ahead at the broad river. His hand rolled slowly, massaging a polished, elongated, emerald-green stone with the tips of his thumb and index finger. When the man's head finally turned, Bryce stiffened. It must've been a blowout orbital fracture, leaving his right eye higher, with a caved-in look. But Rafi's nose tested Bryce's equilibrium most. The bridge had been smashed, and to the right, the lower third pointed to the left. A stranger might assume he'd been a boxer. But his elegant cap, a Kufi, circular in shape and resembling an upside-down cup, with its bronze embroidered front edge, argued against street matches. Bryce took his head adornment as an effort to demonstrate dominance.

"We've got a problem," Bryce announced.

"What? The dead guy?"

Bryce tucked Milo in a little closer. He usually wasn't at a loss for words.

"Do you realize I know everything about this project?" Rafi spoke with a gravelly voice, snarling. "I have eyes and ears all over this deal."

"Yeah, well. We're not taking any more of your referrals until a trained replacement for Damon Grady settles in. I've acted on the snoop problem I told you about, but we've got detectives on our asses right now."

"Watch yourself." His divergent eyes narrowed, a dizzying display.

"It's under control," Bryce snapped. "When we start again, the envelopes will be fatter. Sloan will be handling those." While Michelle was his main spy monitoring Leslie's inquiries, Lynn occasionally provided valuable information.

"Whatever." Rafi's word hissed like a snake's warning. "Shit, man. You are full of messes." A wave of something resembling seasickness passed over his face before he spat into the grass. "We're not stopping referrals. Not for a minute. It's time for me to take over."

Yellow-brown foam at the water's edge swirled into eddies as the wind gusted.

"I'm running this operation. Have from the start." Bryce's tone left no room for doubt. "My power drives the bus." He re-cycled seething resentment. "And we're not taking any patients who've been MAT patients before. We've got an opportunity here to find more candidates. I need your help to find Damon's replacement. I can start taking your referrals in a week, but not sooner. We need to land a computer guy with know-how and loyalty to the project."

"Here's the deal." Rafi's gut visibly jumped, as if his diaphragm had squeezed down on its own. "The bitch doctor is gone, like I told you before. We can take care of her." His left eye protruded, laser-focused and dialed in. "Move the nurse in there. I've got someone in mind already for the computer shit."

A momentary silence accompanied Bryce's impatience. He squeezed Milo again, rethinking his gambit with the medical board. It wasn't a good idea to have Leslie go missing, and right now he needed to leave for the detectives' interview. He had little time to talk Rafi into anything.

"We can't have another police inquiry right now. I'll deal with Dr. Schoen and get her out." Bryce jerked to cup the dog's muzzle just as Milo let loose a low growl.

"You'd better."

"You know I'm in the middle of a plan. Don't mess with it."

Rafi slammed his fist, stone in hand, onto the park bench.

"You're the mess." His face took on a serpentine twist as he squared up to Bryce. "If that bitch isn't gone soon, my man's takin' her down." He pushed himself to stand. "One week, and the referrals flow again. And I'll get the computer guy. There ain't nobody I can't replace."

Izzy and Leslie's compact family loved the Grant Park neighborhood and found comfort in their old-style Tudor home. They'd found a historic 1920s spot with the classic steeply pitched roof and half-timbered stucco exterior. Dark and warm, their living room's original woodwork surrounded a spacious fireplace and mahogany mantel with bookshelves on the sides.

Above the shelves, leaded glass windows opened to trees filled with amber and dusky-rose leaves outside. Leslie plopped into her overstuffed chair next to the fireplace, the day's shock leaving her unsteady. Though nearly dinnertime, her appetite had vanished with lunch. Was it too soon to call Damon's sister? She tossed a woolen throw over her knees and checked her phone.

"Did you reach Susan?" Izzy balanced on the sofa's edge.

"Yeah." Leslie dropped her phone into her lap and stared at her palms.

Her friend Susan, who was Leslie's on-call partner, had been best friends with Jeannette Taylor since medical school. Jeannette, the Deputy Medical Examiner, had received Damon's family contact information from Detective Davis. Portland was such a small town. Through a mutual passion for tennis, Leslie had met Jeannette several months before when the women needed a fourth player. After a text to Susan and a conversation, Leslie had just confirmed that Damon's family had been notified of his death by Dr. Taylor.

"Are you sure you're okay to call Damon's sister right now?" Izzy encircled Baby J with an arm. "You look exhausted. Listen, when did you go to a meeting last?"

"I know you're watching out for me, Iz. I appreciate it. This has been one tough day." Leslie shifted to the edge of her chair. "I haven't missed my home group. I know I usually add a couple more meetings every week, but I'm fine now. Really."

Izzy shook her head. "What a situation. We need to try to keep the stress down for you." Her voice deepened. "We need a break. Let's make some dinner."

"I'm on board for eating. I just want to get this call behind me first. I'll use the study upstairs." Leslie headed toward the staircase.

"Okay. I'll be in the backyard."

Minutes later, as her phone rang with the call, Leslie glanced out the window to see a crowd of crows perched in their backyard maple tree. The birds' distinct caw-caws echoed through the air like an important announcement as she fumbled with her earbuds.

"Hello." A woman answered, her voice soft and flat.

"Hi. Is this Allison Grady?"

"Yes. Who's this?"

"Dr. Leslie Schoen in Portland, calling about Damon." She cleared her throat. "I don't know if he ever mentioned me to you, but we worked together." A broad emptiness stretched between them. "I—I am so sorry for your loss. If you'd like, I'll be a contact here for you and your family in the coming days. You must all be in shock."

She scanned the yard while listening to the silence on the other end of the call. Autumn leaves fluttered in the early evening. The wind had calmed, but the rain continued as a steady mist. Leslie turned to face the room's familiar surroundings.

"I'm sorry," Allison said. "I didn't expect this call. We just got the news a few hours ago." She gave a muffled sniff. "We're trying to take it all in. Everyone's here: my mother, Peggy, our close friend, Sheri. She was Damon's girlfriend, plus her daughter, Morgan." Allison's voice quivered. "I have so many questions. Where to start?"

Glancing out the window again, Leslie spotted Izzy and Baby J in the yard.

"I'd be glad to share what I know." Leslie took a jagged breath. "Though I was one of Damon's bosses, he and I were friends as well."

Outside, Izzy raked in the rain. Soggy, carefully constructed leaf piles grew larger under Leslie's watch. She shared memories with Allison, snippets of time spent with Damon, the bustle of their office, Damon's recent seeming exhaustion. Over the course of half an hour or so, her efforts created an ease of conversation. Their awkwardness was smoothed over, aided by moments of tears and laughter together.

"Did Damon talk much about his work?" Leslie reached for a pen and paper. "Or anything else recently? Anything...different?" She tried not to think about anything Damon may have known related to the missing bupe or her board complaint. Her hope of learning more about those had vanished with his death.

"Not really. We just had a call with two Portland detectives asking similar questions."

Allison recapped some of Damon's personal background. Before living with Sheri, Damon had boasted about his ambitions in competitive video gaming while accumulating student debt. Sheri told Allison he'd gotten into the skins betting market, basically wagering on games. At first, he made some money, but he tried to roll it into serious cash. After a series of wins and losses, mostly losses, he traveled to Madison and the Twin Cities—seeking shady loans, Sheri suspected, to stay afloat.

Allison's conversation with the PPB had led to a plan for Detective Levy to reach Sheri for more details. Of course, they'd asked Allison if she knew of anyone who would want to harm Damon, but she didn't. He'd been so busy lately she hadn't spoken with him as often, especially in the last month.

"I just talked with him a couple of weeks ago, and then he dropped out or something," Allison said. "That wasn't like him. We used to speak several times a week. He didn't even answer my texts much lately."

"Did he say anything about the medications in the office or drugs going missing from work?"

"Not to me."

"Or did you have any concern he might be depressed? Thinking of ending his own life?"

"Oh my god, no," Allison quickly replied. "Honestly, he had a one-track mind lately. Money, money. He said he would come back home and be with Sheri again, but he had to repair his finances first. The way he saw it, his debts broke their relationship."

"Did he talk about having other compulsions? Like drugs or alcohol?"

"No," Allison whispered. "But he sent us money. It was strange. I mean, we needed it. But it was so much. I worried about him having so much cash. I asked him about it. He wouldn't go there."

"What do you mean?"

"Well, like I said, he blamed finances for ending his relationship with Sheri, and maybe money was part of it. But he'd avoided dealing with some family baggage for a long time. He wanted to believe if he just paid off his debts, built a bank account, and held down a job, all would be fixed for him and Sheri. It's true she was over his money problems—but more than anything, she was tired of his escape into video games and computer stuff."

A muffled thud sounded in the background. "Allison?"

"Yeah. I moved into the mudroom." She sighed. "My brother had this pattern of running away from stuff. He was so angry. I mean, our mother has her problems. Our dad was gone for long stretches on the road with his trucking job. One day, he just never came back. Mom started seeking other men. She got sick with HIV. We were on our own."

Though the rain had stopped, a damp coldness had seeped through the windows as the light faded toward dusk. Having gleaned this level of personal detail from Damon's sister surprised Leslie, especially after Allison had just learned about her brother's death. The leaf piles were still visible, and Izzy was rolling out the compost bin.

"I don't mean to pry, Allison, but how much money did Damon send you?" She settled back in her chair, not prepared for the answer. *Over ten thousand.* "I see what you mean." She quickly calculated the chunk out of his yearly salary—too large to give away and still afford living in Portland.

"He knew our mom had hospital bills, and Sheri always has medical costs for Morgan. She has Crohn's disease." Allison's voice caught. "Now we'll have a funeral."

Leslie paused to consider making a unilateral decision. "It's a lot to deal with." She wanted to help, and she believed Izzy would understand. Also, keeping Damon's family close was her only shot at learning about Damon's part in the missing bupe, if any. His death couldn't be unrelated. The timing was just too telling. Getting inside his apartment might be the key.

"What if you all stayed at our house when you come out? You know, to save on the hotel, and you'll have home-cooked meals. Talk it over with your family. At some point, they'll release um…Damon's body, and his flat will have to be packed." She sat taller in her chair. "I can—my wife and I can—help you all with this."

Doubt entered Allison's voice. "Uh…"

It wasn't just about getting information to save her skin with the board. Damon had been her friend, and he'd been friendly with Izzy, too.

"You are kind to offer," Allison said. "Let me think this over. Can we speak again in a day or so?"

"Of course."

After they ended the call, Leslie stared at two of her mother's boxes, taped shut and stacked in the corner. Fatigue washed through her body. Other than the light from the desk lamp behind her, the upstairs was dark. A gloomy sensation arose in her gut, like a noiseless warning siren. The box labels stared at her for the umpteenth time: Dining room. Kitchen. *Jean Schoen's world packed away.*

Kitchen. Dining room. A band of blackness dimmed Leslie's periphery as she dropped into a well with no ladder. The smell of burned toast and stale coffee brought her back to her family's Midwestern dining room. Four worn wooden chairs had surrounded her grandfather's old oak table, its weight an anchor giving ballast to the space.

"What did you do?" Her father's voice had echoed throughout the room. Young Leslie peeked through the cracked door, both drawn to the scene and afraid of what she'd find.

The fear in her mother's face. The tears streaming down.

Heart pounding, mouth dry. The image blinked, then faded as Leslie gripped the arms of her chair. She pushed her way back from the boxes, away from the study, and made it to the bathroom sink. Drowning in dread, she splashed water on her face, toweled herself off, and left to find Izzy and Baby J.

Thirteen

Friday, October 18th—Early evening

The officer's noisy fan blew papers around her counter at the PPB Central Precinct. The drab reception area was empty. Bryce pushed his business card through a carved-out slot in the clear divider. "Here for Detectives Aaron Davis and Adrienne Levy. I'm Dr. Bryce Nelson."

Without waiting for a reply, he sat and checked the time. He arrived for the six o'clock appointment on the nose. The little chat with Mr. Indigestion had left him stewing with indignation. Only one other man, long ago, had created the same effect. As Bryce raked his hand through his hair, the rattling fan lulled him into meandering through a past moment.

"Mr. Bryce, I said, get in here!" Bryce's father had a booming voice that always made him cringe.

His excitement from thrashing the little twerp next door dissipated. Dreams of sixth grade King of the Mountain, nearly at hand, vanished. He ran into their sprawling North Shore Chicago home, not daring to be late.

"I'm here, Father." Bryce rushed into the den, out of breath and wiping blood from his lip. Best not to keep this giant waiting—if he wanted to avoid the belt. The owner and big boss of a successful shipping business, Mr. Daniel Nelson didn't wait for anyone.

The man sat behind stacks of cash at his expansive wooden desk, a cigar smoldering in the ashtray. The room stunk of old smoke and dirty money. A metal fan, buzzing in the corner, had little chance to clear the stinking air. He counted bills into bundled piles and tossed them into a green army canvas bag on the floor.

"No matter what I say, you don't seem to understand, boy. I'm thinking you're just never gonna get with the program." His father's face took on an ugly, bloated scowl. "You've got to stop wasting your time beating up other boys and start focusing. There's a lot of money here, and you'll be in charge someday. Do you hear me?"

"Yes, Father." Young Bryce stood at attention, his head tipped down. "What do you want me to do?"

"Come over here and help me with this cash."

A flutter of pages slipped to the floor after the counter fan at Central Precinct increased a notch. Bryce shifted from the past helpless moment to sulking in the present. No wonder his mother had died young. Now, he needed to surmount the fortune his father had lost. Not only did Bryce understand the importance of cash, but he'd show the bastard who-beat-who when it came to money.

Damon Grady's unfortunate death wouldn't stop him. He'd reach his monetary goal and get out of Portland. Costa Rica might be the ticket to ditch his wretched wife and her dismal family. No need to stick around for her inheritance since the mother-in-law had kicked off and left everything, all those millions, to charity. *For God's sake!* Even with his grandson's health.

With an offshore account established and flourishing, he believed he was on the glide path, free and clear. Now this.

"Dr. Nelson, can you come with me?"

Detective Levy gestured to the reception area exit, waving those ridiculous blue nails around. She seated him in a blank interview room. He stared at her back as she shut the door. Alone in the vacuous space, the silence weighed heavily upon him. This dismal police precinct wasn't his rightful neck of the woods.

Five minutes later, he sat at the table with two seated detectives. The woman had placed a closed folder between them. He crossed his arms, looking from her to Davis as she switched her recorder on.

"And I'll get an audio as well." With his Dictaphone displayed, Bryce fished for a business card in his jacket pocket and handed it to Davis. "I've elected to leave my attorney out of this today, but please include his information in your records." He scratched the stubble on his face after flipping on his device.

The two detectives exchanged a glance before beginning. Davis asked about the origin of Bryce's mental health practice, Psych Recovery, the timeline, and the progression of his Medication Assisted Treatment Program—the Suboxone clinic—over the last few years. They covered every professional and office member since the clinic's inception, including the previous psychiatrist who'd retired just before Nelson had recruited Dr. Schoen. Mannon had affiliated with him for over two decades.

"Yes, Dr. Mannon was with me at the start of the MAT clinic in 2013. So was Michelle. We had a small group, no more than thirty opioid addicts annually, for two years. Then we grew to one hundred cases yearly until 2018. Damon Grady joined us then... around early 2017." He pressed on after clearing his throat. "Less than a year ago, we expanded to a two hundred seventy-five case limit, and Michelle became more active in MAT.

She'd been involved before but recently took on more duties." Bryce paused. "As you can see, there's been successful growth."

Bryce leaned back in his plastic chair, the corners of his mouth rising subtly. He steepled his fingers, causing his shirtsleeves to drop, revealing an obvious Rolex on his wrist. "Our success hasn't come without its challenges, but lesser men might have failed."

Davis pushed his chair back a few inches, scraping it against the floor while remaining seated.

"And was Dr. Schoen ever a part of the MAT clinic?" Levy gathered her folder and tapped it on the table.

"No. Leslie came in right after Damon."

Levy's face gave Bryce an opening. Though mostly neutral, she slipped with an eyebrow lift, strikingly micro-bladed, at the mention of Schoen.

"Maybe that's why they got so friendly. She had poor boundaries with him. As you likely know already, there are some problems with Dr. Schoen."

Detective Davis leaned in, placing his elbows on the table with his hands folded. "We've learned a recent medical board complaint alleged Dr. Schoen stole addictive drugs from your practice. And your recent DEA inspection confirmed the shortage. Is that correct?"

Bryce nodded. "I believe she took the missing buprenorphine, based on Michelle's observations. I made the license complaint, although they're still withholding that fact. You're probably aware Dr. Schoen is an alcoholic with a drug abuse history." He shrugged. "Public information. She's said as much at work as well."

"Did you know about this when you invited her to the practice?" Davis tapped his notepad with his pen.

A moment passed as Bryce looked to the side.

"I'm unable to speak about my professional history with Leslie before she joined our office, except I recruited her a year or two before she came aboard. At the time, I considered her talented and healthy. I don't imagine homicide detectives get involved in a death like this unless it's suspicious." He looked from one to the other. "I believe Dr. Schoen would be a logical suspect if foul play existed. She and Damon were so cozy. Maybe he knew Dr. Schoen stole the drugs. Leslie would've preferred to keep it quiet. It'd ruin her career. Or maybe Grady was a witness, like Michelle. Or maybe Grady and Leslie stole the drugs together." Bryce checked the time on his phone. "Sorry, but an important phone appointment is limiting my time with you tonight."

"The missing medications are essential to our investigation." Levy lightly cleared her throat. "We'll need to examine your safe, of course, in your presence. Can we arrange that?"

Bryce crossed his arms.

"I need to talk with my attorney." He nodded at Davis. "You should reach him for a response."

For a few seconds, no one spoke.

Levy opened her folder and placed a drawing in front of Bryce.

"Dr. Nelson, do you recognize this man?"

Leaning forward, within a foot of the picture, Bryce gathered his surprise into a shielded expression.

"This is interesting. Where did you get this?"

No doubt Rafi's associate. How should he soften the blow of this news to the scumbag?

"Please answer the question, doctor," Davis said. "Do you know who this is?"

"Is there a scar on the right?" Bryce pointed at the likeness.

"Again, doctor. Can you identify this man?" Levy tapped her nail on the table.

"No, but—" Bryce looked at Levy, then squarely at Davis. They'd noted his reaction. He had to cover somehow.

"But what?" Davis asked.

"It looked like someone I saw in the hallway at the office the other day." Bryce swallowed with care. "But no. I can't tell you who this is."

Levy retracted the drawing, glancing at Davis. A phone vibration interrupted them. Bryce grabbed his mobile, sliding his chair away to glance at the screen.

"Do you own a handgun, Dr. Nelson? And if so, where do you store it?" Levy pushed her folder aside.

"I'm a registered gun owner. It's a matter of state record. I store it safely."

Davis stopped taking notes. "Going forward, doctor, please answer our questions." He laid his pen down. "Where do you store your gun?"

Bryce pulled in a crisp sniff. "I have a safe at home and at work. Presently in the one at work."

Davis's eyes narrowed. "Where were you last evening, and into the early hours of today, doctor?"

Bryce placed his car keys on the table. "At home with my wife all night. She can verify that."

"Do you know anyone who might want to harm Damon Grady?" Levy placed her hand on the table. Bryce turned toward her.

"As I said, Leslie Schoen might have a reason to remove a threat to her career. She had his address. She went to his house that night. Beyond her, I can't imagine why anyone would have it out for the kid. He was a good young fellow, as far as I know."

The little pissant.

"Did you observe anything unusual between Damon Grady and Michelle Wichim at last Monday's MAT team meeting?" Davis persisted.

"No, not at all."

"Any conflict going on in the previous two to three weeks between Grady and Pearl Blanco?" Davis flipped some pages in his notebook.

"Not that I'm aware of." Bryce checked his phone again.

"Was it Damon Grady's job to do chart edits on your patient encounter notes?" Davis lifted his eyes. "And if so, what did the chart edits entail?"

His face tight, Bryce took a beat. "I don't know what you mean. No one writes my documentation but me. There are places in the record for the medical assistant's notations. Vital signs, phone calls, messages."

Davis's quiet stillness came across as deliberate. Bryce lightly tapped his foot.

"Dr. Nelson, we need to go through Damon's office and examine his computer. Are you in agreement?" Levy stated firmly.

"Or, we can get a warrant," Davis said.

These intrusive assholes. He'd had enough.

"Another matter to discuss with my attorney." Bryce snatched his recorder, squeezing the power off. He rose to his feet. "I must move on to my other commitment, detectives."

Levy and Davis also stood. "Take my card, doctor." Davis extended his information. "If you think of or come across anything else that might help us understand Damon Grady's death, please reach out."

"I'll show you out." Levy gestured to the exit.

"No need. I can find my way." Bryce grabbed the card, his lips pinched together. He left without looking back.

Fourteen

Friday, October 18th—A brief time later

Sloan needed caffeine before his police interview, even at six-thirty in the evening. As he walked through Portland's downtown Pearl District to his go-to spot on Washington Street, waves of nostalgia pounded his brain. Concrete, old buildings, people milling about on a Friday at dusk. Gallery windows shifted into observers, cataloging his carefully concealed secrets. He surveyed cobblestone streets glistening from earlier rain, warehouse shadows pooling like spilled ink across the Pearl. Staying present was a challenge. At the next light, he reflected on a small maple rising from dirt inside cement, the early scent of fallen autumn leaves mixed with the crisp tang of craft beers and fragrant spices of Peruvian cuisine from surrounding establishments.

The season transported him to his original St. Paul, Minnesota home, another spot with abounding fall colors. Sloan pictured their family home on Lincoln Avenue in the Summit Hill district.

He was the last of the Mannons. In mid-'80s Minneapolis, life had turned down a blind alley when Sloan entered grad school. He vowed he'd never have children. When his mother abandoned her husband's injury and chronic pain, Sloan's father resigned from life. Their Ken-and-Barbie dream relationship died, and the man's unending agony—the misery of pain pills, rehab followed by psych meds, and eventually the same cycle—unfolded to a wretched end. From a fractured pelvis to a self-inflicted gunshot wound to the chest.

Just before his tragic loss, Sloan met Bryce stewing in big trouble at the university. After an enormous blunder through hubris before a clinical crowd, Bryce faced two choices: get kicked out or accept individual supervision with Sloan's psychology department chair. He and Bryce had cemented their connection then.

Their schemes and skeletons kept growing since they'd both graduated and joined clinical work. Bryce wielded plenty of leverage over him. If he'd only had the balls to resist this latest cabal. But Bryce had thrown up the idea when Sloan was vulnerable. And Bryce was outraged then—he'd failed to fathom his son and grandson's loss of health insurance. Didn't they know who Bryce Nelson was?

We're in it knee-deep.

Before long, Sloan found himself inside the Insomnia Bean Café, known for its late-night hours. The bouquet of a powerful brew pulled him toward the pastry case. He ordered his usual chai.

Only three years ago, Sloan had faced foreclosure on his coveted condo in the trendy downtown Pearl District. Against the wall in gambling debt, he'd run out of options. Not even his bookie friend Stan would bail him out or get him additional extensions. The new project yielded extra thousands just in the nick of time. Soon, Sloan was not only in the black again but paying for almost everything with cash, wiping his debts clean.

As he turned south on Second Avenue, approaching Main Street, he braced himself for the police interview. *What to say about last night?* Announcing his arrival at reception sent him straight back to a meeting room in the Central Precinct. In almost no time, he was well into answering the detectives' questions.

Sloan repeatedly cautioned himself to avoid speculating and not to elaborate. The less he said, the better.

"Do you expect the DEA audit to identify problems, Dr. Mannon?" Levy asked.

"They found a simple mistake with our active MAT patients' log. The staff corrected it. I'm unable to address anything about prescribing buprenorphine or medication samples since I don't prescribe. You'll have to speak to Dr. Nelson about medications." He drummed his fingers on his knee. "With the counseling requirements, we were spot-on. That's my bailiwick. I believe we've met the standards there."

Sloan crossed his legs while studying Detective Levy. She had a certain confidence, not just in a physical sense. The jawline was tight, and the dark mole on her cheek punctuated her facial angles. Her brown eyes, large and piercing, posed the question: *So, what about it?*

"There was a MAT team meeting last Monday. Were you there?" Davis asked.

"Yes. I was." Sloan turned toward the man whose chiseled expression showed years of experience. Even while his face was attractive, with its striking symmetry, nicely spaced nose, and well-proportioned lips, there was a roughness. Behind their gloom, his eyes reflected a frightful tone suggesting he'd seen plenty.

"Was there any confrontation between Damon Grady and Michelle Wichim during or at the end of the meeting?" Detective Levy's long lashes, coated with too much mascara, waved as she blinked.

He paused. *Be careful here.* "Not that I noticed."

"Were you aware of any recent arguments between Pearl Blanco and Mr. Grady over billing matters?" Levy asked.

He looked her over again. Did her outward 'het' demeanor make sense? *This is gaydar, baby. Does she have last-to-know-itis?* If so, poor thing. She'd have a mountain of hurt ahead of her. Squinting his eyes, he recapped the matter tied to last-minute patients, concluding there were no arguments, just conversations over accurate charges for services rendered.

As Levy opened her folder, Sloan's gut sank when he saw what she had in mind. She snapped the page down. He failed to hide the heat in his face. The detectives looked at each other before Davis jotted a note.

"Do you recognize this man, Dr. Mannon?" Levy asked.

He swallowed. "Oooh, nasty-looking scar." He cleared his throat. "No, I don't know who that is."

A momentary quiet encased the room.

"Dr. Mannon, where were you last evening and early this morning?" Davis set his pen down, projecting a deadpan expression.

Here it comes. Sloan inhaled deeply.

"I live alone in the Pearl District. After work yesterday, I headed home, maybe seven-ish, and stayed in for the evening. I returned to the office this morning around eight directly from my condo."

"Did you see other people in the lobby or parking lot last night on your return home?" Detective Levy brought her hand to her chin.

"No, not that I recall."

"Do you know anyone who might want to harm Damon Grady?" Davis's face remained unmoved.

"No, I can't say I do."

"Call me if anything at all comes to mind later." Detective Levy pushed her card toward him. "One last thing. Will you tell us how Damon Grady came to work at Psych Recovery?"

Sloan slowly lifted the card. He focused on it for a prolonged moment.

"I saw Damon in a consultation a few weeks before he started. At the end of the hour, he said his concerns had been addressed, and he wasn't interested in becoming a patient. We were looking for someone with his work experience. After the appointment, I told him about the open position, and he mentioned he was interested. Things developed from there, and we hired him."

"I see." Detective Levy jotted a note. "So, your system would have a medical record documenting that consultation. Correct?"

"Yes."

"Thank you. We may be in touch again," Davis rose.

Sloan pushed his chair back and stood. Without delay, he sought to be outdoors, retracing his path. Once breathing the night air, he plugged in his earbuds and tapped a call in a matter of minutes.

"Yeah?"

"It's finished. We're in deep shit." Sloan's eyes darted to the streetcar rolling toward him.

"What are you talking about?" Bryce's touchy tone often came out under pressure.

The man is unchangeable.

"You saw the drawing, too. You must have."

"Hey, it's no big deal. Might be anyone or no one." Bryce's dismissal left Sloan increasing his pace as if he might get away from the idiot.

"Oh, yeah. With the lovely slash under his right cheekbone. I hear it's all the rage these days. Everybody's doing it." Remnants of spicy chai rose to his throat.

How can I escape this man? Stick with him, you'll sink with him. But if I bail, who comes after me? Sloan chewed on his nail.

"I met with Rafi." Bryce spoke quickly. "We're taking no more people from them for a week. And he's got someone in mind for the computer job. Right now, our focus should be on moving Leslie out. Getting Michelle in there to see more MAT patients. The pure bupe crowd. Then we'll be ready again as soon as you and Michelle train in the new guy."

The devil and the deep blue sea.

"Right. No problem. The police are breathing down our necks, probably talking with the DEA as we speak. Hello, confiscated computers." Sloan bit off a hangnail and spit it out. "You're in La-La Land."

He hurried past a sidewalk construction zone, dodging his way around a city bus.

"My attorney will keep them out of our office." His voice escalated, nearly breaking into a yell. "We're on track, buddy. Keep your eyes on the prize."

The man believes what he wants to believe.

"We've got some heavy hitters on the other side. And they won't stop at anything, including us."

"You leave Rafi to me. I've got this. I can do it."

Sensing the hair rise on the back of his neck, Sloan brushed his bald crown. "What next, then?"

"Stay tuned. I'll let you know when I'm ready."

The line went dead.

Fifteen

Saturday, October 19ᵗʰ

The Wildwood Trail often enticed Izzy and Leslie into early morning exercise for Baby J's boundless energy. From Portland's northwest corner, it circles uphill into Washington Park. The three crunched through twigs and pine needles, descending an outlet skirting the Japanese Garden, planning to rest at the Rose Garden.

The dog ran forward and back countless times throughout the hike, never seeming to tire. Leslie inhaled deeply as if drinking in the rich earth, moss, and forest cedar would mollify their tension. An unseen woodpecker, its rat-a-tat-tat pecking above, rattled as they approached a trail turn.

Izzy hadn't taken it well—the unilateral offer of their home to Damon's family. Leslie was surprised by Allison's prompt response, a text stating that she alone would travel to Portland and accept the accommodations. Izzy assumed Allison's visit would be soon and preferred that she and Leslie spend the time planning around the pregnancy. Her silence overpowered the space between them.

"It's such a crazy set of events." Leslie trekked a few steps behind her wife. "Damon dies just as the DEA audit finds opiates gone." She crossed a small wooden bridge over water tumbling to a ravine below. "Maybe he took the drugs and OD'd."

Izzy released an exasperated "Brother," bringing them both to a stop. "When are you going to forget about your office?"

"Hey, this whole thing is worrying me. For us. I just want to keep our income steady, especially now."

Izzy turned to face her, hands on her hips. "We should talk about our *family*." She glared, lifting her chin.

"What?" This was getting to be a difficult juggle. "You mean, will we tell everyone about the baby?" Leslie scrambled to think of some concession, a way to assure her wife this was important to them both, and learning more about the reasons for Damon's death was in their best interest. All without the part locked away.

"Yes!" Izzy leaned down to catch her breath, then came back upright. "The pregnancy and making plans for the baby together. We need to sit down and research those amnio doctors and determine who to call in what order. They get booked way in advance."

The dog made an abrupt turnaround as their voices changed.

"There's plenty of time. Look, you've got a busy Saturday at the nursery, and I'll find Jeannette before spending a few hours at the office. Since I know her through Susan and tennis, I'm hoping she'll give me some ideas about why Damon died. Maybe I'll try the doctor-to-doctor thing."

Baby J jumped and landed with her front paws at Izzy's waist. She quickly pushed her off.

"Why would a Medical Examiner talk about an active case? Besides, we need to focus on us right now. You were melting down in the car yesterday. When will we talk about how Damon's death is affecting you? It's like you're bouncing from one work mystery to the next with no time to stop and deal."

The last thing Leslie wanted to revisit was Damon's death—the improbable idea of suicide that caused her meltdown the day before. Why was Bryce coming after her? How would she defend herself if she didn't put the problem back where it belonged? In his practice.

"Hey, how about giving me a break? It hasn't been twenty-four hours since a key player in my office was found dead." The tension in Leslie's legs grew into restlessness. She tromped ahead a few steps, ducking to avoid a hanging cedar branch.

"You should stay out of it and let the detectives do their jobs." As Izzy fumed, the ruddiness in her face deepened. "You are running from something. What is it? Is it telling Grace about the baby?"

Leslie hadn't talked with Grace, her only known family member, since her mother's funeral. Knowing their eventual reunion might include tough stuff, she had avoided her. *When all this settles, now that your mom's gone, I've got something I'd like to talk with you about,* Grace had said. *It's waited years, but the time is now.*

"What?" The pulse in Leslie's neck pounded. "This has nothing to do with Grace. You know I cared about Damon. Of course, I want to know what happened to him."

Besides the office situation and the pregnancy, Izzy recently had another huge issue on her plate. Her business, the nursery—usually a steady income generator—had landed in the red. Examining the financials uncovered a longtime employee pocketing cash. They needed Leslie's practice production to be the rudder while Izzy's business recovered. Should Leslie emphasize that with the baby arriving in a few months, she was now concentrating on keeping their finances together? How far could she push the financial issue before they both got overheated?

In the past, Leslie had spoken terrible things—words with the power to permanently destroy a relationship. She didn't want to create an even bigger mess.

Damn, I hate this.

If only she'd been transparent with Izzy about everything from the start.

"You don't understand. They've got me on their suspect list for Damon's death." Leslie squeezed her eyes shut, wincing before she looked at her wife again. Izzy stood with crossed arms. The dog sat quietly by her side. "Let's keep moving. I want to catch Jeannette at the courts if I can."

Resuming their path toward wooden stairs, they emerged from the forest under a canopy of moss-covered limbs and fall colors. Their silence had stretched too long. Leslie reached the end of the staircase. Izzy and the dog had taken the lead.

"What if we talk about this later at home?" Leslie spoke to Izzy's back as a sickening churn settled in her gut. Her wife stopped and turned.

"We're not done with this."

And that was the thing. It was just the beginning.

Washington Park's tennis courts were prime real estate between the Rose and Japanese Gardens. Weekend early mornings offered those late to the schedule their only chance at play. Leslie scanned the packed parking strip, looking for Jeannette's SUV before spotting her on the court, deep into her match. Grateful for the momentary distraction from the uneasy conversation she'd left behind with Izzy, Leslie paused to stretch. The smell of decaying leaves in musky-sweet piles signaled endings. Shadows cast by blue-gray clouds and centuries-old trees before an early sun crossed her shoes.

Surely a friend of a friend, another medical type, would come to her aid. She needed an insider at the investigation's center to help her understand Damon's demise. Soon, the Deputy ME sauntered away from the court with a racket bag over her shoulder, smiling and waving to friends.

"Hey, Jeannette." Leslie walked to meet her. "How'd the match go?"

"Hi Leslie, good to see you." Jeannette wiped her forehead with her wristband. "A great way to kick off the weekend. Wow, I needed that. What's happening?"

The natural multicolored elevation concealing the Japanese Garden stretched to the sky behind Jeannette's car. She clicked the rear door open and tossed her gear bag inside as Leslie walked alongside her.

"Can I bend your ear for a minute?" In a case with homicide detectives involved like this, and not one of Leslie's patients, texts or emails to the Deputy ME would be ethically out of bounds. "Wanted to ask about the Damon Grady situation—off the record, of course. He was my medical assistant, you're probably aware."

Jeannette cocked her head, eyes narrowed as she pulled her hair tie back tighter.

"I don't know, Leslie. The legal issues here are sizable. I wouldn't want to make any problems for my chief."

She nodded. "I respect that, Jeannette. I do. I spoke with his sister in Wisconsin. Of course, his entire family is struggling to understand what happened. They have so many questions and need to arrange the last services and deal with his apartment. It's a lot to handle long distance."

Jeannette didn't reply.

"I haven't heard anything official yet, but this must be a suspicious death based on questions the investigators are asking. I overheard Detective Aaron Davis on a phone call. He said at first it looked like a suicide." She scrunched her nose. "It's not a suicide, is it?"

Jeannette stepped back.

"You know official determinations and cause of death never come out until all the labs are in. I don't think they're due until next week, at least."

Leslie considered another angle. "Let's just say, in a generic case of suspicious death in this county, how long would it take for the ME to release the body?"

"Well." Jeannette turned and peered at the courts. "Some general guidelines on the toxicology—it might turn as quickly as forty-eight to seventy-two hours. But it might go out past a week if it's complicated or needs highly specialized input. A body discharge also takes days to weeks, depending on the type of testing needed and the overall circumstances."

She mentioned toxicology first.

"The best advice I have is to tell the family to stay in touch with our department. I gave them a contact person. They can call daily, if they want, for updates and estimates on the body release question." Jeannette paused. "And the homicide detective, Davis, should address the family's access to the apartment."

"Okay, makes sense." Leslie fidgeted with her earring. "Would you be available for a conversation again in a day or two?"

Jeannette's eyebrows pulled together as the chain-link fence gate closed behind them.

"There are complicated legal issues here, Leslie. I don't have to tell you about the statistics in Multnomah County over the last four years. Opioid-related fatalities are higher by more than twenty-five percent. We had about a thirty percent drop in the prior time range." She nodded. "You can see how this might draw some political eyes. I can't help you."

Opioid-related fatalities.

Leslie pressed her lips together tightly. Who would be her insider now? Her drive to understand Damon's death had become a necessity. She had to be careful, though. In the past, having compulsions this driven had resulted in destruction for her. This situation had an especially dark side, with a risk of collateral harm to Izzy and their unborn child.

"I hear you, Jeannette." Leslie reached out for a friendly hug. "And thanks for sharing what you have." She took a step back. "So, keep on with the great weekend."

"Of course. Have a fun weekend yourself."

Leslie walked away without a victory—except for confirming Damon's death was opioid-related. Had she tossed a noose around her neck by revealing her license investigation to the detectives and snapping photos in Damon's office?

Oh yeah. She was likely the top suspect on the investigators' list.

Sixteen

Saturday, October 19th—Mid-morning

"Lynn, can I get my messages and schedule for next week?" Leslie spoke across the hallway from her clinic office. The office was quiet for a mid-morning on Saturday—just her and Lynn. Good thing. Here was a chance to pry information from their office receptionist, the worker who had her hand in everyone's business.

"Sure. Anything else?" Dressed in sneakers and jeans, she appeared in Leslie's doorway. "I'm about to meet with Dr. Nelson. He just arrived. We'll work on dividing Damon's job, but I have some time before we start." She turned and peered across the hall at Damon's once-occupied room. "I can't believe he's gone." Her voice trailed off to a whisper.

"Yeah, we'll all be in shock mode for a while." Her attention was drawn from Damon's empty room to a text. "I'm just hearing from Damon's sister. Allison's coming this week to stay with Izzy and me for a couple of days. I may need to juggle my schedule a bit to help her out. Details will come, but I don't want to shift work to Michelle. She's swamped as it is."

"Okay. No problem."

"Has she said anything more to you about missing sample medication?"

Lynn met Leslie's eyes. "She doesn't talk much to me about medication matters. But you're right about her being over-loaded. I thought she'd go out of her mind with this pregnant lady the other day." The receptionist shook her head. "Talk about improvising under pressure."

The number of MAT clinic pregnant women in their offices had visibly grown in the last year.

"I remember. Wasn't it two weeks ago? Michelle used the kitchen to meet with her. The woman was beyond distraught."

"I know." Lynn unloaded books from a chair and sat down. "I guess Michelle uncovered some bruises while getting her vitals. Domestic abuse."

"Terrible. What happened?"

"She went to the lady's apartment later and helped her move her stuff out. Can you believe it? Downtown, in the Park Blocks. Took her to a women's shelter." Lynn scooted her chair closer. "And get this. Michelle protected them the whole time because she brought a gun. She had her foster father's pistol in her purse, just in case." She repositioned her glasses. "He died a few years back."

"I didn't know Michelle was a foster kid. Geez, a gun."

Lynn nodded. "The mother that moved into a dementia home a few weeks ago—it's her foster mom. I guess her foster parents never went through with a formal adoption. Michelle was fourteen when she and her younger brother lost their bio mom. Their real dad died later—a cocaine-related heart attack."

"I had no idea. Poor Michelle."

"Her bio parents were both addicts, and her father physically abused them all. Eventually, her mom left so she wouldn't lose Michelle and her brother to Protective Services. But by then, her mother was an IV drug abuser with a heart infection. She died on the operating table trying to get a new valve." Lynn shook her head. "Luckily, her foster parents came into the picture soon after. The mom was a nurse. Even worse, Michelle's brother got into alcohol and drugs in middle school. He ran away at sixteen. She hasn't seen him since."

"What a tough background." Michelle's functional work level definitely belied her upbringing. "I feel for her."

"Yeah, she looked like a ghost when she finished the appointment—but the next day, it was as if nothing had happened." Lynn rose and smoothed out her sweater. "I'd better meet with Dr. Nelson. Your schedule and messages will be in your box."

"Thanks." Leslie reached for her laptop case. "I'll text you as soon as I know about changing appointments. Can I get a couple of minutes with Bryce first?"

"Sure."

Between Michelle and Bryce, Leslie wasn't clear who'd changed more over the three years she'd been around. Michelle had maxed out on intensity. Bryce's charisma was history, as far as she was concerned. She'd had enough of him. She knocked on his office door.

"Enter."

Leslie caught a glimmer of Bryce's prior self, surprise on his face as he reached down for his Boston Terrier's collar—then it was gone.

"I have something to say, Bryce." Without waiting for a response, she closed the door. Milo let out a subdued woof.

"What is it?" He didn't veil his annoyance.

"This stunt with the medical board has to stop here. I want you to contact them, withdraw the complaint, and explain it was a mistake." Leslie slipped the computer bag off her shoulder and set it on the floor. "You know I'm not responsible for any bupe missing from your safe. There's no evidence whatsoever because I didn't take it. You're trying to force me out of here, and I'm not about to chase you around in circles to find out why. But I'm not leaving before the lease expires." She paused, taking a breath. "Now, if you'll pay my portion of the remaining lease obligation, I'd be willing to reconsider."

Darkness encased Bryce's face, and his lips twisted into a snarl.

"What's about to happen with you and the board is no mistake. Of course, my intimate knowledge of your background and personal history will shape what I say to them." He put on a broad smile. "Happy to see you leave this office as soon as possible. For encouragement, I will pay half of your responsibility in monthly installments over the next year."

He refreshed the grin again. "I would reconsider the complaint if you were moved out within two weeks. After settling the lease."

"Not going to happen, Bryce. Let's see, would this be bribery or extortion?"

Leslie forced a broad grin as well. "And I wonder if sharing why the last biller left with those detectives would be helpful?"

He turned away. Whatever collegial connection they'd once enjoyed had eroded to dust.

"As if they'd listen to their top suspect's deflection."

Her anger was now emitting steam. Reporting this conversation to the police held such an appeal. But untangling her lie with Izzy needed to come first—and fast. Better to keep this powder dry for now.

"You are a piece of work, Bryce." She lifted her bag, hoisting it to her shoulder. "I promise you this: I'm going to find out what happened to Damon, no matter what it takes." She locked eyes with him, sensing this mission would take her to twisted places. But she would get justice for Damon.

Bryce's tone was pure ice. "Back off, Leslie. If you know what's good for you—and your family—you'll do it."

With a big exhale outside the third-floor public bathroom door, Leslie splayed her fingers before shaking them out. The outer building hallway extended back to the clinic's office suite and forward to the central elevator. Just before noon, there was no time like the present for self-talk. She sharpened her focus on her next steps: a quick restroom pit stop, home to create a lunchtime peace offering for Izzy, then pinning down Allison's travel plans. As she entered the washroom, Pearl appeared around the sink partition, drying her hands. The biller, her solid figure wrapped in a purple coat, nearly walked into Leslie.

"Pearl, what the—" Leslie stepped to the side, avoiding a collision, and tossed her bag onto a foyer chair.

Caught by surprise, Pearl uttered, "Oh, my." She flung her paper towels into the trash.

"Hold on." Leslie waved toward the two chairs stuffed into an entry alcove and circled to check the stalls.

"No one else is here. I was just coming in to grab my book-keeping."

"You've talked to them already, right?" Leslie searched the other woman's face.

"I'm still in shock." Pearl slowly shook her head, then raised an eyebrow. "The detectives showed me the drawing we found. What does this mean for you—you snapped photos of Damon's stuff?"

Leslie stepped back. "Let's sit down." She flumped into one of the chairs.

"First, this is heartrending." Leslie brought her hands to a steeple as Pearl took the other seat.

"I barely knew Damon." Pearl's low, quiet voice resonated off the hard bathroom tiles. "But it's such a tragedy. I've been reliving the loss of my son's father." Her lips trembled before she pressed them together. "Didn't you also lose someone close to you recently?"

Leslie nodded, the banker's box labels flashing in her mind. Her mother's boxes: *Dining room. Kitchen.* Her visual recollection paired with a crushing sense of responsibility.

"Yeah. My mom," Leslie whispered in the trance of loss before the specter of more recent, threatened loss slapped her awake. *Izzy. The baby.* "We've got some things in common, Pearl. Maybe we can help each other out."

Pearl brought her hands to her face. "This is getting dangerous."

The silence in the room finally broke with the automatic air freshener kicking on.

"Do you think it's murder?" Pearl dropped her hands and fished through her purse as if searching for the answer. "Detective Adrienne Levy, Homicide Division." She read from a business card. "The writing is on the ..."

"Yeah." Leslie dismissed the word 'homicide' with a mental *cancel-cancel.* She might be their top suspect in Damon's death. Well, she and the guy in the drawing, probably. But who was he?

"Listen, Pearl. We have a shared interest regarding the office: the scheduling issue in the MAT clinic and the add-in patients."

It was an ethical dilemma for Pearl. If nothing changed, the woman would likely go the way of the last billing manager. She was at risk for jail time if found knowingly involved in healthcare fraud. She'd leave. But she was a single parent, raising a ten-year-old boy.

"I'm listening."

"Well, when Patrick quit, my practice billing stopped for weeks. And when I went to investigate, the next thing was an attack on my license—my livelihood, how I make money for my family. So now, I'm getting pushed out of the office." She wasn't about to share the pregnancy news yet. But her gut instincts said Pearl would relate to protecting the family. "You can see how this is an ambush on Izzy too. Not just me."

Pearl remained quiet, nodding her head as she listened.

"You asked 'what it meant for me,' the detectives zeroing in on the drawing." Her eyes darted to the door, then back. "I'm afraid the police consider me a suspect. Of course, it's a suspicious death, or they wouldn't be asking all these questions. There's so much stacked against me: I took those photos in Damon's office, the missing opiate samples, a medical board complaint against me alleging I stole them."

"It's a lot when you put everything together." Pearl's tone lowered. "And you're right about the scheduling problem. It does smack of insurance fraud. Dr. Nelson is just stonewalling there."

The hard lump in Leslie's throat made it difficult to swallow. This was an opportunity to seize—some help to follow the clues. She needed to get a likeness of the drawing, with the crazy numbers, to Pearl. It was on her phone. But an electronic copy would leave too many breadcrumbs. How should she recreate it on paper, emphasizing the digits?

"Everything has to be a part of the bigger picture. It's all unfolding in a timeline." Leslie tucked her chin down to clear her throat. "Let's work together on understanding this."

Pearl looked straight ahead, her face chiseled in concentration. After an elongated five or ten seconds, she nodded.

"What do I do?"

In hurried words, Leslie explained how analyzing the add-in patients over the prior six to twelve months might reveal a helpful pattern and possibly tie to the numbers grid in Damon's drawing. Her instructions to Pearl: review all those files, noting details and key numbers—names, ages, dates of birth, chart IDs, diagnosis codes, and payment types. Keep all the results on paper, in her possession only. She would shred them later. Leslie assured Pearl she'd get a printed copy of the drawing, with the digits emphasized, to her as soon as possible. Together, they'd work to glean what Damon was trying to communicate.

A click of the bathroom door handle sent them both out of their chairs. As another woman walked in and turned to the stalls, Leslie grabbed her mobile from her bag and turned to Pearl.

"I'm texting you my number."

SEVENTEEN

Davis tossed his notebook onto the Central Precinct kitchen table where Levy ate yogurt. The cramped space reeked of burnt coffee and leftover pizza, fluorescent lights buzzing above its institutional walls, and a sink piled with unwashed mugs. A small table and four chairs fit into the corner, the table piled with napkins, takeout silverware, and numerous condiments in little packages. Refreshed, with new purpose flowing through his pores, he'd left the gym before ten after a high-spirited racquetball game with Brad. Hoping to get home to his wife before dinner, he launched into a strategy session.

"We have time to organize here."

"I spoke with Julie while you were out." Detective Levy licked her spoon.

Julie Faraday and her investigative team had been gathering information on the Grady case while Davis and Levy sorted possible coworker suspects from witnesses. With Levy's help, Davis expected Faraday had finished verifying alibis by interviewing multiple neighbors and family members.

"Great. Let's weave it all into our group review unless I need to know something now." Alone with Levy in the break room, Davis closed the door. He glanced at the trash, filled to the brim, including pizza boxes and leftover slices. The counter was filled with dishes and cups—someone needed to clean the coffee maker. The earthy, bitter smell of days-old brew sent him to the fridge for a water bottle. "Want to start?"

"Sure. Just a couple of things." Levy opened her notebook. "I'm waiting for the landlord to call me back, thinking he might've seen visitors to Grady's apartment recently. But nothing else from the neighborhood about odd behavior from Grady or guests. We're done contacting the families of the receptionist, billing manager, and Leslie Schoen. Their alibis all check out. No neighbors for the nurse can verify her story. So far."

"Okay." Davis took a long pull on his water. "What about Mannon and Nelson?"

"A bit more before them." Levy sipped some nasty-looking coffee. "Of course, every office member could probably find where Grady lived. The personnel files are easy to access, at least the basic data is."

"And then there's Google." Davis smiled.

"Right. I reached Sheri, the former girlfriend in Wisconsin." Her eyebrows lifted. "Interesting. She verified Grady's gaming history and added he was sending funds back to his family. Multiple money orders for a grand each from Walmart. I've got a call into the sister to get more details."

"Copy that." Davis yanked his notebook from his pocket. "Good finding. I'll add bank statements to the search warrants list. Let's see, Nelson's safe... Oh yeah." He raised his head. "We want to see the medical record showing Sloan Mannon saw Grady as a patient. Get the family authorization while you're talking with the sister. I'm getting phone records and connecting with the DEA."

"Sure."

"Let's get to Mannon and Nelson. You've got the team working on their alibis. And the prior billing guy. What was his name?"

"Patrick Walsh. We already know he's out of the picture—he moved to Florida. He was out of state during the events in question." She flipped a page. "We should have more information soon. Outstanding items—the garage security cameras at Mannon's condo and all the neighbors around the nurse. We haven't spoken with Nelson's wife yet either. I'll get it all to you when I have it."

Davis nodded. "So, depending on his alibi, Nelson might have had the opportunity. We've considered a motive. Maybe Grady had some information to give to the DEA, but what would be seriously damaging?" He flipped a page in his notes. "Oh, also, I reached the medical board's executive director and clarified a few questions using hypotheticals. They wouldn't call in the DEA on any allegation of stolen opiates without completing an investigation themselves. The complaint about Schoen has no direct relationship to the DEA coming in on Nelson's practice."

"Got it."

"We know Nelson has a gun. He put the 'chart edits' squeeze on Grady before he went missing. If any of these people are defensive, it's Nelson. And he's busy pointing the finger at the woman doc."

"Seems Nelson made a sound case for checking her out closely."

"Yup." He jotted a question mark between Nelson and Schoen on the page. "Not sure if it's either-or. Maybe both Nelson and Schoen are hiding something."

Nodding, Levy grabbed her pen again. "I've got Faraday checking back with Izzy Turner, too." She squinted over her coffee cup. "I want to check out Leslie's friendly relationship with Grady. Like, maybe they were too close. Just crossing all the t's, dotting the i's."

Davis bit his tongue. Levy's focus on Schoen didn't pass the gut-check test for him—not yet. But there was no denying a state governmental agency investigation into her and the missing drugs.

Levy sat straighter. "Take the interview with the nurse. She showed how easily Schoen might access the safe and steal the drugs. Then there's Leslie's addiction problem and her closeness to Grady. Odd, right? Why would a woman boss—doctor even—be so friendly with a much younger male medical assistant?"

"What evidence of an affair do we have?"

Levy shrugged. "I mean, we're just getting started."

Davis checked his list. "I sense bigger trouble in the clinic somewhere. On to Mannon—his reaction to Grady's drawing was obvious. Still, unless he's in cahoots with someone else, I can't imagine a motive yet. We have nothing suggesting he took the drugs. But we need Grady's medical record. Let's come back to him after the alibi check."

"Right. And you've got forensics working on the drawing, the numbered background?"

"Yeah." Davis took a seat at the table. "Have you started the database search for felons with facial scars?"

Levy nodded, swallowing more coffee. "Gave it to Julie to expedite. Shouldn't take too long." The investigative team's lead, Julie Faraday, was shouldering a pile of work. Levy checked her phone. "I can't think of any good means or motives for the receptionist, Lynn Tidings. Can you?"

"She's at the bottom of my list." He swigged some water. "But what about Michelle Wichim? She had some strange reactions. Maybe there's more to it than her obvious quirkiness."

"Right. And so far, there's no verifying her alibi."

"The nurse definitely aligns with Nelson. I've got to chew on that some more."

"Anything from the ME's office?" Levy wore navy blue again, slacks, and a shirt and jacket.

"The tox is due in a day or two. They're looking for buprenorphine, heroin, and all typically abused opioids. Some materials in the scalp may tell us about the head blow. I'm expecting homicide in a drug abuser, another opioid-related death. We'll see."

She jotted some additional notes.

"Will you start a whiteboard back at the North Precinct?" Davis asked. "We need to hit it hard Monday morning."

"Sure."

A knock on the door interrupted them.

"Enter." Davis turned to the door.

"Detectives." Another officer leaned into the kitchen. "An Allison Grady is calling. She's returning your call. Line four."

"Take the call, Levy."

When she nodded and left the room, Davis looked down at his notes again, taking a moment to start listing all the details he'd need for search warrants.

A moment turned into half an hour.

Levy poked her head in. "The sister on the money details."

Davis wrinkled his nose as he rechecked the time on his phone. "Whatcha got?"

"It's a crazy lot of cash he sent them." She came into the kitchen and sat back down. "I'll get stuff ready for you. But there's one more thing on your list for the sarge."

"Yeah?"

"How about mentioning your former partner's daughter is married to Leslie Schoen?" Levy cracked her knuckles. "And you're playing racquetball with him during this case? Really? Brad Turner?" Her eyes narrowed. "Just sayin'. Full transparency. We don't want the appearance of bias."

Here we go. Davis pinched a scowl. *She's forgotten who's in charge.*

"Listen, Levy." His stone-cold, impersonal voice matched the look on her face. "I'm not answering to you or anyone else about my gym attendance. Mind your own business. Put your head down and get the cash information together. Be warned. You're looking at your superior. Don't forget it."

He slammed his notebook shut and stepped into the hall.

Eighteen

Saturday, October 19th—Later afternoon

At four-thirty, Leslie dragged her weary body later than she'd planned through their kitchen door and went straight to the backyard patio. Eager to get back to the morning's discussion with Izzy, she mentally ticked off the important list: the baby's room, the doctor's appointments, and maybe it was time to tell Izzy's parents about the pregnancy. She focused on the orange Japanese maple, a new dwarf tree planted near their patio border, shimmering in the late afternoon light. Its tightly curled leaves looked as taut as the tension across her shoulders. Inhaling the Bluebeard shrub's clean, herbal aroma with its slight menthol note confirmed she had returned to her favorite place.

The meeting with Pearl had left her even more charged than she was after confronting Bryce. She needed an ally. Unfortunately, the squeeze he'd placed on her brought more complications. Explaining his pressure for her to move out wasn't possible without talking about the board investigation. Of course, she'd be leaving Bryce, just not how he suggested. She shouldn't rely on him—he wasn't reliable—to pay any part of the remaining lease. Not to mention, moving out in two weeks was impossible. She had just enough time to plan a smooth transition before the lease expired. Over two hundred in-person patient appointments a month meant an office was critical. Plus, she needed the money for any lease buyout to get started elsewhere. Yikes. She'd be moving her office right before the baby was due.

The screen door slammed. Izzy arrived with cold drinks and the dog trotting behind.

"I got my custom flowerpots today." She set the drinks on a table near two chairs and reached for her phone. "Look." A crisp, colorful coleus settled into a glazed ceramic pot that sported her business name, *Tip Top Nursery,* and her logo, a hemlock tree with its signature drooping peak.

"Looks great. We need some code words. Nursery for your business and nursery for the baby, you know?" Her broad smile broke with the loud ring from Izzy's phone.

"Hey Dad, what's new?" Izzy switched to the speaker as they sat.

"Finished playing racquetball with Aaron Davis earlier today. Hold on." A moment later, the volume came back louder. "Your mom's here, too. We wanted to call you right away."

"Hi, Kathy. Hi, Brad." Leslie reached for her water, scooting closer to Izzy.

"Hello, you two. Your dad has some heavy news, I'm afraid."

"What?" Izzy met Leslie's eyes.

"Damon's death was a homicide." He waited for the information to soak in. "The formal announcement will probably come out Monday. Aaron's been talking with the Medical Examiner's office."

Leslie reached for the back of her neck. She'd been expecting it, but... How was she a suspect in a murder case? This was unreal.

"I can't believe it." Izzy reached to hold Leslie's knee. She put her hand on Izzy's.

"Leslie," Kathy spoke with a steady, reassuring tone. "They have multiple suspects."

"They're considering every coworker," Brad interjected. "So, you're on the list."

"They can't be thinking Leslie is an actual suspect." Izzy flopped into her chair's backrest. The dog came to her feet, looking worried.

"This is tricky because Aaron's talking to me, and I've got a family member involved in the case." Brad's voice was quiet. "We need to keep all of this just between the four of us."

"Of course." Kathy and Izzy spoke in unison.

"Aaron said the team was checking out Leslie's alibi."

"They talked with me twice." Izzy sat forward. "There's no way they can place her there late Thursday night."

"Well, I don't see how she would be high on their list either, but he mentioned his partner, Adrienne Levy, isn't so sure." Brad paused. "I've got some more details from Aaron."

"Like what?" Leslie noted the caution in Izzy's eyes.

"They haven't found Damon's mobile yet. A search warrant for the phone records won't take too long—but it looked like Grady let the killer into his apartment. They're after someone he knew who fled out the kitchen window."

The cold drink had lost appeal as the breeze gave Leslie a chill. A furtive squirrel at the base of their red cedar dug furiously.

"Davis suspects something's off in the opioid clinic. But his partner focused on your friendship with Damon, Leslie. She thinks it's unusual since you were one of his bosses."

"Jeez, Brad. I think I need a minute to absorb all this." Leslie nearly screamed. The next thing would be the missing drugs, then the allegation. She had to steer the boat. The good news was that Brad could be the insider she'd hoped for, but she had to speak with him alone and put some parameters on what they would say in front of Izzy. With Izzy having no issues with the pregnancy, this was the time to tell her parents about the baby. Brad would surely help Leslie with inside information if he knew his daughter was pregnant.

"There's one more important thing." Brad cleared his throat.

"What?" Izzy squeezed her knee. Leslie held her breath.

"They have a drawing Damon made of a man, and they think it's a real person. A man with a nasty facial scar."

Leslie and Izzy exchanged glances. At the restaurant earlier, they'd just been looking at it.

"They're running a search for felons with similar marks. It's possible a known criminal killed him. They expect it's a drug-related death." His voice dropped even lower. "Brings in the Portland underworld."

"Should we be extra worried?" Izzy grasped the hand Leslie extended.

"Listen, anyone looking into this case might be in danger," Brad spoke slowly. "These people are vicious. They kill without a second thought. Leslie, you must be careful not to probe into the case, even by asking questions. If the drug world is involved, you can bet they've got eyes on everyone involved."

The air thickened in the early descending dusk, the sky cloud-packed and gray, while a pair of backyard crows argued in grating rattles and clicks.

"Right. I hear you, Brad." Leslie nodded at Izzy while making an 'eeks' face.

"It's best to leave this to the police, Leslie." As ever, Kathy offered sensible advice. "Damon's murder is bad enough. Now the drug world's involved. It's scary. We don't want you two in any danger."

A vibrating tension raged under Leslie's ribs. "I hear you both. I'm underground as of this moment."

After the call ended, she regretted spilling so much to those detectives the day before, placing herself under their microscope. But at least she'd been honest with them. Now, she had no choice but to investigate further—she had to show it wasn't her. This all had to tie to the missing drugs and getting her ass out of hot water with the board. *But who killed Damon?* She had to meet with Brad alone.

"Hey, you." Izzy stood next to the kitchen door, the dog already inside. "Want to take Baby J over to the sushi place on Fremont? They have outdoor tables." Hands on hips, she added, "You mean it, right?"

"Yes. I promise I'm underground. Let's eat."

"With all this happening, Iz, is it time to tell your parents about the baby?"

Leslie pulled into their driveway as Baby J whined in the back seat, tugging at her seatbelt. Some tension between her and Izzy had released after each blast of wasabi during their meal. They'd gotten their game plan in sync: which obstetrician to do the amnio, how to put the baby's room together. Reviewing it all had settled some strife. The night's stillness had drifted in, with dense cloud cover. It was dark and going on eight. They'd finished an after-dinner walk around the restaurant neighborhood and drove home.

But their home looked darker than usual. Leslie scanned the front yard before garaging the car. The walkway landscape lights were out.

"What's with the lighting? I just reset the timer." Izzy fumbled with the car door, then reached around to let the dog out.

"Should we recheck the timer now or in the morning?" Leslie opened the kitchen door. "I swear I locked this when we left."

The dog leaped inside, growling.

"And I turned these table lights on, too. What's—"

"Something's not right." Izzy followed the dog from the dim kitchen into the dining area.

"Wait, Izzy?" Leslie sprang after her. Was someone else in the house? A tightened vibe hung in the air. Izzy stood frozen in the living room, arms dangling and mouth open. She looked marble-white as she stared at the barking dog by the coffee table.

"What the—?" Leslie's hand rose to her lips. Something was out of place.

"Oh, my God. Someone's been in here." Izzy knelt beside the collie, shushing her. "There, there, it's okay, Baby. Quiet, Baby."

A mustard-colored ceramic flowerpot—identical to the one in Izzy's photo but missing its plant—sat centered on the coffee table.

"How did it get there?" Leslie crouched next to Izzy, helping to soothe the dog with a shush. "Is someone else here?"

"I left the box of pots in the nursery yard by the shed." Izzy rocked on her knee. "Someone's been there, too." She glanced at the stairs. "Are they in the house now?"

"Shit!" Leslie ran to the kitchen, rifled through drawers, and returned with a large flashlight and a hammer. "Stay here. I'll look around."

"Take the dog." Izzy planted herself on the couch. "I'll call the police."

Leslie switched on a lamp and rushed to check the foyer closet. She followed Baby J down the basement stairs. After punching the lights to full blast, she ran from window to window, finding nothing amiss. Before venturing to the second floor, she found Izzy looking queasy by the main floor stairs.

"There's nothing downstairs. Are you okay?"

"Scared. Should I call my dad?" Izzy's hands covered her stomach. "I gave the report to 911."

"Yeah, call him." Leslie paused at the stair landing. "I'll be right back. Baby—go."

The dog soared upstairs. Leslie bounded after her. With every room checked, she finished a window-to-window inspection, concluding they must have entered through the backyard garage door and crossed inside to the kitchen. Her sushi dinner sat like a rock in her gut. Did they pick the locks? She headed downstairs and turned, nearly crashing into Izzy in the foyer.

"Ooh!" Leslie jumped, jerking a hand to her chest. "Damn, you scared me."

"We cannot have this!" Izzy stepped back, her face ruddy. "It's beyond creepy."

"I'll say."

Izzy paced, ignoring Leslie's hand signals—palms down, arms extended.

"I struggled to think of what to say to the 911 dispatcher." Izzy dropped onto the lowest step, heaving an exhale. "What—we've got a flowerpot burglar? I just said someone had broken into our house. I called my dad. Voicemail. I texted him—911."

"Let's see what your dad—"

They both jumped as Izzy's phone rang. Brad arrived in less than ten minutes and immediately scoured the house with them again. Leslie had suggested Izzy go to bed, but she wanted in on the plan to safeguard their family. Having bolted the garage doors and locked everything, they created as much security as possible for the evening and outlined what needed further work tomorrow. Almost an hour after the 911 call, Izzy and Leslie sat with Brad at the kitchen table.

"I can't believe the police aren't here yet." Brad raked a hand over his wind-tossed, wiry hair. "But we need to get a police report. I can try to grease the wheels. You're both beat."

Leslie looked at Izzy, her eyes weary with circles underneath. They nodded at each other. "You'd better call."

Brad reached the Northeast Precinct Captain, who called for a cruiser, then patched Leslie on the line to give details to the officer. While waiting, Brad called Kathy to provide an update. He insisted on staying the night on guard. Kathy's plan was to join them first thing in the morning. Though Leslie had brought blankets and a pillow for the living room couch, he assured them he wouldn't be sleeping.

The cruiser arrived, and they walked through another house check after giving the officer more information. Leslie's mind drifted again and again to the conversation with Bryce hours before. Her hands were clammy recalling the warning, his words replaying in her head: *Back off, Leslie. If you know what's good for you—and your family—you'll do it.*

She never imagined he would act this quickly. *Was this some sort of chilling notice? Was he coming after her?*

When the police left after eleven, Leslie and Izzy hit the sack. Leslie flopped onto one side, then the other, while Izzy passed out almost immediately. Their bedroom—on the second floor at the end of the hall, across from the nursery—fit a king bed, two nightstands, a dresser, and an adjoining master bath. Baby J's bed fit nicely between the bathroom and the French doors leading to a balcony. A small bedroom chair fit on the other side of the balcony doors.

The dog's soft snoring settled into silence. Leslie's senses jumped over endless scenes. Monkey mind—images leaping from one branch to the next. She pushed tears away, unable to be still. Why was she hiding things from Izzy? What was she afraid of?

With her forehead and facial muscles tensed, she replayed the words exchanged in Bryce's office earlier. If she hadn't laid it on him so thick. Her promise to figure out Damon's death threatened him. Why else would he have said "what's good for" her and her family? She put all of them at risk, but if the break-in was at Bryce's behest, who had carried out the order?

Why didn't she just pack her office and get away from him? Did she simply want to leave on her own terms, not his? But how would it look if she hightailed it out of there in the middle of a murder investigation—where she was a suspect? *Damn.* Thank God she wasn't craving a drink. The slippery idea—*I'll just have one*—might rear its ugly head at any time. How ironic! Her original rationale to shield Izzy from the full truth was about not stressing her and the baby, but what could be more stressful than the events of this evening? Her stomach churned as she hugged herself tightly, goosebumps on her arms despite the room's warmth.

Better not to go down a rabbit hole. Easing out of bed, she tiptoed down the hall to her study and closed the door. As she flipped on the desk lamp, a fleeting, vague scent of rosewood hit her. Her mother's boxes—just days before, she'd found space for two in the study, taking the rest to her garage workbench. *Geez, there are only four boxes left. Why was it so difficult to sort four boxes?*

She'd left the box with the light, woody-sweet fragrance on top. A hollow ache behind her breastbone was tied to the realization—her mom was gone. Jean Schoen would never meet her grandchild.

Upon moving the top box to the floor, she tore at the packing tape, upended the cover, and shoved some contents to the side. An empty bottle of rosewood oil, its lid cracked, rested next to an olive-green velvet sack jammed into the corner. Leslie pulled to free it, staring at the color.

She held the purse-sized pouch in her lap. So much was undone, unfinished. Yet her mother had been dead for six months. She ached for a connection to something unseen, a link to her family. Where was her father now? She'd never been able to shut down these emotional waves, not that she didn't try to drown them out. Vodka had made her think they were gone.

Don't fight it. Surrender completely. Ride this thing.

She winced when she stared at the smooth bag—the same nauseating interior color of her father's beat-up Oldsmobile from more than thirty years ago

As a child, she rode in the back seat, transfixed by the velvety upholstery, and tried to ignore the arguments between her parents in the front. An oozing blackness settled around her navel. She found herself rubbing the bag's plush material in her lap.

Leslie closed her eyes, willing the image of her mother and grandfather to be in her mind from a void and ocean of loss. *Just let me untie it.*

Her trembling hands worked the cords holding the bag shut and pushed it open. She peered inside.

Letters. Addressed to her mother from her cousin Grace, postmarked 1986 and 1987. Underneath, a diary, its pages stuffed with entries in her mother's writing.

She held the bundle close to her chest, hugging it as her body iced over, freezing and shivering. Should she venture into reading these now?

Too much.

She shoved everything back in the pouch and tucked it into her laptop case.

Nineteen

Sunday, October 20th

"Okay, we've got our list." At eight in the morning, Leslie addressed Brad in the living room she shared with her wife. Izzy and her mom crowded close together with Baby J on the couch. Leslie's hand trembled slightly as she held the notepad, her vision blurring around the edges. She set down her glass of water. The words she'd carefully printed—"new deadbolts," "window sensors," "motion lights"—danced on the page. She hadn't slept more than twenty disjointed minutes at a time, her body heavy with exhaustion yet her mind refusing to quiet.

They'd regrouped to create a plan after another early morning home inspection, this time with the benefit of Kathy's sharp eye. The night before, Brad hadn't been willing to leave his post to buy new locks. Because Izzy had looked so exhausted after the police visit, Leslie persuaded him to delay calling for a locksmith.

"I think you had it right, Leslie." Brad shifted on the ottoman. "The intruder picked the locks to go through the garage into the kitchen. We have the basement window problem, updating locks, and a couple of security cameras to install."

"You two ought to be staying at our house for now." Kathy rested her hand on Izzy's knee. "It's no inconvenience to us."

"How long will it take to get all this done, Dad?" Izzy glared at Leslie.

"I've got Bureau friends with connections to security companies. All the lock upgrades and security cameras will definitely be done today. The basement issue might take more time. We'll see what the best solution is for the old casement. But we'll have a camera covering the spot today." Brad tapped on his phone. "I've got a meeting over lunch. We can get started after."

Izzy's face turned pasty as she inched herself away from Kathy.

"Are you okay, hon?" As Leslie moved towards her, Izzy raised her hands, palms forward.

"This is just too much!" Her face tightened, lips and chin trembling. "I've had it with the crazy shit at your work. Why didn't you just stay out of everything?"

Leslie's breath caught, leaving her voiceless.

"Honey, are you scared about the basement window?" Kathy leaned back.

They'd found an old, possibly original, casement in the furnace room vulnerable to tampering. The choices—steel bars in front or a new, secure opening.

"No!" Izzy's voice rose, her complexion graying and hands covering her gut.

Leslie sat softly on the sofa, leaving plenty of room for Izzy.

"What's happening, honey?" Kathy swung her arm around her daughter's shoulder.

"We're pregnant!" Izzy burst into tears as Kathy's surprise melted into joy.

A tear trickled down the side of Leslie's face. She stood again, smiling. Brad jumped to his feet, meeting Leslie in a hug while Kathy and Izzy seized each other, mom laughing, daughter sobbing.

"It's wonderful, my sweet thing." Kathy stroked Izzy's hair while glancing over at her husband.

"What a beautiful tell, Izzy." Brad beamed. "We're so happy. How far along are you?"

"Eight—" Her cheeks puffed out. "Weeks." She slapped a hand over her mouth and leapt to rush toward the back of the house. "Oh, no." She moaned, gagging.

Kathy followed her and the dog down the hall. Brad grabbed Leslie's arm, holding her in place.

"I recognize the look, hon. We'd better stay here."

Brad's grip on Leslie belied the comforting look in his eyes. He let her go.

"I'm sorry. I meant I think Izzy has morning sickness. Maybe we shouldn't crowd her."

"Oh, man." With a raspy voice, she sat down in the nearest chair. A hollow sensation occupied her body.

"You two really have a lot on board." Brad rested his hand on her shoulder. "How long have you known about the baby?"

She focused on the question, dismissing the headache pulsing behind her right eye. "A week or two." After learning of Damon's death two days before, time had expanded. The days stretched into a seeming month.

"Well, I'm going to watch out for you both." He sat on the ottoman. "I mean, I would have before knowing this. Now, all the more. With this morning sickness, I understand if you two want to stay in your own home. I can come over to stand guard any time. Think we'll do an entire security system—so I get an alert if anything goes awry. At least until this Damon Grady case is over."

"I really appreciate you, Brad." Leslie reached out to squeeze his forearm. "You make us both feel protected."

As the second hand moved on the mantel clock, she debated how much to say. Her original mistake, hiding the board complaint from Izzy, had morphed into a growing beast. The tentacles threatened to strangle her marriage. Her throat constricted as if those extensions were tightening around her neck, but she was even more certain now—staying to fight was the right thing to do.

"Brad, I need to tell you something." Leslie's mouth went dry, a desert replacing the usual moisture. She took a sip of water. "And then ask for a favor."

Leslie faced the ottoman so their feet were inches apart. The story of her failure to tell Izzy about the board complaint and the justification for her deceit gushed out: protecting the pregnancy after the prior miscarriage, emphasizing the threat to their livelihoods, and the stress of it. *This is all bullshit.* The pulsations in her ears only served to heighten her headache. She needed a meeting, or at least to talk with a program friend. She had no clue how this mess would unfold, a new chapter that blindsided her.

"So, I haven't told Izzy about the board investigation yet—I'm going to before Damon's sister Allison leaves. She arrives tomorrow and will be gone before the end of the week." Leslie clasped her hands together tightly. "I told Detective Davis everything I knew, including the board complaint. I just want you to keep this medical board allegation quiet with Izzy."

Brad rubbed his temples. "It's a serious one. But I can go with it, Leslie, *if* it's only a few days."

"You believe me, right? I was with Izzy here last Thursday night. All evening."

"Of course." He focused on her face. "You've got to stay out of this, Leslie."

"I know." Her eyes burned. "I have to explain the board complaint to her myself. But let's keep each other posted. I'd really appreciate your help."

She had no reason to keep information from Brad, but there was only so much she knew.

Det. Davis walked the old red-brick sidewalks along rows of roses in the late morning, heading for a discreet meeting with his former partner, arranged away from any watchful eyes. The screams of children playing and dogs barking echoed behind the historic gazebo overlooking Peninsula Park. More than sixteen acres of land surrounded Portland's first rose garden. He passed the central iconic ornamental fountain where, during the summer months, children splashed in the shallow water surrounding the middle geyser-like spray.

Of course, Brad would be worried about his family. His daughter-in-law was open enough in her interview. With her spouse's corroboration, her alibi had squared up, but Brad had requested they meet. *Wasn't this what friends did for each other?*

He spotted a picnic table beneath aged white oaks on the park's north end and settled, taking a deep breath. The clouds moved as if with purpose, sending shadows in motion below the arching branches. He turned at footsteps shuffling through leaves behind him.

Balancing a packed grocery bag, Brad raised a hand in greeting. The barbecue takeout order had been his wife's idea. Had to hand it to him—the old man had a spring in his step at sixty and still had a killer racquetball game.

"Hope you're hungry, bro." Brad dumped the food bag on the picnic table and unpacked the contents. Sliced brisket and pulled pork, pinto beans, and potato salad spread before them in less than a minute. At the bottom of the bag, collard greens and extra sauce finished the menu. They dug in.

"This is great. I'm famished." Aaron spoke between bites, tugging at his collar to dampen the sweat at the back of his neck. "Oh, yeah." He pulled two cans of lemonade out of his jacket pockets. "Brought these."

"Blessed be us, man." Brad smiled, red sauce dangling off his lip. "Almost like old times. So, what can you tell me about the Grady case?"

Aaron's complete trust in Brad had never wavered, even with his family members tangled in this trouble. But the crawling sensation in his shoulders and the sweat bullets tied to his unease about Levy were undeniable. He launched into a recap, sharing that she had arranged for the composite artist to join the video visit with the landlord in case he'd witnessed any of the decedent's visitors. He'd prioritized keeping her busy while he met with Brad since she'd zeroed in on Brad's connection to the case. They had three sets of fingerprints—two full, one partial—to identify, and they'd scoured Grady's office that morning. The Bureau had seized the medical assistant's computer and examined Nelson's lockbox. Among various preparations of opiate drugs, the safe housed a Beretta with ammunition. Nelson's firearm registration was in order. Grady's phone records arrived and the call with Lynn Tidings had checked out. Grady had also called Leslie early in the month, late at the night, on the ninth. He planned to circle back and question her about it. Aaron included information about Damon's gaming, betting history, and the big chunks of money he'd sent back to his family.

"Your team's been busy." Brad wiped his hands on a napkin.

Aaron put his fork down and pulled a folded photo from his pocket, laying it in front of his friend.

"Keep this guarded." Aaron looked over his shoulder. "It's the guy we're looking for now, Finn Connor. You know Grady left the drawing, right? We've matched it to this character. He's got priors: felony assault and possession with intent to distribute. He was a suspect in a San Diego murder investigation—nice fellow. Total time served so far is around twelve years."

"Never ran into him." Brad cleaned his hands with a hand-wipe before grabbing the picture. "How'd he get the scar?"

"Bar fight. He's a known associate of a mid-level drug dealer in the area, Rafael de Leon. Son of the big boss, we think, headquartered in San Diego. He goes by 'Rafi.' Of course, we're searching for these two." Aaron took a gulp of lemonade. "And one other thing."

"What?"

"Autopsy found wood fragments embedded in Grady's scalp at the head blow site. I swung by his apartment this morning. There's firewood and kindling around the corner of the house, accessible from the sidewalk. I'll have the pathologist look at the samples I grabbed."

Brad grabbed his fork. "No stopping these scoundrels—the lawless ones. As soon as you jail a few, more float to the top. It's like whack-a-mole. I suppose it's the way of things."

Aaron chuckled. "You got that right."

Two Labradors chasing each other sent leaves scattering. He and Brad often laughed often amidst serious matters over the years. Each had saved the other's life more than once. He owed Brad plenty, just like Brad owed him.

"Almost forgot." Aaron pushed his plate aside. "Levy and the team finished checking alibis, except for the psychologist—Sloan Mannon. Some things are still out on him. But Leslie and Lynn Tidings check out. No verification on the nurse. Pearl Blanco checks out fine." He glanced at his notebook. "Bryce Nelson told us his wife would verify. Sounds like they have separate bedrooms, though. He came home that night at about nine, she said. But she has no way of knowing whether he left again since she takes sleeping pills—was out by ten."

"Plenty of office workers on the suspect list." Brad took a swig. "Didn't you say Grady had a stash box in his apartment?"

Davis nodded.

"With the rig in the tub, and the scum dealers involved, aren't you more inclined to think it was some drug deal gone bad?"

"Maybe." Aaron jotted a note. "We don't have the autopsy final. The tox will probably seal it, possibly tomorrow. But still no phone. No match so far on the prints. Bank records aren't in yet. I'm keeping my mind open."

"Just one more little factoid I want to share." Brad added a bite of collards. "My daughter and Leslie had an intruder last night." He relayed the story, including the flowerpot from Izzy's nursery planted at the home. "Got a police report. We've increased our security measures. But doesn't it smack of the dope dealer world? Pardon the pun. Some sort of warning?"

Aaron inclined his chin. "Yeah." Down the road, the police report might tie into the murder investigation.

Whether it was the mountain of food or spending time with his former partner, Aaron relaxed. Working with Levy would never be the same. But if he didn't trust Levy at this stage, at least he did trust the man across the table. Faith by experience.

Twenty

Sunday, October 20th—Afternoon's end

As the garage door closed, Leslie stepped out of her car and checked the time on her phone again. Getting Pearl a readable copy of Damon's drawing, with the numbers enlarged, had taken more time than expected. Now it was after five. While Izzy and the dog stayed with her mother for the afternoon, Leslie, Brad, and his friends tackled more house security work. She'd hoped to get home before Izzy.

The delivery to Pearl resembled a clandestine meeting. Leslie didn't enjoy sneaking around, but Izzy had no reason to know about it. The sound of her footsteps created a growing unease as she moved through the garage toward the kitchen door.

A text exchange with Damon's sister had confirmed her arrival for the following night. Allison's presence added a new layer of tension, and Leslie longed to put it all out of her mind for a while. Damon's sister was unaware of what Brad had told them, so she'd likely learn that Damon's death was murder during her stay in Portland.

Baby J didn't rush to greet her as she entered the kitchen.

"Where've you been?" Her hands were on the counter, and Izzy stood behind the breakfast bar, looking drained and serious.

"Oh, you beat me home." Leslie dumped her purse on the table and walked around the counter.

Izzy's eyes held a silent fury as she slid away from Leslie's attempt at a kiss.

"Where have you been, exactly?"

Leslie cocked her head. "I had to run an errand after we got all the locks and cameras installed. You know the video surveillance is pretty cool. Let's go through the app together."

Izzy shrugged and crossed to the refrigerator.

"This is your act again—sneaking around and avoiding questions." She yanked the fridge door open and reached in. "I'm getting close to being over this whole act of yours." She grabbed a cup. "What happened last night was beyond scary." Setting the mug down with a thud, her hand trembled as she poured milk.

"Jeez, Iz. Don't you trust me?" Leslie slid her hands into her jeans pockets. "I don't want to stress you, or us, with having to track my every move. I said I'd be underground, and I'm telling you I'll be careful."

"Just what scares me." Izzy's words fell flat. She gulped some milk. "It feels like a lyin', cheatin', stealin' routine you'd see in some gaslight movie."

Her disappointment clear, Izzy unloaded her emptied mug in the sink. Before leaving, she stopped at the doorway. "If you don't get your shit together, Leslie, you'll be the one sinking our ship." The dog trotted after her. "I'll be in the tub." While heading for the stairs, she stopped and turned around.

"You're on your own for dinner. I ate with Mom."

Damn.

Leslie replayed the rhythmic phrase—*Lyin', cheatin', stealin'*—in her mind while fussing with her jacket collar. Uncertainty stirred in her gut, pushing her back into the garage—to the security of her workbench and the comfort of her woodworking tools.

She grabbed the rubber mallet beside her mini lathe, her throat tight. With its head in her hand as she gripped the handle, the words—*Lyin', cheatin', stealin'*—replaying mentally. She tapped the hammer into her palm. Why should Izzy trust her? She'd been lying by omission, its original seed sprouting multiple faces now. It was time to cut it off. She'd talked herself into believing the ends justified the means, but the truth of her botched behavior was clear. She was cheating Izzy out of full status as an equal partner in their lives. They needed to face whatever challenges arose together.

And stealing?

The boxes of her mother's things stared at her from the end of the bench. She laid the mallet down and ripped open the closest one. What would her mother say if she were here? Would she have advice about honesty in a marriage? Grace's words resurfaced from their last visit at her mom's funeral. *I've got something I'd like to talk with you about. It's waited years, but the time is near.*

Leslie waded through more meaningless trinkets and things. Her mother's favorite containers, lots of them made with wood. No wonder Leslie created wooden jewelry. A small lacquered jewelry box, a head-popped turtle adorning its top. A miniature basket with a short string of carved fishes, their eyes painted in, tied to the side. Leslie scooted her stool closer and sat, studying the collection of knick-knacks before reaching for the turtle-topped box to open it. Inside, an old prescription bottle, the typed sticker faded and unreadable.

Stealin'—exactly what I'm accused of at work.

Izzy didn't know about the board complaint alleging Leslie stole the drugs. But she did know opiates were missing from Bryce's safe. Did Izzy think Leslie might've stolen them?

Tablet vial in hand, smooth and firm rubbing her thumb over the label, she wandered to the window and looked over their backyard. The scent of rich, musty earth blew in from the open back door. Branches of a bordering cedar waved in the wind, stirring a knot in her stomach.

The muffled sound of a beeping IV line alarm surfaced in the back of her mind. Fear coated her mouth with a bitter, metallic taste as she recalled a middle-of-the-night case in her last training year, a decade earlier. She'd let her junior resident sleep in the call room. In a routine case, she'd consulted on a woman who had attempted suicide by overdose, admitted to the medical floor after treatment in the emergency department.

The young patient lay pale in her ward bed, black charcoal staining her mouth. Out cold. She was sleeping soundly from the depressant drugs she'd taken but stable enough to avoid the ICU. Instead, a compact unit for heart monitoring housed her in one of five beds. They'd put her at the end, away from the nursing station and the other two patients. Now, the challenge was keeping her safe in the hospital and figuring out how to help her.

While the nurse tended to the IV alarm, Leslie read through her chart notes from a call with the patient's sister. She'd been so shaky that day, having sworn off the booze after another weekend debacle. Oh, quitting drinking wasn't so difficult. No problem. But her trouble staying stopped had grown into the shakes and insomnia. When her staff physician saw her tremulousness, he'd asked if she was okay. After she mumbled something about lack of sleep, he warned he would keep an eye on her.

She considered quitting her moonlighting job to get more sleep for real, but then she'd have more time for booze. She didn't trust herself to stay away from drinking when she wasn't working.

At this point, within months of finishing her residency, her life's dream was within sight. She had to control the withdrawal.

Beyond fatigue, with a few hours of sleep over the previous three days, Leslie rubbed her eyes to focus. The room was barely lit at two a.m. A fluorescent bulb hummed in its metal case above the patient's headboard.

"I'll be at the nursing station for a bit." The night nurse left.

With curtains drawn to separate out the woman's quarters, Leslie eyed the chair next to the bed but vowed to remain standing lest she pass out sitting down. Quiet surrounded her when another woman whisked into the area, a canvas bag over her shoulder. She looked younger than the patient. Leslie assumed it was the sister.

"Lisa?"

"I can't stay. My three-year-old's in the car asleep. Double parked." She was out of breath and hurried. "You've got my number. Here's all the pill bottles I found in her apartment." She tossed the bag on the bed, the crackle of tablets on plastic lingering as she dashed out of the room.

"I'll give your information to the nurse," Leslie said while the woman left the room. The quietness returned as she ruffled through the case, reading prescriptions one by one, noting the drugs.

A cacophony of crows calling and cedar branches blown against the window redirected her attention now to the blustery outdoors. A loud thump shaking the casement caused Leslie to startle. A small bird had guided itself right into the glass.

Leslie stared at the prescription bottle in her hand.

The memory crashed through her consciousness like a wrecking ball—something buried so deep she hadn't known it existed until this very moment. The patient's vial for Xanax. She had stolen it while the woman slept, then pushed it down to live in dark recesses where lurid acts scurried to hide.

"Fuck." She'd not remembered this for years. Numbness encircled her chest.

She *was* a thief.

Pocketing the woman's pill bottle had been, she now realized, her answer for treating her own withdrawal.

Oh shit. Her cheeks burned.

She grasped what drove her to lie to the one she loved most. The thievery—it was true. Not Bryce's bupe, but ten years ago. If she wasn't able to look at herself and admit what she'd done until this night, how could she tolerate anyone else looking at her? Especially Izzy. Addiction had eroded away her values, her identity. But now, she knew what she had to do. The old shit didn't have to drive how she dealt with the current accusation. Right away, she texted her AA friend—she would come clean with Izzy after getting clear with another recovering alcoholic. She needed clarity from talking to someone who'd been in her shoes to put things right with her wife and their future child.

But was it too late?

Twenty-One

Sunday, October 20th—Early evening

Bryce stepped around a downtown street musician, muttering under his breath. The brick walls closed in on him as he coursed a narrow passage, his ears burning despite the cold autumn evening. Now near six o'clock, after spending much of the day where he hadn't planned, he begged off dinner at home and traveled down an alley south of West Burnside Street and west of Southwest 5th Avenue. A street dweller yelled in conversation with himself. Street grime and car exhaust filled his nostrils.

He'd been on fire, clutching search warrants as police swarmed his clinic suite, wanting to reach through the phone and slap his attorney, who claimed he had no power to stop it. *Those sons-a-bitches.* Brushing his way past a sidewalk crowd at 5th, he relived the officers tearing Damon's office apart and intruding into his personal safe.

It hadn't helped to call Lynn. He blew his top when she said Detective Levy had already taken the loose-leaf drawing and Damon's notebook. Pearl had told Lynn about it. *What else was in this notebook?* And why hadn't Lynn told him about it on Friday? Apparently, she didn't think it mattered. Besides, she said Dr. Schoen had snapped photos of the notes. All he had to do was ask Leslie to share them.

Damn.

He had no option but to send Rafi a message through Telegram. The risk of police finding Finn outweighed the safety of that dimwit psychiatrist Schoen. Even more chilling, the personal risk if he withheld vital information from Rafi sent shivers down his spine. *What physical torture would that thug bring on?* In his interview with the detectives, the drawing shown yesterday had to be Grady's. *Did Sloan hide his reaction when it was revealed to him? What notes of Grady's had Lynn been talking about?*

A left at the corner and onto Broadway brought Mary's Club into view, touting "Full Bar, Lottery, Games, and Girls." He'd first met Finn at the strip joint, one of Rafi's favorite hangouts. *Such an upscale venue,* he mused, spotting the poster of a black cat next to the door with a blood-red chaos symbol—the eight-pointed star—painted over it. "Classy," he mumbled as he passed two figures cloaked in filthy hoodies. Their cigarette stubs pinched in yellowed fingers sent smoke downwind.

Once inside, daylight no longer existed. While Bryce allowed time for his vision to adjust, the stale booze, body odor, and old tobacco stench hit him between the eyes, sending a nauseating signal. He stepped into another world between the black velvet paintings, dancers writhing around stage poles, and the jukebox blaring. He searched for Rafi.

In the far corner, his back to the wall and facing the bar, Bryce's target gazed at writhing unclothed women, his hand gripping a beverage can. He sported a tattered straw Porkpie hat. As Bryce joined him in the booth, Rafi's belly jumped like a fish tossed on the dock.

"You're late." He burped as forces above his neck moved in opposition, creating an exotic look with divergent eyes. The music shifted gears into a pulsing, oboe-led jungle drum.

"It's been quite a day." Bryce turned to watch the lead dancer agonize around a pole. An opened can of Pellegrino rested next to Rafi's frosty, filled glass. *Just what this windbag needed. More gas to carbonate his gut.* Rafi hoisted the can to his mouth and heaved something into it, the disgusting remnants dripping over.

"I put Finn on alert and in lockdown... for now." Rafi repositioned his drink. "We have to get the pure bupe going strong, and the nurse moved into a private office. We'll deliver the lineup directly, Finn to Sloan. Starting Friday." They locked eyes. "From your message, it's clear the bitch doctor leaked the drawing to the police. I'm sick of her."

Bryce scanned the room, giving the tightness in his chest a chance to dissipate. At least there was sparse clientele filling the pit hole. Less chance he'd run into one of his patients.

"Look, Rafi—I need more time. They came with search warrants this morning and seized Damon's computer. With Finn's likeness in their hands, shouldn't he *stay* in lockdown? Unless you've got a surgeon somewhere who can remove the scar."

"Fuck." Rafi glared at Bryce. He bared the brown of his tiny teeth through clenched jaws. "You're about to be next on my list, *gabacho*."

Bryce shifted on the bench. "Face it." He tipped his chin higher. "You need me."

A moment of quiet passed between them, their eyes fixed on each other as tension in the air hummed. Neither looked away before another idea came to Bryce. Injecting some confidence into his voice wasn't easy. "Besides, the new computer guy should be fully operational before we start. Have you got him pinned down yet?"

"You leave it to me." Rafi hadn't blinked or moved since *gabacho*. "His name's Armie. You'll get the signal. I have to take this thing over. You're flunking out, Mister Doctor-man."

The power shift across the table vibrated like a physical force. Bryce's eyes drifted to an approaching woman, coming from the bar. Flaming pink hair and multiple facial piercings, she chewed gum while gripping a tray to showcase the letter X tattooed at each finger base.

"Anything to drink?" She looked at the floor. "Or eat?"

"Nothing." Rafi bared his teeth. "Leave us."

The waitress turned slowly towards the bar, upper lip curled, while Bryce drifted to private reflection. Whether to give voice to his other problem weighed heaviest. He wouldn't forget Leslie's words at the end of yesterday's meeting. *I'm going to find out what happened to Damon, no matter what it takes.* She wasn't about to slow her inquiries. He couldn't know what else Damon had written in his notebook. Bryce had already spilled the essence of Leslie's threat to Rafi. What if Rafi suspected him of holding back? The idea wrapped around him, squeezing his chest. Like it or not, he was part of this shit show. He reasoned the truth was, Leslie deserved her due.

"We've got a time problem." Bryce scratched his stubble. "I told you I took care of getting Leslie out, but my method needs two weeks." He placed his hands on the table, fisted. "Now we don't have two weeks. We both know Leslie's actively looking into what happened to Damon."

There it was.

Rafi's eyes widened. "She's history!" He crumpled the spit-can. "Finn's gonna take her out. Soon. He'll be free to do some selective assignments."

They sat in silence again, facing different directions.

Nobody would take this special project from Bryce. Not Rafi. Not Detective Whoever. Not Leslie Schoen. *This golden egg is mine. I've freakin' worked my ass off for it.*

Sloan shifted on his barstool while he checked his phone in ritual order: email first, three sources, text threads, sports, and news. Though surrounded by his favorite sports on big screen TVs—MLS, NFL, NBA—his heart wasn't in it. Disaster scrolling the news stole attention from his wagers and the Sunday night, seven o'clock Baltimore-Seattle game at Lightning Will's Bar and Grill. Engaged with two distractions at once, he had failed to achieve his purpose—getting out of his head. His mind hovered darkly over yesterday's meeting with the detectives. Now, free from work duds, he'd be in heaven any other year with the never-ending professional and college sports betting cycle. Tonight, he brooded over the questions they had spun and wound around him like a noose.

His hand jerked with the vibration, and a call came in from Bryce. He debated whether to answer. With the bar this packed, he could barely hear himself think. He needed this distraction. Plenty of noise, crowded booths with patrons pounding beers, the bartender at the other end of Will's lengthy, populated counter. Everyone's absorption focused elsewhere.

Trying to steady himself, he let out a breath. *Stay calm.* "Yeah."

"We've got more to worry about." Bryce didn't bother with greetings.

"What?" Sloan gripped the phone tighter.

"PPB served search warrants today. They seized Damon's computer and ransacked his office." Bryce spoke blandly. "For good measure, they looked inside my safe. So, that drawing they showed us?"

"Yeah. I told you already. I kept a blank face, didn't give them a thing." Sloan lied, glancing over his shoulder, searching for anyone who might be watching, listening. "What about Michelle? Do we have to worry about her, too? She skirted the edge at the last team meeting. I'm not sure how strong she is."

His room scanning stopped on a big screen with a beer ad and some happy dudes playing poker. What he wouldn't give for a carefree card game instead of the mess he was in.

"Don't sweat it—Michelle's fine. And under *my* direction. But Damon—the one *you* were supposed to be keeping an eye on—now he was a mess." Bryce spat into his phone. "He looked green-gray as a ghoul at that meeting. You probably imagined it was the lights in your office."

The bartender was working his way back. The last thing Sloan needed was an eavesdropper, accidental or otherwise, tattling to anyone interested in his affairs.

"You done pointing at me?" Sloan didn't expect much. Met with silence. "I heard him—he turned to me—after Michelle rattled off how she'd given him the cash." The TV above shifted to cheering crowds packed into the Seattle game. Somebody scored. "It was something like, 'She never listens to me. Just dictates what will happen, as if I'm not even there.'"

"He was on defense. She was yelling at him. Although he did sound like a whining wimp. She'd had it with him."

"But did you hear what she said?" Sloan plugged his ear with a free hand. "I had a hard time making it out, but I thought she called him da-da. Is she a risk?"

Damn. Baltimore scored again. He washed it down with a warm IPA.

"Man, you're tilted. She was stuttering out his name." Bryce's disgust was palpable. The question was—which of them he condescended to more. "Her blood pressure must've been through the roof. She was so mad she was purple."

Sloan glanced at the front door. Four people entered, reminding him their MAT team of four was down to three. What was once a solid unit now floundered like a sinking ship. His skin crawled. Should he check on Michelle? No doubt that would push Bryce into outrage. *Would she stay strong under the detectives' continued scrutiny? Would Bryce keep her in line?*

"I'll leave Michelle to you." He shifted the burden and the risk away from himself.

"She's on my list. One last thing."

"What?" Between the detectives on the one hand and Rafi and Finn on the other, the pinch of a vice squeezed Sloan's chest.

"Leslie will be gone soon."

"Gone? Where?" Their office census was shrinking fast.

"You don't want to know."

Twenty-Two

Monday, October 21st

Detective Davis winced at the grating noise of metal blades on concrete and reached to close his car window. The racket and dust of an early morning downtown corner remodel awakened him to find parking at the Multnomah County Health Department, home to the morgue and the Medical Examiner's suite. Fresh air and a river view over the Broadway Bridge had settled his focus onto the case at hand. By now, this drive was automatic, his North Precinct base to Jeannette's office, creating a chance to consider smoldering matters.

"I'm Detective Aaron Davis, here to see Dr. Taylor."

He'd found his destination through patterning, like a horse with a lost rider finding the barn.

"Right this way."

The receptionist showed him to Taylor's space. It always surprised him how she made an office comfortable outside a morgue amid the sharp aroma of formalin and its pungent chemical quality. Maybe it was the warm rug, the light but cozy leather chairs in front of her jam-packed desk, or the floor lamps instead of overhead fluorescent bulbs. Medical journal in hand, engrossed before a shelf-covered wall, she wore a white coat over scrubs and didn't seem to notice his arrival.

"Hey, Jeannette."

She greeted him with smiling eyes over nose-tipped glasses and set her reading down.

"Aaron, hello."

"I'm hoping y'all have the Damon Grady case pinned down. Report coming out today?"

"Yes, it's all written and ready for the Chief's signature." She pulled her chair back and gestured to the front of her desk.

"Can I get the preview?" He took a seat.

"You bet." Her dark hair pulled precisely into a tight ponytail, she rifled through some piles, grabbing a bundle. "This toxicology and some parts of the autopsy are technically thick. Do you want the down and dirty or all the details?"

"Let's say, not the complexities yet. I made an appointment to talk with your Chief, but wanted a first glance from you and a copy of your findings to go over with my sergeant before the meeting."

"Got it." Taylor placed her glasses on the desk. Her analytical eyes cataloged evidence without flinching. "We have the cause of death: mixed opioid overdose with heroin and oxycodone. Given the total picture of the death scene and the head blow, we also have the manner of death—homicide."

Davis jotted the information he'd expected in his notebook.

"Can you say more about the toxicology report?"

"Sure." She flipped through some pages. "Findings include heroin use, given the morphine and codeine, their ratio, and the metabolite known as 6-MAM. The metabolites of oxycodone present and their levels are consistent with ongoing usage, not just a single ingestion. Both drugs were found in the deceased's apartment, identified in a stash box."

Davis shifted forward in his seat. "I'm getting it."

Dr. Taylor cleared her throat, her face youthful and unlined despite her work—facing mortality's darkness.

"The body showed a small concentration of naloxone. Negative for buprenorphine and other substances abused, except for a low-to-moderate reading on cannabinoids. Blood alcohol: zero."

Davis raised his eyes, rubbing the side of his nose.

"Naloxone, but no buprenorphine. I mean, the rest fits with what we expected. The cannabis was at the scene, but there was no packaging for naloxone or Suboxone in the apartment. A bunch of the combination drug with buprenorphine and naloxone went missing from his office." He sat back in his chair. "What do you make of the naloxone positive?"

Jeannette set the report down and took a seat behind her desk.

"I'm going to call that a complexity. My boss will have the final word. Naloxone alone can be given in several ways, including nasal spray. When combined with buprenorphine, as Suboxone or a similar generic, if the toxicology is positive for naloxone, it should also be positive for buprenorphine or its by-product. It's because of a detail about how quickly the two drugs clear from the system." She paused. "This tox result suggests the decedent ingested naloxone but not buprenorphine."

A few beats passed while Davis digested the unexpected information. *Grady might have taken the missing office drugs. He might have sold them on the street. But what explained the naloxone in his system?*

"Is it possible he'd been dosing himself with naloxone? I mean, he worked in an opioid addiction program. Maybe there was naloxone lying around." He made a note to go over what they'd found in the clinic.

"It does happen. I mean, opiate addicts self-administering naloxone." Her eyes narrowed. "But in most case reports I've read, another person was always there to assist. Physicians sometimes prescribe a similar blocking medicine called naltrexone to people with this addiction as a treatment. The idea is that once the person gets clean, the blocking agent prevents them from getting high if they slip back to using. So, I imagine an addict might think to use any available naloxone to manage their disease—to help them stay clean."

They sat in silence for a moment.

"I'll talk it through with your chief. But to me, this means if he's the one who lifted the office drugs, he didn't ingest them. Right?"

"There are several factors influencing how quickly the combination drug is cleared. In the deceased's case, for him to be buprenorphine-negative, I'd expect he hadn't taken Suboxone for at least eight to ten days."

Davis nodded. "Can I get the report today after the sign-off?"

"Sure."

The whirring of an air exchange system kicked on, a welcome relief from the formalin-infused air.

"Also, the wood sample you dropped off matched the fragments found in the scalp. Oak. The timing of the head blow was proximate to the time of death, within a couple of hours. While not fatal, the blunt force trauma was substantial. It likely knocked him out, given the fractures below and internal bleeding. All in the report."

"And what do you make of the fingerprints?"

"Since they were on the egress window, and you told me they don't match any known suspect, they may or may not help." Her expression remained neutral. "Plus, there were no other prints recovered in the apartment. Do you know yet if there were any other people there around the time of the murder?"

"We're working on it." Davis was again intrigued by the similarity of their professions, at least in the investigative aspects. "One other thing is the position of the tourniquet and hands in the tub."

"Yes," Jeannette slipped her glasses on and flipped to a page in the report. "The family confirmed the deceased had been right-handed but adept with his other hand. We found him gripping the hot water faucet using his left. You'd think choosing the cold side would make him alert if that was the intention."

"Yeah. It's unclear who turned the shower on or why he gripped the faucet." Davis shifted to the edge of the chair, his fingertips steepled. "So, the position of the tourniquet and injection on the right is a little odd, but not out of the realm him injecting himself."

"Correct. The shower coming down might have happened before or after the injection. There was minimal blood around the puncture site and on the tub surface below."

Davis closed his eyes, imagining the fatal sequence.

"Seems the blow came first. The oxycodone impaired him, at least to start. Maybe the cannabis, too, before he took a club to the head. Any other injection sites on the body?"

She traced her finger through another page in the report. "No. We didn't find evidence of chronic IV drug use."

"Then the killer somehow got him stripped and into the tub."

"Or killers. We don't know for certain it was a single person." Jeannette was always good for alternative theories. "Also, unless they had a key, the deceased had to have known them well enough to let them in. So, the head blow likely happened inside."

"No signs of struggle outside or inside. Then there's the matter of the heroin getting cooked and prepared for injection."

"Exactly. Where did it fit in the sequence?"

Davis added the obvious question. "And why such a bizarre staging of the murder?"

A knock at the door turned both their heads.

"Come in." Jeannette removed her glasses.

The receptionist arrived. "Doctor, I have a police investigator at the scene of a suspicious death on the line."

"Yes. Tell them just a minute."

Davis stood and checked his mobile as Dr. Taylor rounded her desk.

"Aaron, can we finish later today? I'll call you after the report is signed."

"Sure. Thanks." He headed for the door.

The toxicology result threw a wrench into Davis's latest theory of the case. The PPB interviews with Grady's coworkers and family didn't support longstanding opioid misuse. However, Dr. Taylor had said the tox result indicated his use of oxycodone was more ongoing, not a single dose. *Had there been someone at his apartment the night he died who'd rescued him from overdose by administering naloxone? Someone who knew about the drug use? Maybe used with him? And then something went horribly wrong?*

Phone to his ear at mid-morning, Davis scanned the open area surrounded by cubicles as his team gathered at a North Precinct central conference table. The homicide division's meeting room hummed with the constant percussion of ringing phones and clacking keyboards from surrounding workspaces. Across the room, Levy squinted at the large whiteboard dominating the wall opposite the scarred oak table. The whiteboard was covered with crime scene photos, a victim timeline, and suspect names and faces. She drew lines connecting pictures and labels. Others juggled coffee cups and files while choosing their seats. The air hung heavy with the competing aroma of burnt coffee and the faint chemical tang of dry-erase markers.

Davis turned his back on the group to finish the call with his wife. "Thanks, baby. Tell Brad dinner's on us next time."

His new arrangement with a suspect's father-in-law—to speak as if Aaron's wife was on the line during any call with Brad while working—was a bit cloak-and-dagger, but sneaking around fit the bill. No need to let Levy in on it. He shoved his phone in his pocket before joining the group.

"Okay. Let's get going." Davis settled at the table's head while Levy took the adjacent chair. "I'll start with my meeting at the morgue this morning."

Two members of the original investigative team and one from forensics joined them. Other officers present had been assigned helpers for grunt work.

"We've got murder." Davis lifted his chin. He summarized his visit with Dr. Taylor and the autopsy report.

"Whoever the killer was, one or more whacked the deceased unconscious using the firewood by the side of the house. The cause of death after the blow was the drugs. I think Grady was marinating in oxy and weed. Then the heroin took him out. Either the killer or killers injected him or caused Grady to inject himself."

Davis stood and walked to the whiteboard.

"We've got wild cards. The tox is positive for naloxone but not buprenorphine. Curious, given the drugs reported stolen from the office. The sarge and I will meet with the ME Chief soon. The tox result will be a serious focus, so we understand clearly. And the position of the body in the tub, of course."

Though the table remained silent, a few heads were nodding.

"Speaking of the missing medications, I talked with the DEA agent. The inspection and audit were random. Bryce Nelson, running a buprenorphine clinic since 2013, had expanded to the maximum annual caseload allowed eleven months before. Given the number of patients, his staff size is small, but they refer out much of the counseling. His prescription volume and dose amounts are high. They'll get a slap on the wrist for an out-of-date active subject log corrected before they finished."

He absorbed their interested faces.

"The problem was, the count was short on the opioid drug Nelson's registered to distribute, Suboxone. Not a small number—four hundred units of the 8-2 dose. For an average case, that would cover nearly seven months."

Eyebrows raised.

"Just an FYI." Levy typed into her cell phone. "In 2018, the total street value of this quantity and dose would be about nine thousand dollars. Each tablet contains eight milligrams of buprenorphine, the opiate, with two milligrams of naloxone, the part reducing the likelihood that the drug is abused. The naloxone is the 'opioid blocker' drug."

"Yes." Davis sat again. "DEA confirmed—Nelson alleged Leslie Schoen stole the opiates. They've pended the case to await the outcome of the medical board complaint. Who knows how long that'll take? Another thing—they didn't forensically examine patient charts. They spot-checked cloud-based electronic health records. Didn't find any red flags. They'll go back after the board's decision—problem placed on a back burner."

Levy flipped a page in her notebook. "What do you make of the level of scrutiny on the medical records?"

"No red flags on a spot-check doesn't tell us much."

Levy nodded.

"Okay." Davis looked to his right. "Let's hear about fingerprints."

Too many years of sitting at a desk left the forensics investigative team member, Alex James, with a body density thick below the waist and thin at the crown. Jet-black glasses, large for his angular face, drew attention away from the circles under his eyes. An occupational hazard of forensics work, especially by his mid-forties.

"The one partial and two full fingerprints may or may not prove useful." James stood in front of his chair. "We can tell you who they don't match: the suspect we're searching for, Finn Connor, and his associate, Rafael de Leon. We've also ruled out all the licensed professionals in the medical office—the three doctors and a nurse who gave prints to get their state licenses. We don't have comparisons from the receptionist or the billing lady." He straightened out his spectacles before sitting again. "We haven't cracked Grady's laptop or PC yet."

"The prints may be from an unrelated individual." Davis turned to Levy, catching her eye. "Get those missing comparisons done. Voluntary. Let me know if there's any match. Tell us what you've got from the landlord on recent apartment access."

Levy nodded. "I reached him yesterday. He'll check in after he's back from the coast. He gets back tonight."

"Ask him tonight if anyone else was in his apartment recently." David looked squarely at her.

"Will do." Levy cracked her knuckles. "Julie, will you take the missing comparisons?"

"You bet." Julie Faraday led the investigative group at the crime scene. The fair-haired, blue-eyed agent, with a face full of freckles, gave a thumbs-up. An eager twenty-something, her alert eyes missed nothing. Her medium frame moved with purposeful energy. She wore casual slacks and a simple shell beneath a practical jacket, reflecting her no-nonsense approach to policing.

"All right. Any headway with locating Finn Connor?" Davis looked at all the faces around the table.

"Not yet." Levy tugged her earring. "We're checking established haunts and trying to locate every known associate. It's at the top of our list."

"Let's go over alibis." Davis moved back to the whiteboard. "Who checks out and who doesn't?"

"Right." Levy sat straighter. "So, Bryce Nelson's wife claimed he came home around nine. She popped a sleeping pill—can't verify he stayed in."

"And what about Sloan Mannon and Michelle Wichim?" He pointed to their name tags.

"First." Levy read from her notes. "Lynn Tidings, Leslie Schoen, and Pearl Blanco check out if you believe the spouses and the brother-in-law. With Wichim, there are five surrounding neighbors. We've reached four. None of them saw her that evening. Still working on finding the fifth. We don't have the parking garage camera footage with Mannon, but we expect it later today."

Davis shot her a quick glance. "I want to hear from you when those two details come in. Ask Julie to help if you need to, but decipher those."

"You got it." Levy looked down.

"Now, what about the phone records? I gave those to you, Julie." Davis crossed his arms over his chest.

Julie stood as she launched into a summary. They'd documented a few pertinent calls and texts in the prior month. Damon Grady's contacts with his sister on the ninth and Lynn Tidings a week later checked out. She'd run down another unanswered call placed on the ninth, the day before his death. A man he'd met at an NA meeting years before had missed the call, but he'd swung by Grady's place a couple of hours later. No answer at the door. The guy said it didn't surprise him since Grady had resisted accepting help after going cold turkey roughly three years back. The NA friend had a rock-solid alibi, already confirmed, for the time of the murder.

Davis had raised his hand at the mention of NA. "Just so we all register this part: Grady's drug abuse and NA history. Guess his plan to stay clean didn't work."

Some note-takers at the table drew his eyes. "Go ahead, Julie."

"Leslie Schoen explained two late-night calls. In September, Grady talked with her about a computer issue. On October ninth, he called off sick for work the next day, left a voicemail, but came in around noon on the tenth. He'd also contacted an anonymous prepaid phone several times recently."

"Says something." Davis nodded. "Somebody avoiding an ID. The fact Grady's mobile is missing suggests the killer knew it likely had the information we'd want. The signal's still off."

"Probably at the bottom of the Willamette." James grinned. A few smiles broke out around the table.

"Let's look at our whiteboard," Davis spoke in a lower pitch. "Who benefits if Damon Grady is dead?"

Levy leaned forward over the table. "His sister says he was digging out of debt and sending them cash in money orders. Searching for a will is probably a blind alley, but we're now looking at his bank accounts. It seems he was mailing thousands of dollars to his family from Walmart. Eleven K in the last four months, total."

"That's a chunk, especially for a medical assistant." Davis nodded. "You got that from the sister. Allison, right?"

"Yes."

"Did you get the family's permission to release the health record? With the one appointment Grady had with Sloan Mannon?"

"She wouldn't sign off on it." Levy clicked her nails. "Wants to discuss it with the mother and family lawyer. I didn't pin her down on what they might be afraid of. I'll follow through."

It was a minor item, just a note from a psychologist's visit. But it stuck in Davis's craw, along with the other loose ends. He didn't enjoy lingering details, and mentioning a family lawyer meant this wouldn't get clarified soon.

"So, okay—about the drugs in his apartment." Faraday set her pen down. "We're searching for two known drug-related criminals. Might be a dope deal gone bad. Maybe they fronted Damon Grady product—drugs to sell—and he never paid them back. A vendetta."

She and Levy exchanged glances.

"Also, Leslie Schoen." Levy raised her chin. "If she stole the opiates, and Grady was a direct witness, or they were in it together, she might've wanted to remove him to save her career. It ties the missing drugs and the murder. She might have her wife lying for her on the alibi."

"I'm all for finding a link, but the same claim might work about Nelson or the nurse." Davis shrugged. "And in each scenario, we've got no evidence." He sniffed sharply. "Not yet."

Levy's eyes burned into him.

"Let's consider the nurse, the billing manager, and the receptionist for motives. Anyone have an idea?"

No one responded. Davis shoved his chair back and checked his phone.

"Alex, meet me in my office. We'll gather on the faded numbers behind Grady's drawing and what it'll take to crack those computers." He looked around the room.

"I want Finn Connor found, people. Let's get on it."

Twenty-Three

Leslie's closet was an overgrown mess. She pulled from her sweater stack to finish dressing for the day around seven, set on getting things straight with Izzy. She'd had no chance yesterday with Izzy away from the house until Allison's plane had landed. But time with her mom about managing morning sickness and later with her dad upgrading the garden center's security system were both good things.

The circumstances gave Leslie time to arrange Allison's arrival without having to navigate Izzy's frustration. She'd gotten clarity on how to make her amends. Talking it over with her program friend helped iron out the self-interest and fear-driven lies that multiplied with increasing harm. Untangling her past mortifying actions from current events was the key. It held the promise of freedom, a place she was more than willing to go.

Detective Davis had phoned Allison before she left Wisconsin, right before the official news that Damon was murdered came out. Izzy and Leslie's evening with Allison had been heart-wrenching. She'd arrived in time to catch the local news about the homicide. After all of Allison's travel and tears, followed by a late-night call from her family, there was no way Allison would wake early. Izzy's morning sickness had settled down, and she was already cooking breakfast. Clearing the air at the kitchen table might work.

Once Izzy knew about the board complaint and they had a chance to talk about Leslie's lies, she would share what she and her lawyer were doing to respond. He'd prepared her well. With her past board history, some potential outcomes might hamstring her professional future or even eliminate it. Much depended on the proof provided by Bryce Nelson, of which they had no idea. They'd submitted her written response to the complaint. The investigator appointment would be scheduled within a week. Best to not borrow trouble, as her cousin Grace would say, and avoid anticipating any actions the Board might take.

Leslie had to tell Izzy about Bryce's plan to push her out of the office. She'd already told her attorney, who recommended leaving it out of the written response. Were it to arise in the board investigation, he believed, it would likely be seen as a 'he said, she said' situation. But the decision about moving her practice now needed Izzy's input. Her lawyer had agreed, but precipitously moving her practice and even trusting Bryce to follow through with his offer were not wise moves.

Absent-mindedly stuffing her tote bag for the workday, Leslie snapped out of her mental chatter when she ran into the photo of the man with the facial scar. Brad had shared it on Sunday afternoon, saying she should call immediately if the guy showed up. He'd also given a copy to Izzy before she came home Sunday evening. Though speaking little with each other Sunday night, Izzy and Leslie had agreed—no doubt, this was the man in Damon's drawing.

Leslie's home study window opened to a pink-orange sky glowing through branches, reflecting hazy light. Jogging down the stairs, she followed the scent of food and the blaring range fan. As she entered the kitchen, Baby J sat in her bed, her head cocked with a sad face. The door to the basement guest room was closed. Leslie debated whether to talk over the blasted noise while pouring some coffee.

"Can I help with anything?"

Izzy turned off the vent and spoke with her back turned.

"Just sit down and eat."

Leslie eyed the table vase as she settled. A flower bouquet with warm golds, burnt orange, and soft brown tones, fresh yesterday morning, now drooped. Izzy set their plates down and pushed her scrambled eggs around with her fork.

"So, how's your stomach this morning?"

"Marginal." Izzy crunched a well-done piece of toast, avoiding eye contact. "The OB clinic just called. They had to reschedule our ultrasound for next week. I left you the time by your keys."

"Oh, I was looking forward to it." Leslie extended her hand toward Izzy's.

She pulled away. The quiet grew between them while Izzy focused on her phone. Getting no attention, the dog plopped down on her side. Leslie chewed and swallowed, feeling the empty fluttering in her stomach.

"Listen, Izzy." She gulped some coffee. "It's time for me to tell—"

They both startled as the basement door opened, the sounds of its squeaking hinge melding with footsteps. Leslie's coffee splashed as Allison arrived in her bathrobe and pajamas, yawning.

"I didn't sleep." Allison pulled a chair out from the table. "The basement's totally comfortable. It's just …" Her head turned from Izzy to Leslie.

Izzy stood and gathered her dishes.

"Did I interrupt something?"

"No." Izzy set the dishes in the sink. "I was just leaving to sort through some work things in the garage. I've got to run by the nursery afterward. I'll be back in an hour or two. Help yourself to coffee." The dog followed. "Leslie can get you some breakfast."

"Thanks, but I never eat before noon." Allison turned to grab a cup and headed to the coffeemaker.

"Izzy, I need to talk to you later," Leslie said as Izzy opened the door to the garage.

"Yeah. I'll be waiting." She closed the door.

A bitter taste flooded Leslie's mouth.

"Wow, what a night." Allison ran a hand through her dark, wavy hair as she sipped her coffee. It wasn't difficult to see she was Damon's sister, with prominent cheekbones, a brow above chestnut eyes, and a full-lipped mouth. She looked to be in her mid-thirties.

"Were you okay down there?" Leslie scooted her chair back.

"Sure. I did sleep an hour or so. But I just had the craziest dream." Allison cradled her cup. "It was Christmastime when Damon and I were kids. We had flocked Christmas trees every year, decorated with all green bulbs, but the colors kept changing from one of those rotating floor lamps." Her eyes grew misty as her voice quivered. "Damon's favorite thing was to crash on the couch in front of it, holiday music in the background. The tree hypnotized him—red into blue, orange, green, and so on. In the dream, I was trying to tell him about getting a phone call from our dad after so many years."

A pleasant heaviness settled behind Leslie's eyes. If only she'd had more time with Damon. He was so funny, so kind and sweet. "What phone call?"

"Late last night, after I went downstairs, it was incredible. I hadn't talked with our dad for years, but he found my number and texted me to ask if we might speak." Allison set her cup down. "He'd seen a news piece about Damon's death. I really want to talk with my mom today. She'll be amazed he surfaced after decades."

"Wow—intense. Is your mom's health okay lately?" Leslie pictured reuniting with a father who had been gone for decades. A familiar ache bloomed in her chest, a peculiar mixture of longing and curiosity that often surfaced around father-daughter conversations.

"She's pretty stable, considering. Thanks for asking." Allison found her coffee and joined Leslie at the table. "This is going to sound strange, but I don't know if I would've ever spoken with my dad again if Damon hadn't died." Allison's mouth twisted into a grin mixed with regret. "I mean, what do you say to an MIA father after twenty years?"

"I can't imagine." Yet she had—many times.

"But with this news about Damon being murdered, a whole bunch of baggage just fell away. We shared our shock and outrage." Allison swallowed hard. "He told me he'd been watching us from afar." She wiped some tears from her cheek. "If I wanted, he said we should stay in contact with the police together while they investigate to find the killer. To get justice for Damon."

"Sounds like an extraordinary call." Leslie's eyes dropped to her hands, remembering her father momentarily stealing her voice.

"We had an unbelievable moment of forgiveness. I never knew what happened ... like ... why he stayed away, until now."

She stopped. "Oh, sorry. I'm just going on about my family. You probably had enough of them last night."

"No, not at all." Leslie shook her head. "Hearing all this makes me wish I'd known Damon better. Did he ever talk about having friends here?"

Allison paused. "It's funny. Two weeks ago, when we talked about him coming home, he said he had buddies in Portland. But he didn't mention any friends by name or talk about hanging out with them. He was so single-minded—work, money."

"Did he mention drugs or knowing anyone who was struggling with drugs—besides the clinic patients? I mean, now that they've called it murder, I'm trying to imagine how in the world—"

"No, honestly. When the detective told me some details, I didn't believe drugs were a part of Damon's life." Allison grimaced. "I just don't get it. He never told me what was going on."

They grew silent while Leslie absently ran her fingers along the links of her necklace.

"Damon sent a lot of money back home ... not that it wasn't kind and generous. But with his salary and the fact he was paying off debts ... it's hard to understand." She sipped her coffee. "Did the detective mention when we might pack his stuff?"

"Detective Davis said to check in with him about it today. He'd have more info soon."

"Okay, well," Leslie looked at her half-eaten breakfast, now cold. "Are you sure you don't want something to eat?"

"No, thanks. And thank you and Izzy so much for your generosity in helping me like this." Allison grabbed her cup and stood. "I'll just head downstairs."

With the basement door closed and Allison gone, Leslie gathered her dishes. A peek out the garage door showed Izzy's car was gone. Wondering when her next chance would be, she left her dishes in the sink and assured herself she'd tackle the crucial talk at the next opening. Any further delay would only make things more tense between them. And that would surely stress the baby.

Sloan's morning list of to-dos before the day's appointments had shrunk somewhat, but not enough. Seated at his clinic office desk, he checked the time—eight-thirty. His bouncing leg jumped with the click of his office door opening. He spun in his chair to face Bryce, then took a deep breath.

"You scared the shit out of me. Knock next time."

"Take it easy, man." Bryce held out an arm, palm down.

"Hhhh!" Sloan tapped the desk. The burden of his alliance with this man weighed like a ball and chain. He clasped his hands and stood, forcing a plastic smile.

"All right. Sit down." He moved to close the door. Outer phones rang, and Michelle spoke emphatically across the hall on a hard-of-hearing call. "I'm getting used to just five of us here, but tell me how we're going to get the charting fine-tuned without Damon." Bryce's arrival raised another concern. "Maybe we should lie low until this police thing dies down. Detective Levy called me yesterday. They've upped it to homicide." The muscles across his shoulders stretched taut as a bungee cord at maximum extension.

"I know. Davis rang me." Bryce sat. "Rafi's only willing to hold referrals until Friday. He's champing at the bit. We must forge ahead with the pregnant women group next week."

With the window coverings closed and the overhead lights off, Sloan's cocoon-like office was secure, even if he wasn't. A compact, glossy fan kept the room's air moving.

"Well, Leslie's coming in late today." Sloan settled into his desk chair.

"Don't worry about her. She'll be out of here soon enough."

Sloan raised a hand to stop him. "Your turf. Like Rafi." He grasped his armrests, preparing for whatever direction the conversation might go.

"Look. Rafi is proposing this guy Armie to take over Damon's job." Bryce's nostrils flared as his mouth puckered tightly. "I haven't met him yet, but I'm trying to slow this train down until the police are out of our hair. Let's keep a list of pending patient files needing changes, then get up to date later. I'll meet with the new fellow and get him started like a consultant, working off-site for a while." He scratched below his sideburn. "Where'd Damon store the access code and templates?"

"Got me." Sloan shrugged. "He told me he'd hidden them well, so not to worry. He protected his computers with such crazy passwords that they were unbreakable."

Bryce nodded. "We need to start from scratch in some ways. We'll be okay." He swung in his chair toward the wall, hands behind his neck. "I want you to do something."

"What?" Sloan's gut knotted like a closed fist below his breastbone. "The cash?"

"Find out who has a credit balance. For the rest, prepare lump sums for those patients at their next check-in. Track it—the same as before, like Damon did. Remember, we're exerting more control over cash deposits. But the amounts changed right before the little runt went missing."

Sloan rubbed his bald head. "What about the first portion? You know—of the new amounts we figured. Did Michelle get it to Damon last week?"

"No. She said he didn't respond to her Scrabble game message." Bryce launched himself out of the chair. "He must have been...let's say...indisposed, unable to watch for communication." He looked at Sloan for a moment before turning away. "She gave the bundle back to me. It's in my office. Get it today."

Indisposed? Yeah, sick to death. Despite the circling fan's unending pace, the room's stillness had grown.

"Believe me, it was tempting to just keep that dough." His features compressed into a prune-like scowl. "As you know, my wife's inheritance is history. It's decades I've tolerated her—the bitch. For nothing. Like my dad's money all over again. Gone overnight."

The bitterness in his partner's words and face, pinched mouth upon set jaw, reminded Sloan of what they had in common—miserable family histories. Long ago, Bryce had revealed his father's criminal past. The guy became a snitch to save his own ass, only to see his offshore account go *poof* afterward.

"What about your grandson?" Sloan's voice cracked before he cleared his throat. "Is your son handling the medical costs?"

For years, Bryce had underwritten medical care for the treatment of his grandson's muscular dystrophy since his son had been unable to insure the child. It wasn't lost on Sloan that their arrangement with Rafi had started shortly after that began.

"Nah." Bryce snorted. "But I found a Costa Rican specialist who can get the new drugs for a song, compared to here." He crossed his arms. "I just need one more year."

"Right." Sloan bit his tongue to limit his reply. No way was he following suit and skedaddling to Costa Rica when the wheels fell off this wagon. He wasn't the tropical type.

"So, keep me posted." Bryce tipped his chin, catching Sloan's eye.

Sloan joined Bryce, who was standing, and they walked out of his office.

As they traversed the hallway, Bryce headed to his office while Sloan turned into Michelle's area. Should he count the times Bryce had said he needed one more year with this thing? The more this message repeated, the more Sloan considered leaving before getting left—by Bryce.

Michelle sat at her desk in an odd posture. *Is she talking to herself?* She leaned to the side with one hand shoved into a drawer and the other fiddling with something unseen on her desk. He cleared his throat.

She jumped, pulling her arm out before slamming the cabinet shut. "You're sneaking up on me again! How long have you been there?"

"A second. Are you hurt?"

She rolled back and pulled some papers around her desk, dislodging a tiny figure—a boy sleeping on his knees and elbows, with hair like an acorn, balanced on a lily pad. Swiping it from view, she crammed it into her scrubs pocket.

Lynn emerged from across the back work area, mouthing *"Help!"* to Sloan before returning to her reception window. Positioned to view the encounter, Pearl stood at a filing shelf behind Lynn, reaching for a folder.

"You're not on the schedule, Josh." Lynn faced the patient, an unseen figure except for his fisted hand and forearm on the counter. "Can I give you an appointment? How about tomorrow afternoon?"

"I'm telling you, I need to see the dude right now!"

"Lynn?" Sloan intervened as he walked toward reception. "Is Josh there?"

"Dr. Mannon, yes." She stepped back. "I was searching for an open slot."

The man, looking fifty in his thirties with an unshaven face and what looked like dirt smeared on his jaw, was shaking.

"Josh, why don't you step back to my office now? We'll make the appointment when we're done." After a stiff grin at both Josh and Lynn, Sloan walked the man to his office.

A moment later, behind the closed door, he bent toward Josh. The guy's odor was something like last night's vomit.

"Have you got it?"

Josh dug into his jacket, hands trembling, and yanked out a prescription bottle.

"I need a few of these." He clutched the vial to his chest, sweat glistening on his forehead.

As Sloan shook his head, the man surrendered the pill bottle with reluctance.

"No, don't take those." Sloan's voice deepened. "I've got something else for you." Stepping back to his desk and using the procedure for treating clients in withdrawal, he lifted a small brown sack from a bottom drawer.

"Two days of withdrawal meds here with instructions." His voice lowered to nearly a whisper. "There's a medication for nausea. Just use these. Next time, stop in after you've fixed back to normal."

Josh swiped the bag into his fist, leaving without a word.

Twenty-Four

Wednesday, October 23rd

The Psych Recovery office kitchen was of insignificant size, but it often accommodated weighty interactions. A late Wednesday morning meeting with Bryce and Michelle alone proved no exception. He took slow, even breaths while she spoke her piece.

Bryce glanced at the clock, counting to four on inhales to curb his impatience. He had only twenty minutes to pull off the immediate meeting he'd called with Rafi. Delaying an afternoon patient had created the space. With his back to the wall and Michelle inches from his face, he mentally scrambled to bring the current conversation to a close. He bobbed his head with mechanical nods as she leaned forward to emphasize her next point and stepped to the side.

"I'm telling you, Pearl will not stop harping on this topic." Michelle gestured with her index finger. "Something has to be done."

"I'll say it one more time," Bryce spoke slowly. "I've given this problem to Sloan. He'll bring it to a close by letting Pearl and

Lynn know we will no longer take payments from last-minute, unscheduled patients." He raised his hands in defeat. "Until we've got a modified software program."

Michelle pinched the bridge of her nose, closed her eyes briefly, and left the room. Bryce exhaled and made a dash to his office, driven by a chilling vision of Rafi's reaction if he were late. He found his suit coat and slung it over his arm. A quick rummage through the coat's pockets reassured him the baggie he'd prepared earlier was still there. He'd usually be happy to get outside at midday, but happiness was the last thing on his mind this afternoon.

A brisk walk to Pioneer Square helped him brace against the downtown Portland cold. He needed something hot, and Starbucks was empty. Moments later, while checking his email, he rested on a planter's edge in the open plaza with hot coffee in hand. He didn't hear the person behind him until a blunted hiccup caught his attention.

An oversized hoodie covered the man's coal-black hair. Some bangs fell over his forehead, obscuring the crisscrossed terrain of his face. Rafi settled a foot from him but faced away at an angle.

"This better be good." His gravelly voice made him sound old.

Bryce pulled the baggie out of his pocket and slid it across the cement, pausing for a moment, the implications sinking in. "I want whoever takes her out to plant this."

Expecting the necessary event at any moment, Bryce had scrambled to concoct something to counter two deaths close to him within a week. Leslie and Damon had already taken on a ghostly quality in his mind. This meeting demanded precision, and the rush of uncertainty nipped at him like the leaves spinning in the downtown wind.

"What's this about?" Rafi tucked the baggie into his coat without looking at it.

"Packaging for medication samples." He let his words tread out carefully. "We've got missing opiates and a board investigation into Leslie taking them. The hit needs to look like the stolen drugs were involved."

He'd considered everything. Everything possible. But now, as he looked at the shifty angle of Rafi's eyes, his chest tightened.

"Just know, collateral damage is probable." Rafi sniffed deeply. "Anybody helping her. Living with her. My man's at the ready."

Taking a sip of coffee, Bryce shifted his position. The planter's edge was cold but not as cold as Rafi's raspy voice. It had grown on him—the prospect of losing Leslie's intrusiveness. Her questions were drawing attention. He was certain Lynn had already shared yesterday's add-in patient scenario with her. He'd seen it all from the hall. He'd also caught Lynn and Pearl's exchange after Sloan took the unscheduled patient back. This was the only way to keep Leslie's meddling from spiraling out of his control.

He turned to face Rafi, baring his teeth. The man looked distant, his hood over his head and shoulders hunched. With imposing presence, Bryce delivered each word deliberately, his tone unyielding.

"Target only. Leave my staff out of this. And don't forget—Schoen's father-in-law is a former cop."

"We'll see." Rafi looked at his phone.

They sat in silence. A crowd of crows cawed and pecked at old French fries tossed on the cement.

"I need time before your guy Armie comes into the office. We'll have to start from scratch with him, beginning off-site. We're keeping a list of what's needed once we've trained staff again."

"He starts now. I don't care where he works. Just meet with him and keep the flow going." He yanked the strings of his hood tight. "Here's how you contact him. Get rid of this when you're done." He extended a note from his pocket.

Bryce tucked it away, glancing around them. Every day, more homeless people lined the sidewalks of the square, beaten into the impossible state of their circumstances. Tents pitched. Cardboard signs. Heaps of trash. Bags stuffed with barely enough to survive—a woven cloth of endless need gone threadbare. Helpless. Bryce refused to accept helplessness. He needed to topple this scumbag and run the project on his own terms.

"I'll be the one delivering pharmaceutical bupe. Remember that." He sucked his lips into a tight bud. "And one other thing—about the cash."

"What?"

"We're taking larger up-front amounts. The follow-ups will be less than we planned. About two-thirds to control our deposits. Avoid getting flagged."

"I don't give a shit how you do your laundry." Rafi's brows drew together slightly, the right one arching higher in a challenge. "But you better not fuck me on my cut."

Bryce stood to walk away. "We're done."

Detective Davis stood at his North Precinct office doorway as the afternoon moved from mid to late. He looked across the hall into the break room, his eyes settling on a decades-old poster above the kitchen table. In the Southwest red rocks, on an outcropping of rust-orange layered stone rising to a deep blue sky, a tangled scrub tree sprouted, its branches ending in defiant green needles. The Grady case, barely a scrub tree sapling, had inched forward and fallen back, struggling for life. He reviewed his list of lingering details, searching for a key to jump-start their efforts.

He turned and scanned his office. A second doorway opened into the central conference area where voices drifted through. Files sat in neat stacks on his desk, where his wife Rochelle's photo smiled from their honeymoon setting, positioned so only he could view it from his chair. The Venetian blinds covering the large window into the conference room remained partially open, allowing him to monitor the area without drawing attention.

He'd squelched his earlier irritation. It had taken too long to discover Mannon lied about his whereabouts last Thursday. Levy offered a lame excuse—other priorities after they'd found the parking garage video erased in error. They'd had to jump through corporate hoops to get the backup. There was no reason except laziness. It took five days to learn. The bitter taste of wasted time coated his tongue.

Mannon had said he was home alone all night. But his car, parked by early evening, was gone again at seven-fifteen and not back in place until just after one. *Why did he lie? Where had he gone? How might Mannon benefit from Grady's death?*

A call to Grady's sister confirmed the family would not voluntarily allow Grady's medical records with Mannon to be released. The sister had assured Davis that Mannon had not pressured her family about this. Davis headed for the conference area, knowing he'd need more to take to a judge for a search warrant. *Should he wait to confront Mannon's bullshit alibi? Watch the psychologist's movements in the meantime?*

Grady's sister wanted to pack his apartment and get the body shipped to a funeral home in Wisconsin. There was still no trace of Grady's phone, but they'd been through the records. The phone was probably history.

Levy stood with her back to him at the whiteboard as she adjusted one result, simplifying things. She discovered the house windows had been cleaned professionally, inside and out, about a week before Grady's death. They just contacted the company to arrange comparing the prints found in Grady's apartment to the cleaner's, whose prints were on file with their HR department. No answer yet. Grady's bank accounts were about as boring as no-spice spaghetti: automatic salary deposits, auto bill-pay to the usual utility and phone companies. Plus, lots of Venmo debits without details. That meant another search warrant for his Venmo account. He bought those money orders with cash. *Where did he get it?*

The forensics team leader, Alex James, gulped coffee while turning pages in a folder, his glasses perched at the end of his nose. A file cabinet's tinny screech from an adjacent office sent Julie Faraday's hands to her ears. At the same time, Levy took a seat at the table. Davis cleared his throat.

"How about an update on Finn Connor?"

The conference area quieted.

"In his last contact with law enforcement, a year ago in San Diego, they nabbed him on suspicion of assault with a deadly weapon after finding a man badly sliced in Old Town," Faraday spoke while standing, her tone neutral. "Dice and slice. That's his signature. His felony conviction followed a different brutal knife attack, and the two murder cases where he was a suspect in California were deaths resulting from knife violence."

"How about tracking him in the last few weeks or months?" Davis clenched his jaw.

"Nothing so far," Faraday replied. "Except for a connection in Vancouver, Washington."

She turned a page over on the table.

"Go on."

"We know Finn Connor works with Rafael de Leon, a member of the family crime syndicate with roots in Sonora, Mexico, and a U.S. base in San Diego. He goes by 'Rafi.'" Faraday cleared her throat. "Turns out, Connor has a nine-year-old daughter with Rafi's sister, Maria Santiago. We've been looking for this Maria to get a line on him."

Davis's leg bounced. Maybe this would be the crucial lead.

"Rafi is the de Leon drug trafficking boss in the Pacific Northwest, and Finn is his lieutenant."

"And the Washington link?" Davis glanced at the whiteboard. They'd attached a photo of Maria next to Finn.

"Maria Santiago booked a commercial round trip from San Diego to Portland International, departing two weeks ago and returning last week. Tracking her contacts, rap sheet, and after plenty of calls, we found she stayed at the Heathman Lodge, northeast of downtown Vancouver. We think she lives in San Diego."

Davis raised his eyebrows. "You've connected with Vancouver PD? And San Diego PD?"

"We have. We've got alerts out on all three of them there." Faraday glanced at Levy. "And yes, we're moving on questioning the hotel staff. Security camera footage, visitors, messages, you name it."

Davis nodded. "Good work. Plan to contact me at the end of the day for updates."

"Yes, sir," Faraday said as she sat.

"Let's get to the forensics discussion." Davis looked at his notebook. "How about a review of Grady's computers and the numbers in the drawing?"

Alex James unfolded a poster-sized duplicate of the random digits and taped it to the board. The numbers in bold columns and rows had been superimposed over the grayed-out figure's head.

"Five days with Grady's laptop, three with his work PC, and we haven't broken the passwords." James adjusted his heavy glasses. "Our software's running 24/7. Grady was seriously protecting his information."

He elaborated on the electronic data management at Psych Recovery's office, details gained through reviewing the staff interviews. They housed medical records on a cloud-based system, with one company providing scheduling and billing software. Each of the seven workstations, including Grady's, had a separate sign-on to the software and specific permissions to use different sections, depending on the employee's job function. Grady would've been granted access to charts, billing, and the schedule. He was also the officer responsible for securing their clients' health information.

Because of his various duties, James believed Grady would've had access to the system from his work PC and possibly also his personal laptop. This meant he might've stored health records on either of his computers. Seizing other office computers wouldn't help them learn what Grady had stored on his.

"From a probable cause perspective, our link to seize the work computer was the drawing found in Grady's office," James said. "Was Grady trying to communicate something through those numbers? We can assume he knew Finn Connor. But is there a message in the digits? Is it some kind of numerical 'map'?"

Levy raised her eyes from her copy of the drawing. "So, why are random figures like this typically generated?"

"It may be helpful if we start by assuming what the numbers likely don't mean, given what we know about Damon Grady." James repositioned in front of his poster. "For example, we have no reason to believe he was involved in academic activities or research. So, the likelihood that he used a random number generator to create a representative small sample from a large population, used in experimental designs, is quite low."

"Safe bet." The corners of Davis's mouth curled upwards.

"You can see." James stepped to the side and gestured at the board. "There are hundreds of five and six-digit numbers arranged in columns and rows. Similar numbers are used in raffle-like scenarios. I mean electronic raffle tickets. But we have no information, at least so far, that Grady was involved in any activity like this."

Davis turned to look at Levy. "Correct?"

"I think so." Levy glanced at Faraday. "Would you agree, Julie?"

"Yes, but... maybe we should all ponder that for a while." Some heads nodded.

"So, we're narrowed down to other options I consider more likely." James pushed his glasses up. "The first is two-factor authorization. Like when you log into your bank account and, for extra security, they text you a key. You enter the number, and it verifies you're attempting to log in."

"So, we should consider how Grady might have verified that people contacting him were who they said they were, not imposters." Davis made a note. "For example, he's running drugs for a dope ring, and someone contacts him from a burner phone about where to meet. But he needs to be sure who it is. So, he sends a text digit code to the mobile he knows is connected with that person. If the same number comes back, he believes the contact. The system is prearranged by the parties. Incriminating details are left off private phones. Only the texted numbers would be traceable."

Levy elevated her chin. "Added security on the deal. Like protecting against a rival drug gang trying to get the cash or drugs or take Grady out."

"Might be a possibility." Davis looked around. "Except the phone records don't suggest this."

James bobbed his head vigorously. "Two ways around that, though. He might've messaged people through social media or video games. Not traceable in phone records and difficult to trace even if you have the mobile."

Davis nodded. "Okay, anything else?"

"One last idea on the digits, and this is my bet." James rearranged his glasses.

"Let's have it." Levy leaned forward.

"The guy was obviously adept at protecting his data," James said. "What if he rotated the figures for serial password changes? Number sets would be easily at his disposal. He'd just have to add some letters and characters. And he might've stacked them back-to-back. You wouldn't need to keep track of which numbers you'd used before if the system wouldn't let you repeat the same password."

The room went quiet as the idea settled.

"So, search warrants for patient records, other than the one with Grady and Mannon, make little sense." Davis shrugged. "These aren't medical record identifiers, diagnostic codes, or anything tied to the electronic charts, right?"

"I don't think so. The chart IDs are combinations of letters and digits." James shook his head. "I'd expect birth dates to be eight numbers. And the various numerical diagnostic and procedure codes used in their mental health clinic just don't align."

"Damn." Davis exhaled in a huff. "The background numbers either tell us nothing or are useful, but we don't know why."

James pulled his poster off the board. "Yeah—might be something other than the scenarios I've considered." He looked around the table. "You know what they say—four heads are better than one."

Davis tapped his hands on the table. "Means all of us need to give this some serious consideration. If any other ideas come to you, bring them to me."

Twenty-Five

Wednesday, October 23rd—Early evening

Izzy and Leslie scraped plates into the compost bucket on the kitchen counter. After a simple dinner at Izzy's parents' for six, including Allison and Baby J, they all worked to clean the dishes before dessert. The lingering scent of beef short ribs with Kathy's special sauce on top of the full meal lulled Leslie into calmness. Cream cabinets gleamed under spot and can lighting as steam rose from their generous double sink. Leslie's fingers brushed against the butcher block island, where Baby J's tail thumped rhythmically, the dog working to keep the kitchen floor clean.

Beyond the windows, the evening's restless air threw wild wind in spurts. At the howl of a big gust turning both their heads, Leslie caught a chance to hold eye contact with Izzy for a moment.

Miss you, Leslie mouthed. She whispered, leaning forward, "We'll finally get some time alone tonight." Izzy offered a subtle smile. They'd reached a better vibe after clearing the junk from the baby's room with Allison's help. The prior evening,

Leslie, Brad, and Allison had met at Damon's apartment, with Detective Davis's oversight, to plan emptying it out on Friday morning. Leslie had returned home to find Izzy in bed, sleeping early.

Kathy and Allison chatted while washing and drying dishes. They'd accomplished plenty, securing the death certificate and closing out Damon's bank account, making them fast friends. They'd all seen Finn Connor's face. Allison hadn't recognized him.

As Leslie stacked the last plate next to the sink, Izzy reached to toss something in the trash, bumping into her.

"Oops." Izzy grinned.

"That wasn't so bad." Leslie smiled. *Grab the time with Izzy now.*

"I'll just take out the garbage." Brad hoisted a bag over his shoulder.

"I've got the compost." Leslie followed as they traversed the deck and descended the stairs to the trash and recycling bins below. Leslie tossed the bio-bag. "Listen, Brad. Remember how I've got to tell Izzy about the board thing?"

"You're not done yet?" His eyebrows lifted an inch.

"I've been trying, but keep getting interrupted. Would you mind if Izzy and I took the dog for a walk before dessert? I mean, we'd leave Allison with you and Kathy for a bit."

"No problem. We'll be fine. Go for it." He rested a hand on her shoulder, his wiry hair blowing the wrong way. "Take as long as you need."

"Thanks. Everything's just been so ... crazy. Have you talked with Detective Davis today?"

Brad looked back at the kitchen door. "You're keeping those autopsy results to yourself, right?"

"My lips are sealed." Leslie didn't understand the positive naltrexone but negative bupe on the tox. Getting into Damon's apartment would allow her to look for a naltrexone trail. She hadn't been able to snoop in front of Detective Davis the night before. But was it reasonable that she might find something the police missed? A package insert? A nasal spray cap? "Have you heard anything more?"

Brad turned away from the house and leaned in, his voice almost a whisper. "Mannon lied about being home the entire night. They have CCTV footage. He left at about seven-fifteen and pulled back in around one." He raised an index finger to his lips. "The Bureau is tracking him for now. Not a word."

He looked at her as if to inquire whether she grasped the magnitude of this news. Leslie's mind spun with questions as they returned to the kitchen in less than a minute. The update on Sloan was a shocker. *Did he lift the drugs? If so, was Damon a witness? Had Sloan killed Damon?* And Damon was clearly using. Why would he leave a drawing of the man who *had* to have been his dealer? It didn't make sense. Did he mean for someone to find it if anything happened to him?

"Time for dessert?" Allison raised plates for cake.

"We're totally into more time with you, Allison." Leslie looked at a moping Baby J. "But is it okay if we take the dog for a walk first?"

"Oh, sure." Allison shrugged. "But after everything today, I'm pretty beat."

Brad rested a hand on Kathy's shoulder. "Why don't we stay here with Allison?" Kathy and Brad nodded.

Leslie turned to Izzy. "Want to walk the dog, hon?"

She'd have to be in bed sick to pass.

"Let's go." Izzy grabbed her coat from the kitchen chair. "Baby J, come." The dog bounded to her.

"I've got the leash." Leslie dug it out of her jacket pocket, passing it to Izzy.

As Leslie headed for the door, a bugle riff sounded from Izzy's phone. All heads turned to her. She looked at her cell. "It's my security system at work." They both stopped in the living room.

"Oh, no." A wave of dread flashed in Leslie's gut.

"What?" Brad jumped from the couch.

"Not this." Izzy stared at her mobile, eyes wide as she swiped and tapped. "It's gone on backup power and cellular network. Electricity and Wi-Fi are out. I'll check the cameras."

"Look!" Izzy played video footage from the rear nursery yard as Brad and Leslie peered over her shoulders.

The grainy video captured security lights glinting off the greenhouse's metal frame. Someone in a hoodie ran at a rapid clip through neat rows of plants toward the nursery shed, then darted around the corner and out of sight. Leslie and Izzy looked at each other as the color in Izzy's face paled.

"Do we call the police?" Leslie grabbed her shoulder.

Brad stepped back. "Let's go to the nursery right now."

"Should I call?" Kathy jumped off the couch.

"No, the alarm is set to contact the security company first." Brad grabbed a jacket from the closet.

"That'll be my next call." Izzy jammed her coat on, shoving the phone in her pocket. "To tell them whether to call the police. We can deal with it in the car." She handed Leslie the leash. "You stay with Allison so you can take her home. I'll meet you there. You'd better keep the dog."

Leslie nodded, clutching the leash while imagining Bryce was behind this. The notion Bryce that was terrorizing them by arranging an attack on Izzy's business made her shudder. Was this how he planned to throw them off balance? But maybe she was wrong. Maybe it was Damon's man, though, why would the man with the scar target them since Damon was dead?

"We'll call once we've sorted it out." Brad followed Izzy out the door.

"Leslie." Izzy's voice crackled through the phone, tight with tension. "It was a failed break-in. They went after the security system."

"Are you okay?" Under the lights at their kitchen table, Leslie pressed the phone closer to her ear. "Did they catch anyone?" The bright room hadn't stopped Baby J from sleeping, and Allison had gone to bed.

"We're fine." Her words tumbled out. "Dad's with the officer who took my statement. Whoever it was knew what they were doing—wire cutters, targeted approach—but our system held."

"I'll be there in five minutes." She ended the call before Izzy had a chance to protest.

On a Wednesday night around eleven, the streets were empty around their home. Several neighborhood shortcuts helped Leslie rush to Izzy's business in the Mount Tabor neighborhood.

The Portland Police cruiser's blue light bar pulsed as she turned into the TipTop Nursery, her nerves buzzing with worry about how Izzy would tolerate the stress. Empty of cars, other than Brad's SUV, the parking lot between the street and Izzy's garden center was lit by a dim, lone streetlight. The front nursery counters were illuminated by overhead lights. As Leslie slowed to stop, the outlines of two men standing in the side yard showed her the way. Brad knew all about break-ins and how burglars tried to destroy security systems, having recommended a smash-proof design. She left her car to approach the men.

Next to a uniformed policeman just outside the main door, Brad pointed to an area above glass fragments scattered about the ground. Leslie spotted Izzy seated inside, her arms around her purse, her shoulders rounded.

"Hey." Leslie waved at Brad. "Can I catch you?"

Brad raised his hand to the officer. "Just a moment."

He stepped aside. "I'll be in my car overnight outside your house. Maybe you can let Izzy know."

Leslie nodded. "Thanks, Brad. I'm not sure how we'd do this without you and Kathy."

"I've got a security company coming to board the main door. They'll keep watch on the nursery until opening tomorrow. The security system is functioning. Police report filed."

"Did they catch anyone?"

Brad shook his head. "They found wire cutters near the caged main power hub. Seems the intruder ran after failing to disarm the alarm." He turned to check his surroundings. "We got a gloved, masked, hooded person on video but no face. The officer here thinks it'll be difficult to ID the bastard."

"Damn."

"You should get Izzy home."

"I will." Leslie headed inside toward her wife. She stopped in front of her.

"Oh, hon, you must be so spooked. This thing is crazy. Has there only been one cop?"

Izzy stood slowly. "Another car with two others just left." She rubbed the back of her neck, glancing at Leslie briefly. "They walked the yard. We got the power restored and lit everything. It doesn't look like any inventory was damaged. But it'll take some time to comb through it."

"Is anything missing?"

"Ah, shit." Izzy's face reddened, her hands fisted. "Nothing obvious. So far. Dammit. This feels menacing—so dangerous. Can't you see that?" Her face pressed into a grimace of infuriation.

"You're right. This is too much. Two police reports in four days." Leslie moved toward her wife, stopping within an arm's length.

"Goddammit, this is the last thing I need right now." Izzy heaved an exhale.

"Izzy, I'm going to help with the insurance, or—" Leslie reached gently to hold her wife's shoulders. "Whatever. Just tell me who to call. What to do."

Izzy wrapped her arms around her belly, avoiding Leslie's eyes. "Your office has got to be the reason for this. I'm sick of it." A strangled whine escaped with her breath as tears trickled down her cheeks. She covered her face with her hands.

"We've got to come together, hon." Leslie's frazzled nerves hardened. "We need some time to talk. I've been trying to tell you—" With a hand on the small of Izzy's back, Leslie drew Izzy in, taking her into her arms. "Ah. This just sucks."

Izzy whispered, "I'm so tired."

"Come here," Leslie murmured, drawing a deep breath.

Izzy's taut body relaxed as she rested her head on Leslie's shoulder, aligning her breath.

Leslie rocked slightly, sideways. "Izzy, we can talk in your office here—or go home. But we need to talk right now, privately." Rocking and dropping her shoulders, Leslie looked over to check on Brad. Izzy's tension progressively gave way.

He stood with his back to them outside by the police cruiser. The patrolman got behind the wheel.

"Honey, we've got to figure out how to keep you safe—the baby safe—us all safe." Leslie swallowed against the rock in her throat, listening to Izzy weep, her shoulders bouncing gently with each exhale.

After a few moments, Izzy's weeping dropped away. She sniffed and raised her head. "Let's go home."

Having secured the house for the night, Izzy slumped in the bedroom chair, head bowed and fingers massaging her temples as the dim lights cast shadows within the room. Allison was quiet in the basement below. A sunken heaviness occupied Leslie's eyes, the hour now past one in the morning. The dog snoozed quietly in her bed. A relaxed dinner at her in-laws' house had turned into another nerve-rattling night.

"Are you okay?" Leslie sat on the edge of the bed.

"I think so." Izzy pulled her shoes off. "But I'm taking tomorrow off. My dad said he'd help me get the nursery back in order."

"I'll get with him about how I can help. You've been through the ringer. Should you sleep in?"

She offered a meager smile. "Why don't I see how it's going in the morning?"

"Okay." Leslie shrugged. "Izzy, I'm way overdue on telling you something."

Izzy sat back in the chair. "Yeah. No shit."

"I've been wrong to keep things from you." Leslie swallowed hard. "But not long after you told me we were pregnant, I told myself, don't bring bad work news home. So, I chose to wait to tell you what happened. I figured maybe delaying any stress on you and the baby would be better. But I opened a letter from the medical board right after we spoke—when you were in the exam room. Someone—the board hasn't said who—accused me of stealing sample drugs from the clinic and filed a complaint about it. An opiate called buprenorphine—you know, bupe. I've mentioned it before. It's what Bryce prescribes for his opioid addicts."

Izzy's eyes widened. "What? You're kidding."

Leslie nodded. "And last Saturday, I confirmed—it was Bryce. He wants me out of the office. He all but admitted it—dangled dropping the complaint if I moved out within two weeks."

Izzy placed a hand to her mouth.

"But listen. This is the most important part." Leslie took a deep breath. "By keeping all this secret, I hurt you and our relationship. I caused more stress than if I'd just been upfront from the beginning." She shook her head. "I was full of fear and pride. For a few days, I bought a load of my justifying bullshit. Talked myself into believing my career drama might destroy our plans and dreams… maybe even risk the baby. But the truth was I didn't want to look bad—especially in your eyes." She focused on Izzy's disheartened face, her voice cracking. "And I so regret causing you pain and hurting us."

For a moment Izzy, looked stunned. "What do you mean, fear and pride?"

Leslie clenched her hands together, the heat emanating from her palms. "Getting accused of stealing drugs—it messed with some unfinished business I had in my drinking days. My recovery. I didn't realize at first I was looking bad in my own eyes, not yours—because of stuff from years ago. Even though I didn't take the drugs from Bryce's safe, I was insecure in myself. I didn't trust you'd be—we'd be—okay with dealing with the medical board. Again."

The seconds ticked by at a snail's pace. Izzy's crushed expression shifted to a scrunched-up, skeptical knot.

"Jesus, Leslie. In the meantime, you kept me out of planning what to do. You can't stay working with Bryce Nelson."

The fear in Izzy's voice, the uncertainty in her face, was clear. Leslie nodded, the tension in her face taut. "You're right. It's turned into a dangerous, scary place."

Izzy huffed through flared nostrils. "I'll say—Damon's murdered, someone breaks into our house. Someone's vandalized my business. We're all watching out for some nasty-looking criminal—someone Damon knew. It's more than scary. It's threatening. We have to think about our child."

Leslie sat back, reaching for her next words just as the wind blew a balcony door open, sending Izzy to her feet. Baby J woke, her head and ears perked. Softened outdoor light illuminated water streaming on the tiled exterior floor.

"Izzy, I'm done with causing you stress by shutting you out. By lying to you."

Drained, with circles under her red-rimmed eyes, Izzy's face told the whole story.

"I know these are only words. But going forward, you'll see I mean it." Leslie shifted on the bed's edge. Izzy didn't move from standing by the balcony door.

"So—is there any more you think I should know?"

The pain over Leslie's heart extended into a tight throat. She forced an "ahh" as she tried to clear it, the mistiness in her eyes growing. There was more.

"I found letters from Grace and my mom's journal the other night." She reached for a tissue on the nightstand. "In those boxes. Haven't read them yet." Shaking her head, she dabbed her eye. "I was dragging my feet so much dealing with my mom's stuff that I figured facing those letters and the diary might help me understand. Everything happening lately—Damon gone, Allison talking about their family, how different the office has been—it's all caused some memories from my past to surface. But I don't want us to get sidetracked with that now."

Izzy didn't answer. She narrowed her eyes.

"I want to share it with you, but let's finish talking about the board thing first. I've had my lawyer helping me with the complaint. We responded in writing. They're interviewing me on Monday."

Izzy sat again, holding herself stiff and upright. Her words emerged in a steely, low tone.

"I trusted you. And you violated my trust by not being honest."

Ouch. "I did." Leslie's hands fell to the bed. There it was. Ten years sober didn't mean she wouldn't royally screw up.

"No, now you listen." Izzy leaned in, her hands on her belly. "You bungled it big time. Yeah, we'll talk about this more. But the question is, will you rally and get with me? We need to be partners here. To... work together. We need to keep all three of us protected, out of harm's way."

"Yes. I will keep you and the baby in mind first."

In a moment of silence between them, Leslie contemplated the future. The various possibilities.

Izzy blinked through heavy eyelids. "I don't know. I've got to sit with this for a while."

Leslie pulled her head back, curling the tissue into a ball. She'd never known love to be as powerful before her relationship with Izzy. The prospect that she'd driven away the person she cared about most stunned her beyond belief. Would her family of three begin as a fractured unit? She took a deep breath, telling herself that future-tripping and searching for a better past were fools' games.

Of course, Izzy needed time to think.

"I understand. The past few days have been ... overwhelming. Let's come back to this after some time. Maybe after Allison's gone. Like how we go forward from here."

Her head nodding slightly, Izzy tipped her head and rubbed her temples. "All I can say is, I've got to get some sleep."

Leslie stepped toward the hallway. "Sure. Would you like the room to yourself?"

"That'd be good." Her answer hung in the air as she studied the floor.

Leslie turned and left her alone with the dog.

Twenty-Six

Thursday, October 24th

Around seven in the morning, Sloan gripped the Albers Mill Building deck rail, slouching to view the water's edge. The restored six-story red brick building displayed faded ghost lettering along its weathered façade. Solid and weighty, the rust-colored Broadway Bridge, intimately viewed from the old building's veranda, spanned the turbulent river below, churning with whitecaps. A solitary mallard bobbed in the rough waters, the rest of his flock having left without him. A cold blast of air lifted Sloan's cap before he slapped it back onto his head.

He retreated from the deck edge, from the early morning sunrise behind gloomy clouds, and stepped back to find shelter near the building, a historic shoreline relic. A lone figure shuffled toward him from the parking lot. It was Stan, his bookmaker—and these days, his only friend. Stan's crooked posture, permanently leaning left, was his signature mark.

Stan walked as Sloan's father had, periodically slowing to take a step to the right lest he start trudging in a circle. The recollection of that coward, who'd left Sloan vulnerable and alone in his twenties, still made him livid. Not to mention the "fuck you" to Sloan's mother. After everything Sloan had done to support his dad's lost ass, swimming in pain and pills? No wonder his mother had left. The bastard had pushed her away from them both. Then she died.

Sloan dragged himself to a lower deck suspended over the river's edge. He scanned the opposite shore where a moored barge with the name *TIDEWATER* painted on its side rocked gently with the current. A flood of doubt and loneliness, rage, and tension rose as he fought to curtail the entire emotional brew. He would never follow in his father's footsteps and take himself out. He looked directly below at the roiling waters. Besides, death by jump was so overdone in Portland. No originality.

The worn wooden deck wobbled as Sloan stepped toward Stan, whose weather-beaten face seemed to calculate odds beneath his deep-set eyes.

"Hey. I need you to find me a hideout. Hope I won't have to use it."

"You already owe me." Stan's hoarse voice cracked. "When are you gonna even up?"

"Right now." Sloan reached into his jacket and handed over an envelope. "That's all of it."

Stan ripped the wrapper open and thumbed through the bills, his nicotine-stained fingers nervously handling the prize. "Okay, then. Whatcha thinkin'?"

"They have the image of Finn—the pissant Grady drew his picture. Who the hell knows why. With the slash-face, it's just a matter of time before they ID him." He bit on a hangnail.

"I told you Finn and Rafi and their whole crew are the devil." Stan blew on his hands, rubbing them. "Why'd'ya need a hideout? They're comin' for you?"

A bundled-up woman passed on the sidewalk to the building's entrance nearby, keeping Sloan quiet.

"You saw Finn and me last Thursday night at Will's." He lowered his voice. "It wasn't exactly a lovefest."

"I'm surprised you two didn't bat it out then." A soft whistle escaped with Stan's irritation. "What the fuck were you up on each other about?"

"What do you think?" Sloan grumbled. "Little shithead, Grady. The dead guy." He leaned his head to the left, loudly cracking his neck as it echoed in the humid air. "You don't want to know. Let's just say he made a grand mess. And guess which one of us had to take care of it."

"You're right. I don't wanna know what happened to him. I don't wanna know where Finn is... or Rafi."

Sloan shook his shoulders to release the tension in his upper back, to no avail. His plan to skip town created an out, but the proposition left him wondering. *Would I be even more alone in some faraway country, starting all over? But what are my alternatives? Keep hiding behind the bullshit I gave those detectives?* With Finn's likeness in their hands, they'd be coming for him soon. Either the cops or Rafi's gang—not a pleasant prospect facing either.

"Look." Sloan reached into his outside pocket. "Here's a down payment for your guys preparing me to travel on a moment's notice. I'd prefer to land on another continent—maybe South Vietnam or Indonesia. No extradition agreements there. I need a new ID, passport, and place to land." He held out a second envelope.

"How much time do I have?" Stan kept his hands in his pockets.

"I would have preferred it yesterday—but as soon as you can get it works, too."

"One condition." Stan pushed his torso taller, as straight as it would go.

"What?"

"You keep this to yourself. Nobody knows the plan or where you got the papers."

"Of course. No problem." Sloan stared in disbelief at the last man he called a friend. Did he think he wanted to get them both killed? "I'll be long gone before you know it."

Leslie drove her Subaru over the downtown Burnside hill toward work at eight in the morning, dark storm clouds gathering in her rearview mirror. The morning rush hour slowed to a crawl as her windshield wipers struggled to keep pace with the sprinkle that had turned into an abrupt downpour.

The Bureau's theory—that Damon's murder resulted from a drug deal gone wrong—left Leslie increasingly skeptical after her last two updates with Brad. It just didn't explain enough. Like Bryce demanding Damon complete "chart edits."

Leslie pulled into her office parking garage as she neared the end of a call with her on-call partner, Susan. "So, I'm handing you the baton, my friend. For tonight, Friday, and Saturday. Okay?"

"I'm good. No conflicts." Susan sounded sharp for eight in the morning.

Leslie's practice needed an on-call schedule for those urgent situations arising after usual office hours. A psychiatrist's availability by phone was key. Between Susan covering for Leslie's patients at night—three days on, three days off—and the reverse for Leslie's duty, they'd met the mark. Some nights there were no calls. Not so yesterday during Leslie's on-call. She'd been awake when the phone rang late, after her night with Izzy. She now needed to discuss a separate issue with Susan.

"One other thing." Leslie turned into her parking space. "Remember when I told you about the conversation between my office partner and our medical assistant—the demand for chart edits?"

"Yeah. Like there'd been some sort of covert meaning, given the whole picture."

"It was a tense atmosphere, for sure." Leslie turned her car off. "But I've been thinking about what Bryce asked Damon to do." She scanned around the garage, which was dim and mostly empty. "Like adding, subtracting, or changing patient record entries."

"Makes sense."

"But...can you think of anything else it might have meant? A covert meaning?"

After a few moments passed, Susan uttered, "Huh."

"What?"

"My only idea concerns hackers and the whole social engineering concept." She chuckled. "Hey, this is one for a spy thriller, okay? Like when an evildoer tries to deceive a victim to gain control over a computer system. Maybe to steal personal or financial information."

The courses on computer security during Leslie's corporate medical job and residency years covered this. "You mean like with shareware or diversion theft?"

"Right. If hackers somehow got inside the software system, they could make changes without leaving a digital footprint. Or at least the easily spotted digital footprint left when a chart is modified normally."

Startled, Leslie glanced over her shoulder toward a sudden sound, like a car door opening. "You've got me all jumpy with the spy thriller idea." There wasn't another car in close range to her eyes. "But thanks. I'll consider it."

"No problem. We'll talk soon."

Within a minute, Leslie had her purse and laptop bag slung over her shoulder for the uphill trek toward the elevator. Eeriness surfaced in her chest, compelling her to stop and look back. Again, she spotted no other person or new vehicle. The sensation of something touching her back, someone's eyes on her, wouldn't leave.

The mechanical journey to her office from the third floor usually provided daydreaming time. But this morning, tugging at her shoulder bag, she stared into the elevator corner, unnerved. Inching closer to the elevator door, confined to a box less than six by eight feet, she sought to put more space between herself and the stranger. He must have ridden to the parking level, then turned around. But her disquiet wasn't due to the odd-looking man next to her. He bore no resemblance to the suspect in Brad's photo. The height and weight Brad had given were way off.

The truth was her heebie-jeebies had begun the night before with the scare at Izzy's nursery. The second break-in was within a week. *Had it been another warning? Were they expecting to find Izzy there at night?*

Izzy's frosty response when Leslie acknowledged her wrongdoing hadn't helped Leslie's nerves either. Not that she would blame her. But having had no chance to talk with her this morning worsened her wired-and-tired state. Izzy rolled over, covering her head with a pillow, when Leslie checked on her before leaving for work. Now Leslie wrestled with sensing someone watching her—yet there was no sign of anyone around. Was she starting to come unglued? She stepped more quickly toward the office suite.

While standing in the building's outer hall, outside their waiting room, the impression that someone's eyes were boring into her back returned. In an over-the-shoulder glance, Leslie spotted a tall figure dressed in a long, hooded raincoat ducking behind a corner. Her suspicion rose with the person's height and black clothing. *Should I follow them to try to catch a face?* She grabbed her forehead and froze, her chest pounding.

What am I thinking? I'm losing it. The fact that she would even consider following someone was nuts.

She spun around and walked quickly to their waiting room. Were the security cameras in the building able to capture the face? Brad might know or be able to determine that.

Leslie entered the back office and found Lynn with the phone at her ear. She gave her a nod. Was anyone else in yet? Were any of them trustworthy?

No doubt Pearl was on her side, and Lynn was okay. Michelle was a bit peculiar, Bryce's minion, but she'd done nothing suspicious. No—it was Bryce and Sloan she shouldn't trust. *Why am I staying here?* If it weren't for the hundreds of patients she'd inconvenience with a precipitous move, she'd get the hell out fast.

While sitting at her office desk, she took a deep breath and swallowed against the heartburn rising into her throat. No—she wouldn't escape this office without securing justice for Damon and clearing her name. Her gut had steered her to investigate the add-in patient group. She had Pearl's and Brad's help. Besides, who's to say she and her family wouldn't still be a target if she left?

Thirty minutes later, having called and left a voicemail for Brad, alone at her desk, she'd sorted the day's new information and prepared for her clients. It looked like early evening through uncovered windows and with all the lamps lit before nine a.m. Heavy gray and black clouds had evolved from a light sprinkle an hour before to a full-on thunderstorm. Below, the sidewalk trees waved in strong winds, blurred by pounding rain on glass.

Leslie tapped her desk phone intercom. "Hey, Lynn? Is my first patient here?" She rubbed her hands together, wishing she'd remembered her wrist warmers.

"Not yet. I'll buzz you when she's here."

"Okay."

"One other thing."

"Yeah?"

"I've scheduled your medical board interview for Monday afternoon at three. You've got travel time added in. I've already confirmed with your attorney's office—he can be present."

"Good, thanks. The sooner, the better." The wait for her chance to respond in person had been grueling.

Ending the intercom, she rose to look out the window, the cold seeping in. Slapping, wet gusts pounded in sync with a low rumble of thunder. Surely Izzy had risen by now. Maybe Brad was with her. The idea of a short call with Izzy was tempting.

She pictured her wife pulling the pillow over her head that morning. No—she needed to give her some time to digest their conversation last night. She'd text Brad instead.

Pulling her streetside window blind closed in her clinic office hadn't shut out the storm's noise. Just after nine a.m., the harsh winds whistled past, causing the windows to vibrate as rain pelted the glass. Leslie stared at her phone, then tapped a video call with Brad. Her shoulders tensed as a chill crawled through her spine. She tried to ignore the tightness in her chest and the slight tremor in her fingers. He answered before the second ring.

"Leslie, are you okay?" His face showed a mix of concern and static from the dim light flickering behind him.

"Just shaken a bit." Her voice quivered. "I don't know. I reviewed everything that happened again in the parking garage and while walking into my office. Maybe I'm reading into things."

His eyes squinted as if trying to focus. "What'd you see?" He plugged his ear against a hammer pounding in the background.

"Nothing concrete." She shrugged. *Just the oppressive sentiment of being monitored.* "I got this eerie feeling someone had their eyes on me. I looked around in the garage but saw nothing or anyone suspicious."

The more she considered it, the more her instincts yelled danger.

He nodded, keeping his eyes directly on her. "Well, we all had a pretty harrowing evening last night. What about walking to your office?"

"The same sensation. Then I caught sight of this tall person right outside our office. I think it was a man." She brought the memory to mind. "At least six feet tall. Lean. Long black raincoat with a hood. I didn't catch a face. They dashed around the corner, but... I don't know. It's storming hard out there. Maybe it was nothing."

"Which floor? Were they carrying anything?"

"Third. I didn't see anything. Just a brief look, though." A thunderclap beyond her other window startled her. "I shouldn't have bothered you with this, but do you think we could get access to security camera footage? Is the nursery patched together yet?"

The pounding had stopped. Brad's face zoomed smaller.

"I want you to call if anything's off, Leslie. We're nearly done here. Izzy said she's going to the morgue later with Allison. I'll run through your building today to see where the security cameras are and who to ask for a viewing."

"Thanks, Brad. Your watching over us helps a ton."

Twenty-Seven

Thursday, October 24ᵗʰ —Afternoon's end

After a full day at the clinic, Leslie shouldered her gear for the journey home, operating on a dangerous undercurrent of wired fatigue. On her way out, she popped her head into Pearl's office. Its gentle lamp lighting and calming white noise, paired with the artwork and personal touches, created a soothing space. "Hey, can we walk to our cars together?"

Pearl glanced at the clock—nearly five-thirty. "Sure, Dr. Schoen. I'll gather my things."

At a shrill voice behind her, Leslie turned. A younger woman with dyed scarlet hair in tangles leaned over Lynn's counter. The unmistakable odor of skunk weed wafted through the air.

"I've got to get in to see Dr. Mannon. It'll only take a minute."

A composed Lynn explained the client wasn't on the schedule, though an appointment would be available soon.

Pearl stopped her packing and looked at Leslie.

"Oops. I forgot something. I'll just be a few." Leslie dropped her bag and slipped past Michelle's desk, her pulse quickening. The nurse was glued to her headset. Leslie crossed quietly through the hall, the waiting room, and out of the office suite, her eyes fixed on the floor.

She paced a few steps in the outer hallway, considering how to approach a patient from Bryce's clinic.

The flaming-haired woman rushed out the door, her purse stuffed under an armpit.

"Excuse me." Leslie stepped forward.

The woman jumped. "Scared the shit outta me."

"Sorry. I might look familiar. I'm a new doctor in this place."

"Yeah?" The woman juggled the purse with her hand but not from its protected nook. Plenty of dirt under her nails distracted somewhat from her pinned pupils. She looked rail thin under her tattered, knee-length apricot coat. The colors of her attire drained her complexion, leaving her face pallid and lifeless.

"Were you just in with Dr. Mannon?"

"It's how it goes, you know?" She bounced a bit on her toes.

"Did you get everything you needed? I mean, since he's not a medical doctor."

She eyeballed Leslie with a snort of disgust. "You mean, did he get what he needed?" She turned and darted down the hall, punctuating her exit with a "Ha!"

What was that supposed to mean? Should she talk it over with Sloan? But how would she explain questioning a patient who wasn't hers?

Leslie and Pearl stepped off the elevator into the parking garage five minutes later. Dim fluorescent lights flickered above smooth, polished cement, revealing empty cars and concrete pillars. A blast of frigid air hit Leslie in the face and blew Pearl's coat sideways. During their short trek from the office, Leslie had shared her exchange with the woman in the apricot coat. Neither Pearl nor Leslie witnessed this last woman carrying anything out. But who knew what was in her purse?

"Ooh, the wind is nasty." Pearl buttoned her blowing coat. "And the weekend's supposed to be worse."

"It's almost Halloween, I guess. We know what we're up against." Leslie smiled.

They descended the ramp to their cars, their footfalls resounding in the oil-scented air. The well-illuminated concrete provided solid footing under a cloud of mist, nearly water, in the air.

"I've found something about the add-in patients... It's not about the numbers, though."

"Oh, yeah?" Leslie stopped.

"I finished the full year." Pearl faced her. "Every single add-in appointment was cash pay. And each time the patient saw Dr. Mannon—never Dr. Nelson."

"Hmm, what's the breakdown of payors in the MAT clinic?"

"It should be two-thirds self-pay." Pearl tipped her head to the side. "The rest insurance. And there was another one I saw on Tuesday. Josh, I think his name was. He was detoxing. I know what withdrawal looks like. My brother-in-law's son." Her voice trailed away.

"A tough one with your nephew, Pearl. If I can help in any way, even someone to talk to, I'm here for you."

"Thanks, doctor."

They resumed walking.

"I don't know why the man didn't get in to see the medical doctor. Instead, the psychologist cared for him in less than three minutes."

"You're right," Leslie said. "The payer mix, and all the add-in patients seeing Sloan, seems fishy. Did this Josh guy carry anything in or out of the office?"

"I saw nothing on him going in and a small brown bag in his hand on the way out."

"Huh. Sounds like a medication sample bag." Leslie had prepared samples using the office's bag supply hundreds of times. But why would Sloan, a psychologist—not a prescriber—use sample bags?

Leslie stopped again. "So, Damon was in charge of arranging these last-minute appointments."

"It's what Michelle said... but they show up without an appointment anywhere." She shrugged. "And sometimes what happens, like with Josh, is Dr. Mannon will say at Lynn's check-in counter they'll deal with scheduling after the visit. Then it never happens. The patient just walks out after they're seen."

Leslie hadn't checked whether the woman in the apricot coat had dealt with the schedule before leaving. They started walking again.

"What if all these things are connected? What if Bryce got the board complaint rolling just before he left on vacation?"

"That's when he told Michelle your office would be hers."

Leslie nodded. "The drugs would have been missing by then, and Damon appeared his usual self. Maybe a bit worn."

"I thought so." Pearl shifted her purse to the other side. "And the unscheduled appointment problem was going on the same as before. Always cash. Dr. Mannon, every time."

Leslie stopped. "How did Bryce get the timing down? Right before the inspection? I mean, scapegoating me gave him a reason his drugs were short. It was like he sensed the audit coming, but the DEA showed up unannounced."

Pearl shrugged. "Wouldn't you say he's got a leg up on the board? Maybe he had some insider information. Or some kind of sway."

"Mm."

Things didn't fit quite right. The board and the DEA were separate agencies—one federal, one state. Plus, she'd already learned from her lawyer that the board complaint against her was unrelated to the DEA's audit of Bryce's practice. But what if Bryce knew someone within the DEA?

"Well, something nefarious is happening with the bupe." Leslie pulled out her keys. "No doubt." As she and Pearl moved down the ramp, bruised clouds filling a sky frozen into blue-gray mush loomed between parking levels.

"Uh-huh." Pearl looked down.

"And we can't forget the fallout between Damon and Michelle. After he started looking wiped out. Right before he went missing."

"Right."

Pearl likely wouldn't be surprised to learn about Damon using drugs. But Brad had warned her about the autopsy results. Not a word to anyone.

"Damon had to be in on whatever was happening with the bupe. Or he found out about it."

"He looked more than wiped out. More like out of it. But the way he arranged those last-minute clients was broken, even before he got so...exhausted." Pearl opened the passenger side door of her Volkswagen Passat and threw her bags in. "Here's my car."

Leslie stopped again as Pearl returned to stand a few feet away, her expression gentle yet frank. "This whole thing is taking its toll on you, huh?"

Although taken aback by her observation, Leslie seized the invitation. "I'll say. It's got its ripple effects. Not just with my family on the outside, but with me on the inside." She offered a half-pint smile. "The hardest part is the worry about the effect of these investigations on Izzy." *And the baby.*

"Are you getting any other messages?"

Leslie raised her brows. "Messages?"

"Well, you got the idea to dive into details about the add-in MAT patients. It led us to learn about the all-cash-pay deviation. Seems like gut instinct."

"I suppose so."

"It's several things coalescing together." Pearl's voice hit a low pitch again. "Sometimes I'm starting to get it before I know what *it* is." A deep breath escaped her. "And there's no changing how it plays out. There's just living in the unknowing until it unfolds."

"Huh. The unknowing." What those numbers signaled in Damon's map.

"You've got what's happening around you and what's going on inside, where your gut speaks." Pearl's eyes were penetrating. "They're linked. I don't know about you, but for me, when intuition speaks, Pearl listens."

"Yeah. It's my gut speaking about those drawing numbers. Would you look again at the figures associated with the group you just went through? Phone numbers, street addresses, zip codes, emergency contacts, whatever you find. See if you can identify any patterns tying to the numbers in the drawing."

"I can do it." She smiled, looking at the sky. "Got a feeling I'll be inside plenty this weekend."

Leslie glanced at her side mirror again before braking at the first light past the Burnside Bridge. At around six, she was heading home. She was surrounded by commercial buildings, a car dealership, and traffic—cars heading east with her, while others crossed north and south at the intersection. With her window open, the crisp, wet air kept her alert. She bounced her foot on the brake as her eyes shifted to scan the vehicles behind her.

There. The same truck again.

The light turned green.

A battered black pickup had followed her since she'd left the parking garage downtown. It stayed too far back to read the license plate. It wasn't clear whether a plate was on the front, but was there a Chevrolet emblem on the grill? A decades-old Silverado. Was she imagining things? Was this guy following her?

A single figure sat high in the truck cab, wearing a brimmed hat tipped down.

Leslie bolted left without signaling one block later. Just in case. A right turn two blocks down, then another sharp turn. Was this what they called 'alcoholic paranoia'? Gripping the wheel with her eyes on the mirror, she saw no sign of them. Her pulse pounded. Within fifteen minutes, she was home in their driveway, the last moments a blur. She made her way into the kitchen, pulling in a deep breath.

"Hey, everybody." Tossing her bag on the table, she freed her hands to greet Baby J, the dog jubilant at her arrival.

"We're in here." Izzy's voice made the dog jump.

Behind the hopping border collie, Allison and Izzy sat before a blazing fire, the room toasty and a teapot prepared. An empty cup sat on the coffee table. Leslie's mouth was as dry as her mother's cornbread. She preferred to run the latest driving scare by Brad rather than talk about it with Allison and Izzy. She rallied for a smile while Baby J settled next to Izzy.

"We've got some chamomile medley." Allison raised her cup. "This is so smooth. Just what I needed."

Puffy eyes and smeared mascara on Allison's face suggested a rough day.

The empty cup found a home in Leslie's hand. "Are you okay, Allison?"

"Yeah, tough day."

Just as Leslie bent down to meet Izzy with a kiss, she turned her head to the side. "Did you get some rest, hon?" She lightly kissed Izzy's forehead.

"It wasn't sleep. It was hibernation."

"I'm in on this plan." Leslie reached over Izzy to grab the honey jar and poured herself a cup of tea. "Whew, what a day. You two tell me what happened first." Leslie plopped down next to the fire.

Allison's hands cradled her mug as she sipped. Izzy did all the talking. They'd arranged the transport of Damon's body to Wisconsin. The Rhinelander funeral home had been so helpful.

The dog moved to Allison on the couch, lightly resting her head on her knee. Damon's sister smiled weakly as she scratched and squeezed Baby J's ear.

"I'm glad we got this behind us." Allison's voice cracked. "Izzy, I can't tell you enough how your presence helped. And Leslie, thanks to both of you for everything. This entire week feels like I'm in a movie or something. It's unreal."

"We're getting there." Izzy's face softened. "And you're welcome."

"Yeah. Still going back home tomorrow afternoon?"

"I don't want to be away from my mom for long. The detective had no reason for me to stick around. Packing his apartment is the last thing." Though the apartment had been released a couple of days before, Allison chose Friday morning to clear Damon's belongings. "I feel good about Detective Davis. He seems to be working hard on Damon's case."

"My dad really trusts him." Izzy adjusted herself to sit cross-legged, facing Leslie. "Did you get caught up at work?"

"Yup. I'm free to do the apartment in the morning."

"My dad's coming over with boxes and packing stuff." Izzy grabbed her phone. "He's an orphan while my mom's at book club. She'll meet us at the restaurant. Here's his text: *How about pie for dessert tonight? There's a spot a few blocks from the restaurant."* She looked at them both. "I'd say yes."

"I'm in." Leslie widened her eyes. "Allison?"

"Sure." Her preoccupied look lightened.

"I'll go upstairs and change." Leslie took her tea and retrieved her bag from the kitchen. Soon, in comfortable jeans and a sweater, she stepped into the study for a moment. Another text to Brad:

Tell you about my drive home tonight - followed? Not sure.

Twenty-Eight

Friday, October 25ᵗʰ

Early morning haze shrouded the barren concrete under the I-405 freeway, between Northwest Lovejoy and Marshall Streets, not far from Sloan's condo in the Pearl. The area's highlights included concrete barriers and chain-link fences topped with barbed wire. He stewed while waiting, his hands cold despite gloves. Careful not to step on any street dwellers sleeping it off, he made his way in the dark just before dawn.

How much longer did he have—before the detectives discovered he'd lied about where he'd been the night Damon died? There was no way to explain and stay out of trouble. Now he was about to meet with the slimeball who'd been where he was then. Many others witnessed Sloan with Finn in a meeting at Will's Bar and Grill the night of the murder.

Footsteps approached before anything else. He turned in time to spot the tall, lanky figure stepping out from behind a concrete pillar. With his hood pulled to cover his face, Finn gave away his identity by his actions. He fished something out of his hoodie pocket and chomped down on it, removing part with a snap and returning the unused portion to his pocket. Chewing and walking. The oddball was eating chalk again. The only person he'd ever met with pica.

"We got a new relationship between us, dude." A portion of Finn's face showed as he tipped his head. Cruel eyes settled in hollow sockets beneath his perpetually furrowed brow. His taut, pale, and scarred skin looked even more menacing with his dead gray eyes.

"Want to tell me how you and Damon did this?" Sloan looked away from his mangled right cheek.

"It's simple." Finn scanned him from head to toe. "Here's the next list of dupes already on the books—with the IDs you'll need and their numbers." He handed Sloan an envelope. "You prepare an envelope for each one, with the forms and cash. Then get it in the right hands just before the appointment. Up to you to arrange those meetings."

Sloan nodded, stashing the envelope in his jacket and wondering if they *should* make this work. He was probably looking at a heartless killer. The weathered case at his hip, no doubt, held a fighting knife in leather—maybe ten to twelve inches in length. Finn scrutinized him carefully.

"You need to get on our side of things, bro. There's a lot more protection over here."

Sloan's eyes flittered in every direction as his pulse quickened.

"I tried to make the little guy see." Finn licked his upper teeth. "You know I was looking for him that night."

In fact, Finn had sought Sloan out at Will's the night Damon went missing. They'd nearly come to blows in the back alley.

"And you found him?"

"Why would I tell you anything?"

"You just invited me over to your side, dude." Sloan waited while Finn popped in another chalk. He chose pasty white today, the color of his complexion, over the various colors during their past meetings. "We were both interested in where the little fuckup was hiding. You said he owed you money."

The crunching sounds of teeth on chalk filled a gap as Finn looked doubtful.

"I found him all right—over at the big gal's house. The nurse." He jerked his head around. "The little rat rode there on his bike."

Sloan raised his brows. "Why'd he owe you money?"

"Dealin' for me. But let's just say it was obvious he'd been partaking in the profits." Finn sniffed. "Now had he kept his head on and his mitts off the product, sooner or later, he'd have been workin' for us. It's what you need to consider, man. Comin' over to the smart side."

Sloan stole a look at the weapon on Finn's hip again. "What's so lovely over there?"

"Money, dude. Lots of it." He reached into his jeans back pocket, pulling out a note. "Just look at these numbers."

Sloan glanced at a penciled-out chart. Three columns. Three rows. The letters H, W, and O named the rows.

"First number is what you pay me. Second is what you make selling it all. You can see it's basically double." Finn smiled, the right side of his face moving little. "You make what we make. Just unload it to the friends and family of all those addict patients you see." He nodded, laughing. "Maybe even the patients, man. Before long, you're richer than you can imagine."

With an audible intake of breath, Sloan curled his upper lip.

"The first supply is free. Once you get the horse, weed, and oxy down, then we layer in the fentanyl and meth. It's a piece of cake."

"Just like what Grady was doing for you?"

"Nah. He never made it past the second box. The little guy was weak. But you? You've got class. You'd take someone out if needed. You'd do it right."

Sloan swallowed. "So, what'd Damon say when you found him?"

Finn broke out in hilarious laughter. "Oh, man! The little guy fell asleep and missed his day at work. Slept through his commitment to me. He was shitting his pants scared—the little weasel."

Sloan took a step back. "Why was he at Michelle's?"

"He said she was supposed to deliver something to him." Finn shrugged again. "I don't know. The nurse was as disgusted with him as I was."

Sloan looked at the paper before he tucked it into his pocket. No way did he plan to tell the police where he really was that night. In those detectives' eyes, he'd be aligned with this lowlife.

"I'll have to think about it."

Around nine on Friday morning, after more than an hour of packing at Damon's apartment, Leslie imagined what she might be looking for. Evidence of naltrexone? Damon's phone? Something to break the drawing numbers puzzle? She'd covertly been tapping walls around light switches and outlets, but Detective Davis's people had given the entire place a vigorous go-over. A heavy quiet descended over their chore—putting a young man's life into piles and containers.

Allison embraced a framed photo. "I took this picture." Tears rolled down her cheeks.

Looking over Allison's shoulder, Leslie recognized Damon, Sheri, and her daughter Morgan at a party.

Allison whispered, "Damon and Sheri wanted a gathering. Morgan was celebrating her seventh birthday."

Leslie's eyes fixed on the girl. *Seven years old. A time for innocence.* Her heart sank as Allison's shoulders shook in quiet sobs.

"They must have been so happy." She rested a hand on Allison's shoulder.

Allison laid the photo on the desk next to Damon's Green Bay Packers jersey, his name and number nine printed on the back.

"I've been thinking back to our first phone call, Allison." Leslie grabbed the football jersey. "Was there anything Damon mentioned in your call with him the week before that was surprising?"

Her eyes red and swollen, Allison blew her nose. Her head rose abruptly after staring at the half-packed box at her feet. "I'd never heard Damon mention having a side hustle before. We were talking about the money he sent. I asked him how he managed to save with his salary."

"How does having a side hustle fit in?"

She offered a rueful smile. "He was boasting about how good he was with IT in general. Said he had a side job using his computer skills." She grabbed his baseball cap. "This is how I remember him. Just a kid playing ball and loving sports."

Leslie touched the framed photo. "They did look like a sweet family."

"I've just got to keep going." Dishes rattling in the kitchen turned Allison's head. "Izzy, do you need any help over there?"

"Yeah, a little." Izzy and Allison met at the dining table, boxes piled with flaps opened like arms to accept the discarded.

What "side hustle" did Damon have? He was the most proficient person with computers Leslie had encountered, but he got lost in opiates, drawing pictures of dope dealers.

The addicts' and alcoholics' behaviors were familiar to Leslie: lying for lying's sake, hiding bottles inside an apartment where no one else lived. But what she was looking for wouldn't be the drugs or the rigging. They'd found those already. This would be something small, maybe the phone—something he'd use for a side computer job to communicate with the dealer.

Leslie plopped on the couch, gathering an olive chenille throw onto her lap. The color, the smooth, velvety fabric—deep olive green—brought her back to another time, years ago.

The back seat of her family's car again. A sinking black ooze had coated her gut as her parents fought. Hearing her mother's desperate plea ... *If it wasn't for Leslie* ... If it hadn't been for Leslie, then what would've been different? *What were they fighting about?* Even at age seven, Leslie recognized the state her mother had been in. Now she saw the truth: her mother had confessed something to her father, prompting his shock and outrage.

Leslie looked at the blanket again. How had she carried the burden of responsibility for her parents' separation since her childhood?

"Hello in there!" Brad hollered at the front door. Leslie leaped off the couch, gathering the blanket into a ball.

"Hey, Dad." Izzy walked over with a towel, drying her hands.

"I've got the truck at the curb." He leaned into the room. "Your brother's preparing the back. Are you ready for us?"

"I think we're set." Izzy turned to Leslie. "Is all the furniture emptied, hon?"

"Almost there. Let's load those bookshelves last." Leslie tossed the blanket on the couch. After Allison offered a list—of what to pack on the truck—Leslie led Brad to the patio. They settled at the table, leaving Izzy and Allison to pack inside.

"How's Izzy doing?" Brad lowered his voice.

"She was pretty tired last night. I suggested she stay home and rest today, but she wanted to be here."

"That's our Izzy."

Leslie nodded. "I told her about the board complaint. So, you don't have to hold it back anymore."

"Good."

"By now you probably think I'm paranoid, Brad." She'd told him about yesterday's black pickup, but dinner out with everyone had afforded limited time. "I can't tell if I'm being paranoid or if something's really wrong. Between feeling watched at the office and believing I was followed home yesterday, I might be on edge after Izzy's business break-in."

His eyebrows lifted. "Don't discount what you felt... what you saw."

"I know I keep too much to myself. Really, I'm starting to work on that."

The tightness around his mouth loosened. "I checked out your office building. Know where the cameras are now and the process for getting access. If anything else happens, let me know right away—and where it happened."

"I will."

"You've slept on it. Do you think the person in the office hall and the one driving the truck yesterday were the same?"

"I don't know. I can't even tell you man or woman. Just assumed male in the hall because of their height." She told him everything she remembered again.

"Okay."

She debated whether to mention her drawing numbers project with Pearl. "Any update on Sloan from Aaron?"

"Leslie, I'm worried about you." Brad reached out to place his hand over hers. "You've got to accept that this investigation is being handled by Aaron and his team."

She nodded. "But something else is bugging me." She opened the photo of Damon's drawing on her phone. "I dreamt about these numbers last night."

His face softened with a powerful kindness. "Did you get what I just said?"

"Yes. But—did you notice that whenever there's a five-digit, not a six-digit number, it's always inside the drawing?"

Brad scanned the photo, zooming in. "I'm sending this photo to myself to examine it once we unload this place."

"Good. Text me what you think. Another thing." She took the phone back. "If you omit the last four digits from every number inside the man's head, you're always left with a number between one and twelve—right?"

"I'm not sure, but I'll check it out. Let's get this stuff out of here so I can concentrate."

Leslie loaded boots, winter gear, and bicycle accessories into a mudroom box a short while later. While unloading the coat hooks on the inside wall, she uncovered a rusted-out wall heater with a dead control switch. Her pulse pounded. Corroded metal, crumbling ancient plaster, and unpainted wallboard marked the spot. At the bottom edge of the unit, she spotted a gap of a few millimeters empty of caulking, plaster, or any other sealant. *Had it been removed?* Below, at the floor's edge, the raw end of sheetrock was torn off, exposing the old foundation.

Was there a passageway behind the sheetrock from the floor to the wall unit?

Dropping to her knees, Leslie poked about in the space above and at the back of the tear. She pounded the wall next to the ripped drywall. Her breathing shallowed as she worked quickly. Taking a deep inhale, she pounded again. Her punches extended around and above the grill, sending the upper edge of the faceplate ajar. Packed with dirt and sediment, the vents were nearly fused, but two cap screws popped out when the cover shifted. Tugging on the caps, Leslie released the metal into her hand. A century's worth of dust and spider webs covered the inner workings, but the plate held an unexpected item—a rectangular metal piece, small enough to fit in her palm, held in a sealed Ziploc bag.

"Hey! Izzy, Brad! Come here."

She set the grill on the floor, sat on her heels, and caught her breath.

"What?" Izzy and the others hurried over. "What happened?"

Her butt on cold cement, Leslie sat with the prize in front of her. "Look what I found." Smiling and wiping the sweat from her jaw, she beamed at them. "A hard drive."

"Wait." Brad threw his hands out. "Touch nothing there."

Leslie recoiled. *What further message had Damon left?*

Twenty-Nine

Friday, October 25th—Mid-afternoon

As Callie rose to leave her appointment, her last patient before lunch, Leslie toyed with her wooden necklace, interlaced teak squares dangling from a golden chain. The young woman's expression held quiet excitement. Satisfaction. Freedom. Her eyes were more alive.

A successful session.

"Thanks, Dr. Schoen." Callie paused at her clinic office door. "I can't get over how clearing those old stories has freed me. My mind feels clear, more connected to the present."

Watching Callie leave the room, Leslie smiled. "Good work today." She was amazed again at the power unearthed when a person grasped the distortions in their internal narrative. Moving beyond a past memory, examining the story—the meaning—they'd woven into past events promised such liberation.

Callie's fresh perspective transformed her world—a quality Leslie craved. She'd been anxiously awaiting word from Brad. Would he confirm what her gut and eyes said about the numbers in Damon's drawing? She longed to connect with the sixth sense scratching at her mind's edge. Something told her it might reveal Sloan's lies about the night Damon died and show her just how badly Bryce wanted her gone. How did these facts tie to the threat she and Izzy were facing?

Leslie glanced at the clock, anticipating time with Izzy again if she didn't back out. At least she agreed to dinner at home with Leslie cooking. Allison was safely home in Wisconsin. The two-by-three-inch hard drive Leslie had found in Damon's apartment was now safely in the hands of the police.

A background thrum of rain on windows pulled her attention to her bag on the bookshelf behind her desk. She'd been carrying the bundle of her mother's journal and letters for nearly a week. What story had she woven around the events of her eighth year?

Why am I putting off the letters like I did with my mother's boxes? Have I gotten a clue today? What planted this unshakeable conviction that I caused my parents' separation?

Questions spun repeatedly in her mind, stirring a fog that blocked her understanding of Sloan and Bryce's mischief. The time had come to clear it out.

She scanned her appointment schedule, realizing she hadn't gathered messages since her arrival.

The long route to her inbox ended with the sounds of a typical exchange behind the wall. She caught Lynn's eyes moving toward Michelle's desk with amusement. Lynn gained Leslie's attention, and they nodded slightly to each other. She settled in the doorway—able to see Bryce and Michelle clearly while remaining hidden from their view—and absorbed their words volleyed back and forth like a tennis match in its final set.

"I've got this one o'clock—" Bryce pointed at a printed page.

"Where you're going to need these lab results from Monday." Michelle handed him a slip of paper.

"The cardiologist on my two-thirty—" His face was buried in what must have been his day's schedule.

"Will call you at two-fifteen. I'll get it set up with his nurse beforehand and transfer him over."

"Fine. Meet me in my office in five minutes." Bryce left the room.

Leslie turned to Lynn, smiling with unspoken rapport. Bryce and Michelle were a single unit these days. But now their practice MAT foursome had become a threesome. *How would Sloan take it?* Three's a tough number, even though his position outranked Michelle's.

Lynn smiled back.

"Is this everything?" Leslie lifted some notes.

"Except for the last message. Your next appointment was with great apologies. The lawyer said his client had an unexpected conflict, so they rescheduled. He told me to send the bill, of course."

Two free hours.

"A gift then." The opening Leslie had been hoping for. She paused at Bryce's open door to watch the heightened rain lashing his windows. No Bryce, but the dark sky cast an otherworldly spell upon treetops swirling in heavy wind. His overhead and desk lights failed to recapture the afternoon, leaving the room shrouded in evening's dimness.

A gloom shadow followed Leslie to her office. She'd carried her family's fracture on her shoulders for decades. Swallowing, she glanced out the window. The rain came down sideways. She set her jaw and pressed her lips together. Cocooned in her private space, she spread her cousin Grace's letters on her desk. With her mother's journal opened, she read around the spring of 1986.

...I just avoided telling Matt. I barely faced what I'd done myself. I'd been so hyper there was no sitting still. When Matt said I needed to see a doctor—a shrink—I almost hit him. He was the one driving me up the wall with his drugs and boozing. We hadn't slept together for months. Well, I reached for the spirits myself. It was the only way to slow myself down. But I never should have gone to the bar alone. Before I knew it, with a headache from hell, I came to in some unknown man's bed. Couldn't find my clothes. Then later, no period. Then another skipped menstrual. The doctor said there was no doubt. Damn. Pregnant by the wrong man.

But Matt sensed something was off. We yelled and screamed at each other riding in his old rattrap of a car, right in front of our little Leslie. All I knew was—I had to get away. If it wasn't for our little girl, if it hadn't been for Leslie, I would have packed my bags for Lincoln right then. I have this friend who knows a doctor. It's my only way out. I've got to end this pregnancy and get to it fast, before it's too late...

Her palms clammy, Leslie set the diary down. A bulky, aching wad in her throat held back her howl. The old paper's scent recalled funeral cards as bile rose in her chest. Her stomach knotted while a metallic taste coated her tongue, grief colliding beneath her ribs. Tears spilled for both her parents and the predicament they had been in. She reached for the letter from Grace closest in postmark to the date of her mother's diary entry.

...Jean, you may be older than me, maybe you'll think I'm not mature enough to have an opinion, but stop and think. First, you've sounded so depressed in our letters lately. And now this. I'm telling you—just leaving and running away to Lincoln might have you thinking you've escaped a big problem. But you've got to face what's going on with you and Matt. Maybe your idea of couples counseling is equally as good as his idea for you to see a psychiatrist. Why not do both?

If you go off and end the pregnancy, whatever issues led to your decision will simply follow you around in life. God forbid, it might lead to a repeat performance down the road. Can you pause to consider what effect your leaving would have on Leslie? On Matt? I don't know about you, but when I just run from my problems, it feels like they're going to eat me up. Please wait until I get there, at least...

From one letter to the next, interspersed with journal entries corresponding to the postmark dates, Leslie devoured the materials. Eventually, she understood her father learned about her mother's one-night stand and the pregnancy. Their later kitchen argument followed her mother's trip to Lincoln. A seven-year-old Leslie froze as her father's voice thundered from the dining room, "You did what?" Her father left, never to return, after learning about her mother's choice.

Leslie wiped her face with a tissue. Her parents hadn't split because of her.

A few hours earlier, Leslie's goodbye to Allison precipitated a boatload of envy. Damon's sister had beamed after another call with her father. Looking like she'd been made whole, Allison blurted that her father would be attending Damon's funeral. They would reunite after more than twenty years.

What would Leslie sacrifice for her father's return?

She packed the journal and letters back into her bag, figuring Damon had dealt with his past by escaping it through using dope and video games. He might've been repeating it—by abandoning himself again and again with the choices he made.

Would Leslie operate in a similar style? Her default behavior often took the route of pride and shame. Too proud to ask for help, then pedal-to-the-metal on self-reliance. And when it didn't work, too embarrassed to reveal the fallout. She'd acted out the pattern into a well-worn groove. But not this time. Her plan going forward—ask for help to lay down the self-reliance.

A text buzzed from her phone—from Brad.

You're right on both counts.

He'd double-checked Damon's drawing. There weren't any five-digit numbers outside of the man's head. After deleting the last four digits of every five- and six-digit number inside the head, a number between one and twelve always remained. Those had to be five- and six-digit dates of birth. She clutched her teak necklace over her heart, hoping these numbers tied to the add-in client group. She had to get Pearl to confirm her theory.

Leslie's mobile vibrated again. One more Brad message—

I'm watching out for you. Be careful.

Bryce's jarring "Enter" came before Michelle managed to rap her knuckles on his door twice. She flinched. No matter how hard she tried to meet his needs, the boss didn't bother concealing his irritation these days. Late Friday afternoon, when most offices would be winding down for the weekend, the tension here only seemed to escalate. There'd be no break for things as frivolous as easing up after a long work week—suggesting, "Hey, it's Friday, let's take it easy!" made her stomach tighten. She was again on another mission to keep him happy, though it was never enough. She slipped inside, quietly closing the door, her back to it. He hadn't bothered to sit.

"Listen, Michelle." He pinched his features into a mask of distaste. "What's with you telling me what you *think* I want before I even have a chance to speak? Twice now, recently. What's going on with you?"

"Oh, I—" She looked down at the floor as if the answer was written there. She anticipated his every need, want, whatever, and they both recognized this truth. "Uhh…my mother is going downhill fast. Soon I'll have to tend to her even more. So, I got ahead on the schedule." *How much longer will I manage juggling it all?* If it wasn't her mother, where the demands were even more merciless, it was Bryce.

"Well, I'm sorry about your mother, but knock it off. Are we not keeping you busy enough?"

Given how hard he'd ridden her with work this last year, it was quite the contrary. The way he pushed her to the brink and then questioned her commitment was perverse. Why was she staying along for the ride with this man who'd turned into a snake? What happened to the guy who used to value her loyalty? Beyond being baffled, she was pissed.

"I had to meet with two patients in the kitchen this week." Her voice walked a tightrope between defiance and desperation. "It's awkward taking vitals. Your office and Dr. Mannon's were busy."

Bryce gestured for her to sit. "We're on it. Expect you'll have a private office within a matter of weeks."

"So…Dr. Schoen is leaving?"

"Her board interview is Monday." Bryce leaned back in his chair with a satisfied grin, his voice losing its edge. "So, you're on deck to give witness testimony after they talk with her. Stick to the same script, except I want you to add something about her going pale when the DEA showed up. You should mention she said something about being afraid they were here because of her troubles with the board."

He doesn't care what actually happened. "Okay." Michelle swallowed hard.

"Let's have you write your testimony this weekend and read it to me on Monday. Throw in having caught her making errors on prescriptions that you luckily changed in time during the DEA audit." Bryce squinted, his lips pursed again. He sounded more clipped, the warmth present a moment ago—gone. "Oh, and she's been late with her appointments. Yeah, good."

"I'll gather some ideas." The heaviness in her throat remained. "What about Pearl's problem?"

"You mean Sloan didn't talk with you about it?"

"No." She wasn't about to say more.

He jumped from his chair, sending it backward. "God. Damn. It." Raking his hand through his hair, he moved to the bookcase where she hoped he wouldn't snatch something and throw it. "I'll have to get with him this weekend." His hair stood on end. "He's gone, right?"

She nodded, wondering whether Sloan would bounce it back to her. Her pulse quickened. She was certain this wasn't going to end well.

"Okay. We'll *stop* taking payments on last-minute appointments until we get the software modified." Facing the shelves, he adjusted a framed photo. *A stone fist in a velvet glove.* "And I've got two other jobs for you."

She scooted to the edge of her seat, the weird, squeaking sound behind her eyes again propelling her forward. "I'm arranging a meeting with the practice management software rep and I'm going to get with Lynn and Pearl about adding an addendum field in the software."

He pivoted around and stepped forward, the whites of his eyes flashing. "You're doing it again." She flinched. "What is it? You think you're a mind reader?"

Michelle clamped her mouth shut. A bead of sweat broke out on her forehead.

"Well, you're wrong!" A small spittle escaped his lips.

There he was, giving double messages again. *Keep your mouth shut. Do what you know is right.*

"Shit. This Damon thing has gotten us all off balance." Bryce moved to the window, his back turned.

Yeah, you made sure of that. Michelle warned herself to keep her wits and stay cool.

"Yes, on getting that meeting together with the software person." Back to acting like nothing had happened, he walked over to his credenza and grabbed his soft leather briefcase. "Here, take this."

She stood, unsure if her knees would hold, to accept the tote he had carried to and from work for over fifteen years.

"It's all the new MAT clients in the last month and what's needed to update their charts." He returned to his desk. "The list is in the bag. It's updating the records on reviewing the pharmacy board's controlled-prescription monitoring program. You have my sign-in. Just prepare their charts for me to sign next week."

"Got it." *In other words, cancel your life until you get his in order.*

Well, what else would she be doing this weekend?

Not much.

Though the storm beyond her office windows raged on in chaotic fury, clarity illuminated Leslie's mind for the first time in months. Packing for the weekend took seconds at the end of a Friday's workday—no dragging work home this time. Her work was *at* home, a refuge to iron things out with Izzy, she hoped.

Was she absolved? Not her call.

Grateful for her current and original family? Absolutely.

Inspired... with a second wind on Damon's case? Had to be. The next target—Sloan's lie.

Stepping across the hall toward Damon's old office, she bumped into Michelle, who looked absent and preoccupied.

"Sorry." Leslie raised her hands.

"Right." Michelle's face remained deadpan. She looked spooked and walked straight ahead to her office.

Leslie met Pearl in Damon's room. Quickly, she explained the next approach to the drawing's numbers. She was to put a zero before each five-digit number inside the figure, viewing this subset—every number within the man's likeness—as an old-fashioned six-digit birth date. Then, cross-check those against the add-in patients' DOBs. Pearl nodded and told her she'd be in contact as soon as she got it done. She left through the hall.

Leslie opened the office's second door and looked at Michelle's desk. What a strange shift it was watching her pack her belongings for the weekend. She'd always been a large presence at a half-foot taller than Leslie. There was a solidness rooted in the woman. As she was doing now, she remained fixed in some way when she moved about. And she didn't budge for normal social graces, such as stepping aside when someone walked through.

"Going home, Dr. Schoen?" Michelle hoisted a worn leather case with a loose, fold-over flap to her free shoulder.

"Not soon enough. Can we walk out together?"

She smiled politely. "No problem."

The bag looked familiar. Leslie's curiosity piqued as they continued down the hallway and made their way to the elevator. "Is that Bryce's bag?" *Would it be worth putting pressure on Michelle and Bryce's working relationship to pry into Sloan's secrets?*

"Yeah." Michelle shifted the strap to carry her purse and his case on one side. "He loaded me with work for the weekend."

As they stopped for the elevator, Leslie considered whether Michelle would provide the insight she sought, debating if she should risk complicating things by asking. She waited, not just for the elevator, but to make a connection. Michelle hadn't sounded begrudged by her workload. Was there more to dig into there? Why not discover what Michelle might reveal? *Remember, pushing on Michelle would have ripple effects on Bryce and Sloan.*

"You two work in lockstep sometimes." Leslie pulled a heavy scarf from her coat, wrapping it outside her collar. As the empty elevator arrived, she stepped in to face red-paint graffiti obscuring an ad poster: *I see humans, but no humanity.*

No response from Michelle. Another part of Leslie—the part driving to find clues in Damon's case—told her she ought to go for it.

"I've got the medical board interview on Monday." The elevator doors closed. "We both know Bryce concocted that farce." She hit the garage button and rearranged her coat. "I'd appreciate some help there."

Michelle stayed silent, looking straight ahead.

"Maybe you'd want to take a lifeboat off Bryce's sinking ship. I'll move my practice in with another doc when my lease expires. We'll want someone with your skills." She cleared her throat. "You know, with Sloan lying to the police about where he was the night Damon died, it's just a matter of time before they get to him. And trust me, this fabricated board thing will return to bite Bryce."

The elevator swayed and creaked on its slow descent. Still no response from Michelle.

"Do you think Damon took those drugs?" Leslie pressed in the thick silence. "I mean, something was going on with him, right?" She adjusted her scarf, searching for a hint of reaction in Michelle's eyes. "He didn't seem right in those last weeks. Bryce is covering himself. I'm not sure what Sloan gains by lying to the police. What do you think?"

"Who knows? There's just too much to keep track of." Michelle looked further away and pulled herself deeper into the worn case.

"We should find out what really happened before Bryce pins it on Sloan and gets himself off the hook."

Michelle squinted with her fingers running along the cracked leather showing the lines on her face. She turned to Leslie, her words measured. "It didn't have to be like this, you know."

"Didn't have to be like what?" Leslie's gut vibrated with regret—she sensed Michelle's emotion. Was she lamenting her status with Bryce?

"You know." Michelle looked down. "What with the DEA showing up out of the blue."

The elevator doors opened, letting in the wet chill. Leslie stepped out behind Michelle, no closer to understanding what she meant—it didn't have to be like this—but her instincts told her something was foreboding about Michelle's refusal to engage. Leslie buttoned her coat for the long walk down the ramp. An abandoned old Honda Civic, planted in the corner for over a week, was now resting on blocks, its wheels removed.

"No, really. I don't get what you're saying. It didn't have to be like what?" Lower on the slope, their reserved parking practice area lay close to level ground. Perhaps Michelle was simply immovable after all. She hadn't even blinked at the revelation about Sloan's lie.

The place was deserted, even for a Friday at five. Turbulent air, with the fluorescent lights and Michelle's silence, gave Leslie a shiver. She stopped to search for her keys. Her Subaru was parked several slots lower than Michelle's car, with one enormous Suburban in between.

"Hey, I've got to get going." Michelle opened her car without turning around. "See you Monday." She threw her bags into the passenger side of the front seat.

The scent of heavy onions blew in from a nearby Thai restaurant. The woman was unreachable.

"Okay." Leslie let go, hoping Michelle would add something. "Have a good weekend."

Michelle slammed her car shut and slumped behind the wheel, rifling through her bag as Leslie passed. She didn't start the engine.

Leslie rounded the Suburban and reached for her door handle. Time alone with Izzy minutes away, and it was the chance for a weekend to work things out.

An incessant, honking alarm rang from lower down the gradient, blaring repeatedly. The blasts reverberated on yards of concrete as the garage lights dimmed.

It wasn't enough to drown out the sound of footsteps closing in. The heat of someone's breath behind her reached Leslie's ear.

She turned to the side and dropped her bag.

A huge, gloved hand gripped her shoulder, pulled, and slid to her neck. Her eyes darted to a tall man behind her, his face masked. She gasped. She caught the bright glint of something metallic in his other hand in one quick glimpse. He spun her around, his fingers digging into her skin.

"Help!" Leslie cried, planting her feet wide and tucking her arm into her side. Muscles braced, she shoved her elbow back. It landed in his solid body with a crack. The man's grip loosened at the base of her neck. She donkey-kicked her assailant with her heel, pounding into resistance before landing her foot on the ground. Grabbing his cap, she pulled until it came off. Her weight-bearing knee twisted. Sharp pain spiked in her thigh as her leg buckled.

Stinging pain behind her ear, a grinding noise around her jaw, and trouble at the top of her chest made her wince. She hit the concrete, bracing herself for a blow with her forearm and rolled to her back. A man with an ear-to-mouth scar, red and mangled, loomed over her, knife in hand. Leslie's adrenaline surged, sending her crawling on forearms, knees, and toes under her car. She scrambled at speed, trying to get fully beyond his reach.

He grabbed her ankle.

"Hey!" a voice boomed.

A man's voice. The hand squeezing her ankle let go.

Pounding of boots on pavement. Two sets of feet.

Leslie slid her hands under her chest into a sticky warmth. No stab had pierced her. Sliding on the cold cement, she pushed to get herself out from under the car, gulping air. A biting agony at her collarbone pulsed through to the back of her skull. She clamped her jaws down and forced herself to move.

Slipping and sliding, Leslie inched along, pushing to get free of the car. Grunting in the distance blended with a loud crash.

"Shit!" she yelled, curling to her side. Dimly, she spotted a pair of large ankles.

"Leslie, oh my God." Michelle knelt, a leather bag dropping to the ground beside her. "You're bleeding. Let me help you."

"Vile man." Panting, Leslie choked on her alarm. "There were two."

"He's gone. He took off. It's okay to come out." Michelle pulled at her legs, then hips. Leslie pushed herself to the edge of her car.

"Fuck!" The blood covering her coat and hands sickened her. "Damn. I'm bleeding." She clutched at her collarbone.

"Cover the wound." Sliding her case closer, Michelle cursed. "Shit! Wrong bag! Uh, let's use your scarf." She pulled it off her, folded it, and pushed it into Leslie's chest.

She screamed in pain.

"Sorry. I have to stop the bleeding."

"Call 911." Leslie managed to look again at her chest. She turned her head to the side. Bryce's bag lay open, files and a mobile scattered on the cement.

Michelle followed Leslie's eyes and immediately shoved the entire mess back into the briefcase. "Here. I'm calling. Hold on to this." She lifted Leslie's hand to clutch the scarf as she reached into her pocket. Balancing her phone in one hand, Michelle called 911, then set it down, speaker on. Placing her hands again on Leslie's compress, she pushed.

"Ahh." Leslie moaned and grabbed her face, squeezing against the agony, then dropped her head to the concrete. Flat on the ground, her awareness took a dive. A cold sweat broke over her face.

Breathing heavily, Michelle gave their location and told the dispatcher what had happened.

"Call Izzy." Leslie sputtered out numbers.

Michelle scanned the ground.

"Wait. Hold here now." Michelle pushed Leslie's hand to her chest and stood, dragging Leslie's bag with her. She swung the Subaru's door open.

"What—what are you doing?" Leslie's head swam.

"I'm writing the number down—need a pen."

A zipping sound. Michelle's loud huffing. The alarm still blaring. In a blur of pain, Leslie tried to focus as Michelle knelt again, her hands on the chest wound.

"Did you see what happened? Who it was?" Staring into Michelle's face, Leslie gripped the nurse's arm, pushing against the pressure to no avail.

"The back of him. Again," Michelle whispered. She pushed harder, her wild gaze piercing Leslie as a tear rolled down her cheek. A feverish reflection encased her eyes.

Leslie had met eyes like that before.

But never on Michelle—her final impression before passing out.

Thirty

Saturday, October 26th

The many emergency room hours and police interviews had left Leslie, in the dark early hours of Saturday morning, with a sour taste in her mouth. Her sliced chest and the back of her head were now closed with stitches. She pushed into the pillows at her back. Sheltered in their bedroom, steeling herself for a long-awaited moment alone with Izzy, she pictured her wife's state at the hospital—a mix of distress, worry, and exasperation.

The dim nightstand lamp created a surreal tone as Leslie reached for more water. With a photo of Brad and Kathy inserted, a plastic coaster held the glass. The clock read almost two a.m. She waited, alert for Izzy's return after showing them out.

Had it not been for Brad Turner—his stakeout in the garage and sounding the alarm—she likely would not have survived. He lured her attacker away and chased him down the ramp. She didn't know who called 911 first, Brad or Michelle. Without Michelle, Leslie would've kept bleeding. Brad had probably saved Michelle too. The next thing Leslie knew, she was in an ambulance.

She pressed her bandage over twenty-five stitches spanning her collar to breastbones. The wounds looked bloody, but only affected the skin. The muscles underneath had been spared. Her other dozen stitches, closing the gash behind her left ear, had bled profusely, but were easily closed. She hadn't yet adapted to the drafty sensation around the area where her hair had been shaved.

Brad had tackled Finn Connor, bound his wrists, and held him down until the police arrived. Thank God the thug was in jail now. Between Brad and his distress signal, her sudden movements, and the teak necklace she'd chosen to wear yesterday—its solid wood as a shield—she'd been protected against a murderous attack. And she'd been lucky Michelle hadn't left in her car. *She didn't appear a threat. No, Bryce had to have set this in motion. Or Sloan? Or both? If so, the link between Damon and the two was Finn Connor.*

The weariness in Leslie's arms took hold as she returned the glass to its coaster. Regret weighed her down—each breath required conscious effort, like drawing air through wet cotton. How had she been so naive? Ten years ago, even with her medical license and livelihood on the line, why had she given her life story to Bryce Nelson, especially including her family? Look at how he'd taken advantage of her and her situation. She'd violated her cardinal rule—always keep a cushion in relationships to avoid getting hurt. People weren't trustworthy. But when she was finally on her feet, sober for a long while, married to Izzy and established at work, she'd hooked her wagon to his. Now she stared down the repercussions of her choice: a murdered coworker, her wife intimidated, the baby she wanted so desperately threatened, and some horrid criminal trying to kill her. The board complaint shriveled in comparison.

A creaking wood floor signaled someone's feet, or paws, on the stairs. Baby J leaped to nestle into Leslie's leg. Izzy entered the room and crossed to the far side of the bed. She tossed a pillow onto the chair and settled in.

"They're all gone," Izzy spoke quietly. "I was so scared when my dad called saying you were taken to the hospital ... you've been driving me crazy." She'd mustered ire within her swollen, cool blue eyes, brims rounded in red. She looked away.

"Izzy, it's the last thing I—"

She raised her hand. "This is it." Her chest expanded with air, her breathing noisy.

Baby J lifted her head, cocking it to the side. Leslie placed a hand on the dog's back.

Izzy stood, her face reddening. "I can't live like this, Leslie." Her hands closed into fists. "I'm so angry. I've had enough. I'm just over all of it."

The dog whined as Izzy's voice grew louder.

"Izzy, I—" Leslie's throat clamped down, choking her words.

"You've said you want to start a family. We've clawed our way through months of ups and downs. One month I'm pregnant, then I'm not. We get hopeful, then our hopes are dashed." Her forehead veins engorged. "Then you sabotage the trust we've built in each other."

The weariness in Leslie's limbs turned into lead. "You're right. I can't—"

"Now I've got this pregnancy to take care of." Baby J jumped off the bed and came to Izzy's side. "I can't deal with this deranged life we're having. My parents told you to stay out of this thing. I told you ... you had to ..." She sputtered to a stop, her hands on her head, her face flushed to maroon.

Leslie took a deep breath. "Look. I'll ask Brad to go with me Monday morning. Get whatever I need to work at home for a while. Maybe I can arrange to see patients in person at Susan's office until I can get on my feet."

Izzy glared and shook her head. "I can't think straight." She blew some air out of her lungs and sat again, her hand on the dog's head. Silence filled the room as she slowed down her breathing.

"It's too late at night to make any sense. They gave me a pain pill at the hospital."

"I'm sleeping in the spare room tonight." Izzy looked away and stood, crossing to grab another blanket. "We both need some rest. You look as beat as I feel."

"Okay." Leslie's heart sank.

Izzy sat again, her mouth a tight line. "Susan's on call, right?"

Leslie nodded. The heaviness in her arms had moved to her chest.

"So, let's both turn our phones to no volume. No vibe. Nothing. We're safe in here for six or eight hours. My dad probably dropped my mom home and returned to guard us outside." She handed Leslie her phone and pulled hers out of her pocket. "We'll talk more tomorrow. I need some space." After a few punches on her phone, she looked back. "I have an extra shipment of pumpkins coming in the morning. I'll have to run out for it, but it shouldn't take too long."

Izzy directed Baby J to the hall and added blankets over Leslie. "You should just sleep in."

"Yeah."

The love of Leslie's life walked away.

Awakening with a start from a dream, Leslie's leg jumped, the jolt sending stabbing pain into her knee. Alone in the middle of their king bed, she shifted reflexively under the weight of heavy sheets and blankets, pushing the pile of covers away and glancing at the nightstand clock. Morning. Eight o'clock. Saturday. Lifting her head, she caught her breath and remembered the stitches in her chest. The knife wound. The attack. She'd been buried under a stack of bedding and grinding dreams.

"Oh, shit." She hurt all over.

She gaathered strength to burrow an arm out and dumped the entire mess—duvet, blankets, pillows—to the floor on Izzy's side. A faint whiff of brewed java led her out of bed as she tried to recall her conversation with Izzy last night before she'd passed out.

The place was simply too quiet. She peed.

"Hey, Iz?" She limped down the stairs.

No dog, either. The coffee maker had turned off, but the pot was warm. Izzy's laptop was open but asleep on the breakfast bar. Her car was gone. Leslie checked her phone. No messages, no security notifications. The glint of Izzy's favorite gold hoop earring next to her laptop caught Leslie's eye—just one. She woke Izzy's computer. A bright red banner atop a previewed email read:

Unknown source, use caution when opening, possible phishing.

The logo for Izzy's billing software company, as did the entire note, looked legit. But the scammers were asking for her login information! Yeah, right. They'd be laughing all the way into her bank account. No way Izzy would fall for it.

Leslie glanced at her phone—eight-ish. No voicemails. She rubbed her chin and then shot a text to Izzy:

Where'd you go?

Izzy's fury last night entered her mind, lingering like a stone dropped into a dry well—an impact felt, but nothing to soften the blow. She was gone. *What if she simply had enough of the lies and deception?* The look on her face before Leslie had passed out from exhaustion—it bordered on a breaking point. Never before had Leslie seen her with such enraged, fraught helplessness. But it wouldn't be like Izzy not to leave some message if she planned to go away.

A quick scan of the kitchen, the basement, and the dining and living rooms yielded nil. The foyer. The key tray. Nothing. No note.

Leslie's mobile pinged with a message from Pearl:

The #s inside the figure all add in DOBs!

Now Leslie opened her eyes wide and poured some coffee. She'd tied Damon's map to the add-in patients. Her theory was correct. She texted:

Will call ASAP.

After a few lukewarm sips, her mind came into sharper focus. The knife attack clicked into place—the parking garage, Michelle, Brad, everything following in the hospital. Her talk with Izzy—oh, the pumpkin delivery. She immediately placed a call to her wife, but it went straight to voicemail.

"Hey, call me when you get this."

There had to be a note somewhere. Leslie slogged upstairs. She checked the nightstands, the bathrooms, and the study. Nothing. She tapped a call to Izzy's office phone.

"TipTop Nursery. William speaking."

"Hey, William. Is Izzy there?" Leslie had struggled with the hire of Izzy's cannabis-loving high school friend, but now she welcomed his voice.

"Nope—no Baby J either."

His chipmunk laughter was like chewing glass. Too many gummies. Always.

"Did you hear from her?"

"No. Not yet."

"Has the pumpkin delivery arrived?"

"No. It's not expected until later. Probably around lunchtime." He cleared his throat. "Everything okay?"

"Yeah. Have her reach me when she shows, will you?"

Calling Brad and Kathy was definitely in order now. Finn Connor's vile face flashed in her mind. To be sure, he was in custody—but he had associates. And from what Brad had said, the police were looking for at least one, tied to a major drug lord. Finn must have been working at this guy's direction last night. Would the drug dealers target Izzy to get to her? But the dog was gone, too. *Would they abscond with them both?*

Smacking a hand over her trembling chin, she stopped to remember what Izzy had said. She had to run out for a shipment of pumpkins in the morning. Would she have gone to the supplier directly? Checking her work calendar on her laptop might show the supplier.

What's the date?

Holy feck! The add-in patients' dates of birth... Damon had tied them to drug dealers, inside the drawing of Finn Connor. She had to get this info to the detectives as soon as possible. She'd also need Pearl to tell them about her scrutiny of the records. Leslie had to call Brad.

She hobbled down the stairs as fast as her strained knee and sore chest would allow. She dug through the dining room sideboard. With a notepad in hand, she stopped in the bathroom for a couple of ibuprofen. Strong pain meds were out. She needed a clear head.

Finding Brad's text thread, she hit call.

"Yeah."

"Is Izzy there?"

"No. What's happening?"

"Brad, I woke up, and Izzy isn't here. Her car's gone." Leslie settled in front of Izzy's computer. "We had some tough talk last night after you and Kathy left. She slept in the basement. I can't find a note anywhere."

"Did you call the nursery? Text her? Call her?"

"Yes. Yes. Yes." Leslie heaved a breath. "She said last night she'd have to run out for a pumpkin delivery in the morning. But the nursery said they didn't expect the truck until around lunch." She brought up Izzy's calendar.

"Is there anything else off at home? I didn't get any security alarms."

"No. And she took the dog." Leslie found the pumpkin supplier info. "Can you go to the supplier? There's a number here too, but the website says they're closed. It's about forty minutes south. I need to reach Detective Davis about those numbers in the drawing."

"Sure. Text me the supplier's location and contact info. I'll get back with what I find."

"Thanks." Leslie switched to Pearl's number and called.

"Dr. Schoen. It's incredible. Every number inside the figure ties to an add-in patient."

"The detectives need this info ASAP." Leslie moved to the kitchen table with her notepad. "If I get them to come here, can you join us? I think we'll need you to explain what you found."

"Of course. I'll drop Merle off at his uncle's. Just text me when."

"Will do."

Leslie outlined a diagram on her paper at the kitchen table. Bold boxes encircled each MAT clinic provider's name, connecting them in a web of relationships. Bryce, writing Suboxone and bupe prescriptions. Sloan, taking every unscheduled client, always for cash. Damon, using, so attached to the dealer, arranging all the add-in people. His message from the grave: the add-in patients were also tied to a drug dealer. The pattern emerged slowly—puzzling at first, then revealing unexpected links. A shiver shot down Leslie's spine as she recalled her attacker's horrid face, the same one Damon dealt with. No wonder he had a plan to communicate—the drawing—in case something happened to him.

The 400 doses of missing bupe. Pounding on her phone, Leslie searched for street values and pharmacy costs on a typical Suboxone dose. Her calculation showed a nine hundred percent gain when selling bupe on the street over the going rate at a pharmacy. The amount missing led to a spread of some $7,200.

If Bryce colluded with the dope dealer—Bryce and Sloan, with Sloan's knowledge of all the add-ins—the two of them might've unloaded bupe to the dealer for cash. People use it to get high or treat their opioid withdrawal. But 400 doses would just be a drop in the bucket. Things had been off in the MAT clinic for months.

She rose to pour more coffee and stopped, staring at the refrigerator. The noiseless click of something falling into place caught her attention as she returned to the table. She plunked her coffee cup down. A phrase she'd found in her mother's diary yesterday jumped out at her:

... What's in plain view may be the easiest to conceal....

Leslie's diagram wasn't telling the whole story. What had slipped past her at the office, unregistered? What details had escaped her conscious awareness? Bryce wrote scripts the MAT patients took to the pharmacy to fill. And Sloan...

The moment in their outer hall. The woman with crimson hair and the apricot coat. What had she said about her appointment with Sloan?

"You mean, did he get what he needed? ... Ha."

Aww yeah! She brought her bupe prescription to Sloan! Her pills. Leslie scribbled an arrow back to Sloan's MAT box. A certain group of MAT clients, always with cash. Damon's message tied the subset to the dope dealers. He had to complete chart edits before the DEA went through everything. The charts had to show they were treating appropriate people, those with heroin or other opioid addictions. If the patient was pregnant, they needed a pregnancy test. They also had to do tox screens to prove people were taking the drugs, not diverting them—like selling their supply on the street.

Why the hell did Damon hide a hard drive in his wall? What was on it? Did Finn kill Damon for the hard drive? Or—

Pushing her paper and pen away, Leslie returned to Izzy's laptop. She shook it, bringing the email back again. Phishing scam. But clearly, Izzy hadn't opened it.

Phishing scam. Social engineering. Chart edits. Like Susan's idea.

Another piece, the chart edits, fell into place. What if Damon had hacked into their cloud-based charting system? He might've changed charts without leaving obvious breadcrumbs.

Michelle's strange reactions raised nagging uncertainties about her role. She hadn't responded when Sloan's alibi was exposed as a lie, and she'd avoided talking with Damon for days after the team meeting. In the elevator yesterday, had a moment of regret slipped through her defenses? Had she learned what was happening at the team meeting the Monday before Damon vanished? Would Michelle have come to her aid after the knifing if she'd been in cahoots with this whole sordid scheme?

Leslie scoured her recall again. Did she have everything accounted for? Once Bryce and Sloan got the prescription pills back, they sold them to the dealers. She still didn't know where the missing sample drugs went—did they sell those too? How many misdirected samples had there been? And what determined which MAT patients would go for this scheme? What was in it for them?

Following some cold coffee, Leslie checked the time—going on nine. Why wasn't Izzy answering her texts or calls? If Brad remained silent for an hour, Leslie would call him. She sent another text to Izzy. Another call. Another voicemail.

She grabbed Detective Davis's business card.

Thirty-One

Saturday, October 26th—Early morning

Sloan's hat blew off and landed near a featureless Ford sedan. The cold air needled Sloan's exposed skin as scattered trash tumbled across empty sidewalks. Retrieving the cap, he righted himself and jumped to avoid colliding with a jogger. Coffee grinds and stale beer tainted the morning breeze while a solitary delivery truck growled in the background. A quick glance behind him showed no one else in the freezing morning just before nine. Abandoned storefronts with iron gates stood watch over puddles reflecting leaden skies. Walking from his place downtown to Lightning Will's Bar and Grill, a brisk twelve blocks, gave him time to consider two tough choices.

He needed less than five minutes with Stan. An opening for obtaining false credentials had presented itself—an expensive but viable escape plan. Soon he'd reach that critical junction: flee the country with a fabricated identity or stay put. The cost was substantial: thousands for convincing forgeries and abandoning a respected career spanning three decades. But hey—better to spend and not use it than to be left facing the consequences of the cock-and-bull story he'd told the police. He tapped on the locked front door at Stan's bar, jamming his hands deep into his coat pockets, and waited for the only man he called a friend.

"Get in." Stan closed the door behind Sloan. "Did you see anyone in the last few blocks?"

"No, it's dead out there." The bookie was bent into the letter C, his scant crown hair mussed into a fur ball. He'd clearly just rolled out of bed. "Have you got my papers?"

"Depends on if you have my money."

"Of course."

Sloan extended a stuffed envelope, his fingers reluctant to release it even as Stan reached for it. Stan's brows lifted in seeming gratitude as he took in the weight, giving a knowing nod while producing a paper bundle in return. Sloan inhaled deeply, steadying his nerves as they made the exchange—documents for cash, each package representing a different kind of freedom. Would Stan be available on an international basis for Sloan to keep his gambling life alive? Better to broach it later.

After a crammed Friday night, the bar stunk of stale booze mixed with dirt and tobacco. Upside-down barstools on the counter. An unused mop and bucket. The dirty floor with a few leaves scattered about.

"You're gonna want to know this." Stan tried to straighten. "But you didn't hear it from me."

"What?"

"Finn got walked into a cop car downtown last night. In cuffs."

Sloan rocked slightly, his chest tightening. Finn might blow his alibi. "Shit."

"Yeah. You're lookin' a bit peaked, man."

"How'd you find out? Is he in jail? Don't tell me—Rafi knows."

"Slow down, buddy. I know nothin' 'bout Rafi." Stan sniffed and wiped his nose with his sleeve. "It was one of my downtown guys. I got lookouts keeping track of things. This fella was right there. Near the parkin' garage at 11th and Yamhill." He checked the cash, then pocketed it. "Not only cop cars there but an ambulance too. Somebody mighta been hurt."

"Damn." Sloan swallowed hard. Plagued with regret, he cursed himself for getting into this situation. Bryce said Leslie wouldn't be around soon, twice. Had it been her?

Sloan inserted a statement with the inflection of a question. "So, you've heard nothing from Rafi." Bryce would discover any information Rafi possessed.

"Turn the fuck around. Get outta here." Stan shoved Sloan's shoulder. "And don't even speak his name again."

"Okay, okay... Hey, thanks man. I'll let you know what happens."

"Sure."

In seconds, Sloan was outside and the door slammed at his back. He gripped his hat in the gusty wind as the deadbolt clicked and leaves flew above him, circling the overhang. *Shit.* Sloan did a double take on the surveillance camera above him.

The smack of a garbage can overturning at the curb upped his visceral gut hit. Monitoring cameras. The ones at his condo parking garage. They tracked his car movements, and the one night he drove to Will's...

A stinging indignation rose as he zipped his coat tighter. Across the street, someone in a Ford sedan bent over behind the wheel, looking down. Rafi's thugs or the police might be watching him.

He had little time to avoid being snagged.

Bryce leaned into their Nob Hill garage while handing a bag to his wife. "Here's Milo's food. Now get going." The dog barked steadily, his head sticking out of her car. He backed into the house. "I mean it, Debra. Go to Dan's house, and don't leave until you hear from me."

"But—"

"I'm leaving now, too. I'll get this meeting done as fast as I can. Call you soon." Shutting the door to the garage, he pivoted into their drafty kitchen with its leaky windows and retro clock above the doorway—barely after nine. This damp, century-old Northwest home. Who cared if it was Nob Hill—he hated it. Its charm had long since worn thin. The ancient wooden floors creaked underfoot as he crossed into the dining room and turned to his study. His wife's car ignition signaled they both needed to move ahead.

He grimaced at the cramped sunroom office, its modest dimensions starkly contrasting with the high ceilings and spacious rooms throughout the rest of the house. Leaning into a window over his desk, he confirmed she drove away. Good riddance.

Finding a suitable carry-on bag in the closet, he tossed it on his desk. The call with Michelle earlier had sent him into a mental spin. Of course, if he didn't know already, he had to tell Rafi about Finn's situation. But he wasn't ready for the following Telegram—*South Waterfront at 9:30*. No way was he walking into a shit show. The smash-faced lowlife had an agenda for him, Bryce was certain. He tapped:

Family emergency - can't make it. Will get back.

He checked the time again. *Goddamn it*. Michelle should have called last night from the parking garage. As he stuffed his case, recalling her voice left him uneasy. Sure, she'd had a shock. Probably didn't sleep much. But she'd sounded so—what? Spacey? Not like herself at all. At least she'd relayed the key information: Finn's fuckup. She had his description down pat—it must have been close, since Bryce had been careful to shield her from Finn. But the screwup was on Rafi and Finn, as far as he was concerned. They should have expected Leslie's father-in-law, the ex-cop.

Crap! He was running out of time. Bryce scaled the stairs at the back of the living room two at a time, grabbed a hall closet suitcase, and reached for clothes from his bedroom dresser. He needed to get lost—out of Rafi's reach. No doubt he'd be angrier than a black mamba. He had to pacify him somehow, but how?

Dopp kit in the bathroom drawer. An extra pair of shoes.

Outside of eliminating Leslie, Rafi's priority was keeping the flow of bupe patients growing. Bryce had met Damon's new replacement, Armie, but held off on introducing him to Sloan in favor of getting him familiar with the computer system first. No longer. Now Sloan needed Armie to replace Finn's job as well.

A case under his arm, Bryce ran down the steps again, tossed in a jacket, and closed the bag.

That's it. He'd summon Sloan to meet and strategize on getting Armie ready to do Finn's and Damon's jobs on Monday.

He yanked the drawstring of the living room blinds with a sharp snap, instantly blocking the view of the front door and porch. The covering crashed down as the cord severed in his hand. "Damn it!" He tossed the broken string onto a nearby chair.

Son of a—

The phone buzzed in his back pocket. Encrypted—from Armie, the circus act—those ridiculous tats and piercings. He opened Telegram.

meet with R same swf bench. 1300. No excuses.

The hair on the back of Bryce's neck lifted with a chill. To be sure, Rafi's next step would be to give Finn's failed job to Bryce.

He wasn't sure he had it in him to kill anyone. Unless it was kill or be killed. Would he have to find out?

What if he and Sloan improvised a plan for him to take the meeting with Rafi? Sloan would manufacture some delay—Rafi wouldn't bother with him. Bryce clenched his jaws as he moved to his office. From the bottom desk drawer, he dislodged a wrapped bundle. Uncovering it, he inspected the pistol stored with an extra clip and checked the safety switch. His life jacket on a sinking ship. Maybe he'd give it to Sloan.

Phone in hand, he rang Michelle, counting nine rings before she answered.

"Hullo." *Is she half asleep?*

"I'm called out of town—I need you and Sloan to fill in for me a few days."

"Wha—" Michelle mumbled before a thud sounded in the background.

"Michelle, get with it!" The clock behind him ticked off seconds. "You have to reach Sloan. I need him to come to my house right now."

Bryce stared through the window at the dense black-blue sky, while across the street an ancient tree bent dangerously in the violent wind, threatening to snap at any moment.

"Yeah. Okay."

"I need him in person—it's nothing I can write down or do in a phone call. He'll have to see anyone who can't postpone for three days."

"Wait."

"Review my office schedule through Tuesday with Lynn and check in with each patient. I'll send you a T message when I can call you again. It'll be before the weekend's over." Static crackled on the line. "On the Monday board thing, you're on your own after they talk with Leslie. Tell the investigator my communication's coming by phone, and you'll arrange it."

"Uh—uh—"

"Wake up!" Bryce screamed. "It's going on ten already. Get some coffee!"

Thirty-Two

Saturday, October 26ᵗʰ—Morning: Leslie's home

Early-day rain lashed the living room windows as Leslie pulled on a lap blanket. A chill had seeped through to her bones despite the blazing fire. At around nine-thirty, the front porch camera displayed on her phone caught Pearl walking up their drive.

"Come in." Leslie hurried her into the foyer before shutting out the storm. She covered her stitches and welcomed her coworker with a hug.

"My God. How are you?" Pearl scanned Leslie's face and then unpacked her laptop.

In a second phone call, Leslie had updated her on the details of the knife attack, how Michelle had stemmed her bleeding, and Izzy's absence.

"Has Izzy called back?"

"No, and I'm worried. Neither the nursery nor her parents have seen or heard from her. She might have driven out with the dog to a pumpkin supplier. Brad's running it down right now."

Leslie gestured toward the couch. "The detectives will be here any minute."

Pearl sat at the end of the sofa while Leslie settled on the ottoman. Her diagram and notes were within reach.

"You sounded a bit cryptic about the MAT clinic, but I understand. What about Michelle—do you think she's a part of this?"

"I don't know. I mean, she helped me out big-time last night. I tried to talk to her while we were walking out. She said something noncommittal, like, 'It didn't have to be like this ... with the DEA.'"

"Hmm." Pearl's eyes narrowed. "You look worried. You should call Izzy again."

The void in Leslie's gut carved deeper, pulsing like a second heartbeat. Kathy had called back to suggest she might be out exercising Baby J. Brad was driving to the supplier now. Izzy hadn't answered their calls, either. Leslie checked her phone. Not enough time had passed to hear from Brad. Still nothing from Izzy.

A black sedan stopped at the curb before their front yard.

"Brad said to call him if he hadn't called within an hour." Leslie nodded at the window. "I've tried Izzy a dozen times. She just hasn't answered." She inhaled sharply, hoping to shake the rock-hard pit in her stomach loose. "I'll try again in a few minutes."

If Izzy's in trouble, it'll be my fault.

"The detectives are here."

Sloan hovered over his condo desk at ten a.m., his lips pressed together, massaging his temples as the storm lashed against his near floor-to-ceiling living room windows. With its overpriced furniture and tasteful art, his home stood as a hollow marker of his precarious life choices. He sat in a position that allowed him to survey the kitchen and living room without moving.

The fork in the road was here, down the money-draining avenue and closing in on his profession. In truth, he'd turned in this direction a few years back. Oh, for the times long gone when he'd loved helping people. But these days—these whiners had driven him to unbelievable places. Bitterness, a sourness on his tongue, threatened to swallow him whole. For her entire life, his mother, the cynic, had cautioned—*You'll get burned by life eventually. But will you have the brains to stay the course with your plans, no matter what?* He wished he had the guts to call his ex, someone with whom to hash this out.

Damn, how he'd blown it with that gorgeous man. He'd faced a choice back then as well. Looking in the rearview mirror, it had been a no-brainer. But clarity had eluded him then. On the one hand, the relationship that had nourished him for years. On the other, his corrosive gambling habit. His life partner had drawn a line in the sand, and the man meant it. What a pathetic asshole Sloan had been to choose the latter. Regret hadn't come close to describing the flood of emotions he'd carried since. His chest ached with an emptiness that made breathing a punishment.

He pushed his laptop and phone to the side. The morning was flying by. He needed a plan of action and fast. Studying the business card in his hand, he carefully set it down and grabbed a crumpled note. Which one to call? His mobile vibration broke the trance.

Michelle.

Answer it, or let it go? He stared at the two suitcases neatly placed by the couch. His cell kept buzzing. He grabbed it.

"Yeah."

"Hees leafing tun." Michelle mumbled before coughing. "It's me. I jus' talked with Bryce. Some instructions for you."

She fell silent.

"Michelle? Are you okay?" He paused, listening to a faint noise in the background. "Hello?" Was she chewing on something?

"He'll be gone three days. Wants you to go to his house right now. Talk about covering for him."

Sloan welcomed the answer that arrived with the news of Bryce's planned escape. There wasn't anyone more pitiful than himself except Bryce.

"Got it." Sloan cut her off and looked at the two phone numbers in front of him again.

He chose one and started the call.

"Pearl has some info for us." Leslie addressed the detectives. "Believe me, you'll want to hear it."

With her laptop open and her face inches from the screen, Pearl tapped away around ten-fifteen on Saturday morning.

The four had settled in Leslie and Izzy's living room after Davis and Levy shed their coats. The detectives dragged dining room chairs close to the foyer to sit. Leslie looked at her phone.

Still no response from Izzy.

"Before we proceed," Davis glanced at Leslie. "Brad Turner called me this morning on his way out of town. I'm aware your wife was gone when you woke up today. Her car as well?"

"Yes. We had ... a heated conversation last night. She slept in the spare room. And she hasn't responded to a dozen texts and calls this morning. She took the dog. She might've driven directly to one of her suppliers since she said she had to go out this morning about a pumpkin delivery."

Everyone sat on the edge of their seats.

"Any sign someone else was in the house last night?"

"No. I went through the whole place. The alarms didn't trip, and there were no security notifications." Leslie shrugged. "I don't know whether she's just angry with me and not answering my calls, or out running the dog without her phone, or...if—" She swallowed. "She's in danger."

He nodded to Levy and checked his phone. "We should get a call from Brad soon." Levy readied her notepad and recorder. The detectives already knew of Leslie's discovery in Damon's drawing numbers. She'd told them about it in the emergency department last night.

"So, Pearl." Leslie gestured for her to begin.

"Yes." She turned her laptop to face the detectives. "I took all the five and six-digit numbers—"

Davis's phone buzzed. "Hold on." He grabbed it from his shirt pocket and glanced at the screen. "Excuse me, I need to take this. It's Alex James." He looked at Pearl. "Please wait until I get back. I want to hear what you found." Pearl nodded.

"Use the kitchen, Detective." Leslie gestured at the foyer archway.

Davis stepped back and left the room. Levy rested her notes and pen on her lap.

The room quieted, except for the rain pelting on the windows.

"You're remarkably together after such an assault last night, Dr. Schoen. Luckily, your nurse colleague was in the right place at the right time. And Brad Turner, huh?" While keeping here eyes on her subject, Levy clicked her pen closed, then open. "Do you have any more ideas about why Finn Connor targeted you?"

The right place at the right time.

The pen clicked, then clicked again. A shutter shot—the door by Michelle's office desk—flashed in Leslie's mind. The interruption she'd caused days earlier between Damon and Michelle. Just before Damon went missing.

Michelle said: *So, I'll come by with the material we talked about Monday.*

Leslie turned to Pearl as the pen's clicking continued. Her eyes held a penetrating look again. Did she sense Leslie had just landed another gut instinct?

Aaron Davis walked in and reclaimed his chair.

"Last Saturday, I met with Bryce in the office," Leslie spoke resonantly. "I told him I was going to find out what happened to Damon, no matter what."

The younger detective's eyes grabbed hers. "Are you saying Bryce Nelson and Finn Connor were working together?"

"I'm pointing out Finn Connor tried to kill me just seven days later."

Detective Levy's eyebrows rose. "What motivated you, Doctor, to risk those words? With one man dead by homicide, why would you make such a—declaration?"

Leslie covered the bandage over her left collarbone with her hand. "Whatever my initial motivation, Detective, it's about staying alive right now. When will the next attempt on my life happen? Or on someone else's? An office worker? A family member? My wife—who's missing right now?" From the end table, she grabbed a folded piece of paper. "You know, this is just like realizing you have rats." Leslie paused. "At first, you see one dirty little creature running across your kitchen floor. Then you discover that where there's one, there are many more." She spread the page out on her lap, laying her hands on top. "I think there's a rotten scheme happening within Bryce's clinic, and it involves many players."

Pearl scooted closer to the detectives. "Detectives, may I continue?"

"Please, go ahead." Davis readied his pen.

"I took all the five- and six-digit numbers inside the drawing figure's head, first adding a zero before the short ones, then treated them all as six-digit dates of birth. Next, I ran those by the list of add-in MAT clinic patients in the last year." She turned her laptop toward them, revealing the screen. "Add-in patients are those who see a provider without an appointment. In the last year, every add-in patient saw Dr. Mannon. They simply show up asking to be seen."

Davis cleared his throat. "Means I'll be working on a search warrant for the patient files."

Pearl nodded. "This is just a spreadsheet." She gestured to the laptop. "I removed all the patient names for now and used a numbering system. You can see that each entry in the column titled DOBs from the drawing, in every case, correlates with one of the opioid clinic patients seen without an appointment."

"Damon was sending a message." Leslie turned to face Detective Davis. "All these add-in patients in the MAT clinic are linked to the drug dealer, Finn Connor."

"You've been quite involved in some parts of this investigation." Levy sat forward. "Like unearthing the hard drive in Grady's apartment."

"Let's leave the hard disk out of this, Levy." Davis interrupted. "My call was from Alex James. They just cracked it." The detectives exchanged fleeting looks. "You and I will talk about it after this."

"Before you do, let me guess what you'll find on it." Leslie lifted her notes. "It'll have some of Bryce Nelson's MAT patient records or templates for records, templates to generate fake lab reports, and access codes to enter those patients' charts through the software company."

Levy tapped her nail on her notebook. Davis leaned back in his chair, his brows raised.

"Are you inferring Bryce Nelson killed Damon Grady, Dr. Schoen?" Levy stopped making noise.

"Well, Damon didn't die by the knife."

A soft "um" escaped Pearl, hinting at a question.

"What I know is this." Leslie searched the detectives' faces. "Bryce believes he has Sloan and Michelle at his beck and call. Maybe he once had Damon on the hook." She turned her notes over. "But what if Damon started abusing opiates and became a risk to Bryce? What if Damon identified Bryce as responsible for the missing bupe? Worse for Bryce, what if Bryce was worried the DEA would tag him for the missing office opiates? The penalties would ruin him professionally. The subsequent investigations would expose what he's been doing with those samples, and it involves some of the opioid addicts in his clinic."

Leslie handed her sheet to Detective Davis. "Let me explain with this diagram."

Davis moved his chair closer to Levy. Pearl rose to stand behind them, looking over their shoulders. The three of them peered at the page together.

Leslie gestured to her notes. "I believe this is what's going on at Psych Recovery."

Thirty-Three

Saturday, October 26th—Later morning

Sloan's pulse raced as he strained to tune out a clock's second hand ticking behind him. "Randy, I'm running out of time," he told the man on the other end, swallowing hard.

Christ, it's going on eleven-thirty.

"Did you hear what I just said?" Randy sounded exasperated.

Sloan tapped the lawyer's card on his desk, struggling to concentrate. *Listen.*

"There's too much background noise. Say that last part again." Sloan's fingers trembled as he tried to absorb the reality that Randy was on the line. Instead of scoffing, Randy had agreed to help him, an old friend from Gamblers Anonymous before Sloan had vanished and stayed silent for years. He was amazed he'd kept the man's card. He'd abandoned the idea of getting any real help long ago.

"We're going to have to meet." Randy's voice became louder now.

"Okay," Sloan didn't miss a beat.

Am I finally going to catch a break?

"Tell me where."

Leslie stole a look at her phone—*half past eleven*—while the detectives put on their rain gear. Still in her living room with Pearl, Detectives Levy and Davis, she'd risen to stand as they all had. A river of nervousness flowed through her, and the silence of no word from Izzy pushed her to text Kathy again. In the middle of their exchange, Leslie's phone rang.

"Brad, what'd you find?" Her heart pounded with hope.

"The supplier's got a mess out here. He talked with Izzy by phone early this morning about canceling the shipment. The storms flooded some of his fields. He's having labor issues getting enough crops to meet his demand. Izzy never came out here. She didn't text you?"

"No." Leslie held her forehead in her hand. "Okay, Kathy's going to the nursery to look for her."

"Are the detectives still there?"

Davis had shared he'd texted Brad while out of the room.

"They're about to leave." She glanced at their expectant faces near the front door.

"Where should we look for her next? Both her mother and I have been calling. Nothing."

"She might have taken the dog for a run and left her phone in the car or something." Leslie's chest tightened as she looked at Davis, shaking her head. "Look for her car at the Wildwood trailhead, or she might have gone to the Sellwood Riverfront Park."

"I'm on it."

She tucked her phone back in her pocket and turned to Pearl. "Did you get that spreadsheet sent to the detectives?"

Pearl nodded while loading her bag. "That and the redacted deposit slips."

"With this new information, we'll have medical records and practice financial access today." Davis folded Leslie's diagram and tucked it into his inner jacket. "I'll get those warrants."

Pearl zipped her laptop bag.

"Should we save time with divide and conquer?" Levy spoke to Davis, pulling on her woolen cap. "What can I do?"

"I'll reach out to the sergeant after confirming the hard drive contents, then grab the warrants. We'll go to Nelson next with the warrants. More in the car." Davis glanced at Leslie, rearranging his coat. "Do he and Dr. Mannon typically keep Saturday hours?"

"No, but I'll shoot Lynn a quick text about their schedules today if they have one." Her thumbs tapped away.

Both detectives hovered by the front door, speaking quietly with each other, thick rain blurring the front yard and neighborhood. The blowing hadn't stopped.

Leslie's mobile buzzed, drawing the detectives' attention. "Lynn says nobody had plans to come in today. Last weekend was unusual."

She jumped as an old-school ring blared from the phone in her hand. A moment later, another vibration from Levy's cell startled her.

"I've got to get this." Levy moved into the kitchen.

Phone to her ear, Leslie stepped back to the fireplace and braced herself with a hand on the mantel. "Hello?"

"Dr. Schoen?" Lynn's voice flagged more than concern.

"Yeah, I'm here." She held her breath.

"I just got a text from Michelle." Lynn sounded out of breath. "We'll be clearing Dr. Nelson's schedule." She inhaled deeply. "He'll be out of town through Tuesday."

"What?" *What is he doing?* "Why?"

"No direct answer. But I'm supposed to call patients to reschedule and get back to Michelle later. Dr. Nelson is at his house."

"Okay. I understand." Leslie reconsidered Michelle's role, her mind flashing to Bryce's bag on the parking garage floor. A phone had tumbled out, but had Michelle called for an ambulance with a different phone? "Thanks, Lynn, I'll call you back."

Pearl stood at the foyer arch. "Should I go to the office in case someone comes in?"

Leslie tucked her phone away, lost momentarily in the replay of last night's events. "No. Stay with me here a bit longer, would you?"

"Right."

Leslie moved toward Davis at the front door just as Levy returned from the kitchen. "Bryce Nelson's about to leave town." Adrenaline sharpened her senses, her fingertips tingling. "He's at home, supposedly. For now."

"And while Nelson's getting ready to leave, I just got off a call with Dr. Mannon." Levy turned to Davis, gauging his reaction. "Sir, Mannon wants to talk with his lawyer present."

"Okay." Davis nodded to Leslie and Pearl with assurance. "We'll take it from here. Be safe."

Leslie pushed the door shut as Levy and Davis jogged to their sedan. Was Sloan ready to say where he *really* was the night Damon died?

"Oh, no." Leslie spun toward Pearl, lightheaded and swimming with possibilities. Michelle had Bryce's briefcase in the parking garage. Had there been a second phone in it?

"What?" Pearl grabbed Leslie's arm.

"I gave Izzy's phone number to Michelle last night in the parking garage." Her voice wavered as a realization surfaced. "I told her to call Izzy." She shook her head as if to seal the depth of her oversight.

"I told her to call Izzy."

"Let's go out through the garage." Leslie shoved an arm into her jacket, facing Pearl across the kitchen table. She tried to keep the worry from her voice.

Izzy had said her father had contacted her about the attack on Leslie—not Michelle.

Why hadn't Michelle notified Izzy?

Another detail left Leslie uneasy. Michelle must have viewed the back of Finn Connor during the attack. In the garage, she'd said, *"The back of him. Again."* The word—again—echoed in her mind. Had she looked at him before?

A chill ran down her spine. Was Michelle involved in this scheme to funnel opiates for profit?

Days earlier, she'd mentioned 'material'—what 'material' would she bring Damon? Did she have two phones or one in the parking garage last night? *Shit.*

"Are you going out to look for Izzy?"

The question sank like a stone into water, leaving ripples of tension. Maybe it was only suspicion, but Leslie didn't have time to explain her hunch to Pearl.

"Hang on—my phone." With shaky hands, she checked for texts. Brad again.

Any sign of Izzy?

No. The trailhead?

Not Wildwood. Heading to Sellwood.

"What can I do?" Pearl held a hand over her heart.

She shouldn't drive and keep reaching out to Izzy simultaneously. *Should Pearl help but stay safe at her own house?* "Go home and keep trying to reach Izzy for me. I've got to get over to Michelle's. Here's Izzy's number." She texted the info as they stepped into the garage.

"I'll do it."

Brad wrote again.

Let me take it from here. I want you safe, at home, and out of this thing.

Leslie opened the garage door and checked the driveway. The rain continued and the sky was dark. She sent a text, *heard*, back to Brad, the word like a lifeline of certainty amid their chaos. Maybe she should've asked Brad to accompany her, but she needed him to cover the dog parks and hiking trails. Izzy might not be at Michelle's, but Leslie had another way to bring Brad into it if she was. Besides, she'd gotten Izzy and their baby into danger before. So now, if it had happened again, she'd damn well get them out.

The darkening downpour loomed sinister. "Have her call me the minute you reach her!" Leslie shouted over the storm's commotion. "And tell her I had to run to Michelle's house." She stepped further into the garage air and threw her bag into the car. "Let's go."

"Got it." Pearl covered her head with her scarf. "Call me and let me know what's happening." She headed toward her car, her bags close to her sides.

"Pearl, wait."

Her coworker turned.

"I'd like us to arrange an 'in case' system. Izzy doesn't need to know about this unless we have to use it." She gripped the back of her neck, stretching the tightness.

"What do you mean?"

Leslie's mind raced ahead as her eyes settled on the workbench, her quiet wooden jewelry haven. "Hang on, I forgot something."

She bolted back into the house before Pearl could respond. In seconds, scaling the stairs as quickly as her strained knee allowed, she rifled through the stacked items on her desk until her hand touched the leather cord—Badger. A piece of her core strength.

She squeezed the amulet in her pocket before dashing back down to Pearl.

"I want to have some method to signal you easily." Out of breath, her shoulders burning, her plan was coming together. "Without having to ring, in case I need some backup."

"Okay. Like what?"

Pearl was reliable, and she needed someone else who would act fast in a crisis.

"Let's do this," Leslie yanked her car open. "If you get a text from me with anything, even a single letter, call Brad and tell him to send the police to Michelle's house immediately. Follow whatever he says. I'm texting you her address and Brad's number." She hit send, her jaw tight, and locked eyes with Pearl, who nodded firmly.

"You can count on me." Pearl gripped her briefcase. "Are you expecting trouble?"

Leslie jumped into the driver's seat. "I hope not."

Thirty-Four

Saturday, October 26th—Noon

After a quick dash to his garage, Bryce threw his bag in the front seat and tossed his suitcase into the back of his SUV. Returning to the house, he paced the kitchen floor, eyes darting out the window over the sink, phone in hand checking for messages. The morning passed with nothing from Sloan. *Would he flake out?* The timeframe for him to cover Rafi's meeting was closing. Bryce wasn't about to go. He'd have to justify ghosting Rafi later. Or maybe not, since there was still time for Sloan to show.

Another howling gust shook his house, pushing him to the view from his desk—the drive, side street, and a neighbor's house, visible through the heavy rain. Heat rose from his neck. The wind bent an old moss-covered walnut tree into a pretzel pose. The tightness in his chest clamped down just as a branch snapped and fell to the curb, blown into the road. Surely Rafi didn't expect him to meet outdoors in this horrid storm, but with the weather, he had thirty minutes tops before it would be too late for Sloan to make it.

He checked an email attachment for crucial information. Flight choices to Alajuela's Juan Santamaría Airport were limited. Once he got Sloan off to meet with Rafi, he'd have to dash to the airport. *Damn.* Sloan wasn't answering any of his calls or texts.

Anxieties over his grandson's health and the stress of it for his son had hounded him for too many months. Bryce had paved the way for his grandson to get the medical care he needed, complete with family support. There was a glimmer of hope. Their appointment with Dr. Vegas, a pediatric neurologist at the Hospital Clinica in San Jose, had been confirmed.

Bryce made the call. It was answered after two rings.

"Hey, Bill." He resolved to slow his voice down, not to sound emergent. Taking a seat at his desk, he swung around to face away from the raging storm outside. "You sound surprised to hear from me. I can't believe lawyers don't work on Saturday." He'd always worried Bill was too by-the-book. Handling him carefully would prevent inflexibility today.

"Look, there's a change getting my boys Dan and Danny down to Costa Rica. I'm traveling today to get things set up. They'll go later this week." He waited, spinning a strategy to appear open for discussion but not for negotiation. "Yeah, I'll be back in about three days. Here's what I need from you—"

"Okay Alex, I'm getting the picture." Davis raised his voice over the screech of the windshield wipers in high mode, slapping rubber on glass. "I'll run everything by the Sarge here in a few. Will get back after." He ended the call and turned to his partner, her hands white, tense as she drove through the storm. Twelve-twenty on the dashboard clock.

Levy gripped the steering wheel, inching her body forward as if that would improve visibility in the pouring rain. Through the dim blur, a traffic light switched to red a block and a half ahead. Now he'd have to judge how much rope to give her. He tapped his fingers on the armrest, glancing over his shoulder at the strobe lights mounted on the rear deck.

"While I'm talking with Sarge, I want you or Julie to reach dispatch. We need four cruisers standing ready for backup at Nelson's. Dispatch code two." He rubbed the wet off the back of his neck. "You'll have to meet with Mannon and his lawyer. Take Julie with you."

She took her eyes off the road long enough to glance at him and nodded briskly. "You got it."

"I'll text you as soon as I'm free." Shoving his phone inside his jacket, Davis jerked his head toward the center console switch under the steering wheel.

"Let's go with the lights. Wail siren." He jabbed a finger, pointing at the switch.

"Get there."

"Right. Okay." Bryce sighed heavily, restless in his study, his hope for Sloan's arrival dwindling as the minutes ticked past twelve-thirty. "Yes, I'll call you as soon as I arrive."

Managing one minute with his wife exceeded his tolerance level. *Good news, divorce shortly.*

While checking his messages, a rising fury filled his chest. Slamming his fist on the desk, he rose to his feet. *Damn the sonofabitch!* Not a single word from Sloan. It was beyond time to leave for the meeting with Rafi. Armie would be after Bryce next. His patience expired. He grabbed a book from his desk and flung it into the bookshelf.

"Fuck!" He screamed. A duo of framed photos fell to the floor, their glass shattering.

He paced the tight space, veered into the kitchen, and jogged to the garage. If he left now, he'd evade being hunted down. Rifling through his carry-on in the car, he snatched a gun bundle and ran back into the house to his desk.

Bryce exhaled deeply. Stretching his neck from side to side didn't relieve a thing. He strapped a harness across his chest, holding his gun in a tightly hugged holster. His bomber jacket retrieved and zipped halfway, he raked the hair off his forehead. As he tested his plan for a solid defense, reaching under his arm, the revolver quickly slipped to the ready. But he'd have to leave it in his car before entering the airport.

Loud knocking from the porch startled him. Sloan? A visual of Rafi's latest soldier, Armie, flashed in his mind—spiked hair with tats around his neck and jawline. Face piercings and hooped earrings stretched lobes beyond belief.

The thumping grew louder. Bryce's gut clenched.

To remain hidden from the front sidelight, he circled around the kitchen to the living room and reached a front window with its blinds closed, finding the furthest vantage point. Trembling, he pulled the curtain back.

Not Sloan.

Not Armie.

Detective Aaron Davis stood at the door, folded papers in his grip. Davis looked to the side street as he waited—only one black sedan.

More knocking.

Bryce released the drapery slowly, a bead of sweat dripping down his temple. The lawyer would represent him immediately, but how would it go down with Rafi, the seedy, hardcore pusher? The minute he was out of the police station, he'd have to watch his back. His only option now was obvious. Brushing off his damp forehead, he cat-walked to reach his keys in the foyer.

He caught a glimpse from the study window—no vehicle was parked on the side street. The knocking, paired with a loud "Police," impelled a *go* signal in Bryce's gut. He bolted for the garage and pounded the door opener before he jumped in his car, weapon in hand.

Bryce gunned it in reverse. A splashing screech marked his turn to head north on the backstreet. But a scraping, crunching noise arose at his rear bumper.

"Goddammit!" Adrenaline flooded the pit of his gut.

The rear camera caught his bumper entangled in a fallen tree branch across the curb. Pounding rain and fogged windows blurred his view ahead and behind. He punched the defrost to high and rolled his window down, switching it into drive.

A patrol cruiser approached the corner beyond him, its lights flashing, siren blasting. Bryce aimed his gun at the cruiser's front tire and fired. The vehicle skidded to the side on the flattened wheel, grinding to a halt.

Pushing harder, Bryce lurched his SUV forward, dragging the tree branch. Sirens ahead and in the back overwhelmed his effort to accelerate. Another patrol wagon before him swung widely into the street, screeching and slamming to a stop at a diagonal, blocking the road.

His eyes darted right, then left, his shaking hand hovering over the gear shifter. Retaining walls and trees. He hit the brakes and skidded to a halt, the cruiser a few feet beyond.

"Shit!" He wailed as his chest hammered like a jackhammer on concrete.

A bullhorn blasted. "Show your hands!"

Through blinding floodlights and the specter of guns pointed at his head, Bryce braced for a volley of bullets crashing into his windshield. He carefully raised his arms and drifted the revolver, dangled by the butt, out the window. A shift in the spotlight revealed a crouched deputy, shielded by his open car door, handgun aimed squarely at Bryce's face.

"Drop the gun." The voice carried over the tempest.

Another officer emerged from the cruiser, standing firm despite the pelting rain that battered him. Metal hit the pavement with a clang as Bryce's pistol bounced on the ground. The second policeman stepped toward him, revolver aimed, stopping a few feet from the SUV.

Within seconds, Bryce slumped in the downpour, his wrists bound by handcuffs behind him. A muscled officer gripped his arms from behind as Aaron Davis jogged toward them.

"Bryce Nelson, you're under arrest for unlawful use of a weapon," Davis spoke forcefully, rainwater streaming down his face.

"What?" Bryce struggled against the officer's grip. "I want my lawyer."

A rattling voice recited his rights in the drenching rain before the cop jerked Bryce around to face Davis.

"Take him to Central for booking." Davis tightened his face into a scowl. "I'll meet you there."

He turned to go but stopped. "Oh yeah, Nelson. We came to serve you with home and office search warrants. We'll just send the agents in now."

"Searching for what? I don't see any orders."

"For the electronic and financial records on your dope dealing, fool." Davis yanked the papers from his pocket and shoved them inside Bryce's jacket as he wiggled to avoid the inevitable.

"We were coming to gather evidence to arrest you. But with the lame escape act, you handed it to me." As Davis turned his back, he muttered, "You're lucky you didn't get blown away."

Thirty-Five

Saturday, October 26th—Early afternoon

Low-hanging clouds blanketed the murky front of Michelle Wichim's house. Leslie parked her car at the curb, picturing her beautiful wife, radiant with the news of their pregnancy just weeks ago. As her nerves itched, Leslie clasped the badger amulet in her pocket and surveyed the Overlook neighborhood, its century-old homes hunched against the thunderstorm. Rainwater cascaded from overhanging eaves and gurgled through storm drains as wind-lashed trees bent precariously over the street. She steeled herself.

Focus on a plan. First—signs of Izzy's car.

The rain created an eerie vibe, its splatter flowing out of sync with gusting winds and squeaky wipers. She checked to be sure her text thread with Pearl was open, noting the time at twelve forty-five, and killed the car. Slipping her phone inside her jacket, she trod with her hood up toward the gravel drive. Either the adrenaline pumping through her system, or the ibuprofen, or maybe both, had minimized her earlier pain.

Michelle's old Volvo sedan was parked in front of a gated fence. Washed-out tire ruts ran alongside the drive, marking where vehicles had previously traveled. Opposite the hinged, locked barrier, the driveway continued, ending in a dilapidated one-car garage attached to an angled, covered patio in the backyard. Its door was closed, but a side entry was open. No angle revealed whether Izzy's car waited inside.

"Izzy!" she yelled. "Baby J?"

Straining to listen for a reply or a bark rising above the storm, she heard nothing but rain and wind. She walked around to the front of the house, a four-square standing distinct from its neighbors with its boxy shape, passing basement window wells. Drooping shrubs and pools of water created an obstacle course. Blinds covered every visible casement on the ground and second floors. The porch steps held scraps of trash and an upturned plastic bowl balanced near its edge. A low-pitched, mournful yowl to her right gave away an unsettled cat, shivering next to a wet cardboard shelter.

Leslie's shoulders tensed like an archer's bow as she lifted her arm to ring the doorbell. The front windows gave away nothing. No answer. The furthest casement had an uncovered slit at the bottom. Circling her ankle, the cat pitched a drawn-out moan.

She had to gain entry. With the yard entirely fenced—no scaling it—and the driveway gate locked, her only other way in would be breaking a basement window. But what would her ploy be once she was inside? Maybe something about the attack in the parking garage? Michelle had been wild-eyed with fear before the ambulance arrived. Had she been coming unglued? Leslie scooped the meowing critter and held its shivering body against her chest as she knocked on a window.

"Michelle!" She hit the doorbell again and rocked the animal, moving to the end of the porch. At the far opening, she knelt, balancing the cat in one arm, and pounded on the glass. Part of the room was visible. No Michelle. No Izzy.

"Michelle, it's Leslie. I've got your cat here. She needs help." Urgency edged Leslie's voice, pitched high against the patter of rain. Willing her words to penetrate the thick walls, she repeated the call.

As she rose, the shadowed, dull interior lightened by a bulbous floor lamp in an area beyond the living room. Leslie stood clutching the trembling cat to her chest. A deadbolt's click drew her to the front door, which creaked open slowly, revealing a sliver of the interior. Michelle popped into the gap.

"You've arrived." The nurse's voice held a chilling edge, an out-of-place tremor. "We've been waiting for you." She wore a tattered robe over wrinkled scrubs, her hair hanging limp and unwashed around her face as if she'd dressed from the dirty laundry. Quite a departure from her usual crisp look. A shiver of unease ran through Leslie.

"What do you mean, 'we'?" She searched Michelle's face for a hint of what she might be hiding. "Are Izzy and Baby J here?"

"Andy. My cat." She dropped her chin to her chest, looking hollow. "Give him." Her eyes bore into Leslie with an accusatory intensity before they flicked away.

"Let us in, Michelle." The tremor in its tiny body didn't dissuade Leslie from thrusting the cat forward. "Andy's cold and hungry."

Michelle inched the door open wider, stepping back. "Of course." Her head snapped to attention, her arms out.

Leslie handed off the cat in an awkward exchange, then stepped inside to face Michelle's impassive expression. Her puffy eyes looked painful—purple, with a taut, shiny surface. She gave the door a swing shut with her foot. The foyer held an unfamiliar burnt odor like melting plastic—a nasty, acrid smell threatening to overpower Leslie's senses.

"Is something burning?" She shoved her hands into her coat pockets on a wave of anxiety.

"It's nothing." Michelle juggled the cat before freeing it to flee for hiding, her response too quick and turbulent. She closed the door tight. After snapping the deadbolt closed, she side-stepped Leslie to plant herself in front of the living room.

The unlit room behind her looked as clean as her typical work attire. Everything was ordered. Uncluttered surfaces. Pillows perfectly arranged. The motif was oddly modern for the home's century-old life.

Scanning the room with a vigilant eye, Leslie searched for any sign of Izzy. An archway floor lamp illuminated the adjacent room, casting light on a wide desk positioned beneath elevated windows. What must have been a former dining room had been converted into a study. A trash can sat before the desk, in front of the chair. Steps to a second story abutted the wall behind her, suggesting the basement stairs were off the kitchen, through a foyer arch to her left.

"I want to talk about last night, Michelle." Her voice carried both urgency and determination. "I asked you to call Izzy last night after the attack—you wrote her number down." She side-stepped further into the house interior, but Michelle moved in kind, blocking her progress. "Did you talk to her?"

Michelle jerked her head around in a sudden move and spun toward the front windows. "I know. I know," she muttered.

A shiver ran down Leslie's spine as she struggled to understand Michelle's action. A reflex propelled her into the living room toward the archway before Michelle recovered. A single-row dresser, with Bryce's bag on top, stood at the room's edge. Folders fanned out of the case. Near the dresser's corner, a phone's edge stuck out from under a file.

"What'd you say?" Michelle regrouped.

Leslie recoiled at the possibility Michelle might be responding to something other than her question. *Was the woman talking to herself?* Sweat prickled on Leslie's upper lip.

"Listen." Michelle slid in front of her again, offering a tiny smile, and gestured to the couch. "Let's sit down. Can I take your coat?"

Leslie twisted out of her coat as her solar plexus sounded an alarm. Izzy and Baby J had to be there. She tucked her phone into her jeans, turning to get a full view of the dining room-turned-study—another ordered room with a bookcase nearly reaching the ceiling between two doorways on the back wall. She scanned every inch, her eyes coming to rest on the desk. A matchbox, tongs, letterhead with a scribble, and a pen rested on top. As she handed Michelle her coat, the cat's lapping sounded from somewhere near the kitchen.

"Why don't we sit over here?" Michelle steered her toward the couch, hanging her coat on a rack by the door. Leslie chose the sofa's edge closest to the front door, scanning the room as a disturbing eeriness settled over her. Michelle took the upright chair near the fireplace on the far wall, giving their seating arrangement a cool distance. The animal's desperate drinking gave way to the faint sound of water dripping.

"Michelle, do you know where Izzy is right now?" She forced herself to speak with a measured tone despite her nerves fraying at the edges. "What's going on? You've answered none of my questions."

Michelle stared blankly, her eyes far away and detached, her shoulders braced, as if listening.

Plink. Plink.

"Did you speak with her last night or this morning?" Her question came quickly, but Leslie willed herself to sit back a few inches.

"Again," Michelle muttered, her voice a ghostly echo. "I can't tell you how many times she's left me. He killed her over and over."

Leslie froze, her heart in her throat, now certain she faced psychosis. Michelle moved in haste to shield herself with her arms against something or someone, her face in profile, a mask of dread.

"I do everything he tells me to do." She winced. "Because he plants ideas in my mind." Her eyes grew damp, the end of her nose already crimson. "My mom's away anyway," she whispered, tipping her chin down. "Andy's been gone so long."

Was the woman drugged? Leslie's mind spun as she sat rigid, her whole body primed to launch at the slightest hint Izzy might be nearby. Michelle was on another channel, mentally gone. But her pupils weren't pinned or blown. Her eyes showed something else—her demeanor fractured, her speech erratic.

Leslie leaned forward and spoke gently. "Michelle, are you saying you do everything Bryce says?"

Michelle's shoulders slumped as she brushed something unseen off her lap, her hands sweeping toward two cups on the table. *Two cups.* Had Izzy been there? Leslie scanned the rug and froze when she spotted a hint of gold.

A single earring hoop.

The room dropped an inch, along with her stomach. Was air rushing out of the house—or blood pumping in her ears? Leslie fought the panic attached to a vision of her jumping forward to madly search for Izzy. She told herself to wait.

What about the gun Lynn said was in Michelle's purse? Where was Michelle's large bag? Glancing back at her, she glimpsed the top of a black phone case in her bathrobe pocket.

She does have two phones. They never found Damon's phone.

"Well." Michelle's eyes shot over to the cat creeping toward her. "It's time we got down to business."

"What business? Michelle, where's Izzy?" Her palms clammy, Leslie balanced on the sofa's edge. "She's here, isn't she? Tell me."

Michelle's face distorted with mercurial menace. She tossed her head as if throwing off water, pulling her shoulders back. "I didn't ask for this, you know." Her voice dropped. "The hammer's coming down. And if I don't toe the line, I'll be next." A glassy absence occupied her eyes. She reached out to grasp something unseen on her right.

The cat crouched a few feet from Michelle's knees.

"How can you trust Bryce when he's tied your clinic to dope dealers?" Leslie gripped her thighs, her legs tensed. "He put everyone in the office at risk, including Damon. So vulnerable. So young, Damon," she whispered, searching Michelle's face. "Did you know Damon fell into drugs?"

There'd be no talking her out of psychosis.

"Stop." Michelle squeezed her eyes shut, wincing in seeming pain, covering her ears. She rocked as if she was terrified.

Leslie sprang forward past the cat into the office, stopping near the back hallway, tugging her phone from her jeans, scanning for a clue to locate Izzy.

"Izzy!" Was she barricaded in a room? Locked in the basement?

The cat screamed as Michelle caught it underfoot on her sudden dash for the foyer. A loud banging, like a storm cellar door dropped shut, made Leslie jump. Heavy breathing to her right. Michelle moved to the kitchen. Leslie woke her phone, tapped a letter into Pearl's text thread, hit send, and jammed it back into her pocket.

There was no time to call 911 or Brad. She had to stop the woman's next move, whatever craziness it might involve before it was too late.

Leslie burst into the kitchen and then froze.

Michelle stood next to the stove, her feet planted wide in a solid stance. Her loopy bathrobe belt hung like a noose from her hip. She tapped a piece of firewood into her palm, her shoulders set, her eyes blazing with madness.

Leslie gulped air as she scanned the room for a weapon. A knife. A pot. Anything. Panic rose inside of her, a wild thing seeking to escape. Across from her, Michelle held the splintered club tightly in her gloved fist, a massive figure blocking any chance of getting away. Her stare—a grim mixture of frenzy and sickening resolve—locked onto Leslie.

She's bolted us in.

"Walk over to the door." Michelle jerked her head toward the basement. "We're going downstairs."

"Where's Izzy, Michelle?" She tightened her mouth against the trembling. "Is she in the basement?"

"She's comfortable." Stepping forward, Michelle slammed the club into her palm. "Move."

Leslie's adrenaline surged. Comfortable? Was she drugged? Knocked out? Leslie sent a silent prayer that Izzy was alive.

Was the club in Michelle's hands used to bludgeon Damon? It had to be. Michelle killed him or was a party to it. Leslie stole a glance at the front door. A pang of hope twisted inside her.

I've got to stall for time—get in her head.

Stepping backward, her hands in seeming surrender, Leslie retreated to Michelle's study, the weight of uncertainty bearing down on her. A loud crack of thunder boomed as the steady thrum of rain lashed the casements above her desk. Her eyes darted to the windows, water streaking them like frantic fingers.

"I said we're going in the basement!" Michelle's figure grew larger as she closed in, looming over Leslie—at least half a foot taller—her bulk a wall not easily breached.

"Izzy!" Leslie screamed, alarm clawing at her insides. She swung the desk chair around to set a barrier, however feeble, between her and Michelle. "Baby J, Baby, come!"

Desperation colored her every word. The only answers were heightened gusts of wind shaking the windows.

Michelle stopped in front of the flimsy barricade, tapping the firewood club into the palm of her hand. She looked at the chair as if it were a toy, the corners of her mouth turning upward.

I'm definitely faster. The police will be here soon. Slow things down.

"How did you talk Izzy into coming here, Michelle?" Leslie fought to keep her voice from shaking. Her darting glances about the room landed on a bookend. Stone. On the sideboard behind Michelle.

"Simple. She knew you'd want your office keys." She lowered her voice, eyes narrowing as she jerked her chin toward the basement door. "You're going the wrong way."

Office keys? Leslie flashed on the sticky mess of blood beneath her from the night before. Yelling Izzy's number as Michelle rifled through her car. The woman didn't just grab a pen. She'd nicked her keys. She'd planned this out.

Leslie took another backward step, her palms clammy enough to leave drops on the floor.

"What'd you do with Izzy? Where's the dog?" Her words rose to a frantic level. She had to keep Michelle talking. *The baby!* Izzy would have fought Michelle. Had she acted otherwise because she was pregnant—because she had to protect the baby growing within her?

"Don't make me use this." Michelle's eyes betrayed a flicker of uncertainty as she raised the club in a threatening arc. Close to imperceptible, the doubt in her movement gave Leslie an opening.

Bumping into the small trash bin, she reflexively seized its edge, snatching a glimpse of its contents. Michelle's miniatures. Had she been burning them? Charred figures, twisted, blackened, the macabre arrangement a mass grave.

She needed to stall. Her breathing had turned into a pant. How did Michelle get Izzy down the stairs? Was she aware Izzy was pregnant? Leslie needed both Michelle and herself to stay upstairs. Trying to attack Michelle physically would be a fool's game.

"You clubbed Damon, and now you want to do the same to me?" A mix of accusation and doubt painted her tone with just the right edge. She had to get into her head. "Why, Michelle? Let's talk this out. We can sit back down in the living room."

The suggestion of rationality did it. Michelle glared at her, a crazed, sickened look. The color had drained from her face. Tremors quivered down her arm. "You're the reason for all this—everything spiraling out of control." Her words tumbled out in a scattershot of fury. "If you hadn't been such a snoop—" Her voice trailed off, collapsing like a wave against a rock.

"You don't believe that." Leslie took a step forward. "And neither do I."

A faint trembling took hold of Michelle's chin, her face bearing vulnerability and rage. She blinked rapidly, fighting tears, as her nostrils flared with each sharp breath.

"If you keep what you did to Damon concealed, Michelle, it'll rot."

The club in the nurse's hand drifted down. Maybe she had dropped her guard.

"You need to say what happened to Damon." Leslie raised her hands in surrender. "Tell me."

Michelle blinked several times. A tear spilled over her cheek. The hard border of her mouth softened by a fraction.

"We both know I didn't kill Damon." Words wrapped in a practiced calm, Leslie's voice belied her racing heart.

Michelle kept silent, her arm outstretched with the weapon at shoulder height. Leslie stole a peek at the contents of her bookshelf. She'd packed the shelves with small dramas, living fragments, and manufactured scenes. A little girl ice skating. A boy and a man fishing. In Michelle's hesitation, Leslie darted a glance at the paper on her desk. A single written line: *I'm done.*

Time froze for a fractured second. The gears in Leslie's mind calculated the scene.

"He got what he deserved." Michelle's voice dropped to a dangerous quiet. "And so will you all." Her words struck Leslie with a brutal, final clarity.

The charred miniatures. Michelle's appearance. Her mental state. The letter. The trash. It all amounted to something she should have understood sooner. Leslie's heart pounded with a forcefulness that rocked her to her toes. She grasped the truth. She'd walked into a suicide scene.

Or was this a planned murder-suicide?

Thirty-Six

Saturday, October 26th—One moment later

"We both know I didn't kill Damon," Leslie said.

The words pierced Michelle's chest like an arrow, stealing her breath. How dare she? Memory flooded back—Damon's final moments when Michelle alone had witnessed his death—pale, unkempt, rail thin—the image of a pathetic drug user. The same man who, hours before that night, arrived on her porch just minutes before the thug—the one known now as Finn Connor—climbed her porch steps, too. The thug, the scar-faced goon, had it out for Damon. She could detect a low-life drug dealer in a crowd with ease. They were dead ringers for her father's companions.

"You saw Damon the night he died, didn't you?" Leslie leaned forward, her expression deadpan. "The day before, you said you'd bring him *the material*. Was it Bryce's order? What material?"

Michelle's mind flashed on the image of the horrid man's back as he walked away, warning Damon, *You're dead meat, man, if you don't do as you're told.* The same knife-slashing demon from yesterday in the parking garage. Yes, she'd gotten a good look.

Why not tell her? Bryce would want me to. The two of us will be gone soon enough.

"Damon showed up here. He wanted the cash." Michelle wiped the cold sweat off her neck, repositioning her club. "I said I'd bring the money to his house later that night. I wasn't about to give him a bucket of dough right then—he was a mess. Bryce wouldn't have wanted it."

Another memory grabbed her: Michelle creeping through Damon's neighborhood the night he died. Her car deliberately parked blocks away, next to a funeral home. The sign next to the driveway read, 'Exit Only' beneath the company name, planted in a perfectly green lawn. The cynical irony had stayed with her since. She wondered—who would make those arrangements when her time came?

It wasn't a nightmare. It had been real.

Her pulse pounded at a dizzying rate, filling her head with its urgent noise. Were these just words in her mind, or were they tumbling from her lips? Was she actually talking?

"And?" Leslie's voice stretched time itself.

"Damon was getting scary in the days before then. I was afraid of him when he got loaded... terrified." She raised her bathrobe sleeve on the arm holding the club, drawn to a red-dened, burned, itchy area below her elbow. She scraped the surface vigorously. "He was acting just like my father, who beat the living crap out of us. Especially my mother." Her craving to scratch was irresistible. "He killed her, you know."

Why is there no pain? No relief?

The room before her, including Leslie's figure, shifted into grayscale. Nothing had its proper color. A flat, two-dimensional scene spread out before her.

Maybe this is the nightmare.

Leslie's mouth moved at a turtle's pace, like she wasn't real, like nothing in the room was solid. "Michelle—what happened to Damon?"

The question took forever to form in Michelle's mind. She peered at her hands, dropping them lower, the club growing out of her gloved hand.

"I picked this piece of firewood by the house. The tapered end made it a perfect club." She let the last word hang, looking for any shift in her opponent.

On the floor, behind Leslie's foot, her purse strap lay inches away. The bag was her last lifeline. She *would* get this bitch to move. Because her final exit was in the bag, after she finished the letter. Her parting gift. Her brilliant revenge. Her last words.

"And—?"

The bizarre, squeaking noise returned to Michelle's head—she braced for what always came next. A predictable loop: the queer mental click, the sign of Bryce's intention, his directive, to come. *Take this bitch out. Which one—the bitch right in front of me? Get her whole family. Damn. She's the one. The one who's ruined everything.*

Michelle refocused on Leslie, swallowing. She had to think straight and finish the jobs at hand.

"You can't trust anyone—I know it. But when I met Bryce, it was different. I believed he wouldn't lead me wrong." Her arms and shoulders were drawn wire-tight. "Bryce tied me to Damon, then made me responsible for dealing with him. He considered Damon a liability—a no-show to work. Come on."

Her hand balled into a fist. Sweat dripping at her temple, Michelle shivered at the mention of her employer. Her ball-and-chain. Nausea rose and she raised the club again to examine its contours.

"Tell me about Damon." Leslie's words echoed inside Michelle's head as if bouncing off empty walls—her voice settled into a deadly calm. "When he opened his home to greet you that night."

The woman in front of her—Leslie—who'd lost all color and depth, stared her down. *The bitch.* She'd have to play her body beside the blonde's. Then the dog. "He was tossed. His drugs were all laid out in plain sight."

Her head swayed. This *was* an epic nightmare.

A loud whooshing noise took over, like an arrow whizzing by her ears, landing with a thump. Freeze-frame. Dragging the blonde's dead weight down the hall. Sliding on a tarp.

She blinked, disoriented. *Was it real?*

Whoosh—whiz—thud. Again. Stop-motion. Izzy's wavy blond hair, blue eyes, the smile as she reached for her cup. Filled with drugs.

Bryce materialized before her, laughing as he taunted, *You're next. You're nothing.*

Whoosh—whiz—thud. Motionless scene. The stripped-down body, kneeling in his tub, face in the faucet. No breath. No life.

"Michelle."

Was she screaming? Her mouth opened wide, though no sound left. No breath to make noise.

"What was Damon saying?"

Michelle grabbed her forehead, yanking the memory free. Was it banishable—once and for all?

"*I'm sorry, I'm sorry. I didn't mean to.* All those lame apologies after beating the crap out of us. Just like my father. He'll never do it again. He'll change." Michelle's voice wavered with a moan rising from the deepest part of her throat. "Mmnnhh. One excuse after the next, just like...evil man. The pathetic addict, wretched child abuser."

Infused with a sudden clarity, she stood straighter before Leslie, gripping the chair.

"I took this club and whacked him in the head." Fanatically staring at her outstretched hand, she clutched the instrument of her salvation. "Knocked him out cold."

The blunt force had reverberated into her shoulder as she caught him unaware, his face spinning. He slumped on the couch, unmoving. Unconscious.

"The surrender of a beaten man." Her resolve was clear. "I wanted to lay him flat for decades."

The freedom of it. A domino fell as the memory loosened, fresh and alive.

The mental click, again.

You know what you must do.

THIRTY-SEVEN

Saturday, October 26th—Moments later

"I wanted to lay him flat for decades," Michelle said.

Leslie gulped, trying to swallow more air than her throat would allow. She had to keep her wits about her, her only weapon against this lunatic. Michelle's sweat-slick skin, bleary eyes, and pasty color had intensified as she described assaulting Damon.

As she revealed each detail, her pitch rose, her voice more frantic. Leslie winced, thinking how long it had been since she'd signaled for help. Was she in this alone? She needed more time. "Why don't you... why don't you set the club on the sideboard, Michelle?" Each calming, smooth syllable contradicted her inner flood of terror.

Oh God, let them be okay.

"Right. Nice try." Michelle gripped the sharp, heavy log until her knuckles whitened with a deranged grin. "To the basement, you."

The hall clock ticked, and the wind rattled. The club was marked with a dark spot.

"But you've brought me this far. What would it take to tell the rest?" Standing beside the desk chair, Leslie rolled it a few inches, her chest pounding, keeping her eyes on the blood-stained wood. "There's no hurry, right? You locked the doors."

"Wait a minute." Michelle moved the club to her other hand, swinging it in a madcap zigzag at something beside her as a burst of rain pelted the windows above her desk.

She aimed at nothing visible. Betting on immobility as her only defense, Leslie held herself still, scarcely breathing. "How did you get Damon into the tub?"

"I carry Naloxone in my bag, for God's sake. The nasal spray." A wildness gripped her face—a terrifying abandon, recklessness sapping all hope from the room. "He had to go. That's what Bryce wanted." Her eyes lit like a zealot on fire. She slammed the wood into her palm with a meaty, resonant thud.

"You planned to need an opiate reversal?"

Michelle laughed, an unhinged zeal as sharp as glass. "I always have it. We work with drug addicts, after all." She shifted her weight, thrusting her hip to one side, looking down near the desk. "I'm ready for anything."

Leslie pressed again, stretching her words thin. "But... how did you get Damon into the tub?"

Michelle jutted her hip out further. "I used his gear. Cooked the heroin from his stash while he was out of it. Seen it done a million times with both my parents. I loaded it heavy. Nearly every bit he had." Stepping toward the lamp, she looked again at the floor in front of the desk.

Stay face-on with her. Don't turn. A clammy coldness washed into Leslie's hands.

"I sprayed the Naloxone into his nose once I was ready—less than a dose. He was still knocked out. I had everything I need-ed in the bathroom." Sweat dripped down Michelle's temple.

"Used his kitchen rubber gloves—found 'em when I went for a spoon." She stepped back. "I roused him. Right fast. He deserved to walk the plank. To the tub."

Leslie whispered, stunned, "You flipped him into withdrawal?" She imagined Damon retching over and over. "Why didn't he run?"

"My loaded gun. At his head." She smirked.

The gun—where's her big bag? As Leslie's eyes darted to the sideboard, the window, her heart sank. "You sat there and let him jones?" How Damon had suffered.

"We both know thirty minutes and naloxone wears off. Just enough time to see him squirm. Beg. Plead for mercy." She snorted with disdain. "The bastard. Deserved every bit. An eye for an eye." Leslie drew back as the woman unleashed a guttural yell, her face turning crimson. "He tortured us! My mom died. My brother vanished. He sent everyone away from me."

A single moan escaped Michelle as she clamped her mouth shut. Leslie pulled herself back without moving. *So psychotic—more time, more time.* The police had to be nearly there. "How did Damon die?"

Michelle's eyes darted to the floor near the desk, her hair a wild mess. That was the third time.

"I walked him into the bathroom." The terrible command in her voice. The lurid gleam in her eyes. "Before long, in his miserable withdrawal, he did what I said." Her words spilled out with saliva and spit. "Stripped down to his shorts. Got in the tub. Faced the faucet. On his knees." She closed her eyes tight, then opened them wide. "I sprayed the shower down to stop his whining. Then I gave him a choice."

The room took a subtle spin as Leslie tried to maintain calm. "A choice?"

Michelle's eyes darted to the side again. Leslie stiffened, ready to run.

"A bullet to the head. Or the needle in his arm." Dislodged and disconnected, she spoke as if numb to the contents of her words. "He made the choice in a snap. Shoved the needle in and shot himself up."

Leslie's gut clenched as if she'd taken a round. The horrid cruelty. The heinous craziness.

Her hand gripped the chair for balance. She stepped back against the desk, flattening something. She dropped her chin.

Michelle's bag.

Her eyes bulged and her pasty face was shiny with sweat. Michelle locked in on Leslie's foot. Not eight feet away.

The purse. The gun. Leslie bent to grab the bag, lifting her eyes just in time to spot the club closing in on her head. She rolled to her side. The log whirred past her, landing with a whack of wood on wood.

She jumped to her feet, out of breath. The bludgeon tip caught on the desk.

"You—!" Michelle screamed as she snarled and twisted back toward Leslie, her free arm reaching for the bag.

Inhaling deeply, Leslie launched herself with both legs, pushing with all her strength into Michelle's side, slamming the woman sideways, hoping to catch her off balance. She knocked Michelle away from the bag and onto the floor, still clutching the club. Landing on all fours, Leslie felt her strained knee throb as she hit the floor just two feet away. Each of them sucked air and glared in disbelief at the other.

Righting herself to rest on three points, her bad leg stretched behind, Leslie located Michelle's outstretched weapon. Scrambling to reach the purse, she clutched the strap and dragged it to the edge of the desk. Leslie pulled herself back to sit on one heel, eyeing the prize.

"Oh, no." Michelle gave a throaty warning, rising to her knees as she swung the club behind, then overhead. Leslie yanked on the purse, letting loose in time to rise to a squat. She leaned away. The thwack of firewood into the purse loosened Michelle's grip on the club. But with no chance of shifting her weight in a lunge for the wood or the gun, Leslie rushed to her feet, leaving the bag within Michelle's reach.

The back hallway to the right, the kitchen entry straight ahead, and the stove just past it. Leslie weighed doubling back and charging at Michelle again, but no—taking Michelle on physically was too risky. Her entire family depended on her staying alive. Michelle rifled through the bag for the gun.

Leslie limped into the kitchen, turned around the fridge, passed the pantry, and froze at the foyer closet. Panting, catching her breath, she listened for the next direction Michelle would take. She had to stay in the house, find Izzy, and somehow overpower Michelle.

Surprise her?

Was it her imagination, or did Leslie hear sirens in the background? *Please be close... Please. Be. Close.* She jerked her head to the right and left, scanning for Michelle's location. "Frickin' dammit." Her howling built to a shriek, the sound bouncing off hard surfaces. "You're coming with me."

She had to be in the kitchen. *The floor plan—a big circle.*

A loud shatter. Glass breaking. Sirens getting closer.

Michelle let loose a wild, infuriated yowl as she ran out of the pantry with crazed drive and angled straight toward her target.

Leslie hobbled around the foyer corner, her heart hammering, into the living room past the small chest, hurtling into the study. Without losing a beat, she painfully entered the back hall and ducked into a bathroom across the wall. She left the door partly open with an ear to the gap and scrambled for choices. She could lock the door or exit through the window behind her. But Michelle had the gun, and the police were moments away.

Michelle's panting filled the space between them. Close by—in the study. Leslie treaded softly out of the bathroom. She pinned her shoulder blades to the hallway wall—inching slowly, silently—toward the study, toward Michelle's heavy breathing. Drawing close, she craned her head around for a glimpse past the threshold. Here was her chance. Michelle was gasping for breath, the gun outstretched, pointing away—toward the kitchen.

She thinks I'm in there. No club.

Pounding at the front door brought Michelle's whole body around toward the noise.

"Police! Open up."

Michelle shifted toward the desk on her left just as Leslie stepped out next to the bookcase. *It's shallow!* Not ten inches deep, the tall piece wasn't fixed to the wall. She shoved her hands behind the seven-foot, miniature-packed unit and pulled it away from the wall, down onto Michelle's back. The bookcase fell before she could react. A wild grunt escaped as Michelle spun beneath the falling piece. The gun jerked in her hand and discharged into the window above the desk. As glass splintered and flew through the air, the pistol shot from her hand, skipped across the floor, and came to rest at the archway.

The beating at the front door grew into a loud crash as the police broke it down and poured into the house, weapons drawn, shouting commands. Michelle shrieked as Leslie dragged herself onto the bookshelf, pinning Michelle underneath.

"We're in here!" She bellowed the words again, her arms stretched to the ceiling.

Leslie winced with chest pain from her injury the night before. She slid down the bookcase as the last of the police arrived. A wedge of daylight broke through the broken door, illuminating swirling dust motes as Leslie steadied her breathing. At last, she'd have the chance to find Izzy and Baby J.

"Stand with your hands up." Det. Levy aimed her weapon. "Up." Crouched, the detective moved closer.

"Don't shoot. It's me." Leslie's voice cracked as she moved off the bookcase and stood, lightheaded. Michelle moaned as she struggled to remove the bookcase and sit upright on the floor.

"My wife Izzy is here in the house somewhere." Leslie fought panic as she pleaded, glancing at the officers who swarmed the room. "And our dog. I've got to find them."

"Stay put. You can bring your arms down." Aaron Davis stood behind Levy.

Leslie lowered her arms, her entire body trembling. She stepped on jelly legs and motioned to the hallway behind her. "Can you check the back of the house? Her car has to be in the garage."

Davis approached with quick strides. "Are you okay? Do you need medical care?" His tone softened.

"I don't think so. But not that she didn't try." Leslie jerked her head toward Michelle, who was moaning on the floor. "There's a big piece of firewood somewhere—maybe in the kitchen. She said she knocked Damon out with it before she killed him."

Davis's brows raised. "She confessed?"

Leslie nodded. "Izzy is here. We've got to find Izzy."

Aaron Davis motioned for Levy to climb the second-floor steps. Three other uniformed officers had entered with weapons drawn.

"There's a gun by the floor lamp," Leslie mumbled as she pointed to her right. She took a deep breath and spoke more forcefully. "I believe that's Damon's phone on top of the chest."

Davis directed two deputies to pull Michelle free. She lay face down on the floor with her hands covering her ears. Detective Levy yelled, "Clear!" from the second floor. At Davis's direction, the third officer went for the gun and phone, sealing them in evidence bags. The officer yelled, "Got 'em."

"Cuff her. Read her rights." Davis gestured to the two officers with Michelle. As Levy ran down the stairs, Davis shouted, "Clear the basement! Through the kitchen." He turned to Leslie. "Stay right here."

Her knees weak, body drained, Leslie leaned down and grabbed her thighs. Her stitches throbbed. She closed her eyes briefly, swallowing hard, and sniffed back tears. Davis swept through the bathroom, gun in hand, into a room behind it, then into another room across the hall. *Three rooms off the back hall.* Every nerve in her body screamed not to stand still. When Davis didn't come out, Leslie wasn't staying right anywhere. She hobbled ahead of an officer heading after Davis.

Another loud "Clear!" sounded.

On the floor, at the foot of a bed, Davis kneeled beside Izzy, unbinding her wrists.

"Izzy! Oh my God!" Leslie rushed in and dropped to her knees on the other side. "Oh, hon." She laid her hands on either side of Izzy's face and peered into her eyes. "You have no idea how much I've prayed for this moment." Leslie's tears welled and spilled over. "There wasn't a sound coming from back here!" Waves of fear and relief crashed into her heart. She wiped her tears with the back of a trembling hand, on the edge of laughter with a flood of gratitude.

Her mouth taped shut, Izzy's eyes screamed for help, the skin paling around her mouth where the tape stretched tight.

"I've been so scared that I lost you." She kissed Izzy on the forehead, her lip lingering as Izzy's choked, muffled sobs diminished. "I love you so much."

Davis peeled the tape away, unleashing her now unmuffled cry into the air.

"Are you injured?" He took Izzy's head in his hands.

"Jeezus." Izzy tried to pull away from him and into Leslie's arms. She rubbed her irritated wrists, caught her breath, and trembled visibly.

"Can you tell us what happened?" Leslie's words landed with the force of someone who'd spent hours in pursuit. "What did Michelle do to you?"

If Leslie had only had the chance, she would have pitched the stone bookend into Michelle's skull, though her brain was surely broken in another way.

"I—I'm not sure. One minute I'm drinking a cappuccino and the next thing—something's crashing out there." She rubbed her mouth as tears welled in her eyes. Leslie held her, a brace against her trembling. "The crazed woman drugged me."

"Detective, my wife's pregnant." Leslie pivoted slowly to look at Davis, then the officer standing at the doorway. "We need emergency medical services to check her out." Leslie bent low, bracing her injured knee, and wrapped Izzy in her arms, her breaths more hurried than before. "Izzy, have you had any cramping? Nausea?"

Izzy shook her head, the tears falling down her pale cheeks.

They swayed back and forth, their reunion flowing in tears and sighs.

Izzy gasped between sobs, holding her belly. "I don't think so."

Davis stepped back, nodding at the officer. "Have we called the EMTs for the nurse?"

"Yes, sir."

"Get an ambulance here for Ms. Turner."

The officer nodded and left.

Leslie held her tighter. "You scared the life out of me." She leaned away, holding Izzy's shoulders. "How did she ever get you to come over here?"

Izzy coughed, then caught her breath. "She called me. Said she found your office keys after they took you to the hospital last night. I was coming by Overlook for a last-minute deal on the pumpkin delivery." She exhaled with a sigh. "How would I have possibly known?"

Leslie shook her head, turning to Davis. "Michelle took the keys out of my bag last night." She shrugged. "How did she anticipate this?"

"She just said she knew you'd want your keys before returning to work. Last night, you said you'd go into the office on Monday to get some stuff. And you needed to sleep, so I—" Izzy searched her eyes. "I wrote you a note. Didn't you see it on the bed?"

"No, I..." Leslie stammered, the night's chaos flashing through her mind. "Oh, shit! I pushed all the blankets and covers off the bed." She closed her eyes, envisioning the tangled heap she'd dumped on the floor.

Izzy sat straighter, the edge of panic in her voice. "The dog! Baby J's in the car!"

They both looked at Detective Davis. "Levy!" he shouted. "Check the garage."

Levy stuck her head in the room. "Yes, sir."

Davis turned back to Izzy. "Can you answer some questions after getting checked out at the hospital?"

"Really, I think I'm okay. Sure."

"Let's help you off the floor." Leslie stood, helping Izzy sit on the bed. "How did she drug you?"

"She just invited me in and offered me coffee—said she would make espresso, decaf, or whatever. I waited on the sofa while she went to the kitchen. Couldn't turn it down. I ran out of the house after I saw the pumpkin delivery canceled." Her voice was gaining strength. "I had to set something fast for the garden store, so I arranged to meet a supplier on Highway 30." Leslie squeezed her hand.

"Okay," Davis said, looking at the officer who'd returned. "Search every inch of the kitchen. Look for evidence of drugs, medications, the wood or club... and anything else." The officer nodded and left. Izzy reached to hold Leslie's shoulders.

Detective Levy popped her head into the room again. "The dog's okay. She was in the garage, inside the car. I'll bring her to the front."

Leslie helped her wife to the edge of the bed. "Careful."

Izzy stood gingerly, pausing a moment before they moved. "I think I'm okay." They took a few tentative steps toward the door. Izzy paused, looking a little uncertain, then nodded at Leslie to keep going.

"You should get checked out medically just to be sure. Maybe you should lie down and wait for the ambulance..."

"No, I can walk." Izzy covered her lower belly with her hands. "I want to see the dog. My stomach seems fine."

Michelle's home lay in shambles—the office window shattered, the bookcase toppled, the floor littered with glass, figurines, miniatures, the front door broken open. Leslie found her raincoat on the coat rack in the living room and draped it around Izzy's shoulders. The police officers were stretching crime scene tape around the area as they stepped outside with Davis. Leslie gripped Izzy's hand. They paused on the porch. The storm had dissipated.

Emergency medical technicians were gathered around Michelle, who was strapped to a gurney in front of an ambulance. Two more police cruisers approached the crowd of cars and officers surrounding the place. Neighbors gawked from behind the cordoned-off area, their eyes wide with shock and speculation. They stood under umbrellas and raincoat hoods, whispering to each other. The torrential rain had settled into a light drizzle.

"Let's sit here and wait for the other ambulance." Leslie helped Izzy sit on the top porch step, under the roof eave, and followed her gingerly.

Brad's car flashed blinking headlights at the end of the line before the doors flew open. Brad, Kathy, and Pearl jogged toward them. As they closed in on the house, Pearl slowed to a walk, allowing the family to go ahead, her hand over her heart. Detective Levy arrived at the front corner of the house with Baby J on a leash. Leslie and Izzy stood to greet the dog, her tail flying wildly as she rushed to meet them.

Kathy, Brad, Izzy, and Leslie—the nexus of their tight little family—arms around each other, laughed and cried as they held on to each other, the dog jumping in the middle. Izzy held her belly, then her arms flew out to grab Leslie. Brad wrapped one arm around his daughter and one around his wife, a wide smile on his face. Leslie wrestled an arm free and motioned for Pearl to join. The dog turned in circles inside their rough knot.

Another siren sounded in the background.

"Here's my in-case partner." Leslie wrapped her arm around Pearl.

"Oh Lordy, did we do right?" Tears glistened in Pearl's eyes as she joined in the hugs.

A second ambulance parked beside the first. EMTs emerged and began walking toward the house while rolling another gurney.

Brad threw his hand out to Aaron Davis, who stood behind Izzy. They met in a handshake. "Thank you, man."

"With your help." Aaron nodded.

Leslie asked, "What about Bryce and Sloan?"

"They're both in custody." Davis smiled. "Along with one of the dope pushers."

"Is it really over?" Kathy looked anxiously at the emergency medical technicians who'd arrived with their cart.

"After one more trip to the emergency room, I think." Leslie reached for Izzy's hand and gave it a light squeeze. "We need to be sure about the baby and you."

"I think we'll be okay, Mom." Izzy smiled and squeezed back.

Thirty-Eight

Sloan raised his gaze away from the lawyer's face, shifting to cross his legs in the cramped PPB Central Precinct room. He cursed the damned interruption. Detective Levy and Officer Faraday had shut his interview down within minutes. Levy added she'd be back, but he never expected it to take hours. Now it neared five. At least they'd shuffled him and his attorney off to a conference closet after Randy wisely asked for privacy with his client. But maybe this break was a good thing. In a rush to escape the street before some crazed drug lord's hitman found him, Sloan had only given Randy a sketch of his trouble. Finn Connor was in jail, but Rafi might come after him.

"How'd you ever get started with this, Sloan?"

Randy had already gone through his lawyerly warnings. Make sure Sloan didn't tell him any lies. Better to not know something than to base a defense on a crumbling foundation. Striking a cooperation agreement with the DA's office was tricky business. He'd have to be ready to expose every misdeed in his life.

"So, Bryce came to me with this lame-brain idea when we were both caught between impossible choices. Really, there's no excuse for me, except I was in hock so bad with my gambling avocation, close to foreclosure on my condo. One day, Bryce asked me to sign some witness document verifying he'd followed DEA guidelines on the proper disposal of a patient's narcotics. Of course, he hadn't. I guess a patient didn't tolerate the stuff and just left the med vial on his desk, refusing to take it. He showed me a second client's prescription for the same thing—buprenorphine, combined with another medicine, for opioid addiction. The guy walked out of his appointment, leaving his pill bottle in the chair. Dropped out of his pocket, I assume. Bryce kept it."

The lawyer's face was unmoved.

"Long and short, he held onto the drugs and researched how much they sold for on the street. Said we should use the stuff to make some extra money. He was hurting big-time right then. I'd never seen him so desperate. His son had lost medical insurance for his family because his little boy had muscular dystrophy. They fell between the cracks, I guess—private health coverage, the public sector. You know."

Randy nodded slightly.

"We'd been on the edge with a few things before then, but never over the line."

"How long have you been working with Dr. Nelson?"

"Oh, brother." Sloan scooted around to face Randy directly, straightening his spine. "We met eons ago, in our twenties. He was a resident in training, about to get kicked out. Bryce's always been a prime jerk, but he was a hot asshole back then. I was finishing my PhD and made some stupid moves, trying to get laid. He wasn't into it, but something drew us together." He held out his palms and shrugged. "Past life, maybe. We went our separate ways for a while after graduation, but he contacted me again. We've been practicing jointly ever since."

"Decades, then."

"Yeah, time flies." Sloan rubbed his bald head. "The dude is such a butt-wipe. He'd threaten me every now and again about outing me, for God's sake. So nineties—early nineties. Over time, we gathered dirt on each other, which wove us together even more. But basically, he needed me to be his psychologist … his coach. To teach him how to hide his hubris, his narcissism, as much as possible. I enjoyed the lucrative practice opportunities he offered, like those referrals from lawyers and licensing agencies for independent exams.

"Okay."

"Things were moving along all right until Bryce got his opioid dispensing license and the Suboxone clinic going. Led us to … well, let's just say, meeting some interesting characters."

"Are you getting to the trouble you're in?"

Sloan swallowed. This would be the tricky part. Although he'd known Randy in a twelve-step program years before, working with him as an attorney was another matter.

"Yeah. So, through some of my contacts in the sports betting world, Bryce and I got to know these two thugs, Rafi and Finn. It was the beginning of the end."

"Go on."

"I just learned Finn's already in jail here—which led me to call you. Because Finn's tied to this total sleazeball, Rafael de Leon. Son of a drug kingpin. We met 'em at Mary's Club about three years ago, around the time Damon Grady came to work for our practice." Sloan paused. "The dead guy, Grady."

"Are you implying Grady's death ties to these two men?"

"Well, I don't know who killed Grady, except it wasn't me. But if there's a killer in the circle somewhere, I'd put my money on those two drug guys and their lackeys. Ruthless scum. I guess they've got a new one. Armie's his name. I've never met him, but—"

Sloan's leg was bouncing at a quick, lively tempo. If there'd been something to drink at the station, he would've pounded it.

"Let's get around to the drugs and these...uh, individuals."

"Okay, yeah. Bryce and I concocted a scheme for milking the value out of the buprenorphine using the drug dudes. Their aim, of course, was to unload it on the street for getting high or treating opiate withdrawal. Our job was to get the phar-maceutical-grade product to them straight from the drugstore. Well—with multiple intermediaries. The pharmacies never had a clue, by the way." He heaved a sigh. "And the sample bupe tablets came in handy."

"Okay, lay it out. The actual mechanics."

"So, Finn, the local dealer, recruited a bunch of his addict-ed customers to be patsies in our operation. He twists their arms. Says they won't get their fix, their supply, unless they run this scam with us. And he offers a bargain deal on their dope for cooperating. They come in as fake patients, carrying sham IDs, and everyone is paying cash in our office, so there is no insurance trail. They're fitted with the money needed to pay for appointments, along with the intake forms, et cetera. Damon's job—well, it was. He got the envelopes with cash to the fakes right before their appointments. Sealed, of course. The junkies were under threat of major facial rearrangement if they tampered with the money. The cash came from the bupe sales Bryce and I made to the dope dealers."

"I'm getting it." Randy massaged his temple.

"Yeah, at first, we used the samples to raise some capital to feed the dupes. It's what we call the fake patients. You know, duped by the dealer to be pawns. The whole thing built on itself, and we basically laundered the drug money through the practice to wash it. Not all of it, of course. Plenty went into offshore accounts. There's another discussion, but you get the gist."

"Except the pharmaceutical-grade part."

"Oh, right. So, this is how it went down. Bryce writes the Suboxone or pure bupe prescription. The dupe takes it to the pharmacy to fill. Again, always cash, circled dope money, arranged by Damon. Then the dupes come back in to drop off the filled medication—my job. Just a quick 'add-in' visit to get the drugs to us. I gave the pills to Bryce. He'd meet with Rafi and exchange the drugs for currency. The whole deal was pretty smooth. Damon was also our in-house computer expert. He took care of the medical records on the dupes: fake tox screens, pregnancy tests sometimes—all forged. He engineered hacking into the software company's cloud-based record system—our practice management software."

"Well, what happened?"

Sloan sighed again. "It started with the last billing manager, Patrick. See, the other people in the office—the receptionist, the billing person, the other psychiatrist—they didn't know a thing about our little 'dupes for bupe' operation. But Patrick demanded this new scheduling software to handle all the 'add-in' appointments for the sake of bookkeeping." He shook his head. "No way Bryce was letting the software company go since Damon hacked our way in to move data around as we needed. But the other psychiatrist, Leslie Schoen, started snooping into our billing. She's not in Psych Recovery—just has an overhead share agreement with us to manage her solo gig. Somehow, Bryce told Rafi that Leslie's intrusions were a problem. Then Rafi was determined to eliminate her. I think it's what landed Finn in the can, but I don't know the details."

The message, *You stupid prick*, translated through Randy's stare.

"Anybody else involved in this scheme?"

"Our nurse, Michelle Wichim, became more involved this last year. She didn't learn much of the details until then. As our number of dupes grew, we needed more help. She was going to run a program with pregnant women getting a pure form of the drug, but it never really got off the ground. I don't think she ever dealt with or even saw Rafi or Finn. At least Bryce told me he'd shielded her from them."

Nodding, the lawyer shoved his chair back.

"Okay. We have a lot of work to do."

Detective Davis changed course as he walked down the hall at the PPB Central Precinct. A few minutes before his six o'clock meeting with Julie Faraday, he closed the interview room door and stepped into an observation space for a solitary break—a chance to catch his breath. The interviews and bookings were bound to go into the morning. Getting back with Leslie and Izzy when they were available after the hospital would take a couple of hours. A summary meeting with his sergeant would precede contact with the DA's office.

What an avalanche of a case break on a single Saturday. He'd be lucky to get some sleep anytime soon. Three arrests in one day, within two weeks of the murder. Now some sorting was in order. Based on Levy's news about Mannon and his lawyer, Davis expected their request for a cooperation agreement would help them hook the bigger fish: Rafael de Leon.

Their homicide case was about to mushroom into a large-scale search for the drug lord. He believed they had a strong case with the nurse's confession to Dr. Schoen, Grady's phone found in her possession, and the odd club, which he was willing to bet was stained with Grady's blood. The scumbag already in the tank, Finn Connor, would face more legal proceedings. Speaking of scumbags, there was the supposed addictions expert.

Bryce Nelson's hypocrisy and recklessness sickened Davis. Supposedly a professional, the man privy to the private lives of others was a complete disgrace. The dirtbag should cool his heels in a jail cell. He'd get to him last. His sidekicks, the psychologist Mannon and the crazy nurse, weren't far behind. Relieved he'd be handing them over to the next phase of justice soon, Davis was certain they'd solved the murder of Damon Grady. Except for his having to finish the interviews, talk with the DA, the ME, and testify in court, he was at his finish line. None of the rest—charges, prosecutorial agreements, trials—were his thing. The simple, or not so simple, matter of seeking truth and nabbing the collars was enough for him. But the list of probable offenses, beyond murder and attempted murder, for this crew? Health care fraud. Conspiracy to distribute controlled substances. The state's medical, psychological, and nursing boards were in for a load of fun. Adios, professional licenses. The list went on: conspiracy to falsify healthcare records, unlawfully distributing controlled substances and the financial crimes. Kidnapping.

Their little investigative team was bound to grow. They'd be cracking into the healthcare files, searching out the phony 'patients' used in the diversion scheme. He'd need to thank those who helped his team: Leslie Schoen, his former partner Brad, and the billing lady, Pearl. This job never ceased to amaze. The next challenge he faced was another interview. He'd have to grapple with the disturbed RN, who was now under medical watch in jail. Fortunately, she'd suffered no major physical injuries, but her mental state was a major hiccup.

A brief rap at the door preceded Faraday arriving for their meeting.

"I know you've been busy with Mannon and Nelson," Davis began as the investigator walked in. "But would you help Levy start with Michelle Wichim before I join? She'll be over here soon. I need a chat with her first."

"Sure." Faraday turned around again. "Look for a text around ten if we don't talk before. I'll see if Alex can update us on the forensic findings. Probably a video call."

"Good. I'm connecting with the ME's office on the blunt weapon."

Davis nodded and headed for the door. Once in the hallway, the precinct came alive: electronic locks and keypads snapped and beeped their electronic language, officers' voices bounced off sterile walls, and shoes squeaked against the linoleum with each hurried step. The scent of a fresh pot of coffee led him into the break room.

Levy sat with a steaming cup at the kitchen table. Maybe it was the room's lights or the late hour, but the dark shadows under her eyes gave Davis the first hint of her case fatigue.

"Hey, boss." She managed a weak smile.

"So, you've got Mannon tucked away for now?"

She bobbed her head. "Yeah. He's all prepared for your next steps."

Here was the messy part. The nurse would need a behavioral health evaluation based on reports about her behavior from the EMTs and Dr. Schoen. This whole case would likely move in the direction of the affirmative defense, where the public defender has the burden of proof, that is, if they formally plead Guilty Except for Insanity.

"There's plenty to update you on. But I'd like to get Michelle Wichim interviewed first."

Levy nodded.

"Look, Levy, I need to clear the air on something."

She raised her head. "Yeah?"

"We need some time to get to know each other. I respected Brad Turner when I started as his partner because he had experience. I expect the same from you. Respect. I'm the boss. I call the shots. I'm listening to your ideas and your read on things. Why not start asking some smart questions? Start seeking to learn."

She pressed her mouth tight before saying, "Heard," then sighed. "So, this nurse has a case for insanity, right?"

"We'll let the behavioral health people figure it out. We stay in our lane. Let the public defender choose their angle. In the meantime, we've got a lot more work to do."

In his years at the Bureau, Davis understood the treacherous depths of insanity pleas and the Oregon State Hospital. Michelle Wichim would likely never get out if the outcome was Guilty Except for Insanity. But then, if she were found a murderer, maybe she should be permanently put away. The question was—if confined forever—where? And if she were placed in corrections instead, would she have the chance for parole at some ripe old age? Probably more of a chance there than if she landed in the psychiatric setting. The wheels of justice take some hard turns at times. But better minds than his would bear those responsibilities.

Levy stood and emptied her cup in the sink. "Let's go, boss. I'm following your lead."

Thirty-Nine

A few days later—

"Okay, thanks. Bye." Leslie ended her phone call, grinning at Izzy across the couch. Her lawyer had been working to bring the board investigation to a conclusion. Though the agency had canceled her Monday interview, it took longer for the system to address Bryce's allegation.

"This is officially a no-work zone now." Being alone together in their living room on a Friday near lunchtime couldn't be beat.

"Tell me what your lawyer said first, you wombat." Izzy had taken to addressing Leslie with small, obscure animal names in the last week.

The smile on Leslie's face pulled at her overworked muscles. "The medical board dismissed the complaint against me. And by the time everything else is through, he expects Bryce, Sloan, and Michelle will be all done practicing. Permanently."

Baby J lifted her head, cocking it as if needing clarification.

"Yes!" Izzy pulled her fist down.

"Yeah." Leslie threw her hand across her forehead. "What a week."

"What a month."

Two family emergency room visits on consecutive days had been a record for them. Fortunately, Izzy's ER visit after being drugged had uncovered no complications with her pregnancy or with her. But they recommended an OB appointment soon. Her follow-up visit had just ended an hour ago.

"Run through what the OB said again." Leslie sipped her matcha latte.

"Oh, you know how they never give you any definitive answers. We talked about first trimester exposure to lorazepam."

The police had found packaging material in Michelle's trash, the drug matching what was found in Izzy's labs at the hospital, a common fast-acting sedative. They'd later discovered Michelle had ordered the liquid concentrate form of the drug, exploiting Bryce's dispensing license.

"Otherwise, everything was perfect. She wanted another ultrasound and to adjust the timing on the amnio a bit. It's a less than one percent chance of overall ... what was her word ... malformation. She tried to reassure me, saying she believed the risk was extremely small since it was only one dose."

"It seems like we've done everything we can. How are you feeling about it?"

"What's done is done. I haven't had any other problems. I'm at peace with it. I feel fine, just famished."

"Want to get something to eat?"

"You know I do." Izzy leaned away for Baby J to jump off the couch. "Let's walk down to the food carts in the hood."

The dog was back in a flash, the leash in her mouth, her tail wagging.

"I said the 'w' word."

A twenty-minute stroll at noon highlighted the neighborhood, the weather now calm, leafless trees exposing electrical lines interconnecting the homes. A hot meal outdoors and exercising the dog promised them time to relax and chat.

In a scramble to keep her patients treated, Leslie had offered jobs to Pearl and Lynn after their resignations from Psych Recovery. It was a good thing Pearl had helped secure the bank credit line. The plans were underway for Leslie and her on-call partner, Susan, to form a new group. Susan's nurse was all in. They just had to settle on an office location.

New patients from Bryce's practice were coming into Leslie's and Susan's schedules—the ones who weren't in Bryce's MAT program. Fortunately, his on-call colleagues were helping those people with opioid addiction find appropriate providers.

In a sparsely attended Rose City Food Park, Izzy sat opposite Leslie at a picnic table, enjoying hot Thai noodles. Beneath the food cart pod's canvas awning, Izzy sipped their shared coffee. November's chill kept most tables empty, exactly what they needed.

"Do you want to tell me the rest?"

"The rest of what?" Leslie dabbed her mouth with a napkin.

Izzy asked about what Leslie had found in the letters from her mom's cousin Grace and her mom's journal. Leslie shared that, before her parents' separation, they had both been drinking heavily. Her mother's mental illness hadn't been diagnosed. Her parents argued about counseling and her mother's psychiatric care. Leslie learned her mother had gotten pregnant after sleeping with a stranger, which explained the arguing Leslie had overheard as a child.

They pushed their plates aside after Leslie recounted her parents' argument in the car. Something her mother said left Leslie believing she'd caused the nightmare that ensued: her parents' divorce, her mother's suicide attempt, their homelessness.

"But now I know their rift was all about betrayal and lies," Leslie lightly cleared her throat. "It wasn't about me."

"Shocking." Izzy's brows lifted. "What happened with the pregnancy?"

Leslie took a breath and revealed her mother had terminated it and lied to her father that she was unable to have his children. "She tried to make him suspect I wasn't his child."

"Oh, cruel." Izzy squeezed Leslie's hand again. Leslie squeezed back, adding it wasn't true. Her mother had already asked Leslie's grandfather and Grace to help raise her.

A quiet moment passed, broken by Leslie. "Then my dad left. And her suicide attempt followed." With a knowing glance, they shared an understanding—Jean Schoen was getting things ready for her to be gone.

Leslie misinterpreted this as a child—people left because of her. She took a tissue from her purse and shook her head. "While I was reading her diary, I got it. I wasn't at the center of my universe—it wasn't all about me—then or now." A tear trickled down her face.

"The uncanny part has been witnessing what happened to Damon—he was a mirror, a roadmap, to my story. I bought into another lie since my father left: my mother told me he wanted nothing to do with me, painting him the villain. But somewhere inside, I knew that was bullshit. And her diary proved it wasn't true."

Leslie stifled a cry as a distant dog's bark brought about Baby J's raised ears. Izzy leaned in to speak gently. "But she wanted you to have the truth. I know it. She kept the journal and the letters."

They nodded together. "You know..." Leslie looked to the side.

Izzy waited.

"I hadn't looked at it that way." Leslie sniffed, tossing her tissue on the plate. "You're going to make a fantastic mother. You know?"

Izzy smiled. "So are you."

Within an hour or two, they were settled back in their living room, with Baby J at Izzy's feet. Side by side on the couch, they immersed themselves in the neighborhood scene through their front windows. A middle-aged couple, both graying, walked by. One pushed a stroller, while the other commanded a little leashed dachshund—or was it the other way around?

"There we are down the road." Leslie smiled, facing her partner.

"You've offended Baby J." Izzy nodded toward the dog, light glistening in her moist gaze. "Yeah. We're going to be great parents."

"That's right. And when we botch things, we have lots of family and friends to help us." It was true. Over the last few weeks, the message had become clear about how deep a bench their family 'team' truly had.

"You know..."

"What?" Izzy waited.

"There's something I'd like to start working on next year."

"Yeah?"

"Looking for my father." Leslie had found more clues in her mom's things as she finished going through the boxes. Where he'd gone, at least, those thirty-odd years ago. Durango, Colorado. "I might get a jump on it by getting back in touch with Cousin Grace."

Izzy's eyes widened. "Oh my god, I love her. And all her quirkiness. What time is it there right now?"

Leslie glanced at her mobile.

"Not even dinnertime." She searched her contacts and found the number she hadn't dialed in way too many months. Setting the call on speaker, she put the phone on her lap.

Four rings.

"Hello?"

Leslie and Izzy looked at each other and smiled, saying together, "Hello, Grace?"

MM Desch is the debut author of the psychological thriller "Tangled Darkness," and describes her work as storytelling on the edge. She's a proud marginalized voice in the LGBTQ+ community and a former psychiatrist. When not investigating facets of writing, she enjoys hiking, long walks with her wife and their mini schnauzer, Portland food carts, golf, and the WNBA. She resides in Oregon.
www.marydesch.com